MIDNIGHT ALLEY

Also by Miles Corwin

FICTION

Kind of Blue

NONFICTION

The Killing Season
And Still We Rise
Homicide Special

MIDNIGHT ALLEY

An Ash Levine Novel

MILES CORWIN

Oceanview Publishing
LONGBOAT KEY, FLORIDA

ISBN: 978-1-60809-038-9

Published in the United States of America by Oceanview Publishing,
Longboat Key, Florida
www.oceanviewpub.com

2 4 6 8 10 9 7 5 3 1

PRINTED IN THE UNITED STATES OF AMERICA

For Marius

PART I

GHOST TOWN

CHAPTER 1

The sun was fading toward the horizon, and the breeze sputtered to dead calm when I swiveled around and paddled toward the point. My board split a seam in the still, clear water, and spoons of light reflected off the edges. I could see tiny, brightly colored fish scattering ahead of me. This has always been my favorite time to surf. The evening glass off.

A few hundred feet beyond the point, I pushed myself up, straddled the board, and waited for the last wave of the day. I was used to the over-crowded, polluted beaches down south; catching waves at Rincon, a dozen miles from Santa Barbara, on a Friday in winter, was a rare treat. If I'd driven up the coast alone, I would have surfed until dark. But Robin was waiting for me on the sand, and I figured she was getting impatient.

While I waited for the next set, I looked out at sea. I could make out the craggy silhouette of Santa Cruz Island and a fishing trawler chugging north. On shore, the low tide exposed a sweep of smooth, slate-gray rocks that shimmered in the weak December sunlight. A mound of crumbling cliffs loomed above the Pacific Coast Highway, snaking down the coast.

I spotted a swell of pale green, quickly building in size and speed, rising from the anvil-flat horizon. This set, I figured, would be over-head, at a minimum. The teenagers on toothpicks yelped with excitement, whipped their boards around and furiously windmilled out to sea, hoping to reach the calm water beyond the break line before the first wave crashed. I was grateful that I had a longer board with thicker rails. I didn't mind sacrificing some maneuverability for enough buoyancy so I could knee paddle. I passed a half dozen kids on their stomachs who were racing toward the swell, but looked like they might be caught in-side.

The first wave burst into a sleek wall of water about a hundred yards away, and I didn't think I'd make it. I paddled until my shoulders burned, dipped into the lip of the swell, and was blasted into the air, suspended a few feet above the water, gripping the rails of my board, until it landed with a flat smack just beyond the crashing wave. I had only a moment to catch my breath before the next wave curled off the point. Now I was far enough out to catch it. I waited until I could see the swell rise, then took a few strokes toward shore.

As the wave propelled me forward, I jumped to my feet and flew down the steep face, feeling out of control, like I'd just jumped off a cliff, my heart dropping to my gut. At the bottom I carved a sharp turn, just ahead of the billowing whitewater, and then climbed and skimmed along the face, feeling weightless, like I was flying. For a moment, I was in command, not simply reacting to the vagaries of the wave, but mastering it. I crouched slightly, swiveled on my back foot, scaled the wave, and then swung my hips and plunged back down, sculpting clean, graceful swirls.

As I neared shore and began to lose speed, I inched up to the board's nose, my feet parallel, my back arched, then slid back down the board, and kicked out with a flourish. On the beach, a skinny kid in a wetsuit with long, sun-bleached hair, who looked about ten or eleven, nodded as I hopped off my board.

"*Killer* ride," the kid called out, eyes shining with admiration.

I smiled and nodded, feeling flattered and a little silly.

"For an *old* guy," he added with a smirk.

I laughed to myself as I trudged away. When I reached the sandy beach on the other side of the point, I dropped my board and appreciated the view: a crescent of fine white sand, framed by cliffs studded with sage and eucalyptus trees. This was one of my favorite spots in Southern California: an island on the land, cut off from the highway by the cliffs, separated from the crowded surfing beach by the rocky point, a placid place where the only sound was the crash of the surf. The vast stretch of beach was almost empty. There was only a young woman running along the damp sand with her dog, and Robin, wearing jeans and a sweater, reading on a canvas chair. From a distance, she looked like a little girl: small and slender, knees against her chest, arms wrapped around her shins. She clutched her novel, absorbed.

I recalled when my brother Marty, an attorney who worked for the same corporate law firm as Robin, introduced us. When I first spotted her I thought she resembled those girls from the shtetl pictures I'd seen of prewar Europe—pale, dark-haired, and exotically pretty, with wide intelligent eyes that reflected a premonition of the anguish to come.

I snuck up behind her and flicked my wet finger at her neck.

"Hey!" she yelled, scrambling to her feet.

I leaned over and kissed her.

"Mmm," she said. "I love the taste of salt on a surfer's lips."

As I peeled off my wetsuit, Robin threw me two towels. I wrapped one around my waist and stripped off my trunks. Shivering, I dried off and slipped on jeans and a sweatshirt.

"I was getting damn cold," she said. "December's not exactly beach weather."

"Sorry I was out there so long," I said, combing my hair with my nails.

"It's so beautiful, I didn't mind. How was it?"

"Great. Especially my last ride." I smiled. "Some kid said I was pretty good—for an old guy."

She tilted her chin back and laughed. I'd missed so many things about her, but her laugh was one of the things I'd missed most, that uninhibited, trilling laugh that sounded like wind chimes in a breeze.

"Did that bother you?"

"Naw. I just never thought of myself as an old guy."

"You're *not*," she said, squeezing my biceps theatrically. "But, I guess, for you that might be hard to take."

"What do you mean, *for you*."

"You're years past the boy wonder stage."

"Yeah?" I said, motioning for her to continue.

"You were the first cop in your academy class to make detective. You were the youngest cop to make Felony Special. So all I'm saying is that it's probably hard to see yourself, like that kid saw you: as an old guy."

"That's the last time this weekend we mention the LAPD," I said. "I want this to be a perfect weekend."

"Okay. No more LAPD talk."

"You didn't mind stopping here on the way to Santa Barbara, did you?"

She shook her head. "By the time we get to our hotel, I'll be totally relaxed." A hint of worry flashed across her face. "You *did* make the reservation, didn't you?"

"Of course."

"And you made the dinner reservation for tonight?"

"I took care of everything. This is going to be a great weekend. Like the ones we used to have."

I eased into the beach chair and pulled her onto my lap. She snuggled against my chest as I crossed my arms over her shoulders. We watched the waves break on shore, the spume feathering in the air.

"Being together again today is—" I halted in mid-sentence.

"I feel that way, too," she said softly.

"You know, we've been apart now almost longer than we were together."

"Hardly. Five years together. Two years apart."

"It just seems like that," I said. "I'm glad you're a procrastinator."

"Why?"

"Because if you hadn't put off filing those final judgment forms, and all those other documents you had me sign, we'd already be divorced now."

We watched the water churn for a few minutes. I felt content for the first time in a long while. The squad room squabbles, the anxiety over the impending divorce, the pressure of my cases, all seemed to recede now.

We'd talked very little since our separation. Robin had made it clear that the marriage was over, even though she'd been dilatory in finalizing the divorce. She appraised the house, took out a second mortgage, cut me a check for half the amount, and bought me out. I used the money to buy my downtown loft and tried, unsuccessfully, with the help of an LAPD psychologist, to move on. A few months ago, I was stunned when Robin called to say hello. We chatted for about twenty minutes. The next night I called her and we talked for three hours. We'd met for a few long lunches. I called her a few days ago, and when she agreed to spend the weekend in Santa Barbara with me, I was astonished.

"Well," she said, standing up and brushing the sand off her jeans, "let's get to our room. I want to take a long, hot bath."

I slid my arm around her waist and said, "Maybe I'll join you."

We climbed the wooden steps along the face of the cliffs, panting when we reached the parking lot on the crest. I stuffed the board in the rear of my battered Saturn station wagon.

"You should have let me drive my Mercedes," she said. "I could have put some racks on top."

"Why? You embarrassed to be seen in this old beater?"

"I'm thinking of comfort, not class."

The light was draining from the sky—a mosaic of gold, orange, and pink—and the sun was melting into the sea, leaving a brushstroke of red on the still water. The woodsy smell of chaparral floated up from the cliffs. I reached out for her hand. "This is nice."

"Yeah. Kind of reminds me of the old days when we use to—" she paused and froze, a fox smelling danger. "What the hell is *that*?"

"What?"

"I sure as hell hope that isn't what I think it is," Robin said.

I flipped open the back of the station wagon and fished my buzzing cell phone out of a duffel bag. After checking Caller ID, I muttered, "It's Lieutenant Duffy."

"You *promised* me you weren't on call this weekend," Robin said in pleading tone.

"I'm not."

"Can't you just shut off your cell and pretend you never got the message?"

"You know I can't. I've got to at least check in."

She walked off and stood beneath a eucalyptus, arms crossed, body rigid.

I sighed and punched in a number on my cell.

"Duffy here."

"I thought I was off call this weekend."

"You were—until a few minutes ago."

"Listen LT., I'm on my way to Santa Barbara. I've made plans."

"You taking someone on a romantic weekend?"

"I am."

"Who is he?"

"Very funny. I'm with Robin."

"I thought that bitch dumped you a few years ago."

"I'm trying to make it work," I said, a tinge of desperation in my voice.

"I wish I could spare you, but I'm dealing with a shitstorm here. This is December. Half the unit's out of state, visiting family for the holidays or getting ready for Christmas. At least I know *you* can't use that excuse."

"Look, there's got to be someone besides me."

"Ash, I'm not lyin', you're the last man on my on-call list," he said, his voice softening. "I tried to keep you free. But I'm stuck. I've got to call you in. How soon can you get here?"

"Just tell me what's going on," I said, choking out the words.

"Two rappers ambushed this afternoon in North Hollywood. Then we caught another case in Thai Town."

I glanced over at Robin. She was leaning against the guardrail, shaking her head.

"This is fucked up," I said.

"It always is. But I've got to deal with two other vics. Blacks, early twenties. They're tits up in a Venice alley. In Oakwood, that little ghetto there."

"Drive-by?"

"Walk-up."

"Why can't the Pacific Division guys handle a gangster walk-up? Why's it going to Felony Special?"

"Because one of the vics is the son of Isaac Pinkney."

"The city councilman who's always ragging on the LAPD?"

"One and the same."

"This weekend is important to me."

"Can't do it, Asher, my boy. Wish I could. But I *can* give you a choice. You can head out to the rapper shooting. Or you can run with the Venice double."

"Is it a real clusterfuck at North Hollywood?" I asked.

"Affirmative."

"My partner's on vacation until after the holidays."

"I'll team you up with Graupmann. His partner's out of town, too."

"I don't want to work with that knuckle-dragger. I'll take the Venice double—if I can work it alone until my partner gets back."

"You're an antisocial motherfucker. But whatever it takes to get your ass to Venice."

Robin walked over and said, in an irritated tone, "Listen Ash, you have to tell Duffy to—" I held up a palm, quieting her for a moment.

"What's going on there?" Duffy asked.

"An angry surfer."

"Watch your back," Duffy said. He gave me the location in Venice where the two bodies were found. I clicked off the phone as Robin climbed into the station wagon and slammed the door.

Damn. Why did I have to get called out this weekend. I'd looked forward to this weekend and had such great hopes. Who knows if I'd get another chance at a weekend away with Robin? I felt like flinging my cell phone into the ocean and heading up to Santa Barbara anyway. But I knew I had no choice. I paced beside the car, trying to figure out how to placate her. When we were married, we'd been through this drill countless times: homicide call outs ruining weekends away, vacations, birthday dinners, romantic evenings. During that last year, the marriage was brittle enough. All those cancelled plans hadn't helped.

Sitting beside Robin in the station wagon, I struggled for something to say, for words that might break the tension, but I couldn't think of anything that I hadn't said to her dozens of times before. I finally muttered, "Duffy gave me no choice," and braced for a dressing-down.

She cleared her throat and, in a surprisingly good Marlon Brando *Godfather* impersonation, she said in a gravelly voice, "That is the nature of the profession you have chosen for yourself." Then she turned toward me and laughed. She lightly slapped my cheek and said, "*Capiche?*"

"Look, Robin, I'm really sorry about —"

"Don't apologize. I agreed to spend a weekend with a homicide detective. I knew the risks."

I was so surprised at her equanimity that I didn't know how to respond. Finally, I sputtered, "You used to get so irate."

She stared out the window, watching the western horizon, now a glaring scarlet. "We both made a lot of mistakes back then."

"I know I did."

"I'm not letting you off the hook. When you finish off this case, you better deliver on that weekend in Santa Barbara that you owe me."

"I'll deliver. That's a promise."

"So what's this case about?"

"Councilman Isaac Pinkney's son and another kid found shot in an Oakwood alley."

She whistled softly. "This should be interesting. Isn't Pinkney always going on and on about how the LAPD is a racist, fascist, paramilitary organization whose sole purpose is to keep the black man down?"

"That's him."

"You better be careful on this one, Ash." She reached for my hand, ran her fingers across the palm, and said, "I see a civil suit in your future."

"Just what I need."

"Everything you do, document. Put it on paper."

"I keep a pretty good chrono on my cases."

"Make sure you detail *everything*. I don't know anything about homicide investigations, as you used to remind me, but I do know something about civil lawsuits. So if you run into anything that you think might be a problem down the line, give me a call. I'll reduce my usual three-hundred-dollar-an-hour fee to a weekend in Santa Barbara."

This was the Robin with whom I'd fallen in love, the woman who was wisecracking and funny and smart, who grasped the demands of my job. Years later, when our marriage soured and we were fighting all the time, I knew she had changed. But I'd changed too, something I came to understand too late.

Leaning over, I framed her face with my palms, kissed her softly, and said, "Thank you." I started the car and dropped onto the Pacific Coast Highway, past a giant set crashing near the shore, creating a fine mist that hovered over the road, speckling my windshield. Robin pulled out her BlackBerry and tapped in a number.

After a brief conversation she said, "My friend Amy lives in Malibu. You can drop me at the pier, and she'll pick me up. I'll spend the night with her, and she'll drive me home tomorrow. I know you need to get to the crime scene. This should save you some time."

"You sure?"

She nodded. I cut down a two-lane road in Oxnard, flanked by strawberry fields, rolled onto the coast highway near Point Magu, and sped past Zuma and Paradise Cove, the cliffs sheathed in ice plant and yucca hugging the road to my left, the ocean on my right. On a rise I could see the great sweep of the bay, from Point Dume to the Palos Verdes Peninsula, the lights of the coastline spread out like a glittering necklace, the velvety sea streaked with foam along the swell lines.

We headed south in silence. I was disappointed that the weekend was ruined, but gratified that we resolved the problem so easily and had agreed to another trip to Santa Barbara. Feeling good, driving down the coast, watching the waves, I glanced at Robin and thought, *This could work.*

During the past few years I'd been haunted by my future. I wondered if I'd end up like so many other bitter divorced ex-cops. I wondered if I'd return to an empty loft after my thirty-year retirement party at the academy, realizing I had nothing to show for my years of sacrifice except a drawer of dusty commendations and a few dozen cells at Pelican Bay filled with guys I'd sent up.

But now, glancing at Robin as she gazed out the window, I could envision a different sort of life for myself. A life with Robin. Kids. Family vacations. Dinner at home every night. A house in the foothills. A life that wasn't entirely circumscribed by crime scenes and autopsies and witness interviews and warrant searches. But to attain that kind of life with Robin, I'd have to leave Felony Special for a less demanding division. Was I willing to make that kind of sacrifice?

I nudged the brakes at the Malibu pier and veered into the parking lot. She waved to her friend, who was waiting for her in a sleek black BMW. Robin jumped out of the car, jogged around, bent down through my open window, and kissed me. "Call me," she said, "when you come up for air."

CHAPTER 2

Mullin strutted into the bar. He scanned the room and realized he'd made a good choice. On a Friday night, Hank's gave him a decent selection. On the edge of downtown L.A., the bar was scruffy enough to attract some of the lady artists from the lofts, but close enough to the office towers to bring in a few secretaries. He elbowed his way through the crowd and caught the eye of the female bartender, a tall blonde with tattoo sleeves on both arms.

"Gimme a 7-Up, rocks, with a few shots of orange juice, a bit of grenadine, and two cherries," he said softly, so no one else at the bar could hear.

The bartender smiled. "You mean you want a Shirley Tem—" She stopped in mid-sentence when she saw Mullin's cold reptilian eyes, the biceps bulging out of the tight black T-shirt, the jailhouse tattoos. "Sure," the bartender said uneasily. "You got it."

Mullin took a long sip, sighed with satisfaction, and checked out the action. He noticed a woman sitting alone at the bar, staring at his pipes. That's one benefit of a stretch inside—plenty of free time to throw iron. He glanced at the woman again. Lank brown hair, round face, freckles dotting a nose that was a little too wide, and skittish, syrup-colored eyes. Not much style: shapeless blue dress, cheap Timex watch. That, he figured, might work to his advantage. She seemed out of place. Not from L.A. A little chunky, maybe more than a little, but he didn't mind that. He'd been away for a four-year bid. Any woman with warm blood would look good to him tonight.

Picking up his drink, he traded his stool for one next to hers. He crossed his forearms, flexed his biceps, and grinned. "Curious about the artwork?"

She laughed nervously and stared into her white wine. "Maybe a little."

"You want to know what these tats mean?"

"I guess so," she said.

He flexed his right bicep and pointed to the two tattooed clouds. Inside one of them glared the face of a man, and the other featured the profile of an eagle. On his left bicep floated two more clouds, one encircling the head of an ox and the other with nothing inside. Mullin had found a real pro in the joint, an artist with the needle, not one of those convict scratchers. For eight hours he'd sat on his bunk, gritting his teeth, not moving a muscle. He had to pay the *vato* eleven candy bars. But as he watched the woman stare at the clouds, he knew it was worth it.

"So what does it mean?" she asked.

He noticed she was wearing a small silver crucifix on a cheap chain. "You go to church?"

"I used to. Back home in Missouri."

"How long you been in L.A.?"

She smiled shyly. "Two months. I came out with a girlfriend. We got jobs working for an insurance company downtown. Where do you work?"

Ignoring her question, Mullin said, "You remember Ezekiel from your churchgoing days?"

She twirled a strand of her hair with her forefinger. "Not really."

"There's a book of his prophecies in the Bible. In one of them, he saw four creatures comin' out of a cloud. Each one had the body of a man and a head with four different faces. The front face was human, left one was an ox, the right one was a lion, and the face in back was an eagle."

"What do they mean?"

"This is what Ezekiel said: 'And I looked, and, behold, a whirlwind came out of the north, a great cloud . . . and out of the midst . . . came the likeness of four living creatures.'"

"But what does that all mean?"

"Now that's an interesting question, darlin'. I'll tell you sometime."

"Where'd you learn so much about the Bible?"

"I've had a lot of time for reading these past few years."

"You don't look like a college boy."

Mullin laughed, but his eyes remained cold. "I was inside."

"Inside where?" she asked.

"Salinas Valley State Prison."

She stiffened slightly and her eyes widened.

Mullin wondered if he'd blown it. Maybe he should have saved that tidbit for later. Some women are scared off when they find out a dude's been inside; some are into it. She seemed somewhere in between.

"What'd you do?"

"My old man needed money for some kind of back operation. If he didn't get it, he'd be stuck in a wheelchair for life."

"That's sad."

"I didn't have the bank. I had no choice. So I robbed a grocery store."

She nodded somberly.

"How is he?" the woman asked.

"How's who?"

"Your dad."

"Fine." *What a dumb cunt*, Mullin thought. She believed him.

"Can he walk now?"

"Walk where?"

She stared at him, mouth half open.

"Oh yeah. He got the operation. He could go on *Dancing with the Stars* now."

"Are you born again?"

"My parole agent thinks so," he said, laughing. He downed the rest of his drink in a long swallow, inched closer to the woman, and flashed her his most charming smile. "Listen, darlin'. These bar stools are damn uncomfortable. I got a place not too far from here. You want to head over there?"

"I don't know," she said, picking at a cuticle.

"We can have a drink, kick back, listen to some music. It's been a long time since I've had the company of a beautiful woman." He hoped he sounded sincere. "It'll be nice." Her dopey brown eyes reminded him of a lazy cow staring out at the pasture. *This should be a snap, like falling off a fucking log.* He stood, slipped his arm around her shoulder, and said, "Let's go."

Walking out the door, he said, "Why don't we take your car? Mine's in the shop." Better not tell her he didn't own a car. Anyone in L.A. without a car was considered a total loser. Even a dumb bitch like her might rank on him.

He followed her to a Honda Civic. As she pulled out of the lot he gave her directions. As she drove, Mullin thought, *What the fuck am I supposed to say to her. I haven't talked to a girl in four calendars. How do you make small talk?*

"I used to throw a lot of iron," he said. "I read somewhere that girls go to gyms and are into weights these days. You ever lift?"

"Not really," she said.

"If you ever want someone to show you around a weight pile, I'll be glad to do it."

"Sure. Thanks."

She didn't sound interested, Mullin thought. They drove the rest of the way in silence. When she pulled up in front of the motel in a mangy neighborhood just south of downtown, she glanced nervously at him.

"I got a nice apartment I'm moving into next week," he said, bullshitting. "They're painting it right now. I'm just staying here for a few days until it's ready."

She gripped her knees tightly and looked like she didn't want to leave the car. Mullin hopped out, walked around to the driver's side, and led her outside, down a concrete path to a wooden door with a brass number seven in the center. He traced the number with a thumb and said, "This must be our lucky night."

CHAPTER 3

As I watched her friend's BMW fade down the highway, I wondered if Robin was so easygoing about the call out because she knew we had no real future. We'd given it a shot once, and it hadn't worked out. Maybe she'd approached this weekend as an adventure between boyfriends, not a prelude to reconciliation. Since Robin had left me, there had been a few affairs, ranging from a few hours to a few weeks. What were the odds that I'd find someone else whom I cared about as much? How many more chances would I get before I was too old or simply uninterested in marriage and a family?

I checked my watch, gunned the engine, and peeled out of the parking lot, hoping to beat the coroner investigator to Oakwood. As I raced to the crime scene, swerving between cars, I reviewed the scant information Duffy had given me. I attempted to visualize the two men in the alley and pondered who would want to kill them. By the time I jetted through the tunnel in Santa Monica and exited at Lincoln Boulevard, I felt an almost euphoric rush that was a highlight of the job for me. All my senses were heightened, and I savored the anticipation of adventure and, perhaps, danger. All the moves I would make in the next twenty-four hours would be critical. I always thought a murder was like a pebble thrown in a pond, ripples looping out in concentric circles, first devastating the family, then friends, then traumatizing the neighbors, and sometimes the community and the entire city. The key to clearing a street shooting was to unearth a lead before the clues vanished and the suspects covered their tracks, and nail the case down before the pond was still again.

I cruised down Lincoln, through Santa Monica and into a rundown section of Venice, past tire stores, used car lots, taco stands, and thrift shops. At a gas station, I parked and carried my garment bag—which I always kept in the backseat in case of an unexpected call out—into the men's room. Inside the garment bag, I'd tucked a blue-gray Corneliani suit, white dress shirt, Ike Behar tie, all purchased from Murray Glickman, my contact in the garment district who gave me the cop discount. I quickly dressed, drove down Lincoln a few more blocks, swung right, and headed into Oakwood. Driving slowly, past small houses strung with red-and-green Christmas lights, I checked out the neighborhood. When I was a young cop in the Pacific Division, I'd spent a lot of time patrolling Oakwood, but I'd not been back since I made detective. The neighborhood was still dominated by narrow streets, lined with dilapidated sugar cube shacks on tiny lots and tumbledown Section Eight apartment buildings.

In the years since I'd worked here, gentrification had encroached on the neighborhood. Modern, sharply angled, glass-and-steel two-story homes had displaced some of the ramshackle bungalows. Newcomers had renovated and expanded many of the original clapboard beach shacks, encircled them with thick stands of bamboo, oleander, and tall redwood fences, and installed security panels by the front doors—bulwarks against the havoc outside. Oakwood was probably the last affordable beach neighborhood in Southern California. Residents could live a few blocks from the water—and within walking distance to the yoga studios, art galleries, aromatherapy shops, and coffeehouses on trendy Abbot Kinney Boulevard or Main Street—if they were willing to put up with the occasional gangbanging and late-night crack deals. I'd read somewhere that when Venice was developed in the early 1900s as an Italian-style beach resort, Oakwood was created as a servant's zone, the only area near the coastline where blacks could own property.

As I slowly drove through the neighborhood, I thought of the years I'd spent as a homicide detective in South Central, cut off from downtown and the Westside by the concrete ramparts of the Santa Monica Freeway and a forbidding cityscape. Oakwood, however, was an anomalous checkerboard of poverty and affluence, black gangbangers and white bohemians, Mexican and Central American immigrants, and real estate speculators.

I spotted two uniforms standing in front of their squad car, lights flashing, blocking off the alley where the two men had been murdered. I drove around the street adjacent to the alley and parked—to get a feel for the area. The neighborhood was jammed with blocky three-story apartment buildings, featureless walls of stucco with thick black security bars covering the windows. Stenciled on the façades of several buildings

were misspelled admonitions: NO TRESPASING. NO DRUG DEELING. NO
PUBLICK ACCESS. Two teenage boys wearing do-rags and blue FUBU
jackets lingered on the sidewalk, smoking cigarettes. Newly renovated
bungalows with landscaped lawns or cactus gardens in front bordered a
few of the apartment buildings.

A crackhead missing a few teeth stumbled by, which reminded me
of the old shoot-'em-up days in Oakwood, before the hipsters and artists
moved in. The neighborhood was known as Ghost Town then because
late at night scrawny junkies and desperate strawberries stumbled
through the fog, past the ramshackle houses, in search of drugs. On the
corners, dealers brazenly sold crack and heroin and gangbangers tor-
mented residents and shot at each other.

At one end of the street loomed a Baptist Church with a brightly lit
nativity scene on the lawn: baby Jesus in a straw-lined manger, surrounded by Joseph, Mary, the Magi, and a couple of camels. On the
other corner a daring homesteader had built an impressive two-story
Spanish-style home with a tiled courtyard, a dolphin fountain in the
entry, and a stone wall edged with red lantana. An eight-foot-tall prickly
pear cactus, draped with Christmas lights and crowned with a foil star,
shimmered in the center of the lawn.

I drove around the block, parked by the dim alley, and grabbed my
flashlight. A teenager with a pit bull on a leash, a pregnant woman with
a stroller, and an old man wearing house slippers clustered against the
yellow crime-scene tape, rubbernecking. I ducked past them, nodded to
the uniform with the crime-scene log, murmured my name, serial number, and division. I stepped over the flares that hissed like a wildfire tear-
ing through dry grass. I halted and knelt down to inspect the gravel alley,
which was lined with muddy garbage cans and littered with rusty hub-
caps, old car batteries, soda cans, and a sofa with its cushions missing.
About halfway down, I could see the elliptical silhouette of Duffy, gut
distended, gesturing with his hands and chatting with three men. Another patrol car, flanked by two cops, blocked the alley's opposite end,
light bars pulsating red and blue. A dozen feet from Duffy, an LAPD
crime-scene photographer crouched beside the bodies. I approached as
the photographer snapped a picture, his flash illuminating Duffy and
the others for an instant; then it was dark again, as if a light switch had
been clicked off.

Duffy bellowed, "Welcome, Ash. As the great Ernie Banks might have said, 'It's a great night for homicide. Let's investigate two.'" He introduced me to the other men. I'd never met the Pacific Division lieutenant, Sam Garza, a hulking, somber Hispanic, nor the young detective trainee with a blond crew cut. But I knew his sneering, pudgy partner, Richie Falco, from my days at Pacific Division patrol. He thought he was a comedian, but I never found him funny.

"How come you got this one?" Garza asked.

"We're on call alternate weekends with Homicide Special for the high-profile cases," Duffy said.

"Detective Levine, I don't think it would be in your best interest to take this case," Falco said with phony solicitude. "Now correct me if I'm wrong, but I believe tonight is *your* people's Sabbath," he said turning to his young partner and winking. "Doesn't that mean tonight and tomorrow are sacred days of rest for the Chosen People?"

I turned to Duffy and said, "I had to give up a weekend in Santa Barbara to deal with this dipshit?"

"Richie, may I make a suggestion?" asked Duffy—who'd spent his childhood in Ireland—with a hint of a brogue.

Falco nodded.

"Why don't you shut the fuck up."

"I think this has gone far enough for —" Garza said.

"Okay, smart guys," said Duffy, who towered over both of us. He slipped an arm around our shoulders and squeezed until we both winced. "Now that we know that you two are old buddies, let's move on to the subject of these homicides." He jerked his thumb at the two bodies. "Richie, why don't you fill Ash in?"

"Not much we can say at this point," Falco said. "Looks like these guys were killed by ghetto lightning."

"What're you talking about?" Duffy said.

"You Felony Special guys have been away from the 'hood too long," Falco said. "Nobody saw a fucking thing. Nobody has the faintest idea what happened. So the only thing I can conclude is that they were struck down by a bolt from the sky."

"Just give it to us straight," Garza said.

"Okay," Falco said. "Two male usuals were found in this alley about sixteen hundred. A neighborhood kid riding his bike stumbled on 'em. Both shot in the back."

"Anybody canvassing?"

"Yeah," said Garza. "I've got two teams out there going door to door."

"Get anything yet?" I asked.

"A few of the neighbors said they heard a shot."

"*One* shot?"

"Yeah."

"Might have been a split second apart, so it sounded like one shot," Duffy said.

"Could be," Garza said.

I pointed to a duplex hard by the alley with no backyard as a buffer. "That place's got the best view of the scene. You talk to anyone in there?"

Garza nodded to Falco. "The bottom unit's vacant," Falco said. "Some gangbanger lives in the top with his mom. The mom was out tonight. The kid was home but said he didn't see or hear shit."

"When's the coroner investigator supposed to get here?" I asked.

"You're lucky they're hopping tonight," Duffy said. "Even though it took you long enough to get here, we're still waiting on him."

"Any slugs or casings?" I asked.

"Negative," Falco said.

"Any ID on the vics?"

"Yeah," Falco said. "We know Raymond Pinkney is the councilman's son. By the way, good luck with his old man. He fucking hates the LAPD. He's going to be a handful." He grinned. "That nig—"—he theatrically slapped his palm over his mouth—"I mean that African American public servant is an asshole and a half."

"I know all about him," I said. "Just fill me in on the case."

"Okay. His son was a student at Long Beach State. I found his college ID card. And the other one, Teshay Winfield, is a neighborhood kid."

"Did you run them?"

"No," Falco said, looking uncomfortable. "I was just about to."

"Did anyone do the death notifications?"

"We thought you'd want to handle that," Garza said.

Falco was a cretin, and working with him had always been distasteful to me. But I needed him more than he needed me. He'll walk away from the case tonight, and I'll be stuck with solving it. I knew that the best way to insure his cooperation was to make him feel important, solicit his opinion.

"So what's your take?" I asked Falco.

"Maybe a gangster walk-by. Probably Sho'line Crips."

"When I worked patrol here they ran this 'hood," I said. "And that was a while ago."

"Well," Falco said, "they're still running it."

"You know anything about these vics?"

"Probably gangsters. I don't care if this kid," Falco said, tapping a toe near a body, "was a college student and the son of a councilman. He could still be bangin'."

"Any other takes?"

"Maybe a narco hit," Falco said. "Maybe they were looking to score. Maybe they got burned."

"Okay," Duffy said. "First of all, I want to thank you guys for helping out. The brass wants us to buy this one for obvious reasons. It's not that you guys couldn't have handled it, but we've got a lighter caseload and a few more resources." He turned to Garza. "If you guys could stay on the canvass, I'd appreciate it. Maybe we can meet back at the Pacific station later tonight and compare notes. That might help Ash out. What's a good time?"

"How about a little after midnight, say twelve fifteen," Garza said.

"Does that give you enough time at the crime scene, Ash?"

"For now," I said.

As Falco, his trainee, and the lieutenant tramped down the alley, Duffy grabbed his crotch and whispered, "What a dick. This case is going to be a ballbuster. Falco was right: Pinkney's a piece of work. Don't expect a thank-you note from the family for all of your hard work."

"Believe me, I won't."

"I'll try to run interference, so you don't have to deal with Pinkney."

"I'd appreciate it."

"Just clear this case, and I'll do the rest."

"I don't mind taking the case, I just wish it wasn't this weekend."

"Sorry I had to shitcan your weekend with Robin. But I was in a bind. I tried to keep you clear, but I just ran out of bodies. How'd she take it?"

"Better than I thought."

"There you go. You still got a fighting chance. Listen, I'll stick around until the coroner investigator arrives. You can go off and do your thing."

"I haven't worked a walk-up or a drive-by in a while."

"When we worked South Bureau Homicide, you handled enough for a lifetime."

"All those young black guys killing each other. I'll tell you what those drive-bys reminded me of. When I'd cruise through the desert and stop at one of the gas station bathrooms, the mirrors were always filthy, splattered with insects that had killed themselves by smashing into their own reflections."

Duffy, who had been texting on his iPhone, looked up. "You want to know what I think?"

"What?"

"I think you're full of shit."

Duffy resumed texting, and I stepped on a rock, twisting my ankle—my bad ankle. I'd broken it when I was a boot—I was chasing a suspect down a South Central alley when I slipped on a hubcap—and now, whenever I spent too much time on my feet, my ankle throbbed. The surfing this afternoon probably didn't help. The last time I had it X-rayed, the orthopedist had told me he could see signs of arthritis. I slumped against the fence and massaged the ankle, thinking of Robin, how we'd be eating dinner right now, if Duffy hadn't called. Would Robin blow me off when this case was cleared and I suggested another trip to Santa Barbara? The initial rush of the case had dissipated, and I felt disheartened as I watched the mist swirl above the rooftops. Would I be doing this a decade from now, hobbling around a crime scene on an arthritic ankle, then retreating to my monastic loft at the end of my shift and gobbling down a microwaved dinner while I watched Sports Center?

I sucked in a deep breath and spit on the gravel. I knew I better get to work if I was going to make that meeting at the Pacific Division. I flicked on my flashlight and edged toward the bodies with my head down. I recalled my first homicide scene on a South Central street corner when I was a detective trainee. I'd marched around, swiveling my head, eyes level with the horizon, nervously searching for leads. My supervising detective, a grizzled old homicide dick named Bud Carducci, sneaked up behind me, grabbed my head with both hands, and angled it down. "You know the one thing that's going to help you most at a crime scene?" he'd asked. He slapped foot on the sidewalk and said, "Gravity."

Carducci had told me that blood, shell casings, fibers, and hairs will fall to the ground, in addition to items that could be dislodged during a struggle, such as buttons, watches, glasses, and jewelry. As a bonus, I might stumble across footprints and tire tracks. And, of course, the key piece of evidence—the body—always lands on the ground. So a good homicide detective—after surveying the area—always thoroughly examines the ground, Carducci advised. A detective might take a different approach at an indoor crime scene—with its blood spatter patterns on walls and many other surfaces of potential contact. But when tracking a case outdoors, Carducci's mantra was: "Be a hound on the ground." Afterward, Carducci said, a detective could probe for bullet trajectories and other eye-level leads.

I circled the bodies, shining my flashlight at various angles. Both victims were sprawled on their stomachs, dressed in oversized jeans and sneakers, with brick-colored bloodstains—amoebae-shaped smears—creeping down their backs. Pinkney, the councilman's son, wore a gray Raiders jacket, a braided gold chain around his neck, and a diamond stud in his ear. Winfield was draped in a purple Lakers jacket. I couldn't tell if they were dressed down. But these days, with hip-hop fashion trends, teenagers in Beverly Hills dressed like gangsters.

I'd seen so many stiffs over the decades: first as a paratrooper in the Israel Defense Forces, then as a young patrolman and, finally, as a homicide detective. People often told me that I had a depressing job and, in many ways, they were right. But the first part of an investigation—scrutinizing the corpses—had the opposite affect on me. It forced me to confront one of life's dictums: we aren't guaranteed tomorrow. Standing beside a body splayed on the pavement—with a clear view of the bullet hole and the opaque, lifeless eyes—is an instant perspective check. My problems always seem more manageable, my mood buoyed. I'll appreciate the lush landscaping, the colors of a sunset or sunrise, the sweet scent of flowers in the breeze. When a group of detectives mill around a body at a crime scene, for the first few minutes there often is an almost giddy mood, a joking bonhomie that observers beyond the yellow crime-scene tape can never understand and often misinterpret as disrespect toward the dead.

I was eager to get a better look at the wounds, but LAPD regulations prohibit detectives from tampering with the body until the coroner investigator arrives. I worked my way down from the bodies, illuminating the alley in quadrants. The evening was cold and damp, a thin mist blowing in from the ocean. If I'd known I was on-call, I would have packed my wool-lined trench coat. I buttoned my sport coat and tightened my tie.

"If you had some meat on your bones, you wouldn't be so cold," Duffy said.

Ignoring him, I studied a patch of gravel beside a garage door.

"You'd think that with a mother who can cook like yours, you'd pack a few more pounds." Duffy patted his stomach, which hung over his belt like an awning, and said, "When you've got some reserves like me, you can handle any kind of weather."

I tried to stay in motion and generate some heat inside my sports coat. After I'd searched the alley, I examined the wooden fence near the bodies for bullet holes or splinters where clothing could have snagged in a struggle. The Sho'line Crips and V-13, the neighborhood Hispanic gang, had tagged a few of the garage doors with swirling graffiti.

I circled back to the Saturn, removed a pen and legal pad from my briefcase, and diagrammed the crime scene, sketching out the alley's dimensions and noting the graffiti, where the bodies were found, and the location of the nearest streetlights.

"I'll bet Falco was happy as hell to unload this one," I called out to Duffy. "This crime scene's as clean as a kosher chicken. I'm not finding shit here. No shell casings. No slugs. And with all this gravel, I can't even spot a decent footprint."

"You get anything at all?" Duffy asked.

"Maybe," I said, turning around and striding down the alley, as Duffy followed. About twenty feet from the body, I shone my flashlight on the ground. He bent over and squinted. "I don't see anything except gravel."

"Look closer. At that small brown plug. It's shotgun wadding."

"You think our two knuckleheads were blasted by a gauge?" Duffy asked.

"From what I could see of the blood pattern on their jackets, no."

"Could the wadding be from an unrelated shooting?"

"Possibly."

I returned to my Saturn and grabbed my measure meter from the backseat, a metal rod with small rubber wheels that records distance in feet and inches on a built-in odometer. While pacing off the length and width of the alley, I jotted down the dimensions, how far the bodies were from the street, the locations of the shotgun wadding, the streetlamps on the sidewalk, the wooden fence on one side of the alley where the bodies were found, and the garage door on the other side.

I glanced up when a white van screeched to a halt by the curb. The coroner investigator, Theodore Bryson, a tall, gaunt man with a bobbing Adam's apple, sauntered down the alley like he was out for a stroll on the Venice Boardwalk. He carried a black satchel. "Take your time, why don't you," Duffy said sarcastically. "Me and Ash were having so much fun in our little circle jerk we didn't care if you ever arrived."

"We got a little of everything tonight," Bryson said. "Homicide, suicide, fratricide, infanticide, uxoricide, and every other kind of 'cide there is."

"What's uxoricide?" Duffy asked.

"That's when you kill your wife," I said.

Bryson nodded approvingly.

"If it was my second ex-wife, I'd just call it justifiable homicide," Duffy said. "Why are you so busy tonight?"

"People are just getting into that Christmas spirit," he said with a grin that looked like a grimace. "They're working up to deicide."

"That's Easter," I said. "You got three months to go."

"I thought Passover was the only spring holiday you know about," Duffy said.

"Don't forget Purim," I said.

Bryson crouched beside the bodies like a catcher ready for the pitch. "Damn! It had to be a twofer tonight. My supervisor radioed me that one of your victims is a councilman's son," Bryson said. "Which one is he?"

I tapped my toe beside Pinkney.

"I better get to him first."

Bryson plucked Pinkney's wallet from a back pocket as well as a few loose bills from a front pocket and slipped them into plastic bags. He tugged loose Pinkney's shirt and jacket and pointed to a perfectly round hole, the size of a penny, in the middle of his back.

"Entry wound," Bryson said. "See how clean the edges are?" He peeled down the pants and underpants. I could see that Pinkney's legs were grayish, but the thighs, flush against the ground, had a purple tinge, indicating lividity, or settling of the blood.

"How long you think he's been dead?" I asked.

"A while, but I won't know until I stick him with my turkey baster," Bryson said, chuckling.

When Bryson flipped the body around on its back, air escaped from the victim's lungs, a sibilant rush of air, like a punctured tire. Pinkney's face was pocked with gravel and his hair was flecked with dirt. His eyes were wide open and gazing upward, as if he were communing with a higher power. Bryson pointed to a ragged hole in the middle of his chest. "Exit wound. A nice through-and-through."

"Not much blood on the ground," I said.

"The shot might have rattled around and blown out his aorta," Bryson said. He patted Pinkney's bulging stomach. "This tells you—"

"He's got a belly as big as me," Duffy said.

"He probably didn't before the shooting," Bryson said. "If the aorta was clipped, there was a lot of internal bleeding. That's why he's got the swollen abdomen and why there might not be much blood on the ground."

He snatched a scalpel out of his black bag and cut a neat incision just below Pinkney's stomach and then thrust a thermometer into his liver.

"How long has he been dead?" I asked.

"As you know, detective, most bodies cool at approximately 1½ degrees per hour until they reach room temperature," Bryson said pompously. "But it's quite chilly out here tonight, so I'm going to have to throw that into the equation." He yanked the thermometer out and squinted at the reading. "I'll estimate that this unfortunate fellow has been dead from about five to nine hours."

"Can you narrow it down a little more for me?" I asked.

"If I do, some defense attorney might slice *me* up with a scalpel."

"Never seen a gang marking like that," I said, squinting at Pinkney's bicep, where two large shapes had been burned into the skin.

"Doesn't look like a tattoo," Bryson said, tracing fingers along the bicep. "It actually seems like they're letters that were branded there."

"Why?" Duffy asked.

"No idea," Bryson said, shifting his attention to the other man, Teshay Winfield. He lifted Winfield's shirt and jacket and examined the entrance wound in his back, then rolled him over. His head was shaved and his eyes were hooded and unfocused. Pinkney was average size and fleshy, but Winfield was tall and muscular, with broad shoulders and a barrel chest. After Bryson took the liver temperature he said, "Looks like your shooter got two for the price of one. Similar entrance and exit wounds. Approximately the same time of death. Only thing different: no brands, or tattoos, or whatever they are on this fellow."

When Bryson finished probing the bodies, he photographed their faces with a digital camera. After loading them onto a metal gurney, he wheeled them into the back of the van.

"When's the post?" I called out as Bryson slammed the door.

"Autopsy's probably Saturday. Call the desk to confirm."

When Bryson drove off, Duffy checked his watch. "You going to be able to make it over to Pacific Division for that powwow?"

I told Duffy I wanted to linger in the alley a while, and then I'd meet him at the station for the meeting.

"Okay," he said. "I'm out of here now. I'm heading back to run interference for our guys at North Hollywood. I'll get back to Pacific in time to help you out with the notification."

I watched Duffy shuffle stiffly down the alley. The rubberneckers had drifted off into the night, and the uniforms were stamping their feet to keep warm. I called out to them, "Nothing left to do here. Break it down." After they cut down the yellow tape and drove off, I stood in the center of the alley, hands thrust in my pockets, surprised at the silence. The neighborhoods by the ocean always seemed quieter at night to me; maybe the air was heavier and muffled the noise. The crowing of a confused rooster, evidence of a recently arrived Mexican immigrant, broke the calm.

For the next hour I paced the alley. I envisioned the shooting, speculated on the killer's motives and the victims' pasts, recalled the position of the bodies, the entrance and exit wounds, Pinkney's burn marks. I came to the depressing conclusion that I didn't know much more about the case than when Duffy had briefed me on the phone seven hours ago. I hoped someone at the meeting would provide me with a lead.

CHAPTER 4

The girl slouched on the edge of the bed atop a frayed orange coverlet. Mullin opened the mini-refrigerator, pulled out two Coors, opened them both, handed her one, and sat beside her. Mullin was glad that the lamp on the end table cast a faint light, obscuring the stained walls, worn Formica desk, and splintered pine dresser with two knobs missing.

"So what kind of work have you been doing since you left the, uh, uh," she stammered. "Since you were an inmate."

Mullin jumped to his feet. "I hate that fucking word—*inmate*," he shouted. " I was never an *inmate*. That makes it sound like I was some kind of sick fuck who had to be committed to a mental hospital. You think I'm sick?"

"No," she whispered, her voice quavering.

"I was a *convict*. I knew what I was doing. I knew the risks. And I took 'em. If you can't do the time, don't do the crime. I did the crime. And I did the time. There's a difference between an inmate and a convict. You understand?"

"Yes," she said, slowly standing up. "I'm sorry. I didn't mean to offend you." She backed up toward the door. "I understand now."

Mullin grabbed her arm and threw her down on the bed. Before she could react, he reached into a dresser drawer, yanked out a pair of plastic flex cuffs, and shackled her to the bedpost. She began to scream, but when he unfolded the six-inch Buck knife and raised a forefinger to his lips, she shut up. Slicing up a pillowcase, he deftly ripped off a few long strips, gagged her, and tied her ankles together. She writhed on the bed, eyes frantic, the gag muffling her cries. Mullin kicked the bedpost and muttered to himself, "Stupid fucking bitch."

He hovered over the bed, glowering at her. "You wanted to know what these mean," he said tapping the tattoos with his fingertips. "So I'll tell you." Mullin flexed his biceps, enlarging the tattooed clouds.

"I did a lot of Bible reading when I was inside. Because that's the fastest way to get *outside*. Parole boards and prison counselors like it when a convict sees the light. It makes them feel all warm and fuzzy inside," he said in a mocking voice.

He bent over and tightened the gag. "I did a lot of other kind of reading. Like I said, if you do the crime, you have the time. I read about St. Jerome. He's a Christian dude who did his writing a long time ago. This is what he said about those four creatures coming out of the cloud that Ezekiel saw. He said the lion represented man's emotions. The ox, is, well—" Leering at her, he fondled her breasts. "The ox is man's appetites. And the human face is what St. Jerome called the thinkin' part of man."

Mullin ran his palm over the fourth cloud on his bicep, which was blank inside. "Remember that eagle that I told you about, that Ezekiel saw emerging from the cloud? As you can see, I got no eagle here. Instead of an eagle, I got an empty space. You want to know why?"

She tried to scream again, struggling to free her hands.

"St. Jerome says that the eagle is man's conscience. But there's no eagle here," he said, drumming a forefinger on the empty cloud, "'cause I got no conscience. At least that's what the shrinks in the joint told me."

Mullin ripped off the girl's dress, removed her gag, and every time she started to scream he tapped her neck with the tip of his Buck knife. A half dozen tiny red dots ran down her neck like a rash. He was about to slit the back of her bra, when she looked up at him, eyes red and panicky, and said, sniffling, "You know the Bible. You must be some kind of a Christian. And every Christian's got one. And if you're a Christian, you have to let me go."

"I got something else instead of a conscience."

"What?"

"A lawyer," he said, laughing.

He reached over and as he slit the back of her bra, his cell phone rang. He wanted to ignore it, but he knew only one person had his number—Delfour. And Delfour was not someone he wanted to jack around.

He quickly gagged her and, with a groan, picked up the phone on the fifth ring. "Yeah?"

"I've got a job for you."

"I'm listening."

"I'm coming by in fifteen minutes to fill you in."

"Can't we put it off until morning?"

"You want me to find someone else?"

"No."

"Then clean up that flea trap for me and be ready."

Mullin slammed down the phone and shouted, "Motherfucking cocksucker!"

He uncuffed the girl, threw her torn dress at her, and said with disgust, "Get the fuck out of here."

The girl remained splayed on the bed, tears streaming down her face. Her lower lip twitched. Mullin could see she thought it was a trick. He shoved her off the bed, and she tumbled onto the floor with a thud. She glanced up at him, terrified, and scrambled toward the door, clutching her dress and shoes. Mullin could hear her start her car and burn rubber out of the parking lot.

Mullin slammed his palm on the dresser. He didn't know what to do. Would that stupid cow go to the cops? If she did, would they bust him? She came to his room voluntarily. She asked him to cuff her to the bed, he'd claim. Said she was into that kind of thing. No way they could nail him for anything that would stick. But he better not take the chance. Fortunately, he hadn't been stupid enough to use his real name when he checked in.

Mullin stuffed his shaving kit and clothes into his duffel bag. He slung his room key onto the bed and jogged out the door, through the parking lot and onto the sidewalk. Two blocks away, he called Delfour's cell.

"Had to check out of my motel," Mullin said.

"And why was that?" Delfour asked with strained patience, as if he was talking to a child.

"I went out to the lobby to buy a couple of Cokes from the machine, so we'd have something to drink during our meeting, when I spotted a black-and-white cruising the lot. I thought one of the cops might have recognized me from a job I pulled when I was a kid. I didn't want to take any chances."

"I've never known you to be the cautious sort," Delfour said suspiciously. "But that's just as well. Something just came up. Find yourself another place to stay, check in, get some sleep, and meet me at ten o'clock tonight in front of the Rosslyn Hotel. You know where that is?"

"Yeah. Near skid row. Fifth and Main."

"And one more thing."

"What's that?"

"On your way to the Rosslyn, don't run into any other cops you know."

CHAPTER 5

In the watch commander's office, I poured sludgy black coffee into a Styrofoam cup, and walked through the Pacific Division station, a vault of fluorescent light that housed all of the investigative units in a single cavernous squad room, divided only by wooden signs hanging from the ceiling. The squad room floor, covered with worn royal blue carpeting, was almost empty, except for two robbery detectives interviewing a stringy-haired blond teenager with a red-eyed skull tattooed on his neck.

I was early, so I flicked on a computer in the corner of the gang section and booted up the system we called Cheers because of its acronym—CCHRS (Consolidated Criminal History Reporting System). I typed in Teshay Winfield's name, but he had no record. I then tried Raymond Pinkney and was surprised that he had a rap sheet. I printed a list of his arrests in Los Angeles County and discovered the LAPD had busted him a few times for suspicion of narcotic sales and burglary. Next, I clocked on the CII, the Criminal Information Index, which detailed convictions and criminal sentences. Pinkney was fortunate—or just well connected—because he'd never been convicted. Then I checked CAL/GANG, a statewide computerized gang file for law enforcement agencies, and couldn't dredge up anything on Winfield, but discovered that Pinkney was known as P-Stone and was affiliated with the Sho'line Crips.

After about ten minutes, I glanced across the squad room to the Homicide section, a jumble of nicked brown desks with a row of green metal lockers and, along the opposite wall, stacks of cardboard boxes filled with case files. A huddle of men—Falco, his young trainee, Lieutenant Garza, and four homicide detectives—milled around in front of the lockers, sipping coffee from mugs. I'd worked Pacific Division more than a decade ago and didn't know the four homicide detectives, but I recognized Marva Witherspoon, who wandered over. The senior lead officer for Oakwood, Witherspoon was a tall, willowy black woman in her early forties who still looked shapely in her tight-fitting dark blues. I crossed the room and called out, "Hey, Spoon."

"Asher Levine," she said, slapping me on the back. "Last time I saw you, you were in uniform, cruising Ghost Town in a flattop."

"Yeah, it's been a while. How'd you get involved in this gangbang?"

"They wanted a veterano at this meeting, someone who knows the 'hood."

"Well, you certainly do."

"You still surfing every morning?"

"I wish I was. Since I started working Felony Special, I haven't had the time."

"Boy," Witherspoon said, laughing, "you got to get your priorities straight."

"How are your kids?"

"Not kids anymore. Both in college now. You have kids?"

I shook my head. She jabbed me on the shoulder with her palm. "You better get cracking. You're not getting any younger. Time to give your mama some grandkids."

"That's what she keeps telling me."

Garza rapped his coffee mug on his desk and shouted. "Let's get started."

Falco and the other homicide detectives lingered by their desks. Witherspoon and I rolled chairs over from Robbery. The lieutenant remained standing, shoulders back, a soldier's pose.

"As you all know," Garza said, "Felony Special is now investigating the double in Oakwood. It's quiet tonight, but tomorrow the media will be all over this case."

Falco threw up his hands. "Those pub hounds stole our case when they saw it would get some attention."

"They're a bunch of fucking moths," another detective muttered. "Once they saw the potential for TV lights and press conferences, they were all over it."

I jumped to my feet. "Let's get something straight—"

"Okay, okay," Garza said, waving me off. "Now that we got that out of the way, I can tell everyone at Pacific that Detective Levine had no choice in the matter. This case was handed off to Felony Special by the brass."

"If they're going to steal a case from us, I'm glad it was this one,"

Falco said. He held up his right hand, extended his thumb and forefinger to form an *L*, and wagged it at me. "This case is a loser. Two dickheads with baggy pants shot in an Oakwood alley. Good luck."

"Shut the fuck up, Richie," Garza said. "You're going to help Ash and you're going to start right now."

Falco swore under his breath.

"What was that?" Garza barked.

"I just said that anything that Detective Levine needs, he'll get from me."

"Good." Garza turned to me and said, "Fire away."

"Anybody in the neighborhood see anything?" I asked.

"Of course not," Falco said, chuckling. "I had a case last week. Seven people in an Oakwood apartment. Some clown barges in and caps a guy on the sofa right between the eyes. And guess what?" He grinned. "Nobody sees a fucking thing. They all claim they're in the bathroom. That's one damn crowded bathroom. But that's the way—"

"Anybody hear anything?" I asked.

"Early tonight we talked to the one neighbor who heard a shot," Falco said. "But one of my guys found another neighbor who thinks she heard two shots. But she wasn't sure if it was two shots or a car backfiring a couple of times."

"Anybody else hear anything?" I asked.

Falco nodded. "We found a kid who lives in an apartment down the alley. Says he heard someone yell, 'Where you from?' He looked out his window, but didn't see anything, so he put his headphones on and blasted his music. Says if there was a gunshot, he might not have heard it."

"Did the kid have a take on the voice?" I asked. "Could he tell if it was a Mexican or a black guy yelling?"

"Naw," Falco said.

"A white guy?" I asked.

Falco shot me an are-you-kidding? look. "The kid said his brother was watching ESPN, and he could barely hear over the TV."

"Hey, Spoon," I said, "the Sho'line Crips warring now?"

"Nothing big time," Witherspoon said. "But there's been a few skirmishes in the past year with V-13."

"You think that's what this shooting was all about?"

"Don't know," Witherspoon said. "But I've put a few of my people on it. They're hitting the streets tonight and tomorrow. They'll talk to the ballers, the jackers, and the big homies and try to find out what's up. They'll let me know if this was a payback."

"I did a short background check on the vics," I said. "Winfield's clean. Pinkney had been popped a few times, and it's clear he'd been running with the Sho'lines." I nodded toward Witherspoon and said, "You've been working the streets since I was on patrol here. You ever run into either one of our guys?"

Witherspoon downed her coffee and delicately touched her pinkie to her tongue, removing a coffee ground. "I've had that pleasure, you might say."

"What was Pinkney doing hanging out in Oakwood?" I asked. "He's from South L.A."

"He had a cousin who lived in Oakwood. A Sho-line everyone called Li'l Evil. Pink used to hang here all the time. But I haven't see him much in the past year or two."

"Why don't we snatch up Li'l Evil?" I said. "Bring him to the station and find out what he knows."

"Can't. Got bounced in a walk-up about a year ago."

"What was Pinkney's story?"

"A few years ago, when he was in high school, Pink spent a lot of time down here with Li'l Evil and his associates. We arrested him a few times, filled out F.I. cards on him a few other times. He was a knucklehead, but didn't seem hard core to me. Haven't seen him in a few years. I figured he'd cleaned up his act. I guess not."

"What was the son of a councilman doing with those fools?"

"Who the hell knows," Witherspoon said.

"He was going to college—what do you make of that?"

"Obviously, he didn't learn much. Maybe he'd cleaned up his act for a while, then got bored and wanted some action. Probably came back to Oakwood to thug it up. And look what happened."

"How about the other guy, Teshay Winfield?" I asked.

"He grew up in Oakwood," Witherspoon said. "Mom still lives here. But he was a football player, not a banger. Had a dozen scholarship offers, but he didn't have the grades, so he joined the army. He went in about four years ago. He must have just got out."

"What's your take on this?"

"I think Teshay made the mistake of hanging around with the wrong guy," Witherspoon said. "Pink probably made some enemies when he was hanging with the Sho'lines. Maybe he came back here to bang and got caught looking. Maybe he was sexing up someone's girlfriend. Maybe a V-13 was looking for a Sho'line to take out and recognized Pink. Pink was a target, a guy walkin' round with a great big ol' bull's-eye. Teshay was there—at the wrong place, at the wrong time, hanging with the wrong guy—so he had to go too."

As the meeting broke up, I headed for the door and Witherspoon caught up with me. She apologized for Falco's attitude and said, "I wanted to let you know that my captain authorized me to give you any help that you need. I'll see what I can rustle up for you. A double in a 'hood as small as that—someone will be talking. Soon as I hear anything, I'll call you."

I thanked her and when Witherspoon walked off, I saw Duffy cross the squad room. His forehead was beaded with sweat and he was breathing heavily. I noticed that his wispy silver hair, which was usually disheveled, was neatly combed. "I just met with the chief. Turns out the councilman is visiting Nagoya, Japan—one of those sister city scams. The chief tracked him down and gave him the bad news. So we've been spared the unpleasant task of briefing him. For now. But you better believe that by Monday morning he'll be back in town and crawling all over our asses."

I followed Duffy through the parking lot to his Crown Victoria and suggested we visit the councilman's wife. I figured we might learn something about her son.

We cruised west on the Santa Monica Freeway, exited on Crenshaw, drove a few miles through the dark, desolate streets of South Central, and then cut up into the Baldwin Hills. Duffy pulled up in front of a spacious two-story English Tudor in View Park, Los Angeles's wealthiest black neighborhood.

"The golden ghetto," Duffy said. "If someone blindfolded you and dropped you off here, you'd think you were in a million-dollar Westside neighborhood—not a few minutes up the hill from South Central."

I climbed out of the car and admired the panorama. A swath of lights blanketed the city from the ocean to the mountains, and the downtown skyline twinkled in the distance. The Pinkneys' house featured a lush garden dotted with vivid yellow, pink, and orange roses in full bloom, glistening under the porch light like dollops of sherbet.

"That's one thing I love about L.A.—roses and bougainvillea

blooming in winter," Duffy said. "Back in my hometown of Chicago, all you'll see now surrounding the houses is a gray, snowy slush." He checked his watch. "I hate to knock on the door at two in the morning."

"Nobody's sleeping in there tonight," I said. "It's the only one on the street with the lights on."

"We've got to handle this one extra careful. If we don't treat the family very gently, you know how the councilman will play it to the press. The family of a minority youth mistreated by racist white LAPD cops. Or in your case," Duffy said with a sly smile, "a *technically white* racist LAPD cop."

"Pinkney's living in a fucking time warp," I said. "He still thinks it's the nineteen nineties. He refuses to accept that the LAPD's a different department today."

I rang the bell. A large Christmas wreath with a red bow hung on the front door. I waited a minute, then rang it again. An imposing middle-aged black man, who was almost as tall as Duffy, opened the door. "I'm Reverend Wilkinson," the man said, eyeing us suspiciously, "can't this wait until tomorrow?"

"I wish it could, Reverend," I said. "But I'm sure the councilman wouldn't want us putting off this investigation. I spent a few years undergoing intensive religious training and I'm aware of how important the work is that you're doing tonight. It's truly the Lord's work. But it does take a tremendous toll on the Lord's messenger."

Wilkinson sighed. "Yes, it does."

"I think it would be best if we had a word with Mrs. Pinkney," I said.

Before Wilkinson could respond, Duffy and I slipped inside. We followed Wilkinson, and Duffy whispered to me, "What was the intensive religious training?"

"My Bar Mitzvah," I said, stifling a smile.

As we moved into the room, Wilkinson reluctantly introduced us to the victim's mother and sister, both slumped on a sofa. I surveyed the living room, which seemed unnaturally bright at such a late hour. All the lights were on, including a crystal chandelier, spotlighting the creamy whiteness of the walls, sofa, coffee table, and carpeting. A Christmas tree, strung with ornaments and blinking lights, towered in the corner of the room, emitting a sharp resinous scent. In the other corner there was a Kwanzaa candelabra—with black, green, and red candles—atop a straw mat strewn with ears of corn, a black ceramic cup, and a fruit bowl. Baby pictures and high school graduation photos of Raymond and his sister were lined up on a mantel over the flagstone fireplace. I closed my eyes briefly. I have done it countless times, but I will never get used to interviewing a grieving mother after the murder of her child.

Pinkney's sister, who was in her early twenties and wore her hair in cornrows, stared sullenly at Duffy and me. Mrs. Pinkney seemed the perfect politician's wife, with her immaculately coiffed gray hair, and conservative outfit of camel skirt, beige cashmere sweater, and pearl necklace. She dabbed at her eyes with a Kleenex and gestured toward two lavender chairs. Duffy and I sat as Wilkinson joined Mrs. Pinkney and her daughter on the sofa.

"I want to first extend my sympathies," Duffy said. "I am truly sorry that I have to intrude on your grief. But the department's number-one priority at this time is to find out who killed your son. The LAPD will use every resource available to solve this terrible crime. Normally, in a case like this, the local homicide detectives from the Pacific Division would have handled it. But we're making this a high-priority case. We're from Felony Special, an elite downtown unit with city-wide jurisdiction."

"I thought Robbery-Homicide Division handled cases like this," Reverend Wilkinson said.

"We're part of RHD," Duffy said, "along with Homicide Special and a few other units." Duffy lightly touched my shoulder. "This man is such a superb detective, I handpicked him to investigate this case."

I knew this wasn't true, but Duffy often became so impassioned when he was working a witness or a family member, he ended up believing his own embellishments.

"I can tell you," Duffy said, "that when it comes to this investigation —"

"It's been a very long and difficult night," Wilkinson said. "Let's get to the point. How can Mrs. Pinkney help you?"

"Let me defer to Detective Asher Levine."

I gazed at Mrs. Pinkney and said, "I, too, would like to say I'm very sorry for your loss. And I apologize for having to ask you questions at a time like this. But for me to do my job properly, it's just something I've got to do. And, unfortunately, I've got to do it now."

She nodded.

"Did your son have any enemies?" I asked.

Mrs. Pinkney sobbed, her shoulders trembling. Wilkinson handed her a Kleenex, she dried her eyes and said, "As far as I know, Raymond had no enemies."

"Any idea who could have done this?"

She shook her head.

"Can you tell me a little about your son?"

"He was a sophomore at Long Beach State." Her eyes were glazed and her lips trembled, but she enunciated each word like an elementary school teacher. "He'd had his problems. He'd run with the wrong crowd for a while. But he'd really grown up this past year or two."

"Did he live on campus?"

"First year he did. This year he was living at home."

"Did he spend much time in Oakwood?"

"Not since his cousin died." She stared sadly into the middle distance and said, "My husband and I did not like Raymond going out there. My nephew was friends with a very low element."

"How did he know Teshay Winfield?"

"Teshay spent a year on this side of town going to high school. Raymond and he got to be friends. He lived with his auntie down near the Harbor Freeway. I think the coach at our high school here recruited him to play football. When the district officials began investigating Teshay's transfer, he moved back to his mom's in Oakwood."

"Did Raymond spend much time at Teshay's?"

"I don't think so. Teshay's been gone. In the army. He's a good, upstanding young man. They just got together a few times since Teshay returned from the service. Everyone loved Teshay. He was a churchgoing, clean-living boy. A fine athlete. Very well-mannered."

"I want to talk to Teshay's parents tonight," I said. "You haven't, by chance, spoken to them."

"I just called Teshay's mother, but no one answered her phone. She must be out of town."

"And his father?" I asked.

"I don't know who he is. Neither does Teshay."

"You mentioned that Raymond's cousin hung around a low element," I said. "Are you referring to gang members?"

"Yes, I am."

"After the cousin died, did Raymond continue to hang around these gangbangers?"

"I never said Raymond spent time with these people," she said.

I leaned toward her and said softly, "Raymond had some markings that were kind of like a tattoo on his upper arm. Do you know anything about that?"

The sister glared at me. "You think it was a *gang* tattoo?"

"We don't know what it was," I said.

She banged her fist on the coffee table. "A young black man has a tattoo, and you automatically assume it's a gang tattoo. A young man gets killed, and you automatically assume he's a gangbanger. He's got to be a lowlife thug—so he deserved what he got."

Duffy held up his palms. "That's not what he's saying—"

"I'm not talking to any motherfucking cops! Especially no cops from the Los Angeles Police Department," she said, spitting out the words.

She stormed into the kitchen and slammed the door. I figured it was she, not her brother, who'd taken the mantle of political firebrand from their father.

Mrs. Pinkney tried to speak, but began coughing and slapping her chest. Wilkinson hurried into the kitchen to retrieve a glass of water for her. She sipped the water and said, "I apologize for my daughter's manner tonight. She's very distraught."

"Of course," I said.

"You asked about the tattoo on my son's arm. They're Greek letters. He was in a fraternity. A black fraternity."

"It looked as if it was branded on."

"It was."

"Odd," Duffy said.

"Not really," Mrs. Pinkney said. "A lot of black fraternities do that. A lot of prominent black men have tattoos like that, including The Reverend Jesse Jackson, who's got an omega branded on him. My husband has the same tattoo. Got it when he was in college at Morehouse."

"Another thing," I said, "I'd like to ask—"

"I don't know if I can take much more of this." She extended a trembling hand and emitted a sharp, strangled cry. Wilkinson folded his arm around her shoulder, and she collapsed against his chest. I rose and whispered to Wilkinson, "We won't trouble her any more tonight. But before we leave, can we take a quick look at Raymond's room? We might find something important there."

Mrs. Pinkney slowly lifted her head and flicked her wrist toward the stairs. Duffy and I hustled out of the living room and jogged up the steps. We opened a few doors until we found Raymond's room, which still resembled a little boy's bedroom, with a powder-blue bedspread and carpeting and pale blue walls. Football and basketball trophies lined a shelf above his desk. A signed Kobe Bryant jersey hung above his bed, encased in a large Plexiglas shadow box. On another shelf perched a basketball signed by every member of the Clippers. I assumed the councilman used his connections to procure the memorabilia for his son.

Duffy shuffled a pile of dirty T-shirts, sweatpants, and sweaters from the bed and sat down. I opened all the desk drawers and inspected the CDs, floppy disks, envelopes, and Long Beach State notebooks. When I finished with the desk's contents, I sifted through the closet, checking the pockets of the jackets and the jeans. Finally, I clicked on the computer, but couldn't access the e-mails because the program required a password.

"Maybe you can get someone to stop by on Monday and sweet-talk the family into letting us take this downtown. Our guys in the computer unit can scan the hard drive."

Duffy nodded. "Find anything interesting?"

"Not really. But this is kind of intriguing." I fanned out on the bed three pictures I'd removed from a desk drawer. Pinkney was posing against a fence with a group of shirtless, muscular young men flashing gang signs. Their chests were covered with SLC—Sho'line Crip—tattoos.

"Those guys have that jailhouse buff," Duffy said. He tapped a thumb on the tattoos. "Looks like Raymond picked the wrong fraternity to hang out with this weekend."

I pointed to the date on the photos. "But that's a year and a half ago. Maybe he left that world."

Duffy rolled his eyes. "If it looks like a duck, walks like duck, and quacks like a duck, I'm guessing it's a duck." Pinkney's sister pushed open the door and shouted, "A human being has just been murdered! Not a duck!" She'd been eavesdropping on us.

Startled, Duffy sprang to his feet. "It's just an expression, and I'm truly sorry for sounding insensitive." Moving toward the door, he said, "I think we're done here, aren't we, Ash?"

CHAPTER 6

When we dropped back down the hill toward Crenshaw Boulevard, Duffy called the Pacific watch commander for Teshay's mother's address in Oakwood. It was still dark when we pulled up in front of her house, a tiny clapboard bungalow with a cramped front yard and a roof that was missing so many cedar shingles it looked like a worn quilt.

I rang the doorbell. Then I knocked. Then I pounded on the door.

"She's not home," said an elderly, white-haired black woman standing on the porch next door.

"Sorry to wake you, ma'am," I said.

"You didn't wake me. I'm used to getting up early. I moved out here from Texas in fifty-nine, but I'm still a country girl. I still get up with the chickens."

"We're looking for Mrs. Winfield."

"What's she done wrong?" the woman asked suspiciously.

"Nothing. We just need some background for an investigation. Do you know where she is?"

"She's on a turnaround."

"I'm not familiar with that term."

"A turnaround to Vegas. She and some other ladies went out to the shopping center on Lincoln last night. Chartered bus filled with people feelin' lucky picked them up and a bunch of others and drove all night. Passengers gamble during the day. Bus drives back Saturday night and they get in Sunday morning, in plenty of time for church."

"What time does the bus get in?"

"'Bout mid-morning."

As we walked back toward the car, I said, "Did you find out about the post?"

"After I talked to the chief I called the coroner's office. Autopsies on your double are Saturday morning at zero eight hundred."

I asked Duffy to drop me off at the Pacific station so I could pick up my Saturn.

"I've been meaning to talk to you about that. You know, you're never going to get remarried driving that pile of junk. No decent-looking woman in L.A. would be seen in a wreck like that."

I ignored him, stepped into the Crown Vic, and stretched my legs.

As Duffy drove down Lincoln, I closed my eyes and thought about the interview with Pinkney's mother and the pictures of him posing with the shirtless gangbangers.

"You want some backup when you come back here and do the death notification?" Duffy asked.

"I can handle it. Just make sure press relations doesn't release Teshay Winfield's name when they do the press release this morning. Hold off until I get ahold of the mom."

"Nobody gives a shit about him, anyway," Duffy said, pulling into the Pacific parking lot, packed with patrol cars and cops' personal vehicles. "I'm calling it a night. How about you?"

"Naw. I've got a few more things to check out."

"You always do," Duffy said. "But, remember, I can't authorize any cash overtime. This budget deficit is kicking our ass. So all you get is comp time."

"I don't care about that."

"If you were still married, you would."

I drove back to Oakwood and parked on a street beside an abandoned couch with the cushions missing. In the dark, I grabbed my flashlight and ambled down the alley where the bodies were found. I leaned against a garage door, shivering. The streets were deserted—a rare respite from the crush of traffic—and in the early morning calm I heard the surf pounding in the distance. A flash of color caught my eye: a flock of wild parrots and long-tailed macaws perched on a rain gutter. Backlit by a street lamp, their feathers glowed brilliant yellow, aqua, and scarlet. A moment later they flew down the alley, squawking raucously. I watched the birds dart and dive among the telephone wires and fly off. Then it was quiet again. I knew all of them had been pets once, turned out by bored owners, forced to fend for themselves in the smog.

My reverie was broken by a loud, grating sound. I swiveled around. A wino staggered down the alley, carrying a black plastic garbage bag.

Probably looking for metal cans. I stopped, stock-still for a moment.

I realized that Raymond Pinkney and Teshay Winfield were not shot where I'd found their bodies. They were killed somewhere else and transported to the alley. No gunman walking on that pea gravel could take two victims by surprise. They would have heard his footsteps, like I'd heard the wino's footsteps, and turned around. If they'd been shot, it would have been in the chest or stomach—not in the back.

So that's what it was, I thought. A dump job. Of course. I chastised myself for a moment. Why had it taken me so long to figure it out?

After leaving the crime scene, I drove north on Lincoln. The eastern horizon was ribbed with bands of faded blue and amber, bleeding through the darkness—the first shimmer of dawn. I stopped at an all-night diner, bought a cup of coffee to go, and sat in my car, thinking about the dump job.

I swigged the tepid coffee, crumpled up the cup, tossed it in the backseat, and headed toward the Santa Monica Freeway. As I sped east on the freeway toward the sunrise, streaks of pale pink and burnt orange daubed the sky, like paint dripping down a canvas. The downtown skyline glimmered in a wash of rose-colored light. If Duffy could have spared me, I'd be in bed right now with Robin, the sunrise pouring through our window. Flipping on the radio, I punched in a news channel. I didn't want to be distracted by the lost weekend. I wanted news of the world's tragedies, so I'd be in the right mood for an autopsy.

Just past downtown, I cut off the freeway and sped to the crime lab at the edge of Cal State-L.A., the one that we share with the Sheriff's Department. I hopped out of the Saturn and jogged across the parking lot. The building was eerily quiet, but I found a bald, paunchy criminalist dozing in the coffee room.

"Wake up, Jake," I said, patting him on the head.

He glanced up at me, blinking hard. "Why don't you work normal hours like everyone else, and let an overworked civil servant get some sleep."

"I need some new clothes," I said, "and none of the department stores are open yet."

I followed him into an evidence room. He unwrapped two bulky packages that contained the victims' clothing, tore off two large shreds of butcher paper, then carefully laid out on a table the pants, shirts, un-

MIDNIGHT ALLEY   45

derwear, and jackets. Slipping on a pair of Latex gloves, I bent over and studied a circle in the back of Pinkney's Raiders jacket, about two inches in diameter, filled with tiny black specks—burnt powder and gunshot residue. I found the same pattern on Winfield's Lakers jacket.

"Definitely not a contact wound," I said. "But the gun was pretty damn close. Had to be no more than a foot away. You agree?"

Jake nodded.

I knew my instincts had been correct. Nobody could sneak all the way down a long pea gravel alley, get to within a foot of them, surprise them, and shoot them in the back. For several minutes, I examined the victims' jackets, pants, and shirts.

"What you looking for?" Jake asked.

"This was a dump job," I said. "I'm looking for grass stains, scrape marks, any evidence that they were dragged." I motioned toward the table. "Lemme see their shoes."

Jake tugged loose two packages and dropped a pair of Nikes and a pair of Pumas on the butcher paper. I tapped at the back heels of both pairs. "See those scrape marks? See the dirt stains?"

He nodded.

"First, asshole shoots these vics," I said. "Then he lifts 'em up, slips his arms around their chest, and drags 'em to his vehicle. Their heels scrape along the ground, picking up dirt. Later, asshole sneaks into the Oakwood alley, dumps their bodies on the gravel, and drives off without anyone paying much attention."

"If you're so fucking smart," Jake said, "why'd it take you all night to figure this out?"

I sucked down a deep breath, puffed up my cheeks, and expelled a burst of air. "I wasn't thinking clearly. I was dealing with something last night."

"Problems at home?"

"Something like that."

"What homicide detective doesn't."

At seven fifty, I parked in a lot behind the coroner's office, a featureless low-slung, rectangular building a few miles east of downtown and a block from Interstate 5. I crossed a loading dock in back, past a group of coroner technicians who were smoking, trying to obliterate the smell of decaying flesh. In the locker room, I slipped scrubs on over my clothes, booties over my shoes, and adjusted my mask. I hustled down the hallway and into the vast, brightly lit autopsy room, gleaming with chrome counters and steel troughs. I gingerly stepped over pools of blood and snippets of tissue, past pathologists dissecting corpses on metal gurneys, their voices muffled through their masks, until I reached the corner of the room, where Dr. Ramesh Gupta hovered over Winfield and Pinkney.

I could see that the bodies had already been split open from their shoulders to their navels, the ribs cut, the sternum removed, their slick, veined organs exposed.

"You're late, Ash," Gupta said with a lilting Indian inflection.

I checked my watch. "I'm two minutes early. Lieutenant Duffy said it was a zero eight hundred start."

"No. Seven thirty."

"What a fucked-up department," I muttered.

"You said it, not me," Gupta said.

"Okay, master of horizontal medicine, fill me in," I said, reaching inside my scrubs and flicking off my cell. I didn't want to be distracted.

"We've got two male blacks in their early twenties who were in excellent health. Until, that is, they were shot in the back." Gupta pointed to the X-rays of the two men, posted on an illuminated viewing box. "No bullets or fragments remain in the body. So you've got two through-and-through wounds. You find the slugs?"

"No," I said.

Gupta wagged a finger at me. "That's not like you. You're usually very meticulous."

"Body dump," I said.

"Ah," Gupta said, raising a forefinger. "This is a very challenging case you have."

"What have you come up with?"

"Let's start with the councilman's son, Mr. Raymond Pinkney." Gupta grabbed a scalpel off the chrome counter and pointed to faint streaks around his wrists.

"Ligature marks," I said. "I'm surprised I didn't notice them Friday."

"Nighttime crime scene?" Gupta asked.

"Yeah."

"Poor lighting. Black victims. Not so easy."

"Still, I should have looked closer," I said.

"Did you know it was a body dump then?"

"No."

"Then you've got a good excuse. Ligature marks, as you know, are not uncommon with body dumps."

A few inches above the ligature marks, I noticed a faint tattoo on Pinkney's left forearm: a coiled snake, jaws open, ready to strike. The same place my dad had those pale blue numbers. He was eleven or twelve, and he was shipped by cattle car from Germany to the ghetto in Lodz, Poland, then on to Treblinka. A few minutes after being shoved through the gates, he saw his father shot in the back. He never saw his mother or younger brother again. The next year he was transported to Auschwitz.

"Ash, Ash, pay attention!"

"Sorry, Doc. What do you have?"

"This, right here, is very interesting." He pointed to about ten small squares burned into Pinkney's leg, just above the kneecaps, and another ten burned onto the right forearm.

"Shallow?" I asked.

Gupta probed several of the wounds with the scalpel. "About a half inch."

I craned my neck. "I'd say tortured. Nonfatal wounds. What did asshole use to make those marks?"

"I've been thinking about that," Gupta said. "My guess is a soldering iron, the kind of tool an electrician would use to fuse wires. Something like that would generate tremendous heat. Those are significant burns."

Gupta tapped the side of his scalpel on the gurney. "Here's something else I found interesting," he said, tracing the scalpel over two puncture wounds about four inches apart on Pinkney's chest. Then he ran the scalpel over two other sets of identical wounds on his stomach and shoulder.

"What was used to make those punctures?"

"That I don't know, but I know who might." Gupta said. He crossed the room and returned trailing Alfred Eckstein, a hunched, silver-haired pathologist who'd been conducting autopsies since I was a boot.

"Okay, Dr. E," Gupta said, pointing to Pinkney's puncture wounds, "give us the diagnosis."

Eckstein leaned over the body. I heard a faint clicking sound through his mask. He tentatively dabbed at the wounds with a scalpel. He mumbled something.

"What?" Gupta said. "Louder, please."

"The mechanism is like brass knuckles," Eckstein said, "but with two spikes fist-width apart."

"I've never come upon one of those," Gupta said.

"I've done a few posts here on Guatemalan immigrants," Eckstein said. "Apparently, the death squads there in the 1980s used knuckle dusters like this to extract information from recalcitrant leftists. These guys with the marks escaped Guatemala, but ended up getting killed in L.A." He faced me. "Your victim spend any time in Central America?"

"Don't know."

"That might be a line of inquiry for you, Detective," Eckstein said. He nodded to me and shuffled back to his own corpse.

I pointed to a pattern of burn marks and puncture wounds on Teshay Winfield's stomach and chest and asked Gupta, "They exactly the same as Pinkney's wounds?"

"I assume so."

"Can you verify that?"

"Okay, let's find out."

For the next ten minutes, Gupta counted and measured with a small metal ruler every wound on the two bodies and jotted down the information on a chart. Then he retrieved a small scalpel from the counter, scrutinized Winfield's body and said, "Let's see what we can determine on the subcutaneous level." He sliced the top layer of skin off several of the burn and puncture wounds. Then he shifted to Raymond Pinkney's body and did the same.

"Yes, yes, you might be very intrigued by this," Gupta said, his voice rising a notch from excitement. He jabbed his scalpel at the wounds on Winfield's body that he had just dissected. "See how pink this tissue is? Now look at this." He pointed to the dissected wounds on Pinkney's thighs, forearms, and chest. The tissue was a pale gray. "Explain," Gupta said, like a pathology professor challenging an intern.

"The wounds on Raymond Pinkney's body were made postmortem, after he was killed, after he was shot in the back," I said. "If his heart had still been pumping, we'd see more tissue reaction, more color. The wounds on Teshay Winfield's body were made while he was alive."

I tapped a finger on the metal gurney. A moment later I said, "The killer had to inflict those torture marks on both of them."

"Why?" Gupta asked, looking genuinely curious.

"Because he didn't want to tip his hand."

"What does this 'tip his hand' mean?"

"It means he didn't want us to know who he was really after. It turns out I've been going in the wrong direction. Raymond Pinkney is not the key to this case. He, obviously, was of no use to the killer. He was *not* the target."

The victim who was tortured because he had information the killer wanted, who possessed the secrets I needed to uncover, who I should have focused on from the get-go—was Teshay Winfield.

CHAPTER 7

I slowly made my way back to my car, so lost in thought that I almost stumbled off the loading dock and onto the cement. Straining against the wind, my hair blowing straight up, I flicked my phone back on. I climbed into my car, called Duffy, summarized the results of the autopsy, and told him how I figured out the case was a dump job.

"So the shooter chills them, tosses them in the van, and dumps them in the Oakwood alley," Duffy said. I figured he was driving through downtown because I could hear the rumble of traffic and horns honking as his voice faded in and out.

"Right," I said.

"I've got one question."

"Yeah?"

"Because the shooter's got two bodies in the back of his van, was he able to use the car pool lane?"

I was too tired to laugh.

"Good work, Ash. Keep pushing. By the way, you've got an interview at noon at Pacific with Bruce Pender, Winfield's high school football coach. He called and wants to talk to the investigating detective."

"Does he have anything?"

"Don't know. But here's something that might help. The City Council just ponied up a fifty-thousand-dollar reward. That might rustle up a tipster or two."

After I clicked off, I called Witherspoon. "Hey, Spoon, I just got out of the autopsy. I discovered something very interesting. Turns out Pinkney wasn't the guy our shooter was after. It was Winfield."

"Then why'd they drop Pink?"

"My guess is that he was unlucky enough to be with Teshay, so he had to go, too."

"How'd you figure that out?"

"I'll explain when I see you."

"Just doesn't make sense," Witherspoon said.

"Why?"

"'Cause I was working those streets since Teshay was in grade school. He was a good kid, an athlete. Hell, he was squeaky clean."

"I'm heading out to see Teshay's mom. Let me know if you pick up anything in Oakwood."

It was sunny downtown, one of those rare smogless days when the San Gabriel Mountains were clearly etched against a powder-blue sky. But as I zigzagged west on the Santa Monica Freeway, I encountered a fine mist that thickened as I neared the ocean. When I pulled up in front of Winfield's mother's house, the fog fluttered above the treetops and the air was brackish. I cut the engine and sat in the car for a few minutes. The breakup of my marriage didn't convince me to leave homicide, but one too many death notifications might. This was the part of the job I most hated.

My old mentor, Bud Carducci, had a theory that every cop has a preordained limit of murders. When the detective reached his limit, when he simply could not tolerate another senseless death—then he had to leave homicide. I hadn't reached that limit yet, but I felt I was getting close. During my years at South Bureau Homicide, it seemed like I was doing several notifications a week. When I finally was promoted to Felony Special I was greatly relieved—partly because my caseload was lighter, but also because there would be fewer times I'd have to deliver the four most devastating words I knew—Your son is dead.

One part of the process particularly disturbed me: the immediate lack of honesty. Carducci had taught me that a homicide detective never simply breaks the bad news to family members. Relatives often will become so hysterical that they're unable to provide the detective with any useful information. "Get as much background as you can, first," Carducci advised me, "then tell them." I'd argued that I found it offensive to stall a mother, to casually chat with her, to ask her questions, all the while putting off telling her what she had a right to know.

"Don't we owe her some honesty?" I'd asked Carducci.

"No," Carducci had said flatly. "We owe her only one thing: to use every resource and ploy we have—including snowing her—to solve her son's murder."

Staring out my windshield, I could see the crowns of the palms begin to sway. I rolled down my windows. It wasn't the usual offshore breeze, but a hard wind from the east blowing the fog out to sea, fluttering the silvery leaves of the Texas sage bordering the side of the house. I climbed out of the Saturn, walked up the steps to the porch, and swallowed a few quick deep breaths. "God, how I hate this," I muttered to myself, knocking on the door.

I saw a peephole open.

I held my badge up and said, "Hello, Mrs. Winfield. I'm LAPD Detective Ash Levine. I'd like to talk to you about your son."

She swung open the door and glanced up at me, worried. "What's he done?"

I tried to muster a reassuring smile. "Just need some background information on a case I'm investigating."

"Okay," she said, tilting her head slightly and fixing me with a suspicious look. "But I think you're asking about the wrong person. Teshay's a good boy. He isn't involved in any wrongdoing."

I asked her if we could sit down and she nodded. I followed her to the sofa and sat next to her. The tiny living room was immaculate, with plastic slipcovers on the sofa and the chairs, a small organ in the corner, and on a cabinet, pictures of Teshay in a football uniform, Teshay wearing a graduation cap and gown, and Teshay dressed in army fatigues. A small Christmas tree, boughs heavy with white flocking and red ornaments, stood by a window. A string of lights spelling out JESUS IS LORD glowed above the mantel. In front of the fireplace sat a wooden end table with plastic nativity figurines atop a white doily: Mary cradling baby Jesus and riding on a donkey, with Joseph trailing behind.

"Is Teshay in jail?"

"No he's not," I said, my stomach tensing.

"Then what's this about?"

"Detectives have a certain way of doing things. After I get my background, I'll fill you in."

"All right," she said.

"I understand your son was in the service," I said.

"Got out a little while ago," she said. "He was in Iraq first and then Afghanistan. He's been a little out of sorts since he's been back."

"I know how it is. I went through it when I got back from the service."

"Army?"

"Yeah," I said, deciding not to mention that it was the Israeli Army.

"You see some combat, too?"

I nodded.

"It's been a hard adjustment for Teshay."

"It takes a while," I said. "What's he been doing since he returned?"

"Just looking for a job."

"He found anything?"

"Not yet. But his friend is the son of Councilman Isaac Pinkney. And Teshay just talked to Mr. Pinkney last week. He promised to find him a gov'ment job."

"Who's he been spending time with since he got back?"

"There's Raymond Pinkney, like I said."

"Did they spend a lot of time together?"

"Just got together a few times."

"You know much about Raymond?"

"He was a rowdy boy. Before Teshay went in the army, I didn't like him hanging around Raymond. But I seen Raymond when Teshay got back. He seems to have straightened himself out. He been going to college. And, you know, he comes from a very fine family."

"Did Teshay spend time with anyone else?"

"Not really. He mostly just run to the gym, run home, run on the beach. He do a lot of running 'cause he don't have a car yet. When he not running around, he stay home, and listen to his music."

"Does Teshay live here?"

"Used to. But last month he rented himself a little place in Oakwood."

"Where is that?"

She told me the address, which I knew was less than a mile away, and said he lived alone.

"Did he seem worried about anything in particular?"

"Just about getting a job."

"You mentioned you've seen Raymond a few times recently. Did he have any enemies that you know of?"

"I don't know nothin' about that."

"I just have a few more questions. Was Teshay ever stationed in Central America?"

"No. Just Iraq and Afghanistan."

"You sure?"

"I'm one hundred percent sure. He went from Fort Hood in Texas to Iraq and back to Fort Hood and then to Afghanistan and back to Fort Hood."

"Okay. I was wondering if you could help me with something else. I'm trying to find some of your son's army buddies. Maybe someone who's been discharged."

"Hmm," she said. "I do know one boy."

"Do you know his name?"

"His name's Jerry. Teshay bring him by the house a few times. They worked out at the high school together. He handicapped now. Lost an arm in Iraq."

"Do you know his last name?"

After a long pause, she said, "Ambrose."

"A-M-B-R-O-S-E?" I said, spelling out the name.

"That's it."

She clasped her hands together so tightly that her fingers whitened. "I don't like where this is going." She stood abruptly and shouted, "No more games, Mr. Detective! What you done with my boy? I know how you LAPD detectives do our young men. He a good boy. He never been in no trouble." She jerked her thumb toward the door. "You either get out right now or tell me what's going on."

The interview was over. I sighed deeply and nervously pinched my chin. "Mrs. Winfield, I have some very bad news for you. And I'm very sorry to have to tell you this. But your son and Raymond Pinkney were killed on Friday night."

She froze for a moment, arms out, fists clenched, eyes shut, mouth wide open. Then, like a marionette whose strings have been cut, she crumpled to the ground.

"No, Lord!" she screamed. "No! Jesus, don't take my baby!"

As she wailed and sobbed, I knelt next to her, lightly touching the small of her back. She looked up, eyes wild, tears sluicing down her cheeks, and whispered, "How?"

"Your son and Raymond were both shot. We found them in an alley a few blocks from here."

"Why? Why, Jesus, why?"

"I'm going to do everything in my power to find out. But right now,

I don't want you to be alone. Is there anyone you could call now? A family member or a friend?"

She nodded weakly.

"I need your help with something. Do you have a key to the place your son rented?"

She raised a trembling fist and motioned toward the top drawer of the wooden cabinet. I opened it and pocketed a key on a brass chain. Her chest heaved as she pounded the floor with her fist. "Who? Who killed my boy?"

"Right now, I don't know."

She rolled over on her side, gasping for breath, and looked up at me, cheeks wet, eyes unfocused.

"But I promise you one thing, Mrs. Winfield. I'm going to find out."

PART II

COMBAT MASTERPIECE

CHAPTER 8

The night was cold, with a biting wind, as Mullin walked through skid row on east Fifth Street. The stench of urine brought back memories of the joint. The nasty smell, the jarring noise, the foul food, the lights on twenty-four hours a day. As he drifted west he passed a raggedy-ass army of losers: toothless winos pushing rusty shopping carts filled with blankets and dirty clothes, crackheads in doorways firing up glass pipes, trannies balancing pocket mirrors and applying makeup, wetbacks lugging their gear in plastic garbage bags, psychos huddling in cardboard boxes. As he approached Main, he spotted a sign: Historic Downtown. The buildings didn't look historic to Mullin, just old.

He kicked an empty Thunderbird bottle into the gutter, thinking about last night. What lousy timing. Why did he always have such bad fucking luck? Why did Delfour have to call him just when he was about to pop that bitch? Why couldn't he have called an hour later? But you never know. Maybe it was for the best. He might have tossed her into a Dumpster. And that could have cost him some long time somewhere down the line.

Did she go to the cops? Mullin wondered. And if she did, could they track him down? Probably not. The only thing they had to go on was his tats. And Mullin knew they wouldn't give him away. Street cops, he knew, always described tats in arrest reports. That could lead to an identification and arrest. But he didn't get marked up until he went to the joint. And inside, the guards paid no attention to tats. If they tried to describe every tattoo on every convict, the prisons would have to hire a million new guards.

But why did he have to brag to that bitch about what his tats meant? Showing off again. Trying to prove how fucking smart he was, how much he knew. He had to admit that conscience shit had been on his mind for a while. His buddy who worked in the penitentiary counseling center got him a copy of his psych report. It was written in so much double-talk he couldn't figure it out, but one word stuck out in his mind: "sociopathic." A guy in his cellblock—a former college prof who'd carved up his wife—told him it meant he had no conscience. For so long, he'd felt like a freak, but when he read that psych report, a warmth flooded his chest. The shrinks had determined that he was part of a group. For the first time in his life, he felt like he finally belonged somewhere.

Mullin almost tripped over a drunk, sprawled on the sidewalk, who shouted, "Spare change?"

"Fuck off," Mullin said, stepping off the curb to cross Main. He halted in front of the Rosslyn, beside some dusty plastic plants in pots, under the big curlicued *R* above the doorway. He waited for Delfour and looked around. The lobby, Mullin could see, was a fraction of its original size. Someone had blocked off the center with some cheap drywall. In the back, a hotel clerk perched on a stool behind a sheet of security Plexiglas and handed out room keys and mail. The last time Mullin stayed here, the hotel was a flophouse. It was still an old, rundown, sooty brick building, but the 'hood had changed since he'd been inside. Now the place was called the Rosslyn Lofts. And next door there was some kind of half-assed art gallery with a bunch of splotchy pictures that looked like they'd been painted by a damned kindergartner. The usual parade passed by—bag ladies screaming at the sky and gimps in wheelchairs—but he also spotted a young dude, dressed in black, wearing a beret, and a lady walking a fluffy dog.

Mullin heard footsteps thumping down the narrow street, turned, and saw Delfour. He walked like he had a stick up his ass. That Delfour was a strange one. Mullin had never met a nigger who walked or talked or dressed like Delfour. If you shut your eyes when he talked, you'd swear he was a white dude. No slang. No jive. He carefully pronounced each word. And he always dressed like some insurance agent. Tonight he was wearing brown penny loafers, slacks, a white shirt, and a blue sweater with a collar that buttoned down in front. Jesus, Mullin muttered. What self-respecting brutha wore a sweater like that?

"Mr. Mullin," Delfour said solemnly, extending his hand.

"Delfour," Mullin said, laughing at how uptight the dude was.

"As I told you, I've got a job for you."

"You don't mess around, do you? It's always right to business. What does it pay?"

"Twenty thousand dollars."

"How much up front?"

"Nothing. It's all payable upon completion of the job."

"What if I do the job and you split?"

"You've known me too long. That's not how I do business."

"That's a nice piece of change. Who's the target?"

Delfour handed him a yellow envelope. "All the info is in there. Who the subject is, where he lives, and a picture of him so you don't eliminate the wrong guy. Take a look at it. Memorize it, and I'll take the envelope back. I don't want any incriminating information left at the scene. I've included a revolver and latex gloves. You do the job and drop the weapon. It's untraceable. You can get to work right away."

"Why don't you get me an M107 50 cal sniper rifle. I can drop the dude—easily—at half a mile."

"It has to be done from fairly close range. With a handgun."

"Why a revolver? I'd rather use a semiauto."

"We don't want a semi jamming on you. Revolver's more reliable."

"I want a semi."

"Can't take the chance of it double-feeding or stovepiping on you."

"Okay, you're the boss. What kind of piece."

"It's an S and W Model 15 with a Hogue grip."

"That gun's a fucking antique, at least a couple of decades old. Don't they call that rod the K-38?"

"Smith also calls it the Combat Masterpiece."

"Combat Masterpiece," Mullin said, savoring the phrase. "That's fucking poetry. But I'd still rather use a semiauto with fifteen rounds in the magazine."

"We decided this is the best way to proceed."

"Who's 'we'?"

"You don't need to know that."

"Okay, then gimme a preview of the job, bro," Mullin said.

Delfour told him the guy lived in a loft downtown, a few blocks from the Rosslyn, and the only way in is through the front entrance. Across the street, Delfour said, there's a Dumpster. Mullin knew he could use it for cover.

Delfour fished a small notebook out of his back pocket, tore out the page, and handed it Mullin. "Here's his name and address. Memorize this and then tear up the paper. You're going to have to be careful on this one. The guy's an LAPD detective."

Mullin leered at Delfour. "In that case, the job might cost you a little more."

"Okay. Twenty-five thousand."

"That sounds about right. When do you want it done?"

"The cop's out on a case now. Probably won't be home until sometime tomorrow night. Get it done then. He works long hours. He comes home late at night. His neighborhood is quiet, not a lot of people live on that block. Lots of shuttered buildings. Lots of buildings under renovation. Shouldn't be any witnesses."

CHAPTER 9

I drove over to the Pacific station and was relieved to see that Homicide was empty on this Saturday morning, so I didn't have to deal with Falco. I knew that Bruce Pender, Winfield's high school coach, was on his way. I called the front desk and told them when he arrived, to send him back to Homicide.

I slumped down at a desk near a window, signed onto NECS—the Network Communications System—dug up Jerry Ambrose's driver's license information and jotted his address on my legal pad. He lived in the mid-Wilshire area, not far from the La Brea Tar Pits. As I was signing off, the desk officer ushered Pender back to Homicide. A stocky, florid man with close-cropped blond hair, he was wearing a green Nike sweatsuit. We shook hands and I motioned for him to sit across from me.

"Teshay's mother called me as soon as she found out," Pender said, his voice rough with emotion. "Let me tell you why I wanted to see you. I think it's important you know that Teshay was a good kid. He wasn't a banger or a druggie. I didn't want you to think that this was just another hit on a black gangster."

"Actually, I didn't."

"Do you know who did it?" Pender asked.

"It's still early in the investigation."

"You making any progress?"

"We try to keep the details of the investigation confidential."

"Of course," Pender said, nodding earnestly.

"Did you see Winfield since he got back from the army?" I asked.

"He stopped by the school a few times to say hello."

"Was anything worrying him? Did he seem concerned about anything in particular?"

"He was in good spirits, as you'd expect."

"Why would I expect that?"

"Well, he made it out of Iraq and Afghanistan with all his limbs."

"Of course. What's he been doing since he got back?"

"Just working out a lot, lifting and running. I encouraged him to consider going to community college in the fall, play football again, but he didn't seem interested. He was one of the best D-linemen who ever played for the Venice High Gondoliers." He stared at a wall, eyes distant, as if imagining Winfield blindsiding a quarterback. "Agile, hostile, and mobile. That's what Teshay was."

"Hostile?" I asked.

"Just on the football field. Off it, he was a soft-spoken, polite kid. He was recruited pretty heavily, but his grades scared everyone off. He was bright enough, but he didn't care much for school. So he joined the army."

"Have you talked to any of his old teammates? Have any of them seen him since he's been back?"

"I've talked to a few of 'em. They were pretty damn upset, as you can imagine. But none of them had been in touch with him since he joined up. No one figured Teshay would end up like this. Some of his other teammates, yes. You could very well expect them to end up shot in an Oakwood alley. But not Teshay. He had his head screwed on right."

Pender stood, reaching out to shake my hand. "I guess that's all I wanted to say. I just wanted you to know what kind of kid Teshay was."

I escorted Pender out of the squad room and through the parking lot. When we reached his car, I handed him my card. "If you hear anything, please give me a call."

Cruising east on the Santa Monica Freeway, I exited at La Brea, inched north through heavy traffic, and parked in front of a sprawling apartment complex a few blocks south of Wilshire. The wind swayed a towering sycamore in front. I stopped and listened to the branches creak. It was an extreme winter Santa Ana, and the winds might eventually swell to seventy miles an hour. A hot Santa Ana in the fall will spread wild fires, torch acres of homes on its race to the sea, and make the nightly news. But people outside the area aren't familiar with the winter winds. A cold Santa Ana doesn't heat up as it rips through the desert and down the canyons and mountain passes. It's a biting winter gale that blasts dust, tears the leaves off of trees, and knocks out power lines. By tonight there would be outages all over the valley.

I stood by the security door for a few minutes, shivering, waiting for a resident to punch in the code so I could slip in. I didn't want to buzz Ambrose's apartment; I wanted to surprise him. I felt conspicuous by the door, so I withdrew into the shadows, pulled out my cell, and called Robin.

"It's good to hear your voice," she said. "How's the case going?"

"You sure you want to hear?"

"Don't I always?"

A good listener, she'd always found my cases intriguing, and with her analytical lawyer's mind, she made trenchant observations. I told her about the bodies at the crime scene and explained how my focus had shifted from Pinkney to Winfield.

"Sounds like a challenging case," she said. "A lot more challenging than Duffy had advertised it."

"You surprised?"

"Knowing Duffy, no."

I enjoyed bouncing off theories and getting her feedback, but I had to cut the conversation short when I noticed a resident amble up to the security box. "Gotta go," I said, clicking off the phone and sneaking inside the complex before the door slammed shut. After climbing a flight of stairs, I cupped my ear to the door of Ambrose's apartment. Next door, an old lady lifted the bottom corner of the curtain on her front window and glanced at me. When I looked back at her, she quickly dropped the curtain.

I rang the bell to Ambrose's apartment. A few seconds later he nudged open the door—a sweet spicy smell of marijuana wafted out of the apartment—squinted and studied me for a moment, as if he were concentrating on an intractable calculus equation. Slight and boyish, with stringy blond hair and a wispy mustache, he was wearing a T-shirt and ragged jeans. I tried not to wince when I saw what was left of Ambrose's left arm. Just a ragged stump. When I introduced myself, he looked panicked and tried to slam the door. I wedged my foot against the jamb.

"I'm investigating Teshay Winfield's homicide. I don't care about what you've been doing in your apartment this morning." I flashed what

I hoped was a reassuring smile. "That's not in my job description. All I care about is if you can help me solve your friend's murder."

Ambrose nodded, and I trailed him into the apartment. The walls were bare, and the coffee table, end tables, dining room table, and chairs were a matched set, a cheap Danish blond wood. The bookshelf in the corner was stacked with CDs and DVDs. Crumpled Budweiser cans were scattered on the floor. I swept a stack of newspapers off a dining room chair, pitching them onto the floor, and sat down. Ambrose flicked off the television and disappeared into the bathroom. I heard a toilet flush. I figured he wanted to eliminate all traces of the pot. When he returned, he sat down on a frayed sofa.

"So how'd Teshay get tagged?" Ambrose asked.

"That's what I'm trying to find out."

"Nothin' much I can tell you."

"When was the last time you saw Teshay?"

"'Bout a month ago. He dragged me to Venice High a few times. Got me doing leg lifts and hitting the stationary bike. I went a few times, but I got tired of it. He was into working out." Ambrose glanced down at his stump. "For obvious reasons, I'm not."

He stretched out on the sofa, propped a pillow under his head, and closed his eyes for a moment. "I'd appreciate it if you sat up," I said. "It's kind of hard to conduct an interview like this."

"Fuck that."

"Fuck what?"

"Fuck taking orders from anyone again."

"I'm not giving you an order," I said softly. "I'm just trying to find out who killed your friend. And it would be a lot easier for me if you sat up."

Suddenly, Ambrose sat up, saluted smartly, and shouted. "*Sir*, is this better, detective, *sir!*" I decided to shift gears and try to initiate a conversation.

"Lot of LAPD guys I know are in the reserves. They weren't too happy about the way they were treated over there."

He flexed his fist and hyperventilated for a moment. "Fucking A right—it was totally fucked up from the gate!" he shouted.

I was surprised by the vehemence of his response. "The LAPD guys I talked to were pretty bitter when they got back."

"Bitter ain't the half of it. Got to *I*-raq and got issued a 'Nam-era flak jacket. Wouldn't even stop an AK round. Why? Because there weren't enough Interceptor vests for my platoon. Right before our first patrol, our gunny, guy named Gillespie, lent his Interceptor to some pimply faced kid from Idaho who was scared shitless. Two minutes in, Gillespie took one in the gut, spewing everyone in the Humvee with blood and intestines. That was my welcome to an *I*-raq moment. When I finally got my Interceptor, not enough of those ceramic-plate inserts around to protect the old vital organs. I saw some good boys go down 'cause of that shit. If those plates had of been there for us, some of my buddies would still be here. I finally got my plates. You know how?"

I shook my head.

"You want to know how, sir, detective, sir?" he asked sarcastically.

"How?"

"My mom had to take a week's pay, buy the plates, and ship 'em to me. Can you believe that shit?" he asked.

"That's not right."

"You better believe that's not right. You ever been in the service?"

"Not here. In Israel. There were problems, but nothing like that. At least they sent us out properly equipped."

"That's not the motherfucking half of it. We were going out on patrols in unarmored Humvees. When I arrived, less than half of all the Humvees in-country had no bulletproof windows or armored doors. Every day it was like driving into a shit storm of hot lead in a Volkswagen convertible. Pathetic," he said with disgust. "We're the richest country in the world. But us guys were protecting our Humvees with hillbilly armor—welding on strips of scrap metal from old Iraqi tanks, nailing on plywood panels, stacking up sandbags, anything to get a little protection. We called 'em cardboard coffins."

"That how you lost your arm?" I asked.

Ambrose stood and stretched. "Naw. It was a miracle, but I survived those *fuck it, shit happens, drive on* patrols. My girlfriend was pregnant and I had a job in a machine shop waiting for me. I was a short-timer, excited as hell to get out. I signed up for four and I did my four. Then I got stop-lossed. Army told me I had to do another fifteen months. I was angry every fucking day."

"That's when you lost your arm?"

"We were cannon cockers, but in Iraq, with all that urban warfare, they didn't want us blasting in the middle of a city, so they turned us into infantry. I had only three weeks left on that fifteen months when this clueless lieutenant colonel decides he wants a truck and a few gun bunnies with an M240 Bravo to set up an O.P. on a hill outside Basrah. He's a rear-echelon motherfucker, so he orders it, then slips back inside the wire where it's nice and safe. His attitude toward us is *KMAG YO-YO*—Kiss My Ass Guys, You're On Your Own. First day, we don't see shit. Next day, he orders us back—same spot. Third day, same thing. You were in the military. Tell me what's wrong with this picture?"

"Never establish a pattern."

"Right. Fourth day, I'm driving the truck. You know when you're driving, and it's hot, and you roll the window down, and you've got half your left arm out the window and your right hand on the steering wheel? Well, I was backing into position, and I ran over a mine. A mine probably buried between day three and four by some haji who'd been watching us. It blew up half the truck. I felt warm water pouring down the side of my body. Only one problem—it wasn't water. It was blood." He wiggled his stump. "I actually saw my arm half covered in sand, about twenty feet away."

He fiddled with a thread on the sofa and said, "Woke up in a combat support hospital. Then off to Walter Reed. I been to veterinary hospitals better than that dump. Then to the VA hospital out here, but they didn't know what to do with me. No plan, no program whatsoever to train me to make a living. Hell, before I enlisted I was a machinist."

He glanced at his stump with a contemptuous expression and collapsed onto the sofa. After a few minutes of silence, he said, "Yeah, I know, all that happened years ago. The army expects me to soldier-up and look to the future."

I dragged my chair closer to Ambrose and said, "I've been in firefights. I've been peppered with shrapnel. I spent some time in a field hospital. But I'd never say to you that I understand what you've gone through, what you're going through now. Because until I've been wounded like you've been wounded, I'll never understand."

Ambrose nodded. "That's the motherfucking truth."

"If you help me, I'd really appreciate it. If you don't want to talk, I understand. I won't threaten you, I won't hassle you. I'll just be on my way and leave you alone."

Ambrose tugged open an end table drawer, pulled out a pack of Winstons, shook out a cigarette, and tucked it between his lips. He then rummaged around the drawer, fished out a Bic lighter, and fired up the cigarette. After taking a few sharp drags, he said, "Teshay was a friend. He was a good fucking dude. We looked out for each other in Iraq. After I got sent home, he finished his tour in Iraq and did another one in Afghanistan. When he got discharged, he used to come around, try to get me out of my funk, out of the apartment, over to the high school to work out. I went along a few times, just to shut him up. We ran the track a few times."

Ambrose exhaled through his nose, two narrow streams of smoke. "I used to be a pretty decent half-miler in high school. But my balance is all off now. Tried to run, but"—he tapped his stump—"this screws up my rhythm. Every time we'd do a lap, it was just was a nasty reminder of what I lost. I went to the track with Teshay a few times, but eventually I just blew him off. I wasn't into seeing anybody. Yeah, I know, there's a lot of dudes way worse off than me. But I been feeling sorry for myself. Teshay tried to square me away, but I ended up driving him off. When I saw that story in the paper about him being shot, I realized I hadn't seen him in over a month."

"Any idea who might have shot him?"

He stared blankly at me. "No fucking idea, whatsoever."

"Was Teshay with you on that hill?"

"Yeah. He held my fucking hand while the medic worked on me. He rode with me on the evac helicopter. Later, we stayed in touch. He visited me at the VA hospital when he was on leave. He would have been out of the army a long time ago, but his mother was about to lose her house, so he re-upped to get the enlistment bonus. They were paying pretty good cash at that time. He sent her the check, and she was able to keep the house."

"You think his time in Iraq or Afghanistan might have contributed to his death?"

Ambrose stared out the window and said, "Why?"

"I've been working this case for a few days and I've come up with very little. I can't dig up anything he did here that would make him a target. So I'm wondering if maybe he did something over there that might have led to his death."

"You think that's why?"

"I don't know. What do you think?"

"You talk to anyone else besides me?"

"A few people. But I haven't got much. That's why I'm talking to you."

Ambrose flipped his cigarette into the beer can, the butt sizzling when it hit bottom. "You heard about all the looting after Baghdad fell?"

"I read about it in the paper."

"Well, they looted the shit out of Baghdad's national museum. Lots of things, valuable things, old as hell, were carted out of there. It was a fucking free-for-all."

"Was Teshay involved in that?"

Ambrose held up a palm like a traffic cop. "Whoa. The First Cav wasn't even in Iraq during the invasion. We got there later. And lots of crazy shit was going on when we got there. Bunch of dudes from the Third Infantry Division stumbled on a couple hundred million in cool cash—all twenties—in some palace complex in Baghdad."

"Didn't they get caught?"

"They got busted all right. But we heard there were some dudes out there, in other units, who grabbed some cash and didn't get caught."

I wasn't sure where Ambrose was leading me and why, but I thought it was worth pursuing. "Where did most of the stuff looted from the museum go?"

"Don't really know. Like I said, we missed out on the invasion. So that shit was boosted before we arrived. But I did hear about a few stupid-ass grunts who got ahold of some valuable antique-like things and fenced them in the bazaars. But someone ratted them out to the MPIs."

"MPIs?"

"Yeah, Military Police Investigators. They busted these dudes and court-martialed their asses."

"You think Teshay could have smuggled something out of Iraq and into the U.S.?"

He lips curled in a half smile. "You catch on quick."

"Well?" I asked.

"It's possible."

"Did Teshay bring something valuable back from Iraq?"

"I don't know."

"But he might have?"

Ambrose shook another Winston out of the pack and lit it. With the cigarette dangling from his mouth, he drawled, "Maybe."

"Teshay's gone," I said. "So, obviously, he can't get in any trouble.

He was already out of the army when he was killed—so there's no benefits his mother stands to lose if it turns out he was involved in something questionable."

"And your point is?"

"I don't care what was stolen, what was smuggled into the U.S., and what was fenced. I'm only chasing this trail because I think it might help me solve your friend's murder."

He fanned the smoke from his eyes and said, avoiding my gaze, "I don't even know if I *do* know something."

"Just lay it out and let me decide if it will help my investigation."

Ambrose sat up carefully and put his burning cigarette on the top of the beer can, wiped his palm on his jeans, and said, "There was only one time that Teshay said anything. It was right after he got back from Iraq. He was on leave and we were sitting around the apartment here, smoking some weed, drinking some beer. He mentioned he was going to do his tour in Afghanistan, come home, and bide his time. Then he was going to cash in big time, move to Maui, buy a boat, cruise the islands, and forget about everything he saw over there."

"Cash in how?" I asked.

"That's what I asked him. He said he lucked into something over in Iraq that he had stashed and it was going to fund an early retirement. I asked him if he brought back a key of hash. He said it wasn't drugs, nothin' like that. When I pressed him, all he would say"—Ambrose twirled an index finger—"and I still remember what he told me. He said that he'd seen Lady Luck, she had had the most beautiful smile he'd ever seen, and she flashed her smile right at him."

"That sounds kind of vague."

"It *was* fucking vague. He really sparked my curiosity, and I asked him about it a few other times. But he wouldn't say shit. I pressed him because I figured if he was going to cash in, maybe there was something in it for me, too. But that's all I got out of him."

"What did he mean when he said, 'bide his time?'"

"I think he meant until he finished his hitch. He did the tours in Iraq. He did another one in Afghanistan. He was just biding his time until he got discharged."

I questioned Ambrose for a few more minutes, but was unable to learn anything more about Winfield's cryptic comment. He stared at a wall and gave me monosyllabic replies.

At the door, I handed Ambrose my card. "If you think of anything else, don't hesitate to call me."

As I was about to reach for the doorknob, I changed my mind, and returned and sat on the sofa. "Would you mind if I just asked you a few more questions?"

Ambrose shrugged. He was slumped at the other end of the sofa. I make it a point not to tell people I'm interviewing any details of the homicide. If I release data, I can never be sure if the information I glean during later interviews is accurate or simply a recitation of what they'd picked up through the grapevine. But I decided to risk it this time. Ambrose was the first person I'd questioned who seemed to have some knowledge about Winfield and his past. I sensed that he knew more than he was letting on.

"Let me level with you. I originally thought the other guy who was killed was the target of the hit. Now I have reason to believe that your friend, Teshay, was the real target. But someone didn't just want him dead. They wanted information from him first. I examined his body very carefully at the autopsy and I could see he'd been tortured bad. Probably for hours. Before he died, he went through hell."

Ambrose's face tightened in a barely perceptible wince. "How was he tortured?"

"I saw a lot of burn and puncture marks."

"Fucking assholes."

"Our medics in the IDF had a phrase they used. 'The golden hour.' You know what that means?"

"It's those sixty minutes or so right after a serious wound when a medic has the best chance of saving the soldier. After that, it's sayonara. I know, because if the First Cav medic hadn't of stabilized me during that golden hour, they would have boxed me up and shipped me home."

"In homicide investigations, we have something like the golden hour, except it's not an hour, it's a day or two. If we haven't made much progress by then, the odds of solving the case drop."

He nodded. I didn't believe in the golden hour theory for most of my homicide investigations, but I thought it might persuade Ambrose, infuse him with some urgency, motivate him to open up to me. Hollywood was convinced that detectives had to solve a case within forty-eight hours, but at Felony Special we often labored on complex cases for weeks without critical leads. Eventually we cleared most of our cases.

"Jerry, this is my second day, and I don't have shit. I better come up with a decent lead because time's running out. Pretty soon, I'll get called out on another murder, and Teshay's case will be put on the back burner."

"That's fucked up."

"I'll probably never catch that psycho who tortured him."

"I didn't know about the torture," he said, massaging the bicep above his stump. "Paper didn't say anything about that."

"That's just for your ears only. That's usually the kind of info I keep quiet."

"So what you want to know?"

"You said he lucked onto something over there that he told you would fund an early retirement?"

"That's right."

"Can you tell me anything more about what it was he lucked into?"

Ambrose lit another cigarette and sucked down a few deep drags, squinting through the smoke. "I might be able to. But lemme ask you something first. Let's say I know about something Teshay did that might not have been legal. How do I know you're not going to come after me?"

"Like I told you before, I'm a homicide detective. All I care about is Teshay's homicide." I inched closer to him on the sofa and said, "I don't care about anything else."

He tugged the cigarette from his mouth and shaved the ash on the edge of the empty beer can.

"Okay. Here goes. When I got to know Teshay at Fort Hood, I'd already done a tour in Iraq. He was getting ready for his first one. I kind of looked after him at first, until he got squared away. He was a straight arrow. Didn't smoke, didn't drink, worked out all the time, went to chapel every Sunday. He was a gung ho grunt. Full-on Huah.

But Iraq blew his mind. Or at least opened it up some. He hears about the government spending a billion a week on the war. But he leaves the base in a thin-skinned Humvee with no armor, wearing a cardboard flak jacket that won't stop shit. He sees his buddies out on the same patrols, riding the same tin cans, wearing the same useless vests getting blown to shit. He sees the medics scooping up their body parts and dumping them into plastic body bags."

Ambrose took a deep drag and then stubbed out his cigarette on the top of the beer can. "You follow me?"

"I heard about all that. Outrageous."

"We started getting better equipment during that tour, but it was too late for a lot of dudes. He sees some rednecks from his units taking potshots at Hajis—not insurgents, but just guys along the roadside—whose skin color was about the same as his. That turned his head around. After the fall of Baghdad, Teshay knew that protecting the Iraqi Oil Ministry was a top priority, but the honchos blew off the Iraqi National Museum and didn't give a crap as the country's national treasures got hauled off in donkey carts. This was just another thing that kind of reordered his way of thinking. He wondered what the hell he was fighting for—for a cheap supply of oil or to liberate the people. At the same time, he hears about them guys from the Third Infantry getting all those millions in twenties and he hears about soldiers getting their hands on some of that booty from the museum."

Ambrose stood, retreated to the kitchen, and returned with a beer. After a swig, he extended the can toward me. "Want one?"

I shook my head.

"Okay, here's what I know. A couple years ago, Teshay was on his second tour while I was at Walter Reed. He was with a platoon manning a checkpoint at Ramadi, about sixty miles west of Baghdad. Some towel head in a Mercedes tried to run the barrier and got cut down by an enfilade of M4s by a group of jittery grunts. A few of the guys patted down this dead towel head; a few others searched the car. Teshay rooted around in the trunk. He fiddled with the spare tire in the wheel well. Underneath the tire was a metal box. He opened it and found a package about as big as a dinner plate. It was wrapped in linen. He slipped it under his shirt, didn't tell anyone about it, and didn't open it until he got back to the barracks."

"This was years after the museum looting. Why'd this object suddenly surface?"

"Teshay figured it was kept secure after that first wave of looting. But a couple of years ago, someone pulled off a big heist, knew what they were looking for and where to find it. It was on its way out of the country when Teshay stumbled on it."

"When did he tell you?"

"A few months ago—right after he got discharged."

"Did you get a look at it?"

"No. But Teshay told me it was some ancient mask with a lot of jewels on it. Said he was going to fence it and cash in big time. Said he'd heard it was worth a shitload of cash."

"Why didn't he sell it right away?"

"Teshay was smart. Knew there'd be too much heat. So he figured he'd bide his time, smuggle it back into the U.S. when he finished his tour, and wait until he got discharged before shopping it around. Last time I talked to him, Teshay said he was ready to look for a buyer. He said that when he sold it, he'd be so flush he'd be able to help me out."

"How did he smuggle it into the U.S.?"

"He sawed off the bottom of an oxygen tank, slipped the mask inside, and welded the bottom back on. He tossed the tank into a pile of generators, GPS units, computer equipment, and a bunch of other crap from our battalion that was being packed up and shipped back to Texas. When it got to Fort Hood, Teshay was waiting. He grabbed the oxygen tank and was in business."

"You know where in L.A. he was storing it?"

"No idea."

"Any idea who else might have known Teshay had the mask?"

"As far as I know, just me. And I didn't say nothin' to nobody."

"If I want to find out more about this mask, any ideas how I could do that?"

"Not really. But Teshay said the mask's worth millions 'cause it was some kind of rare antique with all kinds of jewels. I know there were rubies, but I'm not sure what else. But I know one thing that might help you. Teshay did some research and he found out that this mask is some kind of national treasure and it's got a name."

"What is it?"

Ambrose scratched his scalp with a thumbnail. "Can't remember."

"Can you remember *anything*? Even if you can't remember the full name, can you remember part of it?"

Squinting, he bit his lip. "Sorry. Just can't remember. After I lost my arm, underwent a few surgeries and skin grafts. I may be crazy, but I think that affected my memory."

"If I can come up with the name, could you confirm it?"

"Might be able to."

"Well, that's what I'm going to try to do. I'll get back to you in a day or two."

I rose and shook Ambrose's hand. Ambrose gripped my hand tightly and said, "Are you gonna come after me for knowing about him pinching that mask and slipping it into the country?"

"Like I said, all I care about is the homicide. The City Council's already put up a fifty-thousand-dollar reward leading to the arrest and conviction of the killer. So if what you've said leads to me catching Teshay's killer, you'll get it."

"I just want you to catch the motherfucker who killed my bud. I don't care about no reward—for myself. But when I was at Fort Hood, I got with this girl from Waco. Like I told you, she had the baby when I was in Iraq. We split up after I got back." He stared down for a moment and shook his head. "I'm ashamed to tell you, I've never even seen my daughter."

He tapped his stump. "Didn't want her to see her pops like this."

"I think she'd want to see you anyway," I said.

"Yeah, I know what I said is just a cop-out. Real reason is I been selfish as hell, too bent out of shape to think about anything but my own sorry ass. But if I get that reward, I want to make sure she gets it all."

"If what you've told me helps me solve this case, I'll mail her the check myself."

CHAPTER 10

Back in my car I called a forensic anthropologist from UCLA who had helped me on a case a few years ago, after I had found a pile of bones in a murder suspect's basement. I told him about the Iraqi mask, and he referred me to Dr. Carlton Stewart, a retired UCLA archaeologist who had written several books on ancient Mesopotamian art. I called Stewart at home, and he agreed to see me.

I drove out to Studio City, where Stewart lived on a street that was lined with houses of many different styles—including Cape Cod, Craftsman, Mission Revival, French Normandy—that it resembled a movie set. I climbed out of my car in front of Stewart's two-story English Tudor with a fake thatched roof. A gust of wind blasted the blossoms of a Mexican flame vine entwined in an arbor near the front door, flitting them into the sky like burning embers. When I rang the bell, I heard several small dogs yelping, yapping, and scratching windows. A man with an unruly thatch of white hair, leaning on a cane, opened the door. We shook hands as four frenzied Pekinese nipped at my ankles and chewed on my shoes.

For the next few minutes Stewart, waving and stamping his cane, struggled to herd the dogs onto the back porch, through a door, and into the yard. He circled back to the foyer, panting and wiping his brow with a frayed green handkerchief. After a curt apology, he led me to his cramped office. The floor was a jumble of two- and three-foot-high stacks of books, journals, and papers splayed from wall to wall. He negotiated the maze and sat behind his cluttered desk as I eased into a leather wingback chair.

"I appreciate you helping me out on this case," I said.

"It's a homicide, correct?"

"Yes, it is."

"Well, it's my pleasure, detective. Most of the mysteries I grapple

with are several thousand years old." He laughed, which set off a coughing fit. He grabbed a glass of water off his desk and gulped it down. "It's
nice to help someone investigate something that's a little more, how
should I say it, contemporary." He yanked the green handkerchief out
of his back pocket and blew his nose. "So how can I help you?"

"What I'm going to tell you is confidential, you understand?"

"Yes, yes," he said impatiently.

"Please don't mention this to anyone else. I don't want rumors about
this thing rattling around archaeological circles."

"I can assure you, detective, that I am discreet to the point of ec-
centricity."

"Very good. Now I have information to make me believe that a very
valuable mask, an ancient mask, was smuggled out of Iraq. Apparently,
it's a rare antiquity worth millions of dollars. Have you heard anything
about an ancient mask from that part of the world that might've gone
missing after the fall of Baghdad?"

He listened intently as he rolled a pencil between his palms. "So we
know this mask is extremely old, extremely valuable, and was possibly
looted from the Iraqi National Museum."

"That's right."

"Let me tell you about the two most valuable masks from that part
of the world. The first is called the Mask of Warka. A remarkable piece.
More than five thousand years old. The oldest known naturalistic de-
piction of the human face. Alabaster. Life-sized. The ruffled forehead,
the striking oval face, the meticulously inlaid eyebrows, the mysterious
darkened eyes." He tapped the tips of his index fingers together. "An
unparalleled portrait of realism."

"When the Iraqi National Museum was looted, and thousands of
pieces were carted off, this mask was, perhaps the most priceless piece
taken. A devastating loss. But, miraculously, less than six months later,
it was recovered. An informant walked into the museum and told officials that antiquities were being hidden in a farm in northern Baghdad.
He mentioned nothing about a mask. All he knew was that some very
old things were there. Iraqi police and members of an Army Military
Police company raided the farmhouse. The farmer, initially, denied
everything. But after he was detained for several hours, he finally ac-
knowledged he did, indeed, have an antiquity. It was buried between
some fruit trees in the back of his farm. And there it was, under six

inches of dirt, wrapped in two dirty cotton rags and stuffed into a plastic bag. The Mask of Warka. With not a scratch on it."

"So the mask was recovered?"

"Yes. The recovery was chronicled in great detail in one of our academic journals."

"So it's not missing? It's still in Iraq?"

"Yes. Clearly, that is the case."

"You mentioned you were going to tell me about the two most valuable masks from that part of the world. What's the other one?"

"I've heard nothing about this other mask going missing."

"Is it possible this mask could have been stolen and you wouldn't have heard about it?"

"Not probable. If such a treasure had gone missing, I think the authorities would have made this known."

"But possible?"

He tapped the pencil on his palm. "I suppose so. The U.S. Army, which set up the security system after the first wave of looting, might have tried to hush it up. Could prove to be quite an embarrassment, a public relations disaster."

"Why don't you tell me about this second mask."

"Before I tell you about this most remarkable piece, let me provide you with a bit of background. Will you bear with me, detective?"

"Of course."

"You have, I'm certain, heard of the reign of Hammurabi?"

"Sure," I said. "Didn't he create the first legal code?"

Stewart flashed me a crooked smile. "Very good, detective. Now Hammurabi's rule was roughly during the late seventeen hundreds B.C. This was a remarkable time in that part of the world. Babylon became the first truly international city. Traders began venturing there from as far away as India, bringing cotton cloth; bringing wool from eastern Turkey; bringing pottery from Crete; and bringing many other marvelous things from far-flung destinations."

"So this mask is from Hammurabi's reign?"

"No. From the reign of his son—Samsu-iluna. It turns out Samsu-iluna was battling with another city-state called Larsa," Stewart said, standing up beside his desk and holding forth, as if he was delivering an Archaeology 101 lecture. "So Samsu-iluna diverted the waters of the Euphrates south of Babylon in order to starve Larsa into submission.

Because the king of Larsa, Rim-Sin, knew he could never defeat the Babylonians on the battlefield, he tried another tact to persuade Samsu-iluna to open up the flow of the river so his people could survive. He presented to him an exquisite portrait—perhaps the most remarkable portrait created anywhere in the world up to that time. It was a portrait of Samsu-iluna's wife—the queen of Babylon."

"How do scholars know all this?" I asked.

"By that time, the scribes of Mesopotamia documented much of life there, and many records have been preserved. Now in order to create this portrait, Rim-Sin's traders collected the rarest jewels and purest, whitest ivory. The pearls were from islands in the Persian Gulf, and the lapis lazuli, which has veins the color of gold, might have been transported from as far away as western China.

"And the artist who carved this likeness of the queen was a Michelangelo of his time. He created a stunning portrait that art historians revere thousands of years later. Rim-Sin's emissary presented this remarkable creation to Samsu-iluna, as a tribute to the queen. It was a show of good faith. Maybe even a plea for mercy."

"You ever see this mask?"

"The Mask of Ellasar," Stewart said slowly, savoring the words.

"Why do they call it the Mask of Ellasar when it was made in Larsa?" I asked.

"A very astute question. Larsa was the metropolis of a kingdom that is referred to in Genesis—chapter fourteen, verse one—as Ellasar. The first Western archaeologists to examine the mask found the biblical reference more lyrical and more consistent with their faith, so that's what they began calling it." He threw up his hands. "Sometimes the members of my profession do inexplicable things."

"Have you seen the mask?" I asked again.

"I've never had that privilege. But people who have, described it as quite remarkable."

"What's it worth?"

He snorted contemptuously. "It's impossible to say how valuable the invaluable is. The artistry of the mask is said to be incredible. It's called the *Mona Lisa* of Babylon. The rubies alone are worth—" he paused, gazing at the ceiling as he mustered his thoughts. "I can't even put a price on them. It's incalculable."

I gripped my knees as my heart pounded in my chest. *Damn!* I thought. This sounded just like what Ambrose had described: *Some ancient mask worth a shitload of cash, studded with all kinds of jewels—rubies.*

"So did the mask save the city? Did Hammurabi's son open up the river and save Larsa?"

"I don't know what happened after the mask was presented. The written records are incomplete."

"Let's say someone got a hold of this mask, smuggled it out of Iraq, and into the U.S. Now if—"

"I find that a highly improbable scenario."

"Take it as a hypothetical. Now let's say someone had this mask right now in L.A. Where would he fence something like this?"

"Fence?" Stewart asked, looking confused.

"Where would he sell the mask? A museum? A collector? A private dealer?"

Stewart closed his eyes for a moment. "You've got me there, detective. I don't know anywhere he could sell it. This is a priceless work. It's doubtful someone could get away with selling it. It would raise a lot of red flags."

"But you haven't heard anything about the Mask of Ellasar being stolen."

"Not a word."

I rushed to my car and called Ambrose.

"You ready to cut me that fifty-thousand-dollar-reward check yet?" he asked in a mocking tone.

"Not yet. But if what you've told me about the mask leads me to the killer, you'll get it. I just wanted to ask you a few more questions. You said Teshay told you the mask was studded with jewels. You mentioned rubies. Any other kinds of jewels did he say were on the mask?"

"I think he mentioned there were pearls on it, too. I'm not sure, but I think he said that."

"Anything else?"

As I waited for an answer, I thought of the pearl necklace I gave Robin on our fifth wedding anniversary. I wondered if she still wore it.

"I can't think of anything else," Ambrose said.

"Did he describe the mask at all to you?"

"Naw. He was more interested in the jewels he could get out of it."

"You said the mask had a name."

"Yeah, but I can't remember it."

"Was it The Mask of Warka?"

"That don't sound right."

"How about The Mask of Ellasar?"

"The mask of what?"

"Ellasar?"

"Hmm."

"Is that it?"

"Might be."

"Can you say for sure?"

"Can't say I'm a hundred percent sure. But it does kind of ring a bell."

CHAPTER 11

After checking into another cut-rate motel south of downtown, Mullin bolted the door behind him. Slumping on the bed, he sighted down the Combat Masterpiece. He slid out the bullets, absent-mindedly weighed them in his hand, and then slipped them back into the cylinder. It would have been a lot easier and cleaner with an M107 sniper rifle. But that's not what Delfour provided. And he had to admit, that would be a more complicated job. He'd have to lug that bulky weapon to a camouflaged perch, keep it out of sight, do the job, and then leave the M107 behind.

He'd never killed a cop before. But how different could it be from killing hajis in Baghdad? He'd blasted plenty of them. *Just make sure to get a clean center-mass hit, right in the ten ring. No hotshot sniper blasts in the melon. And make sure to level on the dude before he gets his piece out.*

Delfour said the cop's out on a case and won't be back home until tomorrow. Best plan is scope the place out tomorrow, find a good roost, and wait. He grinned. He should have that twenty-five thousand by tomorrow night.

CHAPTER 12

If Winfield was killed because of this mask, maybe I could find some leads at his apartment, something that could put me onto other people who might have wanted it enough to kill him. I drove to Oakwood, parked a block away from where Teshay Winfield lived, and walked down the street. The front house, painted a hideous mustard yellow, was shaded by an immense redwood. I double-checked the address. Winfield rented one of the two small stucco cottages—also mustard yellow—set side-by-side on a patch of dirt in back.

I assumed the landlord lived in the front house and would let me into Winfield's cottage, but no one answered when I rang the bell, so I snuck to the back. A navel orange tree and a lemon tree shimmied in the frigid wind, both lush with leaves, but the Santa Anas had shaken all the fruit off the branches. The yard was dappled with hundreds of splashes of yellow and orange in the swirling dust.

Using the key Mrs. Winfield had given me, I opened the door and entered a small studio—a galley kitchen, combination living room-bedroom, and a bathroom in back. The place was as spare and tidy as a barracks, with gleaming linoleum floors and a neatly made single bed flush against the wall. *He still lived like a soldier*, I thought. In the kitchen, the chrome faucet and refrigerator handles shined and the chipped enamel stove was immaculate. The refrigerator was well stocked, with a half gallon of low-fat milk, protein powder, a brown head of lettuce, a packaged chicken, a loaf of wheat bread, and a condiment shelf lined with mayonnaise, mustard, salad dressing, and peanut butter.

A brown La-Z-Boy recliner and a lamp stood in one corner of the living room, opposite a wooden desk. On the desk was a large First Cavalry Division patch—yellow with a black diagonal stripe and a horse's head in the corner—in a silver frame. The small closet was as tidy as the room, with a dresser in back, pairs of shoes lined up on the floor, and the clothes on the rack partitioned into groups of pants, shirts, and jackets.

A sharp noise in the bathroom startled me. I snatched my .45-caliber Beretta Cougar out of my shoulder holster, held it in front of me, elbows flush to my ribs, and stepped lightly across the bedroom. Through the bathroom door, I saw a man crawling through a window and dropping to the ground outside. I hurtled through the window after him, clutching the gun with one hand and breaking my fall with the other.

"LAPD!" I shouted, as I chased the man. "Freeze, motherfucker!" But the man kept running. I shoved the gun back into my holster, sprinted, and tackled him by the ankles. He kicked loose, and we both jumped to our feet. I saw that the man was a huge white guy, about as tall as Duffy, with massive shoulders and a bull neck, and dressed in a brown leather jacket, jeans, and a blue baseball cap. He lowered his head, charged me, and bowled me over with his shoulder, like an NFL running back charging for the goal line.

I flew into the air, crashed against a fence, and rolled awkwardly on the ground, coughing and gasping for air. I'd been popped right in the solar plexus. When I managed to stand and dust myself off, the man had vanished.

Who the hell was he? And why was he there? I crossed the yard to the back cottage next to Winfield's and rapped on the door. There was a rustling inside, but no one answered. I knocked a few more times and shouted, "LAPD! Open up!"

A diminutive, gray-haired Hispanic woman—barely five feet— opened the door a crack and glared at me. I showed her my badge.

"Can I come inside?"

"Can't we talk over there?" she said, gesturing to the wicker chairs on the porch.

Beyond her, I glimpsed a teenage boy in the living room, draped over a couch, a large indistinguishable tattoo on his neck. The mother wanted to keep me away from her son, I figured, and she probably had good reason.

"I saw how that man attack you," she said in heavily accented English. "If I know that you are a policeman, I would call the authorities."

"You ever see that man before?"

"Never."

"Did you hear what happened to Teshay Winfield?"

She nodded and quickly crossed herself. "Such a tragedy."

"Did you know him well?"

"We had conversations only a few times," she said. "But he was always very respectful."

"What had he been doing with himself since he got back?"

"He say to me that he looking for work. He work out a lot. Run, run, run."

"Where did he run?"

"He tell me he run on the beach and he run to Venice High School and lift weights over there."

"Did you see many visitors come to his place?"

"Almost never. He live very quiet. A very nice neighbor."

"You said, 'almost never.' What visitors *did* you see?"

She appeared embarrassed and stared at her shoes. "A few time, maybe two, maybe three, he have a lady over."

"Can you describe her?"

"A white lady."

"Young?"

"Yes. Very pretty young lady. A foreigner."

"How do you know she was a foreigner?"

"She talk funny. I hear them talk on his front porch."

"What country do you think she was from?"

"I don't know. Maybe Russia or someplace like that."

"Anyone else ever stop by?"

"No."

"Do you have a job?"

"I did," she said. "Downtown. Garment work."

"My dad used to do garment work," I said. "He was a patternmaker for a dress company."

She patted her back. "Disability for me now." She was perfect, I thought, a nosy, unemployed neighbor. "I'd like you to do me a favor. You saw that man who ran away?"

"I got a look at him."

"Did you see how he got into Winfield's place?"

"Yes. He pulled something that look like a knife out of his pocket and fiddle it into the lock."

I figured it was a jackknife lockpick. "Would you recognize him if you saw him again?"

"I think yes."

"First of all, I want you to know that I'm a homicide detective, I'm not interested in any crime except Teshay Winfield's murder," I said, hoping to reassure her if she was worried about her son, who was probably a junior gangbanger. "If you ever see that man again, I want you to call me. If I'm not at the office, call my cell." I scrawled the number on my card and handed it to her. "If you do see him and you contact me, I'd like to give you a hundred dollars. Let's call it a small reward."

"Okay," the woman said.

"I'd also like to talk to your son for a minute."

She cast a frightened glance inside the house. "He don't know nothing."

"I promise you, it'll just be a brief conversation about Winfield. Nothing else."

"Mando!" she called out.

The boy strolled out to the porch, leaned against a post, and said, "Wha's up?" He wore an oversized white T-shirt and gray Dickies that looked like a size forty. I asked him a few questions about Winfield, but the mother was right. He didn't know anything. Or, at least, he was not inclined to share what he knew with a cop.

Before his mother withdrew behind the door, I said to her, "Remember, if you see that guy I'm looking for, call me. I don't care what time it is. Night or day. Contact me."

"I will do it."

I returned to Winfield's monastic studio and concluded that he hadn't accumulated much since he left the service a few months ago. Inside the dresser his socks, underwear, T-shirts, and handkerchiefs were neatly stacked. I searched the closet, under the bed, and beneath his mattress, but didn't find anything of interest. Sitting at the desk, I was relieved to discover that he'd saved his phone bills, checking records, cancelled checks, military separation papers, and credit card receipts. They were neatly separated, organized, and held together with paper clips. In a manila envelope there were a few pictures of Winfield in uniform, standing tall, chin down, shoulders back. I tucked one of them inside the front flap of my murder book. I hauled a large brown bag from the closet, and as I was tossing all of Winfield's phone and financial records inside, my cell phone rang and I saw it was Duffy. I briefed him on my interviews with Ambrose and the UCLA professor.

"Can you head back to the squad room?" he asked.

"What's up?"

"That cop hater, Councilman Pinkney, flew back from Japan as soon as he heard the news. He'll be in my office in an hour or two. He wants a meeting."

"Can't you deal with it?"

"No. You gotta be there for the councilman. The chief's personally interested in keeping Pinkney happy."

"I don't have time for that shit. This case is spinning all over the place."

"Head over here and tell me about it," he said. "And when you're done with Pinkney, another person wants to talk to you, too. She's a U.S. Army major."

"What's she want?"

"She's one of the heads of army recruiting for the Western region—based in LA. She's concerned that if this story gets played wrong, it could hurt the army's PR image."

"I don't get it."

"She just wants to make sure that Winfield is portrayed as the fine, upstanding young man that he apparently isn't. She doesn't want the press running with some kind of gang drive-by or drug-hit story."

"Tell the major to contact Press Relations."

"She already did. But she wants to talk to the detective in charge. The chief got wind of this and he told me to take care of her. The major and her butt boy are coming by this afternoon."

"Okay," I said, rising and scanning the room a final time. "After I take care of all my PR duties, I might even have time to begin looking into who killed my victims."

CHAPTER 13

I decided to swing by the Felony Special squad room where I could study the paperwork I'd picked up at Winfield's apartment and wait for the meeting with Councilman Pinkney. I could also dump my Saturn and pick up my unmarked Chevy Impala. This case had grown a lot more complex and confusing than I'd anticipated, with tendrils reaching out in startling directions.

I parked in the LAPD garage and gripped my coat around my neck as I fought the wind and hustled up Main, dodging trash that skittered down the sidewalk. When I reached the Police Administration Building, the flags were flapping so hard they sounded like the whap-whap-whap of a helicopter. I took the elevator to the fifth floor, a bland, carpeted warren of cubicles and faintly humming fluorescent light. Above the Xeroxed wanted posters tacked to a bulletin board someone had posted a sign: SANTA'S NAUGHTY LIST. I still missed Parker Center, which had been the LAPD headquarters for most of my career. Our old squad room was jammed with a dozen battered metal desks, lined up in two rows, separated by a narrow aisle of scuffed brown linoleum tile. The walls were studded with the stuffed heads of elk, wild boar, and antelope, bagged by the hunters in the room. Splintered wooden cabinets stacked with old murder books framed the doorway. Ancient venetian blinds, the slats speckled with dust, shaded the windows. Parker Center was ramshackle, but the place oozed tradition and character.

Although it was Saturday, a handful of detectives were in their cubicles, working cases. I walked past the Special Assault Section, which cops still call Rape Special—the unit's old name. I spotted a detective walking a young blonde woman to an interview room. She stopped by a desk, doubled over, convulsed with sobs. Her hair was matted, the tears had streaked her mascara, and her upper arms and neck were striated with bruises. I couldn't do that job, I thought. There would be no respite.

Every time I'd interview the victim, every phone conversation we'd have, she would relive the savage attack, and I'd be filled with impotent rage and anger and anguish.

Give me the dead. With their silences and their secrets and the vague hints and leads that they leave behind. Dealing with the families is brutal, but it is brief, and then I have the luxury of extended periods of quietude, the contemplative serenity of divining glimmers of truth from the deceased.

When I reached my desk, I spotted Mike Graupmann—an LAPD dinosaur—swearing loudly. He dismantled a string of Christmas lights strung across his desk, and boxed up a CHRIST WAS BORN sign and a small crèche that he had displayed by the squad room door.

"It's not our world anymore," Graupmann grumbled to his partner. "It's a suspect's world."

From the neck down, Graupmann looked like an athlete, with broad shoulders and a weightlifter's chest, but his flushed face was fleshy and sagging, with incipient jowls. He shoved the lights and the box under his desk and announced loudly, "This is still a Christian country, one nation under God and all that." He glanced at me. "We don't try to tell the *non*-Christians how to live. So why should they tell us how we can or can't celebrate *our* holidays?"

Oscar Ortiz, my best friend in the squad room, stood up. Known as the worst dresser in the unit, Ortiz wore a purple shirt, purple tie with tiny yellow stars, green corduroy sports coat with leather patches at the elbows, and wrinkled brown slacks. He stroked his impressive Zapata mustache and said, "I think I know what you're saying, but it's bullshit. The RHD captain ordered you to take down all that Christmas stuff. Ash had nothing to do with it. It's an order that came down from the brass to every LAPD division."

"But that rule might be enforced a little more carefully in this squad room, for obvious reasons," Graupmann said. "Pretty soon they'll be prohibiting us from even *saying* 'Merry Christmas.' They might even ban the word 'Christmas.'"

Robert Grigsby, known as "Bible Bob," raised a palm above his head and said, "Mike, don't forget that our Lord and Savior was of the Jewish persuasion."

"Hey," Ortiz said, winking to me, and turning to Grigsby, "if Jesus was Jewish, why does he have the first name of a Mexican guy?"

"If Mexicans are Catholic," I said to Ortiz, "why are so many of them named Israel?"

Duffy darted out of his office, tugged his slacks over his gut, and shouted, "Is this bullshit conversation over now?"

"It's not bullshit," Graupmann said. "I just made an observation."

"Let me repeat what I just said: Is this *bullshit* conversation over now?"

"Over and out," Graupmann said.

"See that it's over—for good," Duffy said, retreating to his office and slamming the door for emphasis.

"I got your back, homes," Ortiz said.

"I appreciate it."

"Let's get a cup of coffee."

"Don't have time. I caught a fresh one Friday night and I've got a couple people coming in today to pester me."

I deposited my briefcase and murder book on my desk. The door to Duffy's office swung open again. He emerged from his office, waving an *L.A. Times.* "Have you seen *Pravda* this morning?"

I shook my head and followed Duffy into his office.

"They're really running with your double," he said, sinking into his creaking chair. "It's bad enough that a councilman's son got popped. But now the Winfield angle's gotten hot, too. It's a pretty predictable story line." Duffy, in a mock newscaster voice, intoned: *Streets of L.A. more dangerous than Afghanistan. U.S. soldier survives war, but is tragically and brutally gunned down in Venice.*

"I just saw a few messages on my desk from reporters. Tell Press Relations to handle all that."

"I'll take care of it. But like I told you on the phone, you gotta talk to Councilman Pinkney. He's here now, waiting for you. But before we deal with him, let me prepare you. Councilman Pinkney's not too happy about the progress of this investigation."

"Are you fucking kidding me. I've been on this case less than twenty-four hours."

"He complained to the mayor. The mayor complained to the chief. The chief complained to our captain. Our captain complained to me. So I'm complaining to you."

"And who can I complain to?"

"If your wife hadn't walked on you, you could've complained to her."

"I don't have to listen to this bullshit," I said, pounding my fist on

Duffy's desk and jouncing his cup. Coffee sprayed over the brim and onto the blotter, staining a sixty-day unsolved homicide report. Dabbing at the report with a Kleenex, he said, "Calm down, Ash. I was just pimping you a little. Don't forget, I've been married three times. I'm not one to talk. And I don't mean to imply you're not doing everything possible to solve your case. I just wanted you to know that this double is getting a lot of scrutiny. But I'm handling all the higher-ups, so you won't be distracted. I'm trying to be the lightning rod here. But I thought you'd want to know what's going on behind the scenes."

"You thought wrong."

Duffy stood, clapped me on the back, and said, "Believe me, I know you're going balls to the walls. And I appreciate it. Just give this prick Pinkney a few minutes right now, and I'll handle him from here on out."

I trailed Duffy to the conference room where the councilman was waiting at a large oval wooden table. He was a stout man with oily processed hair slicked straight back. He was dressed in a sleek blue suit, pale-pink shirt with matching handkerchief in his jacket pocket, a baby-blue silk tie, and wore large gold monogrammed cuff links. Duffy introduced us and I extended my hand. Pinkney stared at it for a moment, as if I was holding out a stinking mackerel, then he finally gave my hand a tepid, reluctant shake.

"Did the chief give you a full briefing?" Duffy asked.

"Yes, he did."

"Is there anything more you'd like to know?"

He rapped his knuckles on the table and said to me, "Why haven't you caught the lowlife who killed my son?"

"I've only been on the case since last night and I plan—"

Pinkney interrupted me and said, "I'm sure you're well aware of the problems I've had with the LAPD regarding the way my community has been policed, the way racist LAPD cops have acted like an occupying army and treated my constituents like enemy aliens; the way LAPD cops have brutalized the people on the street, using excessive force—excessively." Pinkney's voice rose and fell in the rhythmic cadences of a preacher.

"You're talking about the old LAPD," Duffy said. "It's a different department today. As you know, Councilman, times have changed. Daryl Gates was four or five police chiefs ago."

Ignoring him, Pinkney said, "And you detectives can be just as bad.

As you know, I've complained a lot of times about the way LAPD detectives have cavalierly approached the murder of our young black men. I'm sure my complaints aren't new to you."

Duffy stared at him and crossed his arms.

"Given all that, do you think you could put aside your personal prejudices and conduct a professional investigation into the murder of my son?"

"Listen," I said, angrily, "I've got no personal prejudices."

He flashed me a skeptical look. I slapped the table. "I'm offended by what you said. I don't care *who* the victim is. I approach every single case—"

Duffy gripped my knee under the table and said, "I'll make that clear to Councilman Pinkney, but let me handle this."

"If you can't assure me," Pinkney said, "that you'll be able to rise above the conflicts I've had with your department, I'm prepared to ask the state Department of Justice to recuse the LAPD from this investigation because of a conflict of interest, and name an outside law enforcement agency to conduct the investigation into the murder of my son."

"There will be no need for that kind of drastic action," Duffy said in a soothing voice. "I'm sure you're well aware that Felony Special is an elite unit that culls the best detectives from through out the department and only investigates the toughest crimes in the city. I don't care what agency you put on this case, you're not going to find any better investigators than the ones right here," Duffy said, motioning toward the squad room. "I can promise you that whatever disagreements you've had with my department in the past, it will have no bearing on our investigation."

Pinkney frowned. "The chief mentioned that Detective Levine will be handling the case."

"That's right," Duffy said.

"I would prefer to see a task force assembled."

"That, I can tell you, won't be necessary," Duffy said. "You're in very good hands with him. First of all, he's a member of a minority group himself, so he can sympathize with others who have faced prejudice."

Pinkney scrutinized me with a dubious expression. "He don't look like no *real* minority."

I felt embarrassed by Duffy's pandering, but before I could say anything, Duffy added, "We'll save that discussion for another time. But I want you to know that he might be the best detective I've got. I'm sure you've read in the paper about some of the high-profile cases he's solved. Remember the Spring Street Slasher serial case? Well, Detective Levine solved—"

"That's all fine and good, but I'd still like to see a task force created. I'd like more manpower on this case."

Duffy smiled ruefully. "I understand you spoke to the chief about that. What exactly did he say?"

"Well," Pinkney said, clearing his throat and looking uncomfortable, "he said because of cuts in the department's budget, you're down about four bodies in your unit and you can't spare any more detectives to work full time on the case."

Duffy stroked his chin, letting Pinkney think for a moment about his previous campaigns to decimate the department's budget. "Well, of course that's a reality. But I also want to emphasize that despite our manpower shortages, we're freeing up a number of detectives to provide Detective Levine with support. So he'll still have sufficient resources to conduct a thorough investigation. As far as I'm concerned, the murder of your son is our unit's number-one priority."

Pinkney straightened his tie and nodded.

"Any time you want an update or have any questions at all, call me." Duffy jotted on a business card and handed it to Pinkney. "My office number is on this and I've also written down my cell and home phone. Call me anytime, Councilman."

"Appreciate that," he mumbled, shaking Duffy's hand. He then turned to me and shook my hand—a little more firmly this time. After he'd walked out, Duffy whispered, "What a dick."

"So who are these detectives you're freeing up to help me out?"

Duffy flashed me a *don't-be-naïve* look.

"So the chief tells Pinkney we don't have the bodies to put together a task force to stick it to him for all the times he shafted us on our budget. But you offer him a bone, saying you'll free up some detectives, part-time, to back me up."

"I think our chief's a bigger politician than Pinkney," Duffy said.

"What's the chief's endgame?" I asked. "Is he trying to parlay the kid's murder into some leverage next time the department's budget comes up before the Council and Pinkney is the deciding vote?"

"You surprised?"

"That's going a bit far, even for a chief as calculating as ours."

"So what does that tell you about your case?"

"That if I don't clear it, the LAPD's budget woes for the next decade will be all my fault."

"Smart boy," Duffy said.

I rushed back to my desk, but before I could open the murder book, Duffy slapped me on the shoulder. "The cavalry has arrived. The two army officers from the Western regional recruiting office are on their way up. I'll bring them to the conference room, soften 'em up, and then grab you."

I was writing the preliminary investigation report when Duffy called my name and waved me into the conference room. Two army officers— a male and a female—wearing their dress greens, sat stiffly at the table.

"Major Anna Higgins, this is Detective Ash Levine," Duffy said.

A heavyset woman with a severe, pinched expression stood and said, "Good to meet you, Levine. Let me introduce Captain Rex Rilonas."

Rilonas gripped my hand, a shade too tightly. He was a stiff, bulky man with a deep tan and crow's-feet at the corner of his eyes.

"I'll leave you two in the capable hands of Detective Levine," Duffy asked, withdrawing from the room and closing the door. I sat across from them and asked, "Coffee?"

"We don't care for any," Higgins said.

I found it curious that she had decided for the both of them.

"How can I help you?"

"This is just a courtesy visit, Levine," Higgins said. "We want to give you the courtesy of telling you a little about Corporal Teshay Winfield."

"Anything I can learn about a homicide victim is helpful," I said.

"Corporal Winfield served a number of years in the United States Army with distinction," Higgins said. "He had an outstanding service record. Not a single disciplinary infraction. His M.O.S. was field artillery."

"M.O.S.?" I asked.

"Military Occupational Specialty."

"He must have been pretty busy during the early days in Iraq."

"Actually, his unit was not in on the invasion," Higgins said. "But they were quite active in the occupation." She barked, "Captain."

Rilonas threw his shoulders back and spoke in a monotone, as if he were reciting a military regulation, "Corporal Teshay Winfield was a crew member with the Third Battalion, Eighty-Second Field Artillery, a unit that is attached to the First Cavalry Division. This is a distinguished unit with a rich military history. The unit was formed in eighteen fifty-five and—although it had a different designation then—served in a number of major Civil War battles, including Gettysburg and Antietam. In World War Two, this division saw quite a bit of action in the South Pacific, including battles at—"

"Thank you, Captain," Higgins interrupted. "I think he gets the idea."

"So how can I help the two of you?" I asked.

"What can you tell me about your investigation?" Higgins asked.

"I'm not at liberty to release any information at this time," I said.

"Very well," Higgins said, rubbing her palms together. "Can I speak frankly?"

"Please do."

"We're concerned that Corporal Winfield be portrayed in the media with the dignity he deserves. We request that any information you release to the news media be cleared with our Public Affairs Office first."

"I can't do that."

She frowned and said, "I find that answer unsatisfactory."

I swallowed an impulse to tell her to go fuck herself. "Major, I can tell you that there is no indication, at this time, that Winfield was involved in gang activities or drugs. So I don't envision negative stories about—"

"Don't *envision?*"

"At this point, that's as far as I can go."

"Very well," Higgins said curtly. "If you could keep our office apprised of your investigation, we'd appreciate it."

"You got it," I said, knowing I'd probably never contact them.

"Well then, we won't take any more of your time."

As I ushered them out the squad room door, I jerked a thumb at the paratrooper wings clipped to Rilonas's uniform. "I was a paratrooper. Many years ago."

"What division?"

"The *Tzanchanim*," I said, smiling.

Rilonas looked confused. "Never heard of it."

"Not the U.S. Army."

"Ah," Rilonas said, nodding, "IDF."

"That's right."

"You a sabra?"

"No. I grew up in L.A. I dropped out of college and moved over there."

"Damn good soldiers," Rilonas said. "I met some of them who were sent to Fort Benning for some joint training exercises. I like the way they go about their business. The government over there doesn't pussy-foot around and handcuff their soldiers. They let their military do their job without all the political interference that you get here in—"

"Levine," Higgins said, interrupting Rilonas, "thank you for your time."

Duffy rushed over to the door and said, "Major Higgins, you get everything you need?"

"I did."

"If you need anything else, don't hesitate to contact me or Detective Levine."

"Thank you, Lieutenant."

As the major and Rilonas walked stiffly down the hallway toward the elevator, I turned to Duffy and said, "Why'd you say that?"

"Why'd I say what?"

"That if they need anything, they shouldn't hesitate to call me. I've got enough to do without having to deal with the demands of another bureaucratic institution."

"Ash," Duffy said, "you may know a lot about investigating homicides, but you don't know shit about LAPD politics. The chief asked us to take care of these folks."

"That's what we just did," I said. "I don't want them pestering me anymore."

"I doubt if they will. But since taking care of them was a priority of the chief, it's a priority of mine, too. And since it's a priority of mine, it's now a priority of yours. You understand?"

"So what you're saying is: Shit always flows downhill."

"There it is," Duffy said.

I left the squad room, rode the elevator to the ground floor, and headed to First Street toward a Little Tokyo bakery. I bought a large cup of green tea and two steamed buns—called *manju*—filled with curry. Back in the squad room, I chewed the curry *manju* and sipped my tea as I studied Winfield's phone records, utility bills, and the other paperwork I'd removed from his apartment. After sifting through a few bills, I discovered a parking ticket. The car was cited across the street from Winfield's house. His mother, however, said he didn't have a car. I called West Division Traffic, read the license plate number listed on the ticket to the desk sergeant, and she gave me the address and the name of the car's owner: Valentina Revenco.

A woman—possibly Russian—had visited Winfield a few times, the Hispanic lady who lived next door to him had told me. I didn't know if Revenco was a Russian name, but it was close enough. Winfield probably offered to pay for her ticket after she got flagged while visiting him. I decided to pay her a visit.

It was late afternoon as I cruised down a side street in West Hollywood lined with sleek apartment buildings. The Santa Anas were still blowing hard. Parched palm fronds clotted the street, and the buildings' rain gutters were crammed with shriveled leaves and twigs. I parked and entered an apartment building with a courtyard pond teeming with orange koi, through a pathway fringed with white camellias and pale-pink rose bushes. I walked up a flight of stairs to the second floor, and knocked on a door.

A woman glanced at me through the peephole, flung open the door, and flashed a forced grin at me.

"Valentina?"

"Yes, yes. Come in." she said in a thick accent.

She was dressed in jeans, a tight gold T-shirt, and high heels, and she wore her straight back hair in a long ponytail. She had the pale, creamy complexion of a woman who had grown up far from the sunshine and desert air of Southern California.

"I've got the patients," she said, still smiling. "Milan said you can provide the doctors. Yes?"

I figured she was running some kind of medical insurance fraud and was expecting a new scammer she'd never met. Before I'd left PAB, I ran her in the system and could find no convictions, but one arrest for four counts of Medicare fraud, a Russian Mafia specialty.

"LAPD," I said. " I'd like to talk to you."

"There must be mistake, I believe," she said in a heavy accent, a glare suddenly replacing the grin.

The living room was sparsely furnished with just a red sofa, a polished wooden coffee table in front and, flush against the opposite wall, two overstuffed red chairs. A sad-looking white plastic Christmas tree listed in the corner.

She fell onto the sofa, sighing with resignation, and I joined her. "I'm a homicide detective. Do you know what that is?"

"Murder police, I believe."

"That's right. So I don't care what kind of scams you're running."

"There is no scam here, that I can promise—"

"Save it," I said, lifting a palm. "As I said, all I care about is my murder. You help me out, and I'll forget about your little business."

"I am a legitimate businesswoman, sir. Nothing I do is illegal in this country, I am sure. I never had conviction, not a single one, I can tell you."

"No convictions, but you have been arrested."

"In this country innocent until proven guilty. That is why I love America."

She lit a cigarette and exhaled a thin stream of smoke. "What you what from me, officer?"

"I am investigating the murder of Teshay Winfield. I discovered that you've been at his house a number of times."

"I have been to a lot of men's houses. I am single. I date. I am attractive." She stared at me as if expecting a confirmation.

"When was the last time you saw Winfield?"

"I don't think I know this man."

I retrieved Winfield's army picture from my briefcase and held it in front of her. She briefly glanced at the picture. "I cannot remember this man."

I glared at her, certain she was lying. When confronted with the sudden presence of a homicide detective, most people are jittery, uncomfortable with silence, accommodating. But she simply leaned back on the sofa, took long, luxurious drags of her cigarette, and carefully tapped the ash into an empty wine glass on the coffee table.

Stalling for time, I said, "So you're Russian."

"No, I am *not*," she said indignantly.

"Where are you from?"

"Moldova," she said, staring at her cigarette.

"Isn't that part of Russia?"

"Used to be."

"Where is it?"

"It is near Romania."

"When did you meet Teshay Winfield?"

"As I told you, officer, I do not know a man by that name."

The casual, arrogant way she lied infuriated me. I had to get some leverage over her, locate some vulnerability, and then exploit it.

I'd worked a Russian triple out in Reseda a few years ago. Those people took me to school. I discovered that Russian gangsters—and the women were as tough as the men—did not fear American cops. Compared to Russian police, they saw me, an American cop, as a total puss. Those Russian cops will kick your teeth in if you look at them cross-eyed. But I'm not going to do that. And she knows it. Moldova may not be part of Russia, but Moldovian cops were probably trained by Russians when the country was under their control. *If she's not afraid of me, what is she afraid of?* I recalled what my old mentor Bud Carducci advised me about extracting information from reluctant suspects and wits: "Find out their weak spot; figure out what they're afraid of. Then squeeze 'em like a grape."

"Okay, Valentina," I said, abruptly standing up, "Let's go."

"Where?"

"I'm taking you downtown."

"Do I have to go with you?"

"Yes. You have no choice." I gripped her shoulders and guided her to her feet. "I'm taking you to see an immigration official," I said, bluffing.

"INS?"

"That's right. But they don't call it that anymore. Now it's called the Immigration and Customs Enforcement. I don't like getting jacked around by you, listening to you dodge my questions. I'm dropping your ass off at Immigration right now, they'll throw you on a plane at LAX and you'll be back in Moldova by morning. And all the money you've made here—and that includes all your bank accounts and cash we recover at your apartment—will be seized by the U.S. government. You understand?"

She flopped into a chair and dropped her head into her hands. I learned on the Reseda case that the women from Eastern Europe were great businesswomen. Some of them were hookers. Some of them were madams. And some of them, like Valentina, apparently, were simple scammers. Give them a year in Los Angeles, and they'll sock away twenty, thirty thousand bucks in banks all around town, including a sizeable stash at home. Valentina knew if she was deported back to her hovel, she'd lose her nest egg. She'd probably have to work a lifetime to earn that much back home.

She slowly lifted her head and noticed me checking out her cleavage. "Maybe no need for downtown," she said. "Maybe we solve this problem you have with me in some other way."

"I don't think so," I said, embarrassed. I leaned back in my chair, crossed my arms, and said, "You going to answer my questions truthfully this time, or are you going to force me to turn you over to Immigration?"

She stared at me, eyes wide, fists clenched, tears streamed down her cheeks. Blinking hard, she whispered, "Please."

"Please, what?" I asked harshly.

"I cannot be sent back there. I would die first. It is misery there. When I worked there, as secretary, I make fifty-nine dollars a month. I cannot put food on my table. I send money home now. I help my mother and my younger brother to live, to eat, to pay rent."

"So, like I said, are you going to answer my questions truthfully?"

She wiped her eyes with her palms, smearing her mascara. I moved my briefcase—with the voice-activated recorder inside—toward her and said, "Well?"

"If I speak with you, will you not send me back? Will you leave me alone?"

"If you tell me the truth, and what you tell me helps my case, you'll never hear from me again. But if you continue to give me that line of shit that you never met Teshay Winfield, you'll be at Immigration within twenty minutes."

She stared at her shoes, licking her lips. I reached over and lifted her chin. "You understand me?"

"Yes, I understand very well. Now I am willing, very much, to give you what I know about this situation."

"Okay," I said. "I'm glad we understand each other. Let's start with a very simple question. Do you know Teshay Winfield?"

"I will help you, but I beg you to help me. To help my sister, Anika. She has been forced into a house of prostitution. To pay off her voyage to America. She has done this. She has paid it off. But these Russian gangsters still keep her. I want you to release her. To free her. Will you do that?"

I handed her my business card and a pen. "Write down her name and the address where she's kept. I'll see what I can do. Do you have a picture of her?"

After she scrawled on the back of the card, she rummaged around her purse, dug out her wallet, opened it, and showed me a picture of a smiling teenage girl with a plume of blonde hair, holding a kitten in her lap. "This is Anika back in Moldova. Her hair is cut short now." She gave me the picture and the card.

"Is she being held in a house or apartment?"

"Apartment building. Four stories."

"What's the security like?"

"Security?"

"Are there men guarding the place, keeping a close watch on the girls?"

"Yes, very close."

"Are the men armed?"

"Yes, very armed."

"How many?"

"Two, sometimes more. And these men are hard. Military men at one time. They know how to use their weapons. But you are police. You can help. Will you promise to get Anika free?"

"I promise I'll look into it."

"Will you—"

"Look, I said I'll do what I can. But I'm asking the questions here, not you. So let's get back to it. Do you know Teshay Winfield?"

"I do know him, yes."

I showed her Winfield's army photograph again.

"That is him, Teshay," she said.

"When did you meet?"

"A few months past."

"Where'd you meet?"

"At his house."

"Why'd you go to his house?"

"Someone told me to."

"Who?"

"I'd rather not say," she said, fiddling with an unlit cigarette. "That is my feeling."

I slapped the cigarette out of her hand. "Getting information out of you is like pulling teeth."

She wrung her hands and asked plaintively, her eyes wide with fear, "What is, 'pulling teeth'?"

"It means I don't like the way you're answering my questions," I said, exasperated. "I want to know *who* told you to meet Winfield, *why* you met Winfield, and *what* was the purpose of meeting Winfield. And I want you to tell me everything else that went on between the two of you. And if you keep giving me these one-, two-, and three-word answers, well, that's the end of our interview. And your life in L.A." I rapped my knuckles on the table. "You understand?"

"I really must have a cigarette, please," she whined.

"No!" I shouted. "Start talking!"

She crossed her legs and drummed a long fingernail on a spiked heel. "Everything I am not informed about. But I will tell you what I, myself, know about what I have done."

"That's fine with me," I said.

"There is a man named Kolya who tells it to me that I must meet Teshay."

"Is Kolya Moldovan, also?" I asked.

"No. Russian. If I secure an important item from Teshay, Kolya tells me he pays me thirty-five thousand dollars cash. And most important, he tells me he will let Anika go. And if I refuse to help him secure this item, Kolya tells me he will keep Anika for years and he will make life very hard for my family back at home. Very, very hard." She dabbed at her eyes with a pinkie.

"In addition to being a rip-off artist, are you a prostitute, too?"

Her eyes flared. "Never!" she said through gritted teeth. "My sister and many girls I know, yes. That is how they get to this country. Me, no. I'm a businesswoman. I find other ways to pay off my ticket. This is why Kolya come for me to do this job. A prostitute may not be as tricky as me, as smart up here," she said, tapping a temple with a pinkie. "Kolya needed somebody who is smart. I am smart. This is a difficult job. When Kolya come to me, I have no choice. I have to do what I am told."

"How'd you meet Teshay?"

"In the morning, one day, I knock on his door, wake him up, and tell him I'm looking for lady who lives there. I show him address on a piece of paper—a nearby address. 'There must be some mistake,' is his comment. He tells me no lady lives here. I say I must have written down address wrong. That it how I arranged that, and soon he dated me. I make a great effort to find what Kolya wanted me to find out, but I have no success at all. Before I can make a final great effort with Teshay to find out about item, I am informed that Teshay has passed, and that is all I really know."

"What's this item that Kolya wanted you to find?"

"I don't know exactly, except to say that it is some kind of valuable. Very old. From Middle East part of the world."

"What do you mean, 'some kind of valuable.'"

"Kolya uses the word '*anti*-quity,'" she said, mispronouncing the word.

"How the hell are you supposed to find this antiquity if you don't know what it is?"

"Kolya tells me I will know it when I see it because it is very old and it has many beautiful jewels."

"That's fucking pathetic," I muttered. "You're supposed to steal something, but you don't know what it is. Sounds like he doesn't trust you much."

She airily waved a hand.

"So why did Kolya think Teshay had this thing?" I asked.

"Because Teshay lived in Middle East when he was a soldier. But beyond that, I do not know, God's honest truth."

"Can you tell me a little more about this thing you were supposed to obtain?"

"I cannot. I promise you. That is all I know. Kolya wanted me to get close to Teshay and find out this important information about the antiquity with the jewels. But before I achieve the goal, he is gone."

"Did you find out *anything* from Teshay?"

"He passed before I can do this."

"What's Kolya's last name?"

"I do not know."

"Then how the hell can I find him?"

She nodded. "Yes. I can help you. He owns a nightclub for Russian people. The Dacha. In East Hollywood. Not far from my apartment. One moment," she said, raising a finger. She withdrew into the bedroom and circled back with a dog-eared Dacha business card in her palm.

I studied the card. "So Kolya's last name is Maksimov. Is he Russian Mafia?"

"Mafia is something I do not know about."

"What kinds of things is he involved in, besides prostitution?"

"Business. Sneaky financial business."

"Would—"

"I tell you so much. I know I help you. Now will you help my sister?"

"I said I'll look into it. If I come up with something, I'll let you know. Let me ask you something about Kolya. Would he want that antiquity enough to kill for it?"

She chewed on a knuckle. "Not Kolya. He would not get his fingers dirty with that. But Ziven would kill, yes, for something Kolya wanted this much."

"Who's Ziven?"

"He works for Kolya."

"What's he like?"

"As the Russian gangsters say, he is capable. Capable of beating you, capable of stabbing you, capable of shooting you. Capable of anything. You understand what I'm saying?"

"Yes," I said. "I understand exactly what you're saying."

CHAPTER 14

After another night in another rank motel, Mullin checked out, stuck the Smith in his waistband, and made his way up San Julian, through skid row, dodging sidewalk hostesses and stepping over crackheads and losers snoozing on folded-out cardboard boxes. The smell of piss was everywhere. He drifted west and then north, passed a big sign, HIS-TORIC CORE, and found Levine's street. The neighborhood wasn't as bad as the row, but it was still a shithole.

Mullin stopped in front of Levine's building. The place looked like an old bank that had been fixed up. Over the door, some artist had carved a bunch of seashells and seagulls into the stone. What the fuck kind of cop lives in a neighborhood like this? A pretty whacked-out one, Mullin decided. He must be dirty. Didn't most cops in L.A. live in places where the houses were new and clean, with front yards, and campers in the garages and boats in the driveways?

He scoped out the area, looking for a place to hole up and wait it out. Across the street, two buildings over. Perfect. Looked like another old, beat-up office building in the middle of being fixed up. Windows boarded up. A deep entry in front with good sight lines to Levine's building.

Mullin stripped off his jacket, jammed it into the corner of the entry, stretched out, and waited. He kept his eyes on the front of Levine's building.

PART III

SIBERIAN TIGER

CHAPTER 15

It was late afternoon when I swung by the Hollywood station, a weathered two-story red-brick building across the street from a shabby stucco bail bonds office with a flashing red neon sign. I wanted to run Kolya Maksimov's rap sheet. I entered the squad room from the back door, rolled a rickety chair over to a computer, clicked it on, and printed out his relatively short arrest record: four arrests, no convictions. With a yellow felt pen, I highlighted the pertinent data:

> —*1997. Auto theft: Suspect detained during traffic stop in possession of a 1996 Mercedes-Benz reported stolen.*
> —*1998. Extortion: Jewelry store owner alleged that suspect had extorted $11,000 from him for protection money.*
> —*1998. Assault and battery: Suspect accused by known prostitute of subduing her with bodily force and breaking her nose.*
> —*1999. Credit-card fraud: Owner of Hollywood clothing store reported to desk sergeant that suspect stole his credit card and ran up $19,000 in miscellaneous charges.*

I then signed onto the Criminal Information Index and was startled to discover there were no convictions or prison sentences on Maksimov's record. So I called R and I—the Records and Identification unit—and asked them to scan and e-mail me the arrest and follow-up reports. I discovered that all the cases had three variables in common: all the victims had Russian surnames; they all declined to testify at the preliminary hearings; as a result, all charges were dropped. After depositing Maksimov's rap sheet into my murder book, I drove up to Sunset. I swerved into a strip mall near Bronson, a mini League of Nations that housed a Cambodian donut shop, an Indian curry house, a Persian kabob restaurant, a Korean barbecue, and in the center—the largest establishment—the Dacha, a Russian nightclub-restaurant. The front door was locked, so I cut around to the alley in back and darted into the kitchen, suffused with the smell of frying onions, grilled sausages, boiled beets, and steaming cabbage.

A plump, white-haired woman, whose face was as red as a radish, peered into a pot of potatoes. I tapped her on the shoulder and asked, "Where's Kolya?"

"No Kolya here," she said, shaking her head.

"I'm an LAPD detective," I said to the woman. "So, let me ask you again. Where's Kolya?"

She looked me in the eye said, "No Kolya here."

I stepped gingerly across the cement floor, slick with potato peels and onion skins, and made my way through a darkened dining room with a small dance floor and down a hallway. As soon as I stepped into the office, I was startled by a man with an acne-scarred face aiming a blue steel Sig Sauer .45-caliber pistol at my chest.

"I'm an LAPD detective," I said very slowly. "I'm going to move my coat off my belt a few inches so you can see my badge. Do you understand?"

"*Very* slowly," he said in a thick Russian accent. His eyes were as pale and blue as a swimming pool—and contained the same level of emotion. Jailhouse tattoos—or, I figured, gulag tattoos—speckled his hands and wrists. I was surprised at how slight he was. I'd always heard that Russian enforcers were big and burly; this man was skinny, twitchy, and about five and a half feet tall.

In a corner of the room, a man behind a desk leered at me. "LAPD detective, do not be emboldened by the unimposing figure of my bodyguard. I'll tell you what they say about Ziven. He is like the Siberian tiger: you don't notice him until his teeth are around your neck." He turned toward Ziven and said, "You can put the gun away and leave me alone with this gentleman." Ziven cast a suspicious glance at me, holstered his pistol, and disappeared into the hallway, shutting the door behind him.

The office, with its nicked wooden paneling and stained drapes over the windows, had the flimsy feel of a mobile home. But I discovered that Maksimov took security more seriously than interior décor. Inside a closet, I spotted a sleek stainless-steel electronic safe; I knew that someone would need a high-powered drill with carbon-tipped bits to break into that one. I also noticed the sophisticated surveillance system with six video monitors mounted on a wall, displaying rotating stream-ing video shots from each side of the building and views inside the kitchen and dining room. Now I knew why Maksimov's goon was pre-pared for the intrusion.

"I'm Kolya Maksimov. Please excuse the rude greeting." The man rose slowly and gestured with a manicured hand, nails buffed to a gleam, toward a chair across from his desk. He was slender and silver-haired, with the world-weary demeanor of a jaded aristocrat accustomed to def-erence. He wore slacks, loafers, and a pale-green cashmere crewneck sweater. With his neat mustache and short hair—shaved at the sides and close-cropped on top—I figured he was ex-military. His English was excellent, with just a slight inflection. His air of nonchalant ele-gance seemed anomalous amid the seedy office and nightclub. He stared at me with a bemused expression.

"Can I offer you a glass of tea?"

"No, thank you," I said, easing into a chair and setting my briefcase on a frayed carpet. Maksimov was certainly not the Russian Mafia thug I'd expected to encounter.

"So to what do I owe this honor?" the man asked with a serene smile.

"What honor?"

"A visit from Los Angeles's finest?"

I knew that Maksimov, unlike Valentina, could not be intimidated with the threat of deportation. He was a U.S. citizen, his English was fluent, he was a business owner, even though I figured it was a front for numerous scams. Getting information from Maksimov would be not be easy. In fact, I doubted I'd be able to glean anything useful today. This visit was merely an expedition to view the terrain, assess the enemy. I'd return when I was equipped for battle.

"I'm a homicide detective," I said. "I'm not interested in any of your various *business*"—I gave the word a slightly contemptuous emphasis—"dealings."

"What dealings might you be referring to?" Maksimov asked, his eyes glittering with amusement.

"Like I said, I'm not interested in them. I'm only interested in a homicide."

Maksimov opened a silver case, plucked out a long, black cigarette, and lit it with a heavy gold Dunhill lighter. If anyone else flashed a cig-arette case, it would have seemed like an affectation, but Maksimov, I thought, could pull it off.

After a long, languorous drag, he asked, "The homicide of whom?"

I'd spent enough time in Israel with émigrés from Moscow to rec-ognize the aromatic scent: Russian Sobranie tobacco. "The homicide of Teshay Winfield."

"Never heard of the individual."

I opened my murder book and held up Winfield's picture.

Maksimov reached over for the picture and studied it for a moment. "My business dealings generally do not extend to the black element. My customers in this club are all Russian. The closest to black people that I encounter," he said with a half smile, revealing startlingly white teeth, "are the handful of Armenians whom I occasionally number among my customers."

I knew I had no leverage over Maksimov, but just to see what kind of reaction I could spark, said, "You have a very versatile arrest record: assault, extortion, car theft, and credit-card fraud. You're what we call a quadruple threat."

He laughed, stubbing out his cigarette. "I like to see an officer of the law who does his homework. In the Soviet Union, if an officer wanted information, his methods were usually quite rude and quite crude. But here, the officers work hard. Work hard, get ahead. That's what I love about this country. But in this case, officer, your hard work will get you nowhere because, I am afraid, you've been sadly misin-formed."

"How's that?" I asked.

"I know nothing about this Mr. Winfield."

"I know that you do."

"Well, that is where we disagree. And I must remind you, officer, I am a taxpayer and business owner." He leaned over, pushed aside a drape, revealing a decal in the corner of the window. "You see that. I am a member of the Hollywood Chamber of Commerce. I am entitled to all the rights and privileges of any other businessman in this city. So, officer, until you have data that can support your supposition, which, I must say, is entirely unfounded, I must ask you to leave."

"Sure," I said. "But do me a favor."

"What is that?" Maksimov asked, lighting another cigarette.

"Next time I stop by, tell Ziven to keep his piece in his holster."

"Are you sure there'll be a next time?" he asked, cigarette dangling from his lips, holding my eyes.

Irritated by his cocky tone, I said, "I'm sure. And next time I'm coming with cuffs. And I'll promise you one thing. When I put together a case against you—unlike your other four arrests—the charges will not be dropped."

My cell phone rang as I headed back downtown. It was the nosy, unemployed neighbor who lived next door to Winfield. She immediately began shouting and talking so fast I could barely understand her.

"That man who attacked you is here. I saw him. He's here again. He's inside Teshay's house!"

"If he leaves before I get there, will you do something for me? It's very important."

"Remember you said you'd give me a hundred dollars if I called you?"

"I won't forget. But this is very important. I want you to get his license plate number."

"I'll try."

While ripping down the freeway toward Venice, I recalled how big and burly the intruder was, how he had bowled me over. This time, I decided, I needed backup. I reached for the radio and called the Pacific Division dispatcher.

A sergeant and two uniforms were waiting for me in a patrol car down the street from Teshay's house. After I filled them in, we approached the house. The sergeant and one of the patrol officers covered the front door; the other officer and I circled around to the back.

A few minutes later, I heard the sergeant shout, "We got him."

I ran around to the front of the house. The intruder, wearing jeans and a black sweatshirt, was proned out in the dirt, hands cuffed behind his back.

Grimacing, face smeared with dust, he arched his neck and said, "Can I have a private moment with you, Detective Levine?"

"You know this knucklehead?" the sergeant asked, surprised.

I glanced at the man splayed on the ground: mid-thirties, hair cut short, thick neck, and bulging biceps. He was the same guy who had slammed me to the ground a few days ago. "I don't think so. But what the hell. Right now he's harmless enough. Back off and let me talk to him."

The three officers trudged across the lawn and lingered beside an orange tree, while I crouched beside the man and said, "You've got thirty seconds. What do you want?"

"Please reach into my back pocket."

I snatched a black leather wallet from the pocket and opened it. Stunned, I dropped it on the grass. Inside one flap was an identification card with the man's name—Emery Peck—and his picture. Clipped to the other flap was a gold FBI badge.

"How do I know the card wasn't forged and the badge wasn't stolen?" I asked.

"I'll name a half dozen guys in the LAPD's Organized Crime and Vice Division and what they like to eat for lunch," he said, rattling off the names and the menu items. I recalled two FBI agents I had worked with in the past and asked the man to describe them and name their supervisors. After he passed that test, too, I said, "Where's your dark suit, black shoes, white shirt, and rep tie?"

"I'm undercover today."

I stood and called out, "Sarge, you can unhook this guy. Turns out there's been a misunderstanding."

"What kind of misunderstanding?" the sergeant asked, casting a suspicious glance at Peck.

"I'll explain some other time," I said.

"You Felony Special guys with your fucking secrets," the sergeant muttered, unlocking the handcuffs. He retreated, leading the other two cops out of the yard and onto the sidewalk out front. Peck, rubbing his wrists, said, "I owe you one."

"You owe me more than one," I said. " Last time, you knocked me on my ass, and ruined the pants of one of my favorite suits."

Peck, looking sheepish, said, "Sorry about that. I was just trying to get out of there with no questions asked or answered."

I held up a palm. "Wait here one sec."

I rang the bell of the neighbor, who was watching the action from her front window, her face shadowed by a flap of drapery. She nudged open the door, and I surreptitiously reached into my pocket, peeled off five twenties, and slipped them to her.

"Is he the guy who kill my neighbor?" she asked.

"Probably not." I jogged back to Peck and said, "Hop in your car. I'll follow you to the Federal Building."

"Still don't believe I'm FBI?"

"After the shit you've pulled, who the hell knows."

"Can I ask you a very big favor?" Peck said.

"You don't deserve a favor."

"I know that. But if I can help you with your case, can you forget about what happened today and the last time we met? And not put anything down on paper?"

"It depends."

"It depends on what?"

"It depends on how good your information is."

Peck parked behind the Federal Building, a bland, boxy white tower on Wilshire Boulevard in West Los Angeles, across the street from the VA cemetery, just a few blocks from the Westwood high-rises. I trailed him through the security gates—he waved a key card—into the elevator and up to the seventeenth floor. His office was a jumble of boxes and case files, steno pads with an illegible scrawl, and balled up pieces of paper. I glanced at the family portrait at the corner of his desk: Peck, his wife, and three young sons, all wearing beige cords and red sweaters, posed in front of the Christmas tree. Would Robin and I ever get it together and have kids? Maybe. Would we pose with our family before the menorah, candles blazing, for a photo that I'd display on my desk? Probably not.

When Peck slumped into a chair behind his cluttered desk, the cushion sagging and squeaking, I said, "You play football at Michigan State?" I asked.

Startled, Peck said, "How'd you know I went to Michigan State? And how'd you know I played football?"

I tapped the Michigan State University coffee cup on his desk. "When you lowered your shoulder on me the other day and knocked me on my ass, I figured you'd done that a few thousand times before."

"Played my freshman year. Then blew out my knee."

"Linebacker?"

"Right again."

"Middle?"

"Wrong," Peck said. "Inside. But two out of three ain't bad."

I tugged a yellow legal pad from my briefcase and a pen from my shirt pocket and said, "You better have a good reason for breaking into my vic's house. If you do, I'm perfectly willing to keep that between you and me—if you've got some good information to trade."

"I think I do," Peck said.

"I hope so. Because my case is a tough one. I had a break today and rustled up a decent suspect. But I've got nothing to tie him to the murder—yet."

"Who's your suspect?" Peck asked.

"Same old shit," I said angrily. "You fucking FBI guys always want to take what we've got and never tell us what you've got. Don't play that game with me. This is one of those rare cases where I'm holding all the cards. So tell me what you know. Then ask me what you want to know. If I feel that I've learned something from you, maybe I'll throw you a bone or two."

Peck ground his teeth, working his jaw muscles. He, obviously, was used to giving orders to the local cops. "Fair enough," he rasped.

"Take it from the top," I said. "Why'd you break into my vic's house—twice?"

"I didn't exactly break in," Peck said. "As part of an ongoing federal investigation, I felt it was important to protect the safety of—"

"Just tell me what you were doing there."

"Okay," Peck said, tapping a file with a paper clip. "I know you're familiar with Kolya Maksimov."

Startled, I asked, "How'd you know that?"

"I'm with the Russian Organized-Crime Squad. We got court authorization for a tap on his phone and a bug in his office. So when you paid him a visit this afternoon, I found out."

"I'd be solving cases a lot quicker if I could get that kind of authorization," I said. "I ran Maksimov, and those arrests in the late 1990s seem a little low rent for the feds."

"They are," Peck said.

"Tell me what you know about Maksimov and why you're so interested in him. Because I'm very interested in him."

"What do you know about Russian organized crime?" Peck asked.

"Not much."

"First thing you've got to understand is it's not Russian and it's not organized. It's not like the Italian Mafia with its centralized hierarchy. These Russians are split into lots of small syndicates that they call 'brigades' that work independently. Lot of the people we track, who are in what's loosely called the Russian Mafia, are not from Russia, but from former Soviet republics like Georgia, Armenia, the Ukraine—"

"And Moldova?" I asked

"Moldova, too," Peck said. "The first wave of these Russian gangsters came over in the 1970s. There was a big 'Free Soviet Jewry' campaign in the States, which eased immigration, and a lot of the gangsters came over then."

"I remember my parents talking about that. Our temple was involved. They did marches and picketed the Russian Embassy, that kind of thing."

"Well, there were some crooks among those Jews who were allowed to leave the Soviet Union. Others simply passed as Jews or had some remote connection—like a great-grandmother on their father's side. These characters were what I'd call 'paper gangsters.' They were white-collar criminals par excellence. They had so much practice dodging all the crazy Soviet laws and regulations, they really knew how to work the system. So when they arrived in the U.S., it was a breeze for them to defraud the U.S. government and U.S. businesses. They kited checks, scammed insurance companies and Medicare, ripped off the IRS, forged credit cards."

"So Maksimov came over in the seventies?" I asked.

"No. Maksimov came over in the 1990s, during the next big wave of Russian crooks to wash ashore here. That was when the Soviet Union disintegrated. These guys were even worse than the first group. They stepped right into the paper scams, but they also had no compunction about using muscle and getting into drugs, prostitution, extortion, and a bunch of others enterprises. Brighton Beach in Brooklyn is the hub for all this. But L.A.—mainly Hollywood and the Valley—is number two and closing fast."

I jotted a few notes and said, "Maksimov doesn't seem like your typical crook."

"He's not. He's got a very interesting background. His family, way back, was one of the few White Russian families to survive and thrive after the revolution. Apparently they quickly saw which way the wind was blowing, sold out enough of their friends and distant relatives to satisfy the purge meisters, and switched sides. That genetic trait must have been passed down, because Maksimov seems to have the same talent for self-preservation. He's very well educated. Speaks excellent English—as you discovered—as well as Polish, Spanish, and some Arabic. Has an electrical engineering degree from the finest school in the country—Moscow State University."

The electrical engineering background immediately piqued my interest. I recalled those burn marks on Winfield and Pinkney and what Dr. Gupta had said: "My guess is a soldering iron, the kind of tool an electrician would use to fuse wires. Something like that would generate tremendous heat."

"Maksimov even taught at the university for a while. But he eventually found it was more lucrative to smuggle religious icons out of the country in exchange for hard-to-get luxury items from the West that he supplied to Communist Party officials."

"Religious icons?"

"They're highly valued here, but are never supposed to leave Russia. When the Soviet Union dissolved, he seemed poised to parlay the morphing of Communism to capitalism into a fortune, like a lot of the other glasnost gangsters. But he must have pissed off the wrong people—we're still trying to find out who—which prompted him to flee Russia pronto. So he ended up in L.A."

"Why'd a sophisticated guy like that make like a thug and pull a bunch of street crimes?" I asked.

"When he arrived in North Hollywood, he didn't have two nickels to rub together. It wasn't easy for a Russian fresh off the boat, with a degree from a Communist university, to get an engineering job."

"Did he ever work as an electrician here?"

Peck swirled the paper clip across his palm. "I think he did work as an electrician and handyman briefly to pick up some cash. But he soon graduated from menial labor. And he's got a heartwarming, inspiring immigrant story," Peck said sarcastically. "He preyed on his own. He ripped off other Russians. Most didn't go to the cops. But those who did, were *persuaded*"—he smiled archly—"not to testify. So all the charges were dropped."

"When did he graduate from the street stuff?"

"In a few years, as soon as he got some operating capital. And now he's got Ziven—whom I understand you've met—for the rough stuff."

"So what's he into now?"

"He's got the nightclub and a Russian market. But those are just money laundering fronts. His portfolio of illegitimate businesses is impressive. He made his bones with girls from Russia and a few of the old republics. Uses his contacts back home to get the girls tourist visas. Flies them to Mexico City, busses them to Tijuana, and transports them into Southern California harbors on a fishing trawler he bought from a pot smuggler. When he's got the girls, he sells them to madams and pimps in L.A."

"Do the girls know they'll be working as hookers?"

"Some do; some don't. They're told they'll be models, secretaries, that kind of thing. The savvy ones figure it out; the naïve ones don't."

"What happens to the girls?" I asked.

"They work off their passage and then, if they're lucky, the madams cut them loose."

"How do the madams make sure the girls don't run?"

"Because they all employ thugs like Ziven."

"Is Maksimov still running girls?" I asked.

"Occasionally," Peck said. "But he's very diversified now. He stages auto accidents. He's involved in a small counterfeiting operation. He forges credit cards. He shakes down Russian shopkeepers. He's even running a medical lab out of a mobile home, has some nurse running tests on his stooges, overcharges the hell out them, and rakes it in from insurance companies."

"If he's so diversified, why's his office such a dump?"

"Stealth wealth," Peck said. "He's smart enough not to flaunt what he's got. Easier to stay out of the crosshairs of the cops—and the IRS. His office might be a dump, but you should see his house in Beverly Hills—it's a palace."

"Let's get back to why I'm sitting here right now," I said. "What were you doing tossing Winfield's house?"

Peck rose to his feet and paced behind his desk. "We've got a major investigation into Maksimov going on right now. I had a source working deep cover on this."

"What do you mean—source?" I asked.

"You call 'em CIs—confidential informants. In the bureau, we call them sources. Anyway, I haven't seen or heard from my source in a week. This is someone who was reluctant to work this case." He pinched his chin and a moment later eased his fingers away, leaving two red ovals. "But I pushed and prodded and persuaded the source."

"So you feel responsible?"

"That's right," Peck said.

"So how does your missing informant tie in with Teshay Winfield?"

"I picked up that connection on the tap. One time, and one time only, in his office, Maksimov mentioned Teshay Winfield. He was talking to Ziven—in Russian of course. The conversation was brief and a bit garbled, unfortunately. Maksimov said something like, 'He's talked to the mask or knows the mask,' or something like that."

I inched forward in my seat, trying to hide my excitement. *The mask is the missing link that ties Maksimov to Winfield's murder. That's the fucking motive.*

"Our Russian speakers don't know. But my guess is that 'mask' might be slang for snitch."

"So you think Winfield knew where your snitch was?" I asked.

"That's what I'm guessing."

"And that's all you heard about my victim?"

"That's all."

I jotted a few notes and said, "You've got his phone tapped and his office bugged. You break into my vic's house—twice. And you're telling me you haven't heard any more about Winfield than that?" I slapped a pen on my palm. "I don't believe you."

He leaned over, propping two beefy forearms on his desk. "I didn't go into this business to cover up a murder," he said defensively. "If I had picked up anything on your guy, I promise you, I'd tell you."

"So why didn't you just come to me?" I asked. "I might have let you into Winfield's place myself."

"But you might not of," Peck said. "I've got a good relationship with your Organized Crime guys. But I've worked with some LAPD homicide detectives before. Most of 'em have shut me out."

"That's because you guys are such proprietary assholes."

"Maybe. But I couldn't take the chance of you shutting me out, too." He twisted the paper clip and then bent it double. "When I figured that Winfield might know something about my source, I had to move. And I had to move fast. I couldn't take the chance of you jacking me around. My source's life is in the balance."

"So why didn't you get a search warrant instead of busting into the place?"

He halted and gripped the edge of his desk. "Because the agent in charge here doesn't think Winfield has any connection to my source. He's fluent in Russian; he's lived in the country. I'm not fluent; I've never lived there. The agent guesses that 'mask' is a drug term—like a masking agent to water down heroin or crank. He thinks maybe Maksimov is using black muscle for some drug transactions, and that's his connection to Winfield. I know that's not Maksimov's game. But the agent claims I've lost all perspective and am looking for things that aren't there."

"What's the real reason?" I asked.

"If I file a search warrant, then I have to acknowledge that I don't know where the hell our source is. If it's on a warrant, it'll inevitably get out. I've paid this source more than eighty thousand dollars. And now," he said, pausing and opening a fist, "poof. Gone. That makes the bureau look real bad. That makes me look even worse."

"There's got to be more to it than that. I'm wondering why you care about this source so much that you'd break into a murder victim's house and then bowl over a cop so you wouldn't be caught? I'm guessing that this source was more than a source." I studied his face. "I've had a lot of experience with CIs—male *and* female. I'm guessing this one went from source to squeeze."

"That's a lie. I've never cheated on my wife. Not once." I glanced at Peck's family portrait. On the wall, in a frame, was a New Testament quote: "For he is God's servant for your good. But if you do wrong, be afraid, for he does not bear the sword in vain. For he is the servant of God, an avenger who carries out God's wrath on the wrongdoer."

I studied Peck's face. He glared at me, eyes bulging, face flushed, as if he was about to vault over his desk and level me again. I'd built a career on reading suspects and witnesses, and I had confidence in my bullshit detector. I believed Peck.

"Then why take a risk like that?"

"Pierre."

"Who's Pierre?"

"Pierre, South Dakota."

"I don't follow you."

"The agent in charge here told me if I don't find that source, and that eighty thousand dollars, he'd transfer me to the bureau's field office in Pierre, South Dakota. You ever been to South Dakota in January? Unfortunately, I have. The FBI has already dragged my family from

Omaha to Stillwater to Phoenix to L.A. My wife's had it. I don't think she'd make the move to Pierre. I did what I had to do to try to save my marriage."

"That story's so crazy it might even be true," I said. "Let's move on before I start getting into marriage counseling. You ever hear Maksimov mention a girl named Valentina Revenco? A scammer from Moldova."

"No," Peck said. "On the phone, and even in his office, he's pretty damn circumspect. I'm thinking he might even suspect we're listening. Because we're not getting much of anything from him. That's why I felt I had to jump on the mask thing right away. So who's Valentina Revenco?"

"Just someone on the periphery of my case." I didn't want him interfering with my murder investigation. "Since you've got Maksimov wired, if you pick up any chatter about Revenco or Winfield, will you let me know?"

"I will. Look, I'm helping you out, " Peck said, circling the desk toward me. "I'm sharing a lot of information with you. How about something in return."

"You owed me one," I said. "Now we're even. If I come up with anything in the next few weeks that I think could help your case, or if I pick up the trail of your snitch, I'll contact you."

"I don't like your attitude," Peck said. "But what can I do?"

I tucked my yellow legal pad into my briefcase, crossed the room, stood by the door, and said, "Nothing."

CHAPTER 16

The wind was blowing hard and Mullin, huddled in the entryway, watched the dust drift down the sidewalk. He thought of Iraq. The clear, warm days. The freezing desert nights. Those fucking sand storms that left you picking shit out of your eyes and ears for days.

Not much activity in front of the cop's building. But two black dudes were walking across the street, coming toward him. They looked kind of raggedy, dressed in old jeans and sweatshirts. Both had that cocky, rolling, gangbanger walk, but they seemed a little old for gangsters. They were ripped, with thick necks, and they filled up their sweatshirts pretty good. Tattoos on the neck. Dead eyes.

Ex-cons. Just like me.

"We're a little short of cash tonight," one of them said with a phony smile. He was missing a bottom tooth. "Can you help us out?"

Mullin checked out the street. The only person out was a wino pushing a shopping cart full of bottles and cans.

"No," he said flatly.

"We can do it the easy way, brutha, or the hard way."

"I ain't your *brother*," Mullin said.

The other guy yanked a knife out of his back pocket and flipped it open, the blade catching a spangle of light from the streetlamp overhead. "Motherfucker, I'm going to carve you up like a Thanksgiving turkey."

"You skid row niggers are so down and out you can't even come up with a cheap-ass piece," Mullin said, standing up. "All you've got is that little wood whittler."

As the guy with the blade lunged toward him, Mullin snatched the Smith out of his waistband and leveled it. When you saw someone's eyes change from predator to prey; when you saw that greedy gleam snuff out; when you saw that look of pure fear, well, that was a fine feeling, better than sex.

"Get the fuck outta here," Mullin said.

"We getting," the guy with the blade said, backing up.

"Get!"

Mullin chuckled as he watched them hightail it down the street and around the corner.

He reached for his cell and called Delfour. "When's this cop getting home? I'm freezing my ass off out here."

"He'll be home tonight. Might be late, but he'll be home."

"You sure?"

"Yes. He hasn't slept in a few days, and I don't think he can hold out any longer. So just hang in there. How are you doing?"

"Outstanding," Mullin said sarcastically.

"Remember, when you see him, take care of business and make a slick getaway. You shouldn't have any problems. The only witnesses out there are crackheads, winos, and other street trash. This will be the easiest cash you've ever made."

CHAPTER 17

It was dusk by the time I traversed the Federal Building's parking lot and crawled inside my car. A part of me was energized after the breaks in the case, but I hadn't slept in almost forty-eight hours and was so exhausted I couldn't keep my eyes open. I leaned my head back, stretched out my legs, and dozed off. A half hour later, I woke to the ping of pebbles against my car, kicked up by the gusty winds. As I heard the whine of the Santa Anas, I thought of the *hamsin*, that fierce desert wind that blows from the Sahara, sweeps through Israel, billowing clouds of yellow dust and withering trees as it whips up the coastline and on to Lebanon. As I watched a dust cloud drift through the parking lot, that *hamsin* in northern Israel came back to me, like a video in my head.

A paratrooper patrol reconning for Hezbollah guerillas slipping across the border from Lebanon. The dust is thick, visibility only about ten feet. My mouth is parched. I slide my tongue along my teeth, trying to dislodge grains of sand. I sip from my canteen; even the water is infused with dust. I hear a voice, a whispered word. It sounds like, "Jesh." The Arabic term for soldier. I hold up my palm and aim to the left. A silent signal. We swivel around and level our Galils in unison. An explosion behind us. Sounds like a grenade. An ambush. Pinpricks down my back. Warm. Then hot. Then scalding. A moment later, the distinctive pop-pop-pop *of Kalachnikovs. Tamir, on my left, collapses. I flatten out on the dirt and move forward with my arms and feet—we call it "sheela" in the IDF—toward the gunshots. I see a flash of a green kefiyah. I fire. A man sprints toward a dry wadi. I leap to my feet. I fire again. He kneels and fires back. I see the muzzle blaze. He disappears as I advance. The man tries to crawl out of the wadi. I fire. He goes down. I slide down into the wadi and stand over his body, spraying an automatic blast to the head. It dissolves in a red bloom. My first kill. I stare at what's left of the head. I feel nothing.*

I stepped from the car and ran in place for a moment, seeking a distraction, trying to expunge the memory. The short nap revived me. I decided to track down Valentina Revenco's sister, Anika. I drove west on Wilshire, trudging along in rush-hour traffic, until I'd passed Fairfax and reached a neighborhood called the Miracle Mile. When I was a kid, the district was composed of gracious, modest-sized 1920's and 1930's apartment buildings known for their distinctive architecture, many designed with gables and towers, wood-beamed ceilings, and hand-plastered walls. I was in a melancholy mood as I drove through the side streets north of Wilshire. Many drab apartment complexes, shaped like enormous refrigerators, had replaced the gracious old buildings.

The Russian gangsters had stashed Anika in a four-story monstrosity with a two-tiered parking garage and no front lawn. The only vegetation out front was a single, withered oleander with a handful of shriveled pink flowers tasseled from droopy leaves. After checking out the coded security box by the front gate, I lingered beside the garage. Five minutes later, a silver BMW nosed forward. The metal gate rose, and after the car descended into the lot, I scurried inside before the gate rattled down. I crossed the garage, took the elevator to the fourth floor, and staked out the door at the end of the hallway—the apartment where Anika was imprisoned.

I waited a half hour, but I didn't see anyone enter or leave the apartment, so I rang the bell. A towering, muscular man with a blond buzz cut and sharp Slavic cheekbones swung open the door. While Ziven bore little resemblance to my image of a hulking Russian gangster, this guy fit the stereotype.

As I showed him my badge, I craned my neck and quickly surveilled the inside of the apartment. Two young women in T-shirts and sweatpants were sitting on a sofa, watching television. Neither of them resembled Anika. A second thug, who was wearing a red silk shirt, snoozed in an overstuffed chair in the corner.

"I'm investigating a homicide. I'd like to take a look inside and talk to some of the girls."

"You got paper?"

"I don't have a warrant right now. But I can get it."

"No paper, no entry," the man said, slamming the door.

As I lingered in the hallway, I realized I probably wouldn't be able to convince a judge to give me a warrant based on the word of a scam artist like Revenco. I settled on another strategy, but I was too tired to try it now. I knew I better rush home and rack out for a while or I'd be sleepwalking tomorrow.

I rode the elevator to the ground floor, climbed into my car, and sped home, fighting to keep my eyes open.

CHAPTER 18

A car door slammed, waking Mullin. Where the fuck was he? He rubbed his eyes and glanced around. A dark street. Plywood screening some of the windows. A few gutted buildings. Across the street a nice-looking place with marble columns flanking the entry. Detective Ash Levine's building.

How long had he slept? Had he missed Levine? He looked around in a panic. There was a guy climbing the steps to the building. He could see him from the back. He was wearing a sports coat and slacks. Jesus. Was it Levine?

Mullin scrambled to his feet. The guy lingered by the front door. Jangling his keys, he pivoted around and scanned the street.

Motherfucker! It was Levine.

Mullin whipped out the Combat Masterpiece. But Levine had already slipped inside.

Did I just watch twenty-five thousand dollars go down the shitter? What the fuck am I going to tell Delfour?

Mullin collapsed onto the stoop and slammed the barrel on his knee. *I've got to come up with something. Something good. And it's not going to be easy 'cause Delfour's smart. Smarter then me. Best to take a negative and turn it into a positive. That's what his counselor in the joint told him to do when he faced adversity.*

Mullin dialed Delfour's number on his cell phone. "I've got good news."

"Did you take care of business?"

"It's good news, but not that good. I got a positive ID on Levine at his building."

"But you weren't paying close enough attention so you missed your chance."

"Not exactly. He was with several people, kind of a crowd, in fact, as he walked from his car to his place. I couldn't get a clean kill shot."

"I don't believe you."

"You calling me a—"

"Did he see you?"

"No."

"You sure?"

"One hundred percent sure."

"Levine's down for the night. So you've lost tonight. I don't want you back tomorrow night. Someone on the street is going to make you. Hanging around that much is too suspicious. Return to your post in two nights and do the job then."

"Yes, sir."

"I want to make sure you understand. Leave immediately. Don't return tomorrow night. Come back the night after that and do the job."

"Huah."

"And I want you to promise me one thing."

"What's that?"

"When you return, do not, and I repeat, do not, fall asleep."

CHAPTER 19

The next morning as I walked up Main Street, I thought of how I'd been shut down at the Miracle Mile apartment house. I decided to try another approach. At PAB, I rode the elevator to the fourth floor, and knocked on the door of Ralph Baaken's office. Baaken, the captain in charge of the Organized Crime and Vice Division, looked too young to be a captain. He was blond and fair, with a face so round and fleshy there was no evidence of cheekbones or a jawline. I introduced myself and briefed him on my visit to the Miracle Mile apartment.

"There's a lock-down hooker operation going on there," I said, sitting in a chair in front of his desk. "It's tied in with the Russian mob. With your contacts in that world and with a short investigation, I'm sure you can get enough to take them down. This will be a good bust for you. I'd just like a favor. When you take them down, I'd like to be there. They're holding a girl who could help me out on my double."

"I know all about your double," Baaken said. "Councilman Pinkney has a lot to say about this department's budget. If you don't clear that case and find out who killed his son, I'll have to turn in my take-home Crown Vic and start taking the bus to work," he said, laughing.

"Excellent, I really appreciate your help."

He tugged at an eyebrow. "Unfortunately, I can't help you right now."

"Why not?"

"I know all about what's going on in that apartment. We've got a big investigation going on that involves dozens of places like that and a lot of other shit. We're close to a bust."

"How close?"

"Three weeks. A month at the outside."

"I can't wait three weeks. You ever work homicide?"

He shook his head. "Patrol was my specialty. Out on the streets you—"

"With a homicide, three weeks is an eternity. I can't afford to let my leads get stale. The girl who can help me with my homicides is in that apartment. I need to talk to her right now. If I wait three weeks, she might have already been moved to San Diego or Seattle."

"Sorry," he said officiously.

"Look, I don't know how you made it to captain, but at every LAPD division I've worked, homicide trumps prostitution."

"Not on this case," he said with a smug smile.

As I stood, I said, "The tenth floor is interested in this case. Give someone up there a call."

As I backed out of the office, he lifted the phone off the receiver and said, "I am."

When I returned to the squad room, I saw Duffy sitting in my chair, leafing through my murder book. "Let's go," he said.

"Where are we going?"

He jerked his thumb at the ceiling, toward the tenth floor, where the command staff was based. Deputy Chief Ronald—not Ron!—Greever was waiting for us in his office, which was so spacious there was a conference table in the corner. Greever didn't look like a cop. His face was artificially bronzed and glowing—a tanning booth tan. He had the fluffed-out, light brown hair of an anchorman. His eyes were a little too blue—I suspected tinted contacts.

Ignoring Duffy, he said, "Good to see you, Ash. Sit down, sit down. Can I get you anything? Coffee? A Coke?"

"I'm good," I said.

After we joined him at the conference table, he held out his arms. "Frankly, this is a tad embarrassing." He grinned, revealing teeth so white I wondered if they'd been capped. "I understand you've had a bit of a misunderstanding with Captain Baaken."

"No misunderstanding. I told him homicide trumps prostitution."

He smiled again, but it didn't reach his eyes this time. "There's an exception to every rule. So I've got to ask you to back off for just a few weeks. Wait until Baaken's team finishes their investigation and then you can scoop up this girl."

"As you know, I'm investigating the murder of Councilman Pinkney's son and another victim who was a decorated combat veteran. Baaken's case must be pretty fucking important if you're telling me he's calling the shots."

Greever, again, gave me a smile that wasn't a smile. "It is."

"That's the most fucked up—"

"Ash," he said, cutting me off, "let me stop you before you say something you'll regret. I know you have a history of that kind of intemperance."

He turned toward Duffy, acknowledging him for the first time. "I'd like a few minutes alone with you."

I stormed back to Felony Special, taking the stairs instead of the elevator, to work off some of my frustration. Back in Duffy's office, I fell into a chair, stunned. Fifteen minutes later, Duffy burst into the office and slammed the door.

"I don't get it," I said.

"Okay," Duffy said. "Here it is. Baaken's unit has been working a big Russian organized crime case for six months. They're close to wrapping it up."

"They investigating my guy, Maksimov?"

"From what I can tell, no. But it sounds like they're investigating the head of some Russian Mafia brigade who's big-time. Bigger then Maksimov."

"The FBI's got a similar investigation going on."

"Right. That's why Greever and the rest of the tenth-floor honchos have determined that it's vitally important that we make our bust before the FBI."

"Who gives a shit who takes who down first?"

"The LAPD brass gives a shit."

"Why?"

"Okay, listen carefully. Baaken's case involves big-time prostitution. And more important—big-time drugs. And most important—big-time money."

"Big-time money is the most important element of this?"

Duffy shrugged. "There it is."

"There what is?"

"It's all about the do-re-mi."

"Why?"

"You know the city's got a nightmarish budget deficit. Well, it's killing this department. Our shortfall alone is more than fifty million.

We've already got a hiring freeze. The city budget gurus are talking about big-time LAPD layoffs and all kind of drastic shit. Christ, we've got bodies stacked up on the south end, but homicide detectives are sitting at home taking vacation days because we can't pay their overtime. That thin blue line is getting so thin it's almost invisible. The brass is in a panic. They think that by the time the budget gurus get through slashing our budget, you won't be able to recognize the LAPD."

"What does this have to do with my double?"

"Baaken's sitting on this gangster who's not interested in sticking with the typical rackets that these Russian guys run like hookers, and check kiting, and insurance fraud, and tax scams, and credit-card forgery, and that kind of chickenshit crap. He's in business with one of the biggest Mexican drug gangs—the Campeche Cartel. He's moving tar and coke for them, and he's laundering their money. Baaken's got a tap going on this fool."

"The feebs have got a tap on Maksimov, too."

"When it comes to the Russian mob, the judges have been cutting law enforcement a lot of slack. So Baaken finds out on his tap that this Russian has got more than seventy million dollars in cash that he's going to ship in a few weeks to Odessa in a tanker."

"Whose money is it?"

"Some of it is his. Some of it is the cartel's. Hard to launder that kind of green in the U.S. or Mexico. But not so hard in Eastern Europe if you've got criminal contacts in a dozen countries over there."

"So say the LAPD seizes the money," I said. "How much do we get to keep?"

"Our state asset forfeiture laws say sixty-five percent."

"That's more than forty-five million."

"That kind of money will save this department. The DA even gets ten percent of the haul, so we buy a lot of goodwill with them as a bonus. If you start shaking things up with Maksimov's girls, it might make this other Russian mobster skittish. Word travels fast in that world. He might suspect either us or the feebs are sitting on him. He might start making moves that we don't know about and then"—Duffy swirled an index finger—"poof. There goes our forty-five mil."

"Councilman—"

"Yes, Councilman Pinkney is important to this department. And to this department's budget. And I want you to go balls out and find his son's killer. In your pursuit of this investigation I want you to leave no stone unturned. Except one."

"So you're telling me—"

"You probably were going to ask me if forty-five million dollars is more important than the lives of your two victims."

I shrugged.

"Were you?" Duffy asked.

"Something like that."

"The answer is yes."

I needed to leave PAB and clear my head in order to plot my next move. I cut over to First Street, the wind kicking up dust and stinging my eyes, and ducked into Restaurant Aoi in Little Toyko. After ordering the sashimi and tempura special, I sipped green tea and was contemplating the case when my cell rang.

"I've got one for you," Duffy said.

"Hold on a second." I covered the phone and caught the waitress's attention. "Pack up that lunch to go." I swigged down my tea and said to Duffy, "Let's hear it."

"Wilshire just caught a fresh one. They're running with it right now. But their lieutenant called me because he thought we should know that your card was found in the vic's apartment."

I felt my heart thumping in my chest and my throat tighten. "Jerry Ambrose? A one-armed vet?"

"That's him. Wilshire's willing to keep the case. But you can snatch it from them if you want it."

"I'll meet you there."

"You have any ideas?"

I immediately thought of Maksimov and Ziven. "Yeah. Two."

CHAPTER 20

When I arrived at Ambrose's apartment, I hustled through the security door, which was propped open and manned by a uniform. The apartment, I thought, appeared about the same as the last time I was there—but with one exception: a dead body was sprawled in the center of the living room. Duffy, two detectives in suits, and a woman lingered by the dining room table. I knew one of the detectives, Ralph Butella, a rangy man with tired eyes and a sunburnt neck—the D-3 for Wilshire Homicide. I'd worked with him years ago at the South Bureau Homicide. Ralph was no investigative genius, but he was a solid, hard-working detective, and a decent guy. After I shook hands with Butella, he introduced me to the other Wilshire Division detectives: Richie Powers, red-haired and freckled with jug ears, and Joan Guzman, a lean, leathery woman in her late thirties who wore gray slacks, flats, and a black trench coat.

Butella jerked his thumb toward Powers and said, "Opie, here, got all excited when I told him the great Ash Levine was on his way. I think the kid even got a hard-on. You got a real fan."

Richie Powers stared at his shoes and said, "I was working patrol in Central when you put together that serial case against the Spring Street Slasher. It really made an impression on me. That's why I became a detective."

"Are you married?"

"Yeah."

"When you get divorced, you'll be cursing me."

Guzman said, "An honor to work with you, sir."

"Forget the sir-shit," I said.

"Before these two start groping you, let me tell you what we've got," Butella said. "The manager knocks on the door this morning. He wants to invite this kid, Jerry Ambrose, to a Christmas party. The manager's a Vietnam vet and he kind of feels for this kid, who lost an arm in Iraq.

No one answers the door, but he can hear the TV blaring. He finds this kind of fishy, so he let's himself in with the pass key and finds the stiff. We're here, tossing the apartment, waiting for the coroner to arrive, when Opie spots your card in the bedroom. So we thought we'd give you a courtesy call. It's early on, so I don't know much about the homicide. But I do know one thing."

"What's that?"

"My lieutenant won't be authorizing any overtime."

"Neither will Duffy. What else do you know?"

"Like I said, not much," Butella said. "Two guys from patrol have been canvassing the building during the past hour. Nobody heard a shot fired; nobody saw anything."

"This building have a security camera by the front door?" I asked.

Butella lightly tapped Powers's elbow. "Find out, Opie."

"Give me a few minutes to check out the scene," I told Butella. "Then Duffy will make the call on who takes the case."

I crouched on the carpet and examined the body. Ambrose was curled on his side, in a slight fetal position, barefoot, wearing sweatpants and a long-sleeved T-shirt. In the back of his head were two neat round holes, each the size of a pencil eraser—the entry wounds. The hair surrounding the wound was flecked with blood—stiff and spiky, with a brown sheen. Dashes of blood on the beige carpet surrounded the head like a halo.

I edged around the body and studied the forehead, but could find no exit wounds. "Small caliber to the back of the head. Maybe a twenty-two. Two shots. Possibly a professional job."

Powers returned and motioned, thumbs down. "They have a security camera, but it was on the fritz."

"That's a bad break," I said. "So why didn't anyone hear the shots?"

"Suppressor?" Powers asked, tentatively.

"Maybe," I said. "That would go with the professional job."

"TV was blaring," Powers said. "Maybe it obscured the sound. And if it didn't, two shots from a twenty-two might not be loud enough to alarm people."

"Entirely possible," I said.

I lifted the cuffs of Ambrose's shirt with my pen but did not see any ligature marks. I wanted to peel off the shirt and pants, but I knew I had to wait for the coroner investigator.

"Do something to confirm Opie's confidence in you," Butella said. "Tell us what the hell happened here."

I closed my eyes for a moment. "Our shooter knocks or rings the bell. Ambrose opens it up without looking through the peephole or asking who it is."

"How'd you know that?" Powers asked eagerly.

"Because when I stopped by his house yesterday and knocked on the door, that's what he did. He's a pretty angry guy who doesn't seem to give a shit about anything. So, obviously, he's not too security conscious."

I quickly scanned the room. "After Ambrose opens the door, he becomes suspicious and tries to slam it, but asshole forces his way inside."

"Sounds good," Butella said.

I tapped my foot beside a small table beside the door that had toppled over, spilling a pile of magazines. "This is what asshole knocked over after he forced his way inside."

I stepped forward. "Ambrose tries to escape, but probably stops in his tracks when asshole pulls out his piece." I knelt beside the coffee table, which was almost perpendicular to the sofa, and traced a finger along the indentations in the carpet where the table once stood. "Ambrose banged into the coffee table as he was trying to get away." I rose and asked, "Find anything interesting in the rest of the house?"

"Not much," Powers said. "Ambrose lived here with his brother, the manager told us. But the brother was out of town for the holidays visiting his girlfriend."

Butella waved a palm. "Let's hold up for a second. Before we go any further, Ash, why don't you tell us why you wanted to see Ambrose yesterday."

"Fair enough," I said and quickly briefed them.

"So you think Ambrose was killed because he was a friend of Teshay Winfield?" Powers asked.

"Let's just say I don't like coincidences," I said.

"So what do you want to do about this case, Ash?" Duffy asked. "You can have it, but don't expect any overtime. And if you max out on comp time, you'll have to take a few days off."

"Let me spend a few minutes tossing the place before I decide."

"We already did," Butella said. "Not much there."

"I'm just going to give it a quick once-over."

"No problem," Butella said. "Me and Opie and Guzman will finish up the canvass."

Duffy and I entered the bedroom and looked around. An unmade queen-sized bed was jammed against one wall, the dingy sheets and navy comforter crumpled in the middle. A large dresser with a broken leg teetered against another wall. The top was crammed with a CD player, stereo headphones, and loose change. After I sifted through the dresser drawers, the closet, and the bathroom, I searched the kitchen and inspected the drain. I turned to Duffy and said, "Not much to go on."

"Very clean crime scene. How do you feel about it?"

"I feel like shit," I said, sinking onto the sofa. My mouth was dry and I could feel a brutal headache coming on. "I track down this guy, he gives me a lead, and the next day he gets capped. That's fucked up."

Duffy leaned over and gripped my shoulders. "It ain't your fault."

"Wouldn't you feel guilty?"

Duffy hitched up his pants. "Of course—I'm Catholic. I feel guilty about everything. But in a case like yours, I'd just deal with it and move on. Your job is to catch killers. You try to protect your sources of information, but sometimes you can't. So what're you going to do? You're not that smart to be able to figure out everything. Do you know for sure why Ambrose was dropped?"

"No," I said uncertainly. "But my best guess is—"

"Fuck your best guess. At this point, you don't know. The shooter might have been planning to eliminate Ambrose anyway. He might not even have known you interviewed him."

I shrugged.

"Did you deliberately put his life into danger?"

"No."

"Were you negligent in any way?"

"No."

"Was there any way you could have anticipated this?"

"No."

Duffy lightly slapped me on the back of the head. "Then stop wearing the fucking hair shirt."

"I liked that kid," I said. "He reminded me of some guys I served with. Sarcastic and smart. Full of moral outrage."

"So you're pissed?"

"Of course I'm pissed."

"Then get pissed at the shooter and catch him. Getting pissed at yourself is a waste of time."

Duffy and I rose when we saw Butella and Powers saunter through the door. Right behind them was Theodore Bryson, the coroner investigator who worked my double in the Oakwood alley. He nodded to us, set his black satchel beside the body, and dropped to his knees. He tugged down Ambrose's sweat pants and peeled off his long-sleeved T-shirt. "This is déjà vu all over again for me. You too, Ash?"

I held my breath for a moment when I noticed the dozen tiny squares burned into Ambrose's leg just above the right kneecap. "Looks like the wounds on Teshay Winfield."

"That's what I'm thinking," Bryson said. "Pretty damn similar."

"Anybody have any idea what could have made those burns?" I asked.

"Not me," Duffy said.

Butella, Powers, and Guzman shook their heads.

"You think it could be a soldering iron?"

"Could be," Bryson said. "Seems to fit the wounds."

I waved my pen above the bruising on Ambrose's ankles. "Ligature marks?" I asked Bryson.

"It's possible."

"I think he was gagged," I said, pointing to the red striations that ran from the edges of his mouth to his ears. "Give us a second," I said, motioning for Duffy to follow me into the bedroom.

I closed the door with my toe. "This case is connected to the Winfield homicide. But I don't want to be the primary. I got a shitload of stuff to do, and I don't want to get bogged down with the paperwork, the autopsy, the canvassing, the death notifications, and everything else."

"But you might pick up on something that could help you with your double," Duffy said.

"I still want to be involved in the case."

"So you want to cherry-pick the stuff you need, and let Powers and Guzman handle the scut work. Right?"

"You see any problem with that?"

"Ordinarily, yes. But Butella's a pretty squared away guy. His ego won't be bruised by Felony Special big-footing him. And your number-one fan, Detective Opie, sounds like he'll do whatever you want. So I think it'll work. But you better give them a thorough rundown on what you've found on your double so they can connect the dots with their case. You just gave them the CliffsNotes version."

"I need a favor."

"Uh-oh," Duffy said.

"I've kept you pretty up to date on my case. Can you brief them for me? I've got to rush out of here right now."

"Right now?"

"Yeah. Right now. I don't know if I've got much time to spare. I'm worried about this female wit. I don't want to find any other stiffs with ligature marks and those little squares burned into their legs."

"Sure you want to protect the witness, but, my guess, it's more than that. You got a wit who you think is holding out. So you let her know her life's in danger. You help move her. She's shaken up. She's grateful to you. She's vulnerable. You prod her a little bit, and she tells you what you want to know. I know those Russian babes are pretty slinky. Knowing you, you'll want to bang her. Let me warn you off that right now because—"

"Fuck you," I said, storming out of the bedroom, across the living room and out the door.

Back in my car, I slumped in the seat and closed my eyes. Was there anything I could have done to protect Ambrose? Should I have tried to relocate him? I had a throbbing headache. After dry-swallowing three Tylenol, I made a U-turn and weaved through traffic toward West Hollywood.

Valentina Revenco peered through her peephole and angrily swung open the door.

"You again," she said with weary resignation. Barefoot, she was wearing shorts and a T-shirt.

"What are your plans for the day?" I asked.

"In one hour—a business meeting."

"Well, cancel it," I said, shutting the door.

"That is something I cannot do, for my business is—"

"Look, I'm trying to keep you from getting killed."

She nodded and curled up on the sofa, her feet beneath her. I briefly told her about Ambrose.

"So you are here, not for more information?"

"No. I'm here to get you the hell out of your apartment."

"So I do not end up, in the end, like this Ambrose?'"

"That's right."

"So," she said with a crooked smile, "you have come here as my savior. Yes?"

"Just pack a bag."

"How long will I be gone?"

"A few days. A few weeks. I don't know."

"Where are we going?"

"We're not going anywhere. You're going somewhere. I'm going to
walk you to your car and make sure you drive off safely. You should stay
with a friend and not return until I tell you to."

"But I don't have a car."

I shook my head and muttered, "This day is going from bad to
worse."

After she packed, I carried her suitcase to my car. Driving south on
Highland, I said, "I want to take you somewhere where you feel safe, a
place where you can hide out for a while. Any ideas?"

"I will be safe at what kind of location?"

"A place that Maksimov or Ziven don't know about."

"Hmm," she said, tapping an unlit cigarette on her thumbnail.

"Please don't smoke in here."

"What do you expect?" she asked, jamming the cigarette back into
the pack. "Now I am nervous for my life."

"I'm sorry about that. That's why I'm here. So don't waste my time.
Think of somewhere I can take you."

She stared out her window, then turned to me and said, "There is
one place I'm able to think of where I cannot, I believe, be found. A girl
I know from the town where I come from—Chisinau—immigrated here
with her husband. My sister was good friends with her. She is different
from me. Not in my business. She is a hairdresser."

"Where?"

"Lomita," Revenco said and told me the address. I cut over to La
Brea—checking my rearview mirror for a tail—picked up the Santa
Monica Freeway east and then the Harbor freeway. As we snaked down
the freeway through a traffic jam, she said, "Have you thought about my
request?"

"What request?"

"Remember, the last time we talk, I ask you to help my sister?"

"I can't do anything right now because the department is doing an investigation involving prostitution. I have to wait until that investigation is finished. When it is, I'll follow up. I'll see what I can do."

"Please. Don't wait. Don't you understand the kind of hell she is living in?"

"I tried," I said, embarrassed at my feeble response.

"Trying is not good. She is—"

"I promise, I'll follow up. But I can't do anything right now. I've got three homicides that take precedence."

"Precedence? What does that mean?"

"I can't discuss this anymore with you."

She sullenly gazed out the window.

A few minutes later, after checking my GPS, I parked on a cul-de-sac lined with weathered, ranch-style homes. I dropped my card into her purse and said, "Any problems, call me. If you see anyone parked out here who worries you, call me."

She nervously twirled her hair and said, "Yes. I will."

"Make sure it's okay for you to stay with your friends," I said. "I'll wait here. If a cop comes to their door, it might spook them."

She trudged up the walkway to the front door and rang the bell. A woman opened the door, hugged Revenco, and kissed her on both cheeks. They briefly chatted and then Revenco trotted back to the car.

She leaned into the window and said, "I am able to stay here, my friend says."

"Good."

"I know what you do for me is—how do you say it—extra. So I thank you."

"I just want you to be safe."

"When can I come back to my home?"

"Like I said, give me some time. When I clear this case, you should be okay. I'll give you a call. What's the phone number here?"

After she scribbled the number on a piece of paper, she said, "And what happens to me if you do not solve this case?"

"I can always relocate you, but we're not there yet. For now, think of this as a short vacation."

She stared at her friend's house, frowning, looking troubled.

I climbed out of the Impala, shut the door, and said, across the roof,

"I have the feeling you know more about this case than you've let on. If you want to get home sooner, then tell me everything you know. Because you'll never be completely safe until I catch the shooter."

"But this I promise you—there is no more that I know."

"You sure?"

"Yes, I am sure. But I told you, find my sister. Last time we spoke, I give you the address and a photograph. I tell you where she is being held against her will." She circled the car and gripped my forearm so hard I could feel the nails digging into the skin. "She might know something about your case. You help her, she help you."

I fell back into the car, sucked down a deep breath, and closed my eyes. My headache was so intense I couldn't think. "What did you say?"

"You help my sister, she help you."

I massaged my temples. That damn headache was getting worse.

"Will you help her?"

I fired up the engine, glanced up at her, and said, "Yes."

CHAPTER 21

Why had I agreed to free Revenco's sister after I was warned by Duffy and Deputy Chief Greever to stay away from her? First of all, I was anguished and outraged that Ambrose, who had cooperated with me, had been assassinated. Also, Anika might be a potential lead in a case where leads were hard to come by. I had to find her. I owed Ambrose that much. If Anika could help me—and if I could spring her without the LAPD finding out and without interfering with the department's big-money investigation—then fuck the edicts of Baaken and Greever.

I suppose it was a lot easier for me to countermand a superior's order than for most cops. My casual response to authority had been forged in the IDF. Unlike the U.S. military, in Israel there is an absence of hierarchical bullshit that I found refreshing. The noncoms were hard-line about weapons and tactics, but many didn't care if our uniforms were wrinkled, or we marched without precision, or we failed to salute an officer. I even called my commanding officer by his first name. The paratroopers in my unit frequently argued with officers if they thought they were wrong. In fact, a central tenet of the IDF that traces back to the army's origins, is "the purity of arms"—a soldier's responsibility to refuse an order he considers immoral. Unfortunately, in the aftermath of the IDF's many debacles during the past decade, the edict has been watered down. But when I served, I took it very seriously.

I considered the order to ignore a lead in a homicide—and to ignore the plight of a young woman forced into prostitution—immoral. So I would ignore the order, help the woman, and maybe I'd help myself.

I drove back to the Miracle Mile, slipped inside the building again through the garage, and waited down the hall from the apartment. About twenty minutes later a scrawny, balding, middle-aged man wearing black slacks, a white button-down shirt, and a red V-neck sweater crossed the hallway to the elevator. He had to be a john.

I rode down the elevator with him in silence. Outside the security gate, along the sidewalk, I tapped him on the shoulder, lifted back my suit jacket to reveal my badge, and said, "Follow me."

"Shit, shit, shit," he muttered. "I am so stupid."

I nudged open my Impala's passenger door, shut it after he climbed inside, circled around the car, sat next to him, and locked the doors. I pointed to his gold wedding band and said, "You cooperate with me right now, and your wife will never hear about your recreational activities."

He licked his lips and swallowed hard.

"Do the girls ever leave the house?"

"This was my first time—"

"I don't have time for bullshit. If you don't level with me right now, I'll take you to the station and book you for patronizing a prostitute and, maybe, third-degree rape for having sex with an underage girl."

"Oh, my God," he said, burying his face in his hands.

"Do the girls ever leave the house?"

"Yes."

"When?"

"I'm not sure the exact days, but I think it's about three days a week. Once a week they go to the doctor, and a few other days they go to the drugstore to buy things they need for, you know, what they do and, um, for their own, um, what do you call it? Hygiene?"

"What time of day?"

"Late afternoon."

"How do you know?"

He stared at his shoes, sheepish, and said, "I've tried to make three p.m. appointments, but some days I can't get that time. I asked one of the girls why, and she told me what they do some afternoons."

"Do you know if they're leaving the house tomorrow afternoon?"

"I'm not sure."

I showed him the picture of Anika. "You ever see her?"

He tugged at the V in his sweater. "Why?"

"You're not in a position to be asking any questions. Just answer me: You ever see her?"

"Yeah."

"You see her today?"

"Yes."

"Were you her customer?"

"Of course not," he said, looking horrified.

"Why 'of course not'?"

"Simona is my regular girl," he said with a hint of indignation. "I wouldn't see anyone else."

"That would be cheating, right?" I said sarcastically.

"Something like that."

"Can I go, officer?"

"Okay, beat it."

I unlocked the doors. He scrambled out of the Impala, and scurried to his green minivan.

I realized I hadn't eaten all day. I decided to order a sandwich at Café Metropol, in the old brick warehouse building east of downtown, and eat at my desk. I planned to update my chrono, organize my murder book, and spend the rest of the day trying to figure out how to extricate Anika Revenco from the Russian whorehouse.

CHAPTER 22

After killing twenty-four hours at his fleabag hotel, watching *Law & Order* reruns, and bringing back Big Gulps, chips, and candy bars from the 7-Eleven, Mullin was back in the entryway of the building across the street and two doors over from Levine's place. He stood to stretch and his shoulders ached. Spent too much time throwing iron on the yard. What else was there to do? The old-timers said they used to have all kinds of college classes, but not much of that shit anymore in California. That was the worst part of his time inside. The boredom. The monotony of yesterday, today, tomorrow.

He used to pass the time daydreaming of all the exotic places he'd travel to after he got out. He wrote to a bunch of travel agents, asking for information on resorts, and some of them were stupid enough to send brochures to a guy in the joint. Made his cell a nicer place. Instead of naked chicks from biker magazines, like the other losers, he had pictures on his wall: Tahiti, Hawaii, the Virgin Islands, the Dominican Republic, Jamaica. White-sand beaches and babes in bikinis and waterfront swimming pools and people sipping drinks in lounge chairs. He'd spend hours staring at those pictures. His favorite was a resort in Thailand that featured thatched bungalows with hammocks on big front porches right on a beach with pale blue water and creamy-white sand. Each bungalow under a grove of palms, with its own dock and sailboat.

After he finished this job, he'd use his pile of cash to live that fantasy. As soon as he cooled that cop, he was going to walk over to Union Station and take the shuttle straight to LAX, buy a one-way ticket to Thailand, and find that resort.

"Hey, good lookin'," a tall, slender hooker with long red hair called out from across the deserted street, busting his groove. "You want a date?"

She wasn't half-bad looking, but taking her up on the offer would be a big mistake. He was supposed to be sniping. But he was so bored and so cold, he started to waver. A quick blowjob, though, shouldn't be a problem. He could still keep his eyes on the cop's front door.

She sauntered across the street.

"How much for a hummer?" Mullin asked.

"I like a man who doesn't beat around the bush," the hooker said in a high-pitched, singsong voice. "You get right to it, don't you, honey? For an oral experience you'll never forget, I charge a mere forty dollars."

"Let's get started. I don't have a lot of time."

"With me, honey, you pay, then you play."

He dug two twenties out of his pocket, but as he was about to hand over the cash, he noticed a shaving cut on her chin. Or was it *his* chin?

"Motherfucker! Beat it, you fucking freak! And make it quick or I'll blow a hole in your skinny ass."

Mullin slumped back into the entryway and fell onto the stoop. He looked off into the distance and spotted the red-and-green Christmas lights atop the Bunker Hill skyscrapers. He could hear someone in the distance playing a Christmas tune he couldn't recognize on an electric guitar. Christ, this was a depressing night. He thought of all those sad, fucking Christmases in the joint, waking up in the morning and staring at steel and cement; waiting in the chow line for pressed turkey and sour cranberry sauce; and later, sacked out in his cell, listening to Christmas carols on his tinny radio, trying to ignore the farting and snoring of his cellie.

He decided to get a drink, something to cheer him up. If he was still in the service he could get court-martialed for leaving his post, but he was an independent contractor now, so he would make his own rules. He walked two blocks over to one of those hip new bars that had sprung up in this crappy 'hood. Instead of beer signs like a normal tavern, the walls were covered with flat screens streaming scenes from old black-and-white movies and all kinds of other crazy shit. The bartender was a skinny dude with stupid-looking studs poking from his face and a bunch of multicolored, faggy-looking tats on his forearms.

"Gimme a 7-Up, rocks, with a few shots of orange juice, a hit of Grenadine, two cherries, two straws. Make it to go."

The bartender smirked, mixed the drink, and slammed the cup on the wooden counter. "That'll be eight bucks, for your Shirley Temple."

"That's a little steep, homey."

"I'm sure a hard drinker like you can afford it," he said in a snide tone. Mullin translated that to mean: *I'm better than you are, you white trash, ex-con piece of shit who doesn't even know how to order a regular drink.*

He smiled and tossed a ten on the counter. But before the bartender could grab the money, Mullin leaned across the bar and dropped him with a short left hook. Mullin knew that he was out before he hit the ground.

"Keep the change," Mullin called out as he hustled out the door.

Back on the stoop, he sipped the drink, thinking of his mother's ex-husbands. The first one, his real dad, split when Mullin was two. When he was five, she married again. The sound of his mother's screaming woke him up every night after his stepdad came home from the bars. He'd beat the crap out of her, and when Mullin would toddle out in his pajamas and try to protect her, he'd slap him around. Later, he used a closed fist, or a belt, or a shoe, or an electrical cord. Once he used a small frying pan, and his mom rushed him to the Good Samaritan Hospital emergency room. Then it was back to the electrical cord. He'd never forget the sound that electrical cord made as it whizzed through the air. And he'd never forget his stepdad's breath as he bent over him, whirling that fucking cord. It ruined booze for him. He could never stomach anything with that sour, fermented smell.

But the third ex-husband was a stand-up guy with a good job as an installer for the phone company. Every night he'd sit on Mullin's bed and tell him hairy stories about humping paddies in 'Nam. That inspired Mullin to enlist when he was eighteen. On Sunday nights he took Mullin and his mother out to dinner at the Majestic Eagle Bar & Grill near their apartment. He always winked at Mullin and then told the waitress, "Bring the kid a Batman cocktail." That was the happiest time of his childhood, maybe the only happy time. The third ex-husband, of course, eventually split. One day he was there. The next day he was gone. Mullin never knew why. He remembered crying and screaming at his mom, who was stretched out on the sofa. "Why couldn't you leave and he stay?" He expected his mom to kick the shit out of him. But when he looked down at her, he realized she'd passed out. Again.

CHAPTER 23

The next afternoon, I parked down the street from the Miracle Mile apartment building and balanced a pair of binoculars on my thigh. I craved coffee, but I learned long ago never to drink coffee on a stakeout.

Thirty-five minutes after I arrived, a black Infiniti SUV pulled out of the underground garage, with three young women in the back and one in the front. I focused my binoculars and spotted Anika in the back driver's-side seat. I then focused on the driver and realized he was the Russian thug in the red silk shirt who had been snoozing in a chair when I first cased the apartment. He was still wearing the same shirt. Fortunately, he hadn't seen me at the door yesterday.

He made two left turns and stopped at a light. I sped behind him, reached under my police radio, and snapped on my lights and siren. I was relieved when he immediately pulled over.

I badged him and said, "License and insurance."

"Isn't it customary in L.A. for an officer of law to be uniformed and to be driving police car that is black-and-white?" he asked in heavy accent.

"Isn't it customary to operate a motor vehicle with functioning brake lights?"

I was surprised when he produced what appeared to be a valid California driver's license and a Xeroxed copy of his insurance policy. Maksimov was no dummy. He knew it was good business to make sure the front men were legal.

As I returned his driver's license and insurance, he said, "Can I ask, officer, what it is I did wrong?"

"Your passenger-side brake light appears to have an intermittent short. It's going off and on. Have your mechanic check the wiring."

I whirled around, jabbed a finger at Anika, and said, "You! Out of the car."

"What do you want with her?" the driver asked.

"Keep your hands on the steering wheel where I can see them!" I shouted in my best street-cop voice.

I tugged open the back door. Anika reluctantly crawled out, and I pointed to my Impala. "Get in the backseat."

I pivoted to the driver and said, "In roll call this morning, I was told there's a warrant out for a young Eastern European woman who is suspected of being involved in a series of burglaries. She fits the description. After I question her, she will be free to go."

"I am certain this is not her."

You're certain, I thought, *because you've kept her prisoner in the apartment.* "We'll soon find out."

"This makes no sense."

"If you want to come to the station with me, let's go right now," I said, knowing the suggestion would scare him off. He couldn't complain to the desk sergeant, "I demand my rights. An LAPD officer just stole my prostitute." The driver sighed heavily, started his engine, and drove off.

I joined Anika in the backseat. She'd curled up in the corner, arms tightly locked around her knees. Her hair was a brittle bleached blonde. Garish blue shadow circled her eyes. She gave me a frightened look and said, "Who are you?"

"My name is Ash Levine. I'm an LAPD detective. Your sister, Valentina, told me where you were. I'm taking you to her right now."

"Thank you," she said, tears running down her cheek, sobbing. I handed her a Kleenex, and after she dried her eyes, she said, "In Moldova, they tell me I will work here as a secretary. When I get to America, I was forced into this work they make me do." She sobbed again, and I pushed the Kleenex box toward her. When she'd calmed down, we moved to the front seat and I drove to Lomita.

I parked across the street from where Valentina Revenco was staying, faced Anika, and said, "Let me fill you in. I'm investigating two homicides. Your sister helped me out. Things are a little dicey now, so she's staying with a friend. But before I take you to her, I want to ask you a few questions. You might be able to help me with my investigation."

"I will try."

"At the place where you were staying, did you hear anyone talk about a valuable antique mask covered with many expensive jewels?"

"I never have heard anything like that."

"Do you know Teshay Winfield?"

"Is that a man or a woman?"

"Do you know Kolya Maksimov?"

She blew her nose and stuffed the Kleenex in her purse. With another Kleenex, she dabbed at her eyes, smearing her mascara and eye shadow. "I do not know of him personally."

"Have you heard of him?"

She paused and said, "I guess so."

"You want me to take you to your sister?"

"Yes," she said, her eyes misting. "Please."

"Then give me something. Anything."

"About what?"

"About Maksimov."

"I have not met him ever, personally. But yes, I have seen him." She twirled a tendril of hair with a forefinger. "You help me today. You save me. So I am going to give you something. I am going to give you a person. There is a girl named Irina Komarova. She was a special girlfriend of Kolya Maksimov."

"How do you know her?"

"She work with me in the house. But not for a long time. Only weeks. We become friends. She is a beautiful girl. At one time very, very beautiful. Maksimov see her and make her his girlfriend. Or should I say, one of his girlfriends. But he release her loose about six months ago. She knows very much about him."

"How have you stayed in touch with her? You're kind of a prisoner in that apartment."

"After she leave, even though I am not free to go, I am able to answer the phone when she call me. She is permitted to call me because of her association with Kolya. We talk many times. Until recently."

"Why'd Maskimov cut her loose?"

She clenched her fist and jabbed it toward her open arm, like a junkie with a spike. "Very bad."

"Heroin?"

"That's right."

"Where can I find her?"

She stared out the window, forehead pressed against the pane. "I know if I tell you, her life might be in danger, but I take that chance, because her life already is in danger."

"How?"

"Because, already, she is killing herself with the drugs. I am afraid, very much, that sometime soon, she die with the needle in her arm. Cleaning up is something, I believe, she wants. But she has no job, no money. If you are celebrity you go to celebrity drug hospital. If you are a girl who is poor and alone, you go nowhere. Can you get her treatment?"

"Maybe. What's her story?"

"She learn much of the language back home so, not like me, her English is very good. Soon after she did what the people who brought her over to do, Kolya made her his woman and she lived a very high life. The drugs were the big downfall for her. Now she has nothing."

"Where does she live?"

"I hear Glendale," Anika said.

"Do you know the address?"

She shook her head.

"Will she talk?"

"If you promise to get her treatment, she might, I believe. She wants to be clean, she tells me, but she is too weak to do this on her own."

I pointed at a scabby ranch-style home. "This is where your sister is staying. I'll wait here, just to make sure she's home."

She leaned over the seat and clasped my wrist in both her hands. She kissed my fingers, looked up at me, and said, "You save my life. I will never forget you."

She eased out of the car, wandered across the lawn, and knocked on the door. A moment later, Valentina flung open the door and the sisters embraced. When Valentina saw me, she dashed out to my car, leaned through the open window, held my face in both hands, and kissed me on the lips. "Thank you, thank you, thank you. This means everything to me."

"Sure," I murmured, uncomfortable with the outpouring of emotion. She ran back to the porch and kissed her sister on each cheek. I drove off as they burst into tears.

At a stoplight, I called LAPD's Records and Identification Division for Komarova's address. I traversed a few freeways until I hit the 134, and pulled off in Glendale. Irina Komarova lived on the ground floor of a tumbledown triplex next door to a small Armenian market. I rang the bell and waited a minute, then I rang it again. While waiting, I distractedly jiggled the knob. To my surprise, it was unlocked.

Typical junkie. I twisted the knob and opened the door. I was immediately assaulted by the smell of stale cigarette smoke. The apartment was a studio, just a large single room with an adjoining kitchen.

In one corner of the room, Komarova had passed out on a stained mattress. Wearing jeans and a sweater and worn leather boots, she was curled up atop a yellow blanket. The only furniture was a glass coffee table—littered with empty Sprite cans and a half-eaten sandwich—and two metal folding chairs and a chipped wooden table in the kitchen. On the table was an ashtray overflowing with butts and a spoon with a ball of rolled up toilet paper. The walls were bare and pockmarked, with plaster plugs filling tiny holes where previous tenants had hung pictures.

I crouched beside Komarova and tried to wake her, but she wouldn't stir. Then I shook her, but she continued to snore softly. Finally, I slapped her face and pinched her neck.

Her eyes fluttered. "Go away," she slurred.

I hauled her to her feet and led her to a chair. Tall, with lank blonde hair, slate-blue eyes and the cheekbones of a model, she had probably once been striking, but now she was so cadaverous—ghostly pale with deep circles under her eyes—she just looked haggard. She blinked hard, glanced up at me standing, and said in a slight Russian accent, "Who the fuck are you?"

I slapped my card in her palm.

She squinted at the card, moving her lips. "I see you work for Felony Special. I've committed no special felonies."

"I'm sure if I searched this dump, I could find evidence of something illegal."

She looked at me, her eyes half closed, "What do you want from me?"

"I'm investigating a murder, and I believe you know something that could help my case."

Komarova dropped her chin to her chest. I slapped her across the face. "If you don't pay attention," I said, "I'll book you myself for being under the influence of a controlled substance. I want you to listen to me."

She stifled a yawn. "I'm listening," she said impatiently. "You were saying something about a murder. Why do you think I know anything about it?"

"I've been investigating this case for a while, and I've learned—" I halted in mid-sentence when I realized she went on the nod again. I scooped her up and threw her over my shoulder. Teetering into the bathroom, I dumped her in the shower and flipped on the cold water.

She writhed on the grungy tile floor. "Shit! Shit! Turn it off," she shouted.

"No," I said calmly, perched on the lid of the toilet.

"You motherfucker," she screamed. She struggled to her feet but slipped. After another moment, I shut off the shower and pitched a towel to her. Without a hint of modesty, she stripped off her jeans and sweater and dried off, shaking her head like a dog after a bath. She was so skinny her hip and collarbones were visible and her ribs jutted against her pale skin like railroad ties on a track.

When she was dry, she snatched another towel from a rack, wrapped it around herself, and announced imperiously, "You are a bastard. You know that?"

"It's part of the job description."

She glared at me. "I was in a great place—before you got here."

"You were definitely in a great place," I said sarcastically. "Almost dead."

"What do you want with me?"

"Get dressed," I said. "Then we'll talk."

She strolled into the living room a few minutes later, barefoot, wearing loose green cords and a yellow sweatshirt with a hood. We sat in the metal folding chairs, facing each other.

"Like I told you before," I said, "I could probably search this place and find enough drugs to send you away for a few years."

She raked her fingers through her wet hair and dried her hand on her pants. "But if I tell you what you want, you won't?"

"That's right. I've talked to some people who care about you. They believe you want to clean up."

"Who'd you talk to?"

"That's confidential," I said. "But I promised them to get you into a treatment center."

"A bonus," she said acidly.

"I'm serious about that."

"As you see," she said, sweeping her hand around the filthy room. "That's probably not something I can afford."

"There's some residential treatment centers run by the Department of Health Services. You don't need money or insurance. They've got a pretty decent detox program and they'll put you up for thirty days."

"My friend checked out those county programs for me. They told him I'd have to get on a seven-month waiting list."

"I've got connections."

She retrieved her purse from beneath a chair, grabbed a pack of Marlboros, and shook out a cigarette. Lighting the cigarette, she took a quick puff. "So," she said, swallowing a longer, deeper drag, "if I cooperate with you, you get me into treatment. If I don't, you search my apartment and if you find drugs, you arrest me and throw me in jail."

"Jail while you're awaiting trial," I said. "Then prison."

She waved her cigarette in a wide circle. "Not much of a choice, is it?"

"No, it's not."

She studied her cigarette for a moment, then flicked her ash on the carpet. "Who gives a fuck?" she said, testily. "Ask me your questions."

"Do you know Teshay Winfield?"

"No."

"Ever heard of him?"

"Never."

I opened my murder book and showed her a picture of Winfield. "Ever see this guy?"

"No."

"Do you know Kolya Maksimov?"

She stared at her hands. "Yes. I know him."

"But you never heard of Teshay Winfield?"

"I told you, no," she said, fidgeting in her chair.

"Black guy in Venice. Served in the army in Iraq and Afghanistan. Just got out a few months ago. Might be in possession of something that Kolya thinks is very valuable."

She blew a stream of smoke at the ceiling. "I didn't know his name," she said. "But I did hear Kolya talk about a guy like that."

Trying to disguise my interest, I attempted to look bored. "So, why was Kolya interested in Winfield?"

She stubbed out her half-smoked cigarette on the coffee table and fished out another one. She fiddled with it, eyes vacant. "If I tell you about all this, Kolya will kill me," she said. "Can you promise I'll be safe?"

I felt torn. Of course I couldn't guarantee her safety. Ambrose was dead. Valentina was in hiding. And now I was putting Komarova's life at risk. But what choice did I have? I was in too deep. Either I nailed this case, and insured that everyone was safe, or I failed—and put everyone's life at risk. I inched forward, clutching my knees. "I promise I'll do everything I can to protect you—from Kolya and from yourself. Because if he doesn't kill you, you know you'll eventually OD. But if I can get you into a treatment center—you'll be safe for a while. And I hope that by the time you get out, I'll have this case cleared, and you won't have anything to worry about."

"And if I don't talk, you'll bust me."

I leaned back in my chair. "That's a pretty accurate rundown."

With the heel of her hand, she wiped beads of water from her damp hair. She nodded. "Kolya was interested in a black man. Very interested."

"And why was that?"

"Kolya believed that he had something. Something Kolya wanted. More than wanted."

"What do you mean, more than wanted?"

"My feeling was that Kolya thought of nothing else but this object. I believe it was of the greatest importance to Kolya that he possess it. Now, he never talked business in front of me. That is something he made a point of. But one time we were at home." She tilted her head and gave me a sad smile. "I say home because we shared his home in the Beverly Hills. No more, as you can see. I walked into his office at home, and he was talking to Ziven. You know Ziven?"

"Yes, we've met."

"Usually, Kolya stopped talking business when I entered the room. But this time he didn't. He was talking about something that I could see was very, very important to him. He was very excited. He was telling Ziven that he thought he had found the person who was hiding, what he called, 'the treasure.' Kolya motioned for me to sit down, and he and Ziven continued to talk. And that's all I know about. But since you said the name Teshay, I think I remember that's who they were talking about. It's an unusual name."

"What, exactly, is the treasure that Kolya was so interested in?"

She stared at a wall, mouth open, eyes glazed. I heard a dog yapping in the apartment next door.

"Do you want another shower?"

"No," she said, raising her forearm as though warding off a blow. "I am telling you what I heard that day. But I never heard Kolya mention it again. He was talking to Ziven about a mask."

"A mask?" I said, surprised.

"Yes. But an ancient one. Found somewhere in the Middle East."

"Very valuable?"

"From the way Kolya was talking about it, I know it is. It has a great value for museums, I believe he said it's also worth a fortune just for the jewels."

"What kind of jewels?"

"That I don't know."

"Where in the Middle East is it from?"

"Don't know that."

"Why did Kolya think Winfield had this treasure?"

She threw up her hands. "Don't know that."

"What kind of museums are interested in it?"

"Don't know that, either."

"You didn't hear anything else about it?"

"I promise you, that's all I heard and that's the only time I heard it." She clasped her hands on her lap. "Isn't that enough to keep you from taking me to jail?"

"You sure you told me all you know?"

"I told you this much. Why would I hold anything else back?"

I scrutinized her for a moment. "Okay. Bring a driver's license or some other proof of ID. Finish getting dressed and pack a bag."

"Where we going?" she asked, sounding worried.

"Oak Knoll Medical Center."

"I feel like a chauffeur service," I said, heading west on the Glendale Freeway. "You're the second woman today I've driven out of town."

"When I left Russia, I never thought I would end up like this," she blurted out with a sob. She wiped her eyes with a sleeve and said, "What kind of place is this Oak Knoll?"

"In the '40s, it was built as a TB sanitarium. Since the '70s, the county's run it as a drug treatment center. In the whole county, there're only a few residential centers like this. We've got tens of thousands of junkies in L.A., and only a few hundred beds for them. It's a joke."

"So how you going to get me in?"

I swerved into the fast lane. "Four years ago, two nurses there were strangled," I said. "Nobody there had any idea who did it and everyone there was a suspect. All the nurses were scared to death. When I caught the strangler, the director of the center was pretty damn grateful. Last year, I got a witness who helped me out on a homicide into Oak Knoll. I figure the director can't say no to one more."

"How'd you catch him?"

"I had a hunch it wasn't a patient. They don't have that much freedom of movement. So I polygraphed every orderly, male nurse, doctor, janitor, and gardener on the property. Everyone passed. I was stumped. So I decided to poly everyone who serviced the place. I asked the guy who drove the laundry truck to take a poly. He refused. That put me onto his trail, and I eventually put it all together."

I cut over to the Foothill Freeway, skirting the base of the San Gabriel Mountains. The moon was almost full, casting a milky sheen on the undulating hills, backlighting the escarpment in the distance, patches of ice glistening on the peaks.

"Where are we?" she asked.

"Still L.A. County."

"I've never been to a place in L.A. like this."

"This is how Southern California looked before the Spanish got here," I said. "Enjoy the view while it lasts, because it won't last long."

A few minutes later, we passed a saddle shop and a few stables hard by the freeway. When we hit Sylmar, the Southern California blight returned: fast-food restaurants, trailer parks, apartment complexes—the windows sheathed in silver foil, the stucco splashed with graffiti.

A few miles past Sylmar, I exited and drove along a frontage road edged with cyclone fencing topped with barbed wire. I braked at a metal gate, leaned out the window, and pressed the call box. While waiting for a response, I climbed out of the car and breathed deeply, the air dense with the scent of sumac, a sharp contrast from the bus exhaust and factory fumes of downtown.

The call box squawked. A disembodied voice asked, "Code please?"

"My name is Ash Levine. I'm an LAPD detective."

The gate swung open. I hopped into the car and slowly wound up an asphalt road, past acres of dry, rolling grasslands, past the long, low-slung World War II-era dormitories where the patients slept, past clusters of oak trees shading picnic tables. I parked in front of a single-story Spanish-style office with a red tile roof.

Komarova clutched my arm. "Will this work for me?"

"If you want it to work bad enough, it will."

"How do you know?"

"Because someone close to me just cleaned up."

"Here?"

"No. Private facility. He had insurance. But this is a good place. You're lucky for this chance. Make the most of it."

I ushered Komarova out of the car, to the front desk. "Hello," I said to a pudgy, pasty-faced woman who was munching on potato chips. "I've got a patient for you."

"Are you out of your mind?" she said, glowering at me. "You know how long it takes to get on the intake list?"

"I know. But this is a special circumstance. Call Dr. Rebecca Sherry and tell her Detective Ash Levine is here with a patient who needs immediate treatment. She'll clear it."

"I'm not calling her on a Saturday night."

"Did you work here when Hector Corral strangled the two nurses?"

"I did," she said, her eyes widening.

"Don't you remember me?" I asked.

She peered into my face for a moment and then nodded. She picked up the phone, dialed, spoke a few hushed words into the receiver, listened for a moment, and hung up the phone. Turning to Komarova, she said, "I think we can accommodate you, after all."

"Work the program," I told her. I returned to my car, leaned my head back against the seat, and closed my eyes. A moment later, I jerked awake. I needed more than a nap in my car. I started the engine and headed home.

PART IV

SPRAY AND PRAY

CHAPTER 24

I zigzagged through downtown to the outer edge of the neighborhood known as the Historic Core. After parking in an outdoor lot, I wandered down a forlorn street, past a rundown hotel that rented to parolees and pensioners, a grimy minimart with a large canvas sign—We Accept Food Stamps—a 24-hour torta stand, a bail bondsman with a blinking neon phone number above the door, and a Mexican beer bar blaring cumbia.

I darted across the intersection to a street in transition, flanked with twelve-story, early twentieth-century commercial buildings in various states of disrepair. Most were vacant, the lobbies boarded up with plywood. But a few, including the cream-colored stone building with the swirling cornice where I owned a loft, had been renovated and transformed into residential housing.

As I reached the door, I heard someone call out, "Hey, detective!" I pivoted and heard two loud shots. In the middle of the street, about twenty feet away, a man was aiming a pistol at me and firing. It seemed like he was moving underwater, his motions slow and deliberate. I couldn't hear bullets pinging against the trash cans or thudding against the building, but I saw the muzzle flashes. My IDF training kicked in. I snatched my Beretta, pointed and shot without aiming, and kept firing until he buckled. I then sprinted toward the body, about to put another round in his head. This was what I learned in Israel, in case the victim was still alive and able to pull the plug on an explosive strapped to his belly. I stopped myself, reason overtaking instinct and training. A moment later, I heard another series of shots from the other direction. I dove and rolled until I was shielded by a parked car. I raised my Beretta and peeked over the hood, but I couldn't spot the shooter. I punched in 911 on my cell, gave my address, and said, "Officer needs help. Shots fired. Suspect down." A few minutes later, four patrol cars, sirens blaring, skidded to a stop in front of me. I stood, wiping the grit off my pants. I identified myself and returned with a pair of uniforms to Felony Special squad room.

An hour later, two detectives from the Force Investigation Division arrived. They investigate every incident in which a cop fires a gun. They led me to a windowless interview room, its walls scarred with graffiti, the metal table battered and dented. One of the detectives was a tall, skinny Asian named Walter Ying, and his partner was a paunchy, middle-aged Latino with a shaggy mustache whose name I didn't catch. I sat across from them.

Ying nodded to his partner to take over.

"We just came from the scene," he said to me. "Why don't you take it from the top?"

I offered him a brief recap of the incident.

"You get a look at the second gunman?"

I shook my head.

"Where were those shots coming from?"

"Not from the grassy knoll."

"Any idea where?"

"Maybe a hundred yards to the north of the first shooter."

"Two guys busting caps at your ass, and you don't have a scratch," Ying interjected. "Can you explain that?"

"A couple of piss-poor shots."

Ying stared at me. "Can you explain that?"

I stared back at him for a moment before answering. "Like I said, a couple of piss-poor shots. Any ID on the shooter?"

"Negative." Ying flipped open a leather folder with a yellow legal pad inside and scrawled a few notes. "Can you think of anyone in particular who might want you dead?"

"No." I immediately thought of two people—Kolya and Ziven.

"Revolver or semiauto?"

"Revolver."

"Chrome or blue steel?"

"Chrome."

"Did you identify yourself as a police officer?"

"Didn't have time."

"Is that a no?"

"It's a no."

"Did you ask the suspect to drop the weapon?"

"Didn't have time."

"Is that a no?"

"It's a no. Asshole was firing at me. Asshole was trying to kill me."

"What was in your mind at the time you fired the weapon?"

"To kill him before he killed me."

"Okay," Ying said. "Let's hear it again, but with more detail. Don't leave anything out."

I shut my eyes for a moment, running through the incident in my mind, then recounted the details I could recall, from the moment I heard, "Hey, Detective," until the uniforms arrived.

"So, you just started firing wildly on this suspect."

"I didn't say that."

"Sounds like spray and pray to me."

"It wasn't."

"Why didn't you employ the training you were given in the academy?"

"I did employ the training I was given—in the Israel Defense Forces."

"You're not in Israel now, Detective Levine. The LAPD—"

"I was taught to shoot without locking in the sights. We don't have the luxury of time over there. Not when we're dealing with terrorists. We were taught to draw, get into a shooting platform, and point and fire in a single, split-second motion. I know it's a different method than I was taught in the academy, but it's pretty damn fast and accurate. It saved my life on the Lebanese border. And it saved my life tonight."

"Run through it again for me, from the time you first saw the suspect."

"Listen," I said, irritated. "I've told you everything I can remember. Twice."

"We need to hear it again."

I groaned and told him the same story for the third time. When I finished, he said, "Would you object to taking a poly?"

I stood. "Do I have to call the league and ask them to get me a lawyer?"

"Do you?" Ying asked.

"If you refuse to believe me, yes."

Ying flashed me a forced smile. "Just trying to do my job, Detective. Sit down. Relax. I just have a few more questions."

I fell back into my chair and sighed. He peppered me with another dozen follow-up questions. Just as I was about to stalk out of the room, he snapped his leather folder shut and said, "Thank you for your patience, Detective Levine. I'll let you know in a few days if we need that poly. Anyway, we've asked all the questions. Are there any questions we can answer for you?"

Without answering, I stomped out of the room and barged into Duffy's office. "I've had a few shootings in my time, and that was the most hostile damn follow-up I've ever been subjected to. What's with Ying?"

"I've heard he's a humorless fucking grinder. He goes after every OIS like he's got a wild hair up his ass. Too bad he was on call."

"Just my luck. That was the last thing I needed tonight."

"You know the after-shooting drill, Ash. I'm going to have to make an appointment with Behavioral Science for you. If the shrink thinks you need to take time off, you'll have to take it."

"Make the appointment for next week."

"I'll clear it with the captain. Do you want a few days off?"

"Naw. This shooting was so clean, it won't bother me for a second. I'd rather work my case."

He leaned across the desk and tapped the butt of my Beretta. "Give it up."

I knew that after a fatal OIS, it was routine protocol to run ballistics and trigger-pull tests on the cop's gun. I removed the Beretta Cougar from my shoulder holster and set it on his blotter. Duffy pulled a .45-caliber Glock 21 from a drawer and handed it to me. "Here's your tactical Tupperware."

"You know I don't like plastic guns. I'm glad my dad, *olava sholom*, never lived to see the day that I packed an Austrian gun."

"Jesus, Ash, let it go. You don't find me boycotting English shit because of what they did to Ireland."

I shrugged.

"I guess you should have blown me off and gone to Santa Barbara with your ex-wife," he said with a half smile.

"Now you tell me."

"I'm posting a patrol car outside your building for a few nights."

"Suit yourself."

"So what do you think. Those Russian gangsters?"

"That's my guess. I don't have enough to hook 'em up, but by to-morrow I might."

Duffy and I rode the elevator to the ground floor and walked out-side into the night. The wind carried the smell of exhaust fumes, and we both squinted to keep the dust out of our eyes.

"How you going to work it with Press Relations?" I asked.

"Generic. Officer-involved shooting. Self-defense. No names."

"That'll work."

"How about a ride home?" he asked.

"I feel like walking."

"Your little walk tonight didn't work out too well."

"I'm too jacked up to sit in a car. I need to burn off some energy."

"Okay. But watch your back."

I shook his hand, and wandered south to Sixth Street, at the edge of the fashion district, past a desolate stretch of small clothing and fab-ric shops, shuttered for the night, their corrugated metal security doors zigzagged with graffiti. Walking into the teeth of a stiff wind, I hunched over slightly and stuffed my hands inside my pockets, dodging toothless bag ladies, crackheads shouting to themselves, homeless men pushing shopping carts stuffed with cans, winos huddled in the entryways of buildings, swaddled in ragged blankets. After I passed a few USC stu-dents who looked like they were on a downtown pub crawl, I decided to get out of the wind and stopped at a smudged brick building, climbed down the cement steps, and entered Cole's, a basement bar-restaurant that had been around for about a hundred years. I sat at a booth, star-ing out a window, and watched the dust swirl along the sidewalk.

"What'll it be?" the bartender called out.

"What's on tap?"

"We got a German and a Belgian beer."

"Belgian, of course."

"Why *of course?*" the bartender asked.

"It's a long story."

The bartender slid a pint of amber-colored Chimay Ale with a foamy head in front of me. Sipping the beer, I looked around Cole's. At the other end of the building, the buffet-style restaurant had closed for the night. In the bar, there were only two other customers, both old men wearing frayed sweaters. They stared glumly into their beers.

Cole's was a soothing place, and I hoped that a beer in the dim, hushed warren might calm my jangled nerves. The scarred mahogany counter, oak tables crafted from horse-drawn trolley cars, ancient black-and-white tile floor sprinkled with sawdust, and Tiffany lampshades transported me to a bygone era of Los Angeles, an era I would have preferred right now, an era when there was a code, an era when a crook never tried to kill a cop or a newspaperman.

I downed my beer and walked home. As I neared my building, I rested my palm on the butt of the Glock. At the front door, I checked my watch: 9:05. I hadn't eaten in almost twenty-four hours and I was ravenous. But I wasn't in the mood to eat in a restaurant alone or to face my empty loft. I called Robin's cell.

"Where are you?" I asked.

"Still at work."

"I can see that your social life really picked up after you dumped me."

"You're one to talk."

"I was heading out to a Salvadoran place for something to eat."

"Where is it?"

"It's a pupuseria near MacArthur Park." I gave her the address.

"I'll be there in fifteen minutes."

I cruised down Sixth Street, headed south on Alvarado, east on Eighth, and pulled up in front of El Molcajete, a modest storefront restaurant in a sooty brick building. There were a dozen Formica tables and red vinyl chairs on a linoleum floor, plastic ivy spilling over shelves, and a small shrine in back featuring Jesus clutching a cross. At a front counter, a young woman leaned against the cash register. Behind her, a cook hovered over a steaming griddle. The restaurant was filled with Salvadoran couples listening to jangly merengue on the jukebox.

I eased into a red plastic chair by the window. A few minutes later, Robin walked in and sidled up next to me. She surveyed the restaurant and peered out the window at a wino who'd collapsed on the sidewalk. "Who says this isn't like having dinner at a romantic restaurant by the water in Santa Barbara?" she said, laughing. "You're the Spanish speaker. Why don't you order for us?"

Fortunately, when I was in the academy, all the recruits were required to take a basic Spanish class, which came in handy on the street—and at El Molcajete. At the counter I ordered pupusas and sides of *curtido*—a spicy shredded cabbage marinated in vinegar—and sugary drinks made from *arrayan*, a small green Salvadoran fruit. Before I reached the table I could hear the cook making our dinner—the *slap, slap, slap* of his palms flattening cornmeal masa, then a thud, then the sizzle of the pupusa on the griddle.

"I've got some good news and bad news," I said. "What do you want to hear first?"

"The bad news, of course."

I told her about the shooting.

"Jesus Christ, Ash," she said. "You're getting too old for this." She clasped my hand. "I'm worried about you."

"It's a freak thing. This case came together fast. I'm going to arrest two guys very soon and that'll be that."

"Christ," she said. "After that news, what can you tell me that can possibly be good?"

"I'm free for the rest of the night. Why don't you come by my loft. Save you the commute tomorrow from Pasadena."

"You really know how to invite a girl to your place in a romantic way," she said, laughing. "I'd say yes, despite your clumsy efforts at seduction, but I'm starting a trial tomorrow. I'll be working almost all night and up early in the morning."

I tried to hide my disappointment. "What's the case about?"

"Too boring to discuss," she said. Then she began to recount a hilarious story about a trademark-infringement case her firm handled a few months ago involving a penile pump, when the woman from behind the front counter strolled over and served our food.

"So how do I eat this stuff?" Robin asked.

"Watch me," I said. I forked open the pupusa, which was laden with white cheese and speckled with chopped *loroco*, a dark green flower bud. I sprinkled a forkful of *curtido* inside the pupusa, and squeezed a few dashes of spicy tomato sauce from the plastic bottle on the table. When Robin took a bite, I asked her what she thought.

"Pretty pungent, but I like it."

Afterward, we split an *empanada de platano*, a fritter with the rich taste of plantains, dusted in sugar. For the past few years, I'd been returning to my empty loft at the end of my shift, mulling over cases in my mind, pacing and chattering to myself. I sipped my fruit drink and realized how much I'd missed this. Discussing a case over a meal with Robin, listening to her quips and observations, sharing the daily dramas.

Robin pinched my chin and gazed at me. "You didn't get any sleep last night, did you?"

I shook my head.

She abruptly stood and said, "You look like hell. You should head home and crash right now."

"I think I will."

As she turned to leave, I reached out for her hand. "This was nice. Maybe by next weekend things will have calmed down enough so that we can do something together."

She stooped over, kissed me lightly on the lips, and hurried through the door.

I slurped the dregs of my drink and returned to my car. At the first stoplight, in the heart of the Central American barrio, a small dark man with ruler-straight shoulder-length hair, who looked like he just walked out of a Mayan jungle, held out his thumb and forefinger a few inches apart and motioned to me—the signal that he had a green card for sale. I glanced at myself in the rearview mirror. I wasn't as dark as the Mayan, but with my olive skin and black hair, people told me I could pass for a Latino.

I drove back home and crossed the street with my hand on my Glock. I gave a half-salute to the cops in the patrol car in front of my house and said, "Sorry boys. You're going to have a long, boring night."

The one behind the wheel, who looked about sixteen, said, "No problem, bro."

I passed through the towering pale-green marble columns, pushed open the filigreed brass door, ambled through the once elegant lobby with the stamped tin ceiling, and entered the mahogany-paneled elevator. At the top floor, I walked down the chipped tile hallway, and unlocked the door to my loft, a vast single room with exposed steel beams and pipes running along the ceiling, brick walls, polished concrete floors, two dusty gold-trimmed skylights, and two windows, one facing east and one west. Instead of a kitchen, there was simply a refrigerator in the corner of the room, along with a small stove, sink, and cabinet.

I undressed and crawled into bed. Slipping a CD into the player, I skipped past a few cuts. When I heard the silky, evocative trumpet of Miles Davis playing "All Blues," I drifted into a heavy sleep.

CHAPTER 25

I jumped out of bed and reached for the ringing phone. "Hello," I said groggily.

"Just checking up on you," Robin said. "What are you doing?"

"Just lying in bed. Waiting for you to come over."

"I'll just have to put that invitation on my list of rain checks I've got for you."

I checked the clock on my end table: 5:55 a.m. "Why are you calling so early?"

"I just wanted to see if you're okay. I'm worried, with all these people hiding in the shadows and taking potshots at you."

"I'll be all right."

"Stay in touch with me, okay?"

"Definitely."

I called Powers's cell. He and Guzman, who had been up all night, were writing the Preliminary Investigation Report at Wilshire Division. I told them I wanted to meet them at Ambrose's place. I swung by the Felony Special squad room, and compiled two six-packs, inserting booking photos of Kolya and Ziven into two separate sheets, along with five other mug shots from suspects who looked a bit like them. I slid the six-packs into my murder book and hurried to the elevator.

It was cold and clear, with a shroud of steam rising from the pool at Ambrose's apartment building. The surface was stippled with red bougainvillea blossoms, like drops of blood floating in the mist. Powers and Guzman had just sat down at a table under an umbrella. Powers opened a white paper bag and we all reached for coffee. Guzman drizzled Sweet'N Low into her cup.

"I left the scene before the coroner investigator checked the liver for time of death," I said. "What did he estimate?"

"Saturday between noon and five," Powers said.

"Duffy, I assume, told you about Kolya and Ziven."

"He did," Powers said.

"Let's see if we can get someone to ID them."

"Nobody around here saw nothing," Guzman said.

"You two are the primaries," I said. "What do you think?"

"Maybe canvass a second time," Powers said.

"Did you talk to the resident in two oh two—next door to Ambrose?"

"Me and Butella did yesterday," Powers said. "She's an old lady by the name of Eleanor Feinman. She was: see no evil; hear no evil; speak no evil."

"Let's give her another shot," I said. "When I visited Ambrose on Friday, I remember her. She lifted up her curtain, checked me out, and when she saw me looking back at her, disappeared."

"She sounds nosy as hell," Guzman said.

"But she didn't remember seeing anything when we talked to her," Powers said.

"Let's see if her memory's improved," I said.

We mounted the concrete steps and rang the bell at apartment 202. Again, the woman lifted the bottom corner of the curtains by her front door, glanced up at us, and nudged open the door.

Tiny, frail, and in her eighties, Feinman still retained a touch of vanity. She wore makeup, lipstick, pearl earrings, and her gray hair looked like it had recently been styled. Clutching her yellow sweater tight at her neck with both hands, she turned toward Powers and said, "Not much more I can tell you than I told you yesterday."

"Just give us a few more minutes of your time," I said. "Can we sit down and talk?"

Her hands fell to her sides, as if defeated, and she said with resignation, "Oh, well. Come on in."

We gathered around the dining room table. I didn't want to offend Powers and Guzman, who were the primaries, so I waited for them to begin the questioning. But they both glanced at me with an anticipatory expression, so I handed her my card and said, "I'm working with Detectives Powers and Guzman on this case. I'd like to ask you a few questions."

She shrugged.

"Do you remember what you were doing on Saturday?"

"Yes. I was at shul during the morning."

"How about in the afternoon?"

"I was watching television."

"Did you hear anything in Ambrose's apartment yesterday?"

"We already went over this—"

I extended a palm across the table and said, "I understand that, Mrs. Feinman. I'll try not to take up too much of your time. But this is important. I need your cooperation."

She crossed her arms and said sullenly, "Well, all right."

"Did you see anyone enter Ambrose's apartment on Saturday?"

"Certainly not. Why should I?"

"You live next door."

"I still don't make it a habit to spy on my neighbors."

I leaned back in my chair and crossed my legs. "Do you remember seeing me at Ambrose's door on Saturday?"

"What are you suggesting?" she asked, cocking her head to the side and squinting suspiciously at me.

"I'm not suggesting anything. Let me state a simple fact. When I was at Ambrose's door, I saw you move back the curtain and get a look at me."

"So what if I did?" She held her wrists out. "Handcuff me. Take me to jail."

I realized the interview was lurching away from me as she grew increasingly defensive and hostile. It was unlikely I'd be able to glean any information from her. Powers fidgeted in his seat, and Guzman inched forward, as if she was anxious to take over.

Mrs. Feinman reminded me of my mother and a few of my elderly aunts. What would be the best way to approach them in a situation like this? Certainly not by leaning on her, threatening her, or pushing too hard. "Mrs. Feinman," I said, clasping my hands on my lap, "as you know, your neighbor Jerry Ambrose was murdered. His mother, of course, is devastated. Now, we can't bring her son back, but if we can find his killer, that might bring her some small measure of solace."

She closed her eyes and shook her head. "What a terrible tragedy for the family."

"And Detectives Powers, Guzman, and I are very concerned about *you*."

"Me?" she said, bringing her fingertips to her throat.

"Yes, you. We want to make sure you're safe. We want to catch this murderer before he can kill again. We don't want any other residents in danger."

"Yes, yes. I haven't hardly slept at all since I found out."

"Before we leave here today, Detectives Powers, Guzman, and I will check your windows and your doors and make sure they're secure. And we'll be glad to answer any safety-related questions."

"Thank you." She stared at her house slippers. "You don't know how worried I've been." She glanced up at me. "Would you detectives like some coffee?" Without waiting for an answer, she padded off to the kitchen and teetered back a few minutes later, carrying a tray with cups of coffee, bowls of sugar and cream, plates, and a Tupperware container of cookies. She set the tray on the dining room table and filled the three plates with cookies. "Please, detectives," she said. "Help yourself."

Turning to me she said, "If you don't mind my asking, what's someone like you doing in the police department?"

"Someone like me?" I asked, playing dumb.

She studied my card. "Levine? What's a nice Jewish boy doing as a police officer?"

My career choice inevitably emerged whenever I was with another Jew. I usually found a glib way to change the subject, but I felt I owed Mrs. Feinman more than that. I was asking her to be honest with me. And after what happened to Ambrose, she might be putting herself at risk.

"*Tikkun olam,*" I said.

She didn't respond.

"You know what that means?" I asked.

"Of course. To heal or repair the world—one of the six hundred thirteen mitzvahs found in the Torah."

"You really know your Torah."

"So why the police?"

"Everybody has their own talent. I guess this is mine."

"It's a rather unusual choice."

"There's a passage in the Talmud that says something like: if you save a life it's like you saved the entire world."

"So if you solve a murder, it's like you've solved the world's murders?"

"I don't think it's exactly—"

"Where were your parents born?"

"My mother was born here."

"And your dad?"

"Germany."

"You look kind of young to be the child of a Holocaust survivor."

"He was almost fifty when he had me."

"So when did you decide to—"

"All that, Mrs. Feinman, is a very long story. After I catch the person who killed your neighbor, I'll come back to visit you, have a few more of your cookies, and I'll tell you all about my path from high school, to Israel, to the LAPD."

"Ah, *Israel*," she said, slowly pronouncing the word as if she were uttering an incantation. "My niece just returned—"

"But first," I said, "I've got to question you about the case."

"Of course."

"Now getting back to Saturday afternoon. If you can jog your memory a little, do you recall seeing anybody go to Ambrose's door?"

She passed plates of cookies to the other detectives. When she handed me my plate, she said, "I would like you to be brutally honest with me. If I had any information to impart, could I be in any danger?"

"Just to be on the safe side, do you have any relatives you could stay with for a little while?"

"My son has three beautiful children. They live in Orange County. His wife hasn't been too eager about me staying overnight there. Maybe you could call and explain why I need to move in with them for a while. I'll give you the number, and you can call now."

I raised a hand. "Let's wait on that for a little bit. Why don't you first tell me what you remember about Saturday."

"Okay," she said, disappointed.

"Do you remember seeing anybody enter Ambrose's apartment?"

She gazed at the window and said, "I do remember lifting my curtain on Saturday afternoon and seeing who was at that young man's door." She wagged a finger at me and said, "That doesn't mean I'm some yenta who spends her life spying on other people in the building. A widow living alone has to look out for herself. It's a safety issue, you know."

"I understand completely," I said. "You mentioned you saw who was at Ambrose's door on Saturday."

"Yes, I did."

"About what time?"

"Sometime between four and five o'clock."

"What did you see?"

"Two men."

"Can you describe them?"

She chewed on a cuticle for a moment. "One was small and skinny. The other one was tall. I wouldn't say skinny. More like slender. With a mustache. He was handsome."

My pulse quickened. "What color hair did the smaller man have?"

"Gray."

"Anything else you noticed about the small man?"

"Scary looking."

"Scary how?"

"Just scary."

"Can you recall if he had any tattoos?"

She squinted for a moment, lost in concentration. "Yes. Yes, he did."

"Where?"

"On his hands. That struck me as odd because I'd never seen anyone with tattoos on his hands before."

Mrs. Feinman had given me almost enough to arrest Ziven and Kolya for murder. I just needed one more bit of confirmation.

"I'd like to show you some photographs, to see if you can identify the men."

"Could you first call my son? I'd feel more secure." She scrawled a number on a piece of paper and handed it to me.

"Do you have a car?" I asked.

"I do, but it wouldn't hurt him to pick me up. You don't want to know the last time he stopped by to see me." She lightly patted her hair. "I hope you see your mother on a regular basis."

I clicked on my phone.

"Do you?" she asked.

"Do I what?"

"Visit your mother."

"I certainly do," I said, punching in the numbers as fast as I could to change the subject.

After I identified myself and mentioned the murder next door, he sounded concerned and promised to swing by in less than an hour to pick up his mother.

"You ready to look at some photographs?" I asked.

"Well," she said uncertainly, "I guess so."

I read her the admonition—"Keep in mind that hairstyles, beards and mustaches maybe be easily changed. Photographs may not always depict the true complexion of a person."—and then gave her the first photo-display sheet, which included booking photos of Kolya and five random white suspects. She studied each photo and then tut-tutted. "Such a nice-looking man."

"Who?" I asked.

She knocked her knuckles on the picture at the bottom right. Maksimov.

"Is that the man you saw at Ambrose's door on Saturday?"

"Yes, it is. The sophisticated-looking fellow."

"Please circle that picture, initial it, and date it."

When she finished, I said, "Under the pictures where it says, *Additional comments regarding photos.* Describe what you saw the man doing on Saturday."

She scrawled on the card, "I saw the fellow in picture six knocking on my neighbor Jerry Ambrose's door Saturday afternoon."

I handed her the second six-pack. She glimpsed at the photographs and immediately pointed at Ziven's picture. Shuddering, she said, "He's creepy."

"You sure that's him?" I asked.

"Oh, yes. That's a face I would never forget."

After she circled, dated, and initialed the picture, she wrote a few lines at the bottom of the card.

"I want to ask you one more thing," I said. "Did you hear anything that sounded like gunshots the night you saw those two men?"

"I didn't hear anything like that. But I've got to tell you, my hearing's not so good, and I play the television pretty loud." She lightly patted her hair. "What are you going to do now?"

"We're going to wait here until your son arrives."

"I mean, what are you going to do about these two criminals?"

I gathered the two six-packs and said, "We're going to scoop 'em up and book 'em for murder."

CHAPTER 26

Delfour decided to celebrate with a breakfast bottle. He uncorked a dusty Kistler Cuvée Catherine Pinot, poured a glass, and carried it out of the kitchen. He dropped his nose into the glass for a moment and then savored the first sip. Remarkably proportioned, incredible depth, and a fabulous finish.

He looked around the living room. Wood-beam ceiling, Batchelder tile fireplace, hundred-year-old thickly varnished oak floors. Not a bad place for a rental in Long Beach. Pretty soon he'd be able to buy his own place. He'd earned it. But the place he envisioned was far from Southern California.

When Delfour finished the glass, he picked up the phone and dialed a number. After he heard the beep he spoke: "As our former comander-in-chief once proclaimed, 'Mission Accomplished.' But in this case, we're talking reality, not wishful thinking."

CHAPTER 27

Powers, Guzman, and I gathered around a table by the pool. The sun was bleeding through the clouds and undulating ribbons of light spangled the water. Guzman asked me, "How you want to work it?"

"I think we should bust Kolya and Ziven simultaneously. If we grab one, and there's any lag time, the other one will be in the wind."

"Sounds like a plan," she said.

"Why don't Richie and I take care of Kolya. You can grab some backup and pick up Ziven. Let's stuff both of them in interview rooms at Felony Special. When I'm done with Maksimov, then you and I can question Ziven." I checked my watch. "It's still Sunday morning. My guess is these guys keep pretty late hours at that cheesy nightclub. I'm betting they'll both be at home this morning."

I cut west on Sunset, past the all-nude shows and massage parlors, past the boutiques and fashionable restaurants with the tables on the sidewalks, past the sprawling estates with parklike front lawns in Beverly Hills. I swung north on Palm Drive, jogged left onto a side street and braked at Maksimov's tall metal gate. I pressed the button on the call box.

"Identify yourself," a female voice squawked from the box.

"LAPD Detective Ash Levine."

About two minutes later, the gate swung open. We cruised down a long winding driveway flanked by plush Italian cypresses pruned to pencil points. Pomegranate trees, with brilliant gold leaves, dotted the sweeping lawn. I drove past a massive persimmon tree, the bare branches heavy with shiny orange fruit that glowed in the sunlight like Christmas tree bulbs.

"The key here," I said to Powers, "is to get Maksimov to make one simple denial before he lawyers up. If he denies that he ever stopped by Ambrose's apartment, he's bought and paid for. Mrs. Feinman's testimony will be very damaging. And if SID was able to lift either of their prints at the apartment, they're really screwed."

"These guys sound like a couple of pros," Powers said. "You think they'd leave prints at the scene?"

"Remember, Mrs. Feinman said that she spotted tattoos on Ziven's hands?"

Powers nodded.

"Well, he obviously wasn't wearing gloves then. Maybe he left a print on a door jamb before he slipped on the gloves. Even a pro gets sloppy sometimes."

When I pulled up in front of the house I was surprised because it was not the tacky, columned, overbuilt mansion I had expected. The house was a Mediterranean Revival beauty, probably built in the 1920s, with ornate Spanish ironwork around the balconies, whitewashed walls, a terrazzo path leading to a trickling fountain in the courtyard—a dazzling brocade of Italian tile. Over the glazed terra-cotta entry was an elaborate arched molding inlaid with shields. The place looked like the mansion of some silent film star.

We walked to the entryway, past pots of red poinsettias, and rang the bell. "This guy," I said, "has got taste."

"And a lot of dough, too," Powers said.

A few seconds later, I heard Kolya Maksimov's muffled voice, "Just a moment, Detective Levine."

Maksimov, who was wearing a royal-blue sweat suit and black velvet house slippers, opened the door. I could hear Christmas music in the distance.

"Good morning, Detective Levine. As a Los Angeles business owner, I appreciate the diligence of a public servant like yourself. But, as I told you the last time you paid me an unexpected visit, either arrest me, or get off my property."

"Okay," I said.

Maksimov started to nudge the door closed.

I grabbed his arm. "I'm arresting you."

We drove downtown in silence, Maksimov in the backseat, legs crossed, gazing out the window, appearing serene and unconcerned.

In the austere Felony Special interview room, Powers and I sat across a gray, hard plastic table from Maksimov.

"So what are you charging me with?" said Maksimov, who studied his gleaming nails, which looked as if they had just been manicured.

"Murder."

Maksimov slightly raised an eyebrow. "The murder of whom?"

"Jerry Ambrose."

Maksimov mumbled something in Russian.

"Would you care to translate?"

"You would find it very offensive."

"That's okay. I have thick skin."

"I decline."

Just to get him talking, loosen him up a bit, I asked him some basic biographical information for the LAPD's 510 form. I was encouraged because he seemed cooperative and cocky—always a disadvantage for a suspect.

"I'm not much of a host, am I? You want a cup of coffee?" I asked genially.

"Yes," Maksimov said. "I'd like a cup of *real* coffee. I can't drink the swill you brew up here."

I laughed. "Obviously, you're a man of discriminating taste."

"Obviously," Maksimov said.

"Well, you better get used to swill. When you're in the chow line at county jail, don't expect continental cuisine."

"I plan to make bail before it comes to that."

"Since you don't plan on being here long, let's get right to it. What did you do yesterday?"

Maksimov jabbed a finger at me. "That's the kind of question I'm not inclined to answer. As a result, I'd like to call my lawyer."

"Of course," I said. "But let me just mention one thing to you first. We hauled Ziven in here about an hour before you. He, of course, refused to say much."

"Of course," Maksimov said smugly.

"But he did say something that I found very interesting. He said he spent yesterday in bed with a girlfriend. He denied ever stopping by Jerry Ambrose's apartment and said, in fact, he'd never heard of the guy."

Maksimov picked a piece of lint off his knee.

"One more thing you might be interested to know," I said. "I know all about the mask. And the mask is what links you to Teshay Winfield and to Jerry Ambrose. And witnesses IDed you and Ziven at Ambrose's front door. That puts the nail in your coffin."

Maksimov gestured, as if he were about to speak, and then shook his head. "I will say only four more words to you: I want my lawyer now."

"That's five words."

Powers and I conferred in the squad room.

"After you linked him up to the homicide scene with the mask, I thought he'd talk," Powers said.

"At least it'll give him something to think about tonight while he's tossing and turning on that cold steel bunk."

"Why didn't you just say that Ziven laid him out?" Powers asked. "If he thought Ziven fingered him for the shooting, maybe he would have turned on Ziven to save his skin."

"If I was dealing with a south side or east side gangbanger, I would have. But Maksimov is too smart for that. Once a smart character like Maksimov catches you in a lie, it's all over. He won't believe anything you say. And he knows Ziven won't scare easily. A guy with all those gulag tattoos isn't going to roll over for a couple of American cops. He thinks we're all pussies. If Russian cops wanted information from him, they'd put his head in a vise and keep squeezing until he talked. Ziven knows we can't do shit to him. And Maksimov knows that he knows."

"You think Maksimov was confident that Ziven wouldn't run his mouth?"

"Yes," I said. "But here's where Maksimov might get thrown off. A thug like Ziven would never blab. But he might be the type to simply deny everything—deny he was ever at Ambrose's house, deny that he knew who Ambrose was."

"And if he did—Maksimov is screwed too."

"Right. He knows we can tie him and Ziven to Ambrose's place. But if Ziven denied ever being there, that's enough to hang both of them. I was hoping that Maksimov would buy that Ziven made the denial. But Maksimov was betting on Ziven not saying a fucking thing. His bet was right."

"So where do we go from here?"

"Why don't you take Maksimov over to the jail and book him. I'll wait here for your partner and Ziven."

At my desk, I was just about to open my murder book when Guzman and two uniformed officers escorted a handcuffed Ziven to an interview room. I thanked the officers and unlocked Ziven's cuffs. Slumping into a chair, he rubbed his wrists.

"Can I get you a cup of coffee?" I asked.

"Yah," Ziven grunted. "Sugar. Extra."

I returned to the room and set the cup on the plastic table.

"Before we get started, let me ask you some basic background information," I said.

Ziven held up a palm and slurped a few sips of the tepid coffee.

"You ready?" I asked.

Ziven swigged the rest of the coffee like a man downing a shot in a bar.

"What's your date of birth?"

"I say nothing to you," he said in a thick accent. "I insist that I speak to my lawyer. Ask no more questions."

"I'll let you talk to your lawyer. But I do have one question. Why didn't you say that when you got here?"

"Jail coffee taste like horse piss. Police station coffee much better."

Guzman chuckled. "This guy really knows the system."

I said to Ziven, "You seem to like our coffee better than your partner in crime—Kolya. I just talked to him, and he told me an interesting story about how the two of you spent yesterday afternoon."

Ziven spit into his empty coffee cup. "No more questions. I will talk only to my lawyer."

After Guzman and Powers booked Maksimov and Ziven, they gathered around my desk. "We don't feel right taking credit for this case," Powers said, nodding toward Guzman. "That mask was the link between our victim and those two Russians. And you found it."

"Plus, you got Mrs. Feinman to make the key ID," Guzman said. "That's the case right there."

I rolled a pencil between my palms. "Why don't we do this? On the arrest report, we'll list this case as a Wilshire clearance. That'll be good for your division's stats."

Powers grinned. "It'll keep our D-3 and our captain happy."

"Clearance rates," Guzman said with distaste. "That's all they care about."

"Well, they'll get their clearance," I said. "But since this case is connected to my double, why don't I run with it now. If I need any backup on anything, I'll contact you guys."

"That'll work," Powers said. "Should keep everyone happy."

Guzman and Powers hunched over computers at Felony Special for the next few hours, writing the arrest reports, while I assisted them and updated my chrono. When the slats of the venetian blinds on the west windows glimmered a molten red from the sinking sun, the two Wilshire detectives clicked off the computers, fetched their coats, and shook my hand.

"I'm glad we cleared the case today," Powers said. "The timing's great."

"Why?" I asked.

"Christmas is, um, next week," he said nervously. "For those who celebrate it."

"That right, I forgot."

"Happy Holidays," he said cheerily.

After they left, I called Robin, but she wasn't picking up her cell or her work phone. I was upset and angry that Ambrose had been killed, and I didn't feel like writing reports in the empty squad room. I hadn't eaten since last night, so I decided to grab a late lunch as a reward for clearing the case.

I crossed the First Street bridge into East L.A., and parked in front of a boisterous Mexican pool hall, across the street from Birrieria Jalisco, a beige stucco restaurant with iron bars over the windows and a sketch of a goat above the front door. The modest restaurant, which served only one entrée—roast kid—was a single square room with a red tile floor, a dozen Formica tables, black metal chairs, and overhead fans. On the walls were hundred-year-old photographs of Guadalajara, where the dish is a specialty.

I ordered at the counter and found a seat in the back of the restaurant. I sipped my *tamarindo*—a sweet drink made of tamarind pods— and mulled over the interview with Maksimov and the shooting of Ambrose. I felt a measure of satisfaction, clearing the case so quickly, but I worried about the two Russian women I'd moved. I hoped they'd be safe, hoped that locking up Maksimov had neutralized him. I thought that I better wait a while until I let them know it was safe to return home. The waitress interrupted my reverie, carefully setting down a platter of roast kid—brimming with spicy broth—and a stack of tortillas. I wolfed down several tortillas that I'd loaded with strips of dripping meat and topped with chilies, lime juice, chopped onions, and cilantro. Pushing aside my plate, I wondered what Robin was doing. I reviewed the drive up the coast, our brief time together on the beach, how I'd felt almost giddy by the prospect of getting back together. I recalled what my father had told me at the hospital, right before he died. *You know the best way to prove that Hitler didn't win? It's to have a family, to have children, to bring another generation of Jews into the world.* Could it work this time with Robin? If not, would I ever get another shot at marriage and kids? Another few dozen demanding cases and, before I knew it, I'd be retired and alone. Still eating dinners in restaurants by myself.

After ordering coffee, I called Robin. Again, no answer. I downed my *tamarindo* and headed west toward the freeway.

CHAPTER 28

The Santa Anas had blasted the smog out to sea, and as I headed up the 110 toward Pasadena, I slipped on my sunglasses. Although it was late afternoon, the sky was a brilliant fluorescent blue, flooded with sunlight. When I exited in Pasadena, the air was remarkably clear for Southern California, and I could see every crevice, canyon, and shadow in the corrugated San Gabriels. I checked my watch. Robin might get home after five. I knew when she was in trial she liked to prepare in her home office, away from the distractions at work. She didn't answer her phone. I decided to kill some time and then stop by the house.

I drove up the side streets, past parked cars speckled with dust blown down from the mountains, to the edge of the Angeles National Forest. I parked on a rise, in a grove of live oak trees, with a sweeping view, from the foothills to the sea, the humpback silhouette of Catalina sharply etched on the horizon. The wind was roaring through the Mojave Desert and down the mountain passes, snapping branches off the trees. I closed my eyes for a moment, listening to the acorns rattling down the ravines, the rocks peppering my car with metallic pings, and the groaning and creaking of the old oaks. I must have dozed off because when I awoke, the light had faded from the horizon. I started the car, dodged the fallen branches, and veered over to a residential street bounded by cone-shaped liquidambar trees, their leaves a palette of brilliant orange, red, rust, and gold—a New England landscape. The next block was veiled by a graceful arbor of camphor trees, trunks grooved with deep striations, their pungent leaves twirling down like green snowflakes. It was almost dark now, and Christmas lights were starting to flash on the houses as I passed.

I parked in front of Robin's house. *Robin's house.* It used to be our house. I hadn't lived here in two years, and I spent the time trying to get over her. But her call to me a few months ago set off a chain of events—

the phone conversations late at night, the long, lingering lunches, the drive up the coast to Santa Barbara—which ended with me right back where I was when she first walked out.

I glanced at the house. She'd planted a row of pale-pink azaleas in front, which were in full bloom. A gust of wind ripped the blossoms off the stalks and they bobbed along the lawn, caught in an updraft, and flew over the house like a flock of birds. I walked up the pathway, bending slightly, fighting the wind, and lingered at the door. The house was a 1909 Craftsman with a wraparound porch studded with arroyo rock, a low-slung roof with a peak in the middle, dormer windows, and a clinker brick chimney. I rang the bell.

Robin swung open the door, stepped out onto the porch, and hugged me. She patted the Adirondack chair on the front porch. I collapsed into it, she sat on my lap, and I wrapped my arms around her waist. From the sheltered porch, we watched the pair of palm trees on the lawn across the street, the wind rattling their fronds.

A few minutes later, I followed her into the living room and sat next to her on the sofa. I told her I'd just locked up two suspects. "You know what that means?"

"What?"

"We can make that trip to Santa Barbara next weekend."

"Count me in," she said. "This calls for a celebration."

"You have a beer?"

"Just wine."

"That'll do."

As she withdrew into the kitchen, I glanced around the living room and felt a bittersweet pang. So many memories in this room. A lot of them bad. But some pretty damn nice. She hadn't changed the place much, just added a few paintings, some wooden shutters, a Persian rug. She returned with two glasses of white wine. We clinked glasses and she said *l'chaim*. I told her more about the cases, and she listened intently. After we emptied our glasses, we finished the bottle. She leaned back on the sofa and laughed.

"Neither of us are really drinkers," she said.

"We're going to pay in the morning."

"I guess I'm nervous."

"About what?" I asked.

"About us. It's been a long time."

I slipped my arm around her shoulder and kissed her.

"It's nice having you back," she said. "How'd I ever let you get away?"

"You didn't let me get away. You kicked my ass out."

"Well, I might do that tomorrow morning. But I'm not letting you get away tonight," she said smiling. She stood, clasped my hand, and guided me to the bedroom.

I awoke to my cell phone's buzz.

"Ash, it's Powers. Kolya Maksimov wants to talk. He says he's got something to tell you. Something you'll definitely want to hear."

"I'm on my way."

Robin peered at me, one eye open. "Ash, it's two o'clock in the morning."

I leaned over, kissed her, and said, "It's my case. Sorry that I—"

"Don't worry about it," she mumbled sleepily.

"We still on for next weekend?"

"Of course."

"Good, 'cause I'm carving that weekend in stone. I'm not even going to take my cell with me."

As I was dressing, Robin called out, "Ash, I made a lot of mistakes."

"We both did."

"I think it can be different."

"That's what I'm counting on."

A stout female guard led me to the cells. I missed the old lockup, which had just closed. It was called the Parker Center Jail and it looked like a jail, a dank, fetid warren of claustrophobic hallways ribbed with pipes on the ceiling, the cells echoing with clangs and shouts of the prisoners. This new facility was called the Metropolitan Detention Center and, with its sterile, hermetic chrome-and-cement corridors and video monitors, it had the tidy, efficient ambience of a high-tech navy vessel. At the old jail, at least, the grime and crumbling walls reminded prisoners that they had fucked up, were stuck in a shithole, and were facing serious consequences.

The jailer ushered me into a boxlike attorney interview room where Kolya was perched on the edge of the table. He was wearing the same royal-blue sweat suit, but it was now rumpled and stained.

"How's the coffee down here?" I asked.

Maksimov pretended to spit.

"You should have had a cup yesterday when I offered it."

"Maybe."

"So I understand you're ready to talk."

I dragged a chair across the room, the metal screeching on tile.

"My attorney has advised against this," Maksimov said.

I waited for him to continue.

"But I've thought about it. And I know it looks bad for me. I know you detectives don't look beyond the surface. I know juries don't, either. What you've got, so far, could be enough to send me away. For a very long time."

"You got that right."

"Even if it's all erroneous, all inaccurate?"

"But it's not."

Maksimov's shoulders slumped. "It doesn't really matter now. My only chance, I feel, is to set it all before you and hope you pursue the *true* leads, not all the false ones, like you've been doing."

"I don't have time to listen to this shit. I was doing something very important when you asked to see me."

"What I'm going to tell you is not shit. It is the truth."

I jabbed a thumb toward the cellblock. "I'll bet if I talked to every guy in here, not a single one of them would be guilty. They'd all tell me they'd been framed, or screwed by the lawyers, or locked up by crooked cops. So why should I believe you? Whatever you've got to say, I guarantee you, I've heard it before."

"And I guarantee you, you haven't heard the story I'm going to tell you. Can you spare me a half hour? I promise you that what I'm going to say will not be tedious. And I promise you, at the end, you'll view your investigation in an altered light."

"Thirty minutes," I said impatiently. "Then I'm out of here."

Maksimov squinted and nodded to himself, as if he were conjuring up some kind of image. "I have a scientific mind, but I also have an appreciation for things aesthetic and artistic. You understand?"

"I saw your house; I got that impression."

"My training is in electrical engineering. I have an advanced degree from a very fine university in Moscow—you can view it as the Stanford of Russia. Very early in my career I was sent overseas to work on projects with what you might call the client states of the Soviet Union. You understand? I was in Poland. I was in Cuba. And I was also sent to countries we had close ties to, countries that were important to us strategically. That's how I ended up in Iraq. I don't know if you're aware of this, but the Soviets and Iraqis, for many years, have had very close ties on many different levels—in the Foreign Ministry, in the military, in the intelligence services. During the Cold War and during the Iran-Iraq war, Soviet advisors were intimately involved in the affairs of that country."

He cleared his throat and asked for some water. I left the interview room, walked down the hallway, returned with two Styrofoam cups of water, and set them in front of him. He gulped one down and flipped it upside down on the table. "I was sent to Iraq fairly early in my career to advise on a large military construction project. Soon I was asked to become involved in activities that exceeded the parameters of electrical engineering."

"You were recruited by the KGB?" I asked.

"No, the PGU—the Russian acronym for the First Chief Directorate. That was the KGB's unit for foreign intelligence gathering."

"Never heard of it."

"It was later known as the SVR."

"Still never heard of it."

"This agency and Iraqi intelligence shared information. In fact, some of my superiors helped reorganize Iraqi security. Many Iraqi unit heads spent time at our Special Training Center in Moscow. In return, they gave us critical data on Middle Eastern countries we had no ties with. They also gave us information about Muslim terrorist groups targeting Chechnya. So you see, the two countries had a close relationship. And I had a close relationship with a few of my counterparts in Baghdad."

I checked my watch. "Let's get to the point here."

"Very shortly," Maksimov said. "You'll soon see how this all ties in. Now, when I was in Baghdad, I developed an interest in the country's rich cultural history. It is, as you might know, the cradle of civilization. And you also might know it was necessary for a Soviet civil servant such as myself to find ways to supplement his salary to even sustain a modest lifestyle. So I found a way to combine this love of Middle Eastern culture with a need to enhance my income."

He ran his finger along the side of the empty water cup and said, "A close friend in the Foreign Ministry provided the diplomatic pouch. I had associates in Baghdad who provided the cultural treasures. The functionaries in Moscow found the European markets. And everybody was happy."

"Except, maybe, the Iraqis who didn't want their country's cultural heritage looted," I said curtly.

He sipped from the second cup.

"So how'd you fence them?" I asked.

"There's an international treaty that was drawn up to stop the trade in these kinds of artifacts. The U.S. and most European countries have signed it. A few countries, including Germany, Switzerland, and Belgium, haven't. So dealers there, of course, were our most enthusiastic purchasers. In addition to Japan, of course. There's always a market there."

He fidgeted with the cup, swirling the water. "At one point I got ahold of a remarkable set of Sumerian bronzes. They were very old, cast about three thousand B.C. This time, unfortunately, I didn't have the benefit of the diplomatic pouch when I transported them out of Baghdad and into Moscow. When certain associates of mine became aware that the bronzes were available on the international art market—and discovered I was the source—they became rather vexed."

"In other words," I said, "you hustled the art out of the country and tried to sell it yourself. And your partners were pissed because you burned them, you cut them out of the action."

"That was *their* interpretation," he sniffed. "That's why I love this country. Here you'd just consider it using some business initiative."

"And because your Moscow associates were heavy hitters, you had to get out of the country fast to save your skin," I said. "So you disappeared and washed up here. Broke. But not for long."

"That's right. I'm an embodiment of your nation's mythology—the American dream."

"Hardly," I said.

"So that's the background."

"Let's get to the foreground."

"There was a curator at the Baghdad National Museum I did extensive business with. He was a remarkable man. A great scholar—but also an astute businessman. He made me aware of one of the country's greatest artistic treasures. I soon devoted quite a bit of time trying to find this treasure. This was something very different from many of the nation's most valued and revered antiquities. Many of them—bronzes, gold anklets, cylinder seals, ancient jewelry, Assyrian reliefs, copper busts, carved limestone vases—date from as far back as five thousand years before the birth of Christ. Some are among the world's earliest representational sculptures. It is their great antiquity and historical interest that make them so valuable. But this treasure that I soon was determined to possess, was not quite so old."

"The mask," I said.

"Ah, yes, the mask." For a moment, Maksimov stared into his water, as if he could discern its image in the reflection.

"The mask," I reminded him.

"Let me start with Hammurabi. Now in Babylon—"

"I know the history of the mask. I talked about it with a UCLA archaeologist."

"Do you know about the artist who created this masterpiece?"

"I have no idea."

"Neither do I. Neither does your professor, or anyone else. But I can tell you that the artist who carved the likeness of the queen of Babylon was the Michelangelo of his time. He created a work so lovely it simply takes your breath away."

"You ever see this mask?"

"The Mask of Ellasar," Maksimov said slowly, savoring the words. "It was never on display at the Iraqi National Museum. They didn't have the security to protect it. But many years ago, I was at a state dinner in Baghdad. A small group of us were escorted to the museum, taken down to an underground vault, and briefly shown this superb creation. I don't have the words to describe such beauty, but I'll try. The face is carved from the finest Indian ivory. The artistry, delicacy of the features, the brilliance of the portrait, in itself, would make the mask one of the world's great art treasures. It has been called the *Mona Lisa of Babylon* because of the singular nature of her expression that is so lifelike you almost expect her to speak, because of her cryptic smile, her astounding beauty. Like I said, that in itself would have been enough to spark my fixation. But the jewels inlaid in the mask are—"

He paused and squinted at a wall. "Let me just say that two of the world's most remarkable rubies are inlaid in the mask to represent the queen's eyes. Remarkable because of their size. Remarkable because of their clarity and color—the reddest of red, like they were on fire. Remarkable because of their luminosity—perfectly transparent, without a hint of a flaw, radiating with razor-sharp six-point stars. Transported by donkey caravan from as far away as what used to be known as Burma. And the rest of the mask is inlaid—and here the artistry is unmatched—with pearls from Bahrain and lapis lazuli from Western China, with streaks of gold and silver animating the visage."

"So when did you try to steal it?"

"What?" Maksimov asked, his voice tinged with irritation.

I repeated the question.

"Several times. Once I saw it, I knew I had to have it. I was simply blinded by its magnificence."

"Not to mention the millions you'd make if you'd put it on the market."

"What a cynic you are, Detective."

"Just calling it like I see it."

He smiled, but his eyes remained vacant. "By saying millions you underestimate the value. You need to think in the tens of millions—as a starting point. An Assyrian relief from eight fifty B.C. sold for eleven million dollars in London at a Christie's auction some years ago. Can you imagine what the Mask of Ellasar would fetch? But money was not my primary motivation—although I suspect you don't believe me."

"You suspect correctly."

"So be it. Anyway, while I was struggling to survive in this country, I had to abandon my quest. I wouldn't say I forgot about the mask—once you've seen it, as I've said, you'd never forget it—but I had more pressing concerns. Then when I achieved some measure of success and security here, my thoughts, again, returned to that museum vault and how I could penetrate those many layers of security. But I never really believed I would have a chance—until the U.S. began making plans for invading Iraq. It was then that I—as well as other collectors—saw an opportunity."

"That's right," I said. "I remember reading about the fall of Baghdad and how the Iraqi National Museum was looted. Did your mask get ripped off?"

He shook his head. "Two groups of people did the looting: opportunists who just smashed and grabbed; and art thieves with glass cutters and keys to museum vaults who knew exactly what they were looking for, knew about the basement storage areas. And, in some cases, thieves were actually taking orders for specific items from European buyers.

"So where was the mask?"

"Fortunately I still had some good contacts in Baghdad and I had the financial wherewithal to pay for information. So I was able to determine that the mask had been moved to the basement of the Baghdad Manuscript Centre. A former agent of the Mukhabarat—the Iraqi intelligence service—happened to be a friend of mine. When he received his advanced training in Moscow years ago, I'd been a splendid host. Now, with the Americans dashing through his country, he was aware that his job security—and, perhaps, his life expectancy—was rather short. He believed, and rightly so, that he needed to get himself and his family out of the country quite quickly. But he needed a quick infusion of a lot of cash to do so. I made contact with him and I told him if he could get that mask for me, I'd have someone on the ground in Baghdad hand him a suitcase full of cash—enough cash to solve his family's problems."

"But you never got the mask."

He smiled ruefully. "My contact twisted a few arms to find out where the mask was and then twisted a few more arms to gain admittance to the Manuscript Centre."

"Broke heads is probably more like it," I said.

"Well, let's just say he employed effective methods. He was very good at his job. That's why I relied on him. And I can't tell you how ecstatic I was when he informed me that he had succeeded, that he had secured the mask. It took me a little while to get my transport team—all contacts I'd made while I'd been stationed in the country—ready to truck the mask to Tel Aviv. Then I planned to have it flown to L.A."

"Sounds dicey."

"Not really. That's how everything looted from the museum got out of the country. Sent overland to either Tel Aviv or Tehran. Then flown to Europe."

"Did it ever reach Tel Aviv?"

"From what I was able to piece together, the driver was about sixty miles west of Baghdad, on his way to hand the mask off to my transport team, when his Mercedes was stopped at a U.S. Army checkpoint at Ramadi. Unfortunately, he panicked. He tried to run the barrier and got terminated by some trigger-happy soldiers."

"I'm guessing it was a checkpoint manned by the First Cavalry," I said. "And one of the soldiers at the checkpoint was Teshay Winfield. And he took possession of the mask."

"You *are* a detective, after all," Maksimov said sarcastically. "I did discover all that. But way too late. It took me months and months and quite a lot of money. And by the time I found out that Winfield had the mask—"

"How'd you find out?" I interrupted.

"He showed it to some antique seller in one of Baghdad's maze of bazaars. When the seller appeared a bit too eager to take the mask off Winfield's hands, I'm guessing he caught a whiff of its value. I'm also guessing he calculated that it might be better to fence the mask at home than risk getting court-martialed in Iraq or having his throat slit in some Baghdad back alley. Unfortunately, he was on a tour of Afghanistan when I discovered all this. If I'd have known it when he was still in Iraq, I think everything would have been a lot easier. I'd be admiring the mask right now, instead of sitting here, rotting in this dungeon."

I leaned across the table and jabbed his shoulder with my palm. "You mean you would have had Teshay killed *there*—instead of shooting him here?"

Maksimov waved his cup at me, water splashing onto the table. "That's an entirely false assumption. I would *not* have killed him there. I did *not* kill him here. I am telling you the entire story so you will understand the truth. Yes, I am a ruthless man. You cannot come to a new country at my age and make the money I've made and not be ruthless. Yes, I am a man who is, how do you say it, monomaniacal? Is that the right word?"

"Sounds like it."

"Well, you cannot pursue this mask as I have done without being monomaniacal. This mask has a very interesting property. Anyone who bisects its trail seems to get infected with the virus of obsession. I would not be surprised if you, detective, also became fixated on finding this treasure."

"I doubt it."

"I have broken a few laws in my time, as you know."

"And a few legs, I'll bet."

"I freely admit to some criminal activity," he said. "But I am not a killer. Never have I killed anyone. Never will I kill anyone."

I was reluctant to say too much because I didn't want to let Maksimov know that I'd talked to Valentina Revenco and Irina Komarova. I checked my watch. In another hour or two, Robin would be awake. Should I call her? Should I stop by again tonight? Maybe if I—

"Never!" he shouted.

"What?"

"I've never killed anyone."

"But you've employed a number of methods in your attempt to get Winfield to reveal where he hid the mask."

"That is true. But you cannot and you will not prove that my methods included murder."

"But I already *have* proved that. That's why you're here."

"But that's what I've been trying to tell you." His voice sounded like a whine, pleading, desperate. "You have *not* proved that. *Someone* committed murder in an attempt to locate the mask. But, I swear to you, it wasn't me."

"So you were framed," I said, sounding bored.

"Yes, that it's. Don't you see?"

"Frankly, no."

"Your investigation is not over, I hope."

"Not entirely. I'll do some work through the prelim and before the trial."

"So if I have information for you, you'll pursue it?"

"Depends on what it is."

"The mask is the key."

"And where can I find it?"

"That's all I've been thinking about for the past four weeks. Yes, I did search Teshay Winfield's home. Yes, I did talk to Jerry Ambrose at his apartment. Yes, I employed a young woman in the hopes that Winfield would tell her where the mask was. None of these methods, as you know, were successful."

"So if you couldn't find the mask, what makes you think I can?"

"Because I have a few more ideas. I have some suggestions on where you should look."

"I'm listening," I said.

"When I discovered that Winfield had obtained the mask in Iraq, he was living in that house behind a house in Venice. So that's where I searched. But recently, I had a young man in my employ spread a little cash around Oakwood. And I just discovered that when Winfield first returned home, he briefly lived with his mother. Shortly after that, he moved into the cottage. If I wasn't in this jail, I would be searching the mother's house."

"What makes you think it's there?"

"I had a young woman working for me who was very good friends with Winfield."

Maksimov scrutinized me, like a poker player searching for a hint on a hand. I looked back at him without blinking.

"Now I'm thinking maybe I trusted her too much. Maybe Winfield *did* tell her where the mask was. Maybe he showed it to her. If she got a sense of even a fraction of the value, she might have gone behind my back, had Winfield eliminated, and hidden the mask herself. Her name is Valentina Revenco."

Maksimov told me her address and said, "I suggest you search her apartment."

I wondered if Revenco could have slipped the mask into her overnight bag. But I recalled following her into her room and carefully watching her pack. I wanted to make sure she didn't hide a pistol in her bag.

"You find that mask and get me out of here, and I can promise you more money than you've ever imagined."

"Is that a bribe?"

"Just check her place, Winfield's mother's place, and any place else your investigation takes you. Because I believe that if you find the mask, you'll find the killer. Or he'll find you."

CHAPTER 29

The next morning, I rode up the elevator to the fifth floor in a daze. In a brief span, Maksimov had dumped so much information on me I didn't know what to think. The man was either a pathological liar or—what? Could he be telling the truth? Or was he just like every other cornered killer, spinning a web of lies leavened with enough truth to make the story sound convincing?

At my desk I switched on my computer, cruised a few websites, and read more about the mask. After scrolling through dozens of stories, however, I still couldn't find any mention that the mask had been stolen or was missing.

I decided to contact FBI Agent Emery Peck and camouflage it as a courtesy call, when it was really a fishing expedition. I thumbed through my murder book, found Peck's card, and left a message on his cell. Two minutes later Peck called.

"What's going on?" he asked warily.

"I booked Maksimov and his thug for murder yesterday."

"Teshay Winfield's murder?"

"No. Winfield's friend—a guy named Jerry Ambrose."

"Thanks for filling me in."

"No problem. I'm doing some follow-up and I was wondering if you picked up anything more on the wire about the mask."

"Why?" Peck asked.

"When we first talked about this case, you thought the mask was slang for snitch. But I discovered that the mask is not a who, it's a what."

"Okay. What's the mask?"

"It's a long story. The mask is actually—a mask. It's some ancient artifact. It was smuggled out of Iraq. You never answered my question. Did you hear anything on the wires about it?"

"Not a thing. But since we're involved over there, I'm going to have to pass that along to the higher-ups."

"I know. But can you give me a few days before you do?"

"Why?"

"I don't want the feds or Interpol to step in right now and interfere with my investigation. Will you hold off for a few days?"

"I suppose so," he said reluctantly. "But after Christmas, when I'm back in the office, I've got to file a report."

"I can live with that."

"How's Maksimov involved in all this?" Peck asked.

"It's a long story—too long to tell you over the phone. After Christmas, why don't you stop by Felony Special and I'll fill you in."

As I hung up, I noticed Duffy at his desk, motioning to me. "Fill me in on that Russki bust," he said, as I sank into a chair in the corner of his office. I spent the next twenty minutes briefing Duffy on Mrs. Feinman's statement, the arrests, the interview with Maksimov, and the background on the mask.

He leaned back, hands clasped across his impressive midsection, eyes slitted, looking like an Irish Buddha. "So he cops to stopping by Ambrose's apartment and setting a honey trap for Winfield with that Russian hooker."

"She claims she's not a hooker."

Duffy raised an eyebrow. "But he swears he didn't cap anyone."

"That's right." He jerked upright.

"What are you, some kind of fucking rookie? Sounds like he's laying a bunch of horseshit on you to save his ass."

"Could be. But that mask story is a pretty amazing yarn, don't you think?"

"Who gives a shit about the mask," Duffy said with disgust. "All I know is your collar doesn't do *me* much good."

"What do you mean?"

"Councilman Pinkney's pissed," Duffy said. "He wants those two Russian mafiosi officially charged with his son's murder. And pronto."

"I can't do that. Yet. But I plan to."

"Make sure you do—unless you want the LAPD's budget cut so much that you'll be spending half your days chasing speeders and red light jumpers."

"By the way, you're welcome," I said.

"Oh, yeah. Thanks for doing a good job on the Ambrose hit. But until you book those Russkies for the Oakwood double, I'll still have

Councilman Pinkney on my ass. He wants someone arrested for his son's murder."

"All three homicides, obviously, are connected."

"You know that. I know that. But the councilman doesn't give a shit. He wants someone officially nailed for the murder of his son."

"That's my next step—to tie my Russians to the Oakwood case. And when I do, the DA will charge 'em with two more counts of murder."

"Well, get cracking."

"You know, you're an ungrateful motherfucker."

Duffy circled around his desk and patted me on the cheek. "Ash, my boy, don't be so sensitive. Look, I know you did a hell of a job clearing that Ambrose murder. And I appreciate it." He studied me for a moment and said, "Any chance of picking it back up with Robin after you bag and tag this case?"

"Maybe."

"I say, maybe not. I had a sense from the get-go that it was never going to work."

"Why not?"

"It's a class thing. She's got it. You don't."

"Fuck you."

"Seriously, Ash, she's a big-time corporate lawyer. You're a cop. She's from a rich family who grew up in some mansion. You were raised in a dumpy apartment. You're a fucking oxymoron—a poor Jew. Her dad's a big-time surgeon. Your dad worked downtown as some dress company coolie."

"Patternmaker."

"Whatever. That bitch is never going to be happy being a cop's wife. It's pretty obvious."

"Not so obvious to me," I said, irritated. "I think I've got a shot."

Duffy slapped my thigh. "I hope you're right." As I walked out the door, Duffy called out, "One down, two to go."

Powers dropped me off at my car, but instead of returning home I drove toward the beach and parked in front of a small surfboard shop, which was sandwiched between a parking lot and a Thai restaurant. Inside the shop, I breathed deeply, inhaling the distinctive surf shop scent of neoprene rubber wetsuits, laminating resin, and sugary surfboard wax. I lingered by the far wall, where a dozen boards were lined up in racks, and traced my fingers along the smooth rails. I grabbed a single-fin long-board and raised it up like I was staring down the barrel of a shotgun, following the spruce stringer from the center of the board to the slightly kicked up nose.

A voice called out, "Ready to ease into a longboard?"

Razor Reed emerged from a back room and gripped me in a bear hug. I knew he'd been shaping a board because his long, wavy gray hair was speckled with polystyrene foam. He was wearing baggy shorts, rubber thongs, and a long-sleeved T-shirt with *Razor Reed Surfboard Creations* emblazoned in front. Even though it was a cool winter afternoon, his skin glowed with a bronze tinge, like he had just stepped out of the sun.

When I was a young cop, working Pacific Division patrol, I'd saved Reed during a mugging in Venice. He'd made me a board in appreciation, and over the years we had stayed in touch and occasionally surfed together.

"So what's cracking, Ashman?"

"I need two things. One is personal. One is professional—something to help me out on a case I'm working."

"You got it."

"Let's start with the personal. Remember my eight-year-old nephew, Ariel? You met him last year when he watched us surf County Line after that big storm. He's had a tough year. His dad was in rehab. I want to do something nice for him, get him a great Hanukkah present."

"He ever surfed before?"

"No."

"You going to take him out?"

"Eventually. But his mother's very overprotective. I talked to her last summer about it. She thinks surfing's too dangerous. She said maybe she'll let him go with me when he's older, but only if I sign him up for one of those surfing schools first."

Reed scowled and drummed his fingers along the nose of a board. "I ain't selling you one then. Fuck those surf schools. They're destroying what this sport's all about. When I was a kid, I hated sitting in class, having a teacher tell me what to do all day. My dad made me play Little League and I hated that too, having some coach tell me: *This is the right way to throw, this is the wrong way to bat, now stand over there and take fifty ground balls.*

"For me, surfing was our way to get away from all that fucking fascism. No adults. No one telling us what to do. No drills. No organization. I'd get out in the water and figure things out for myself. There was no right way to surf. There was no wrong way. No fucking rules. I could develop my own style. Dude, back then it was all about individuality. Out in the water was the only place I felt like I could get away from all that adult regimented shit. That's why I loved surfing from the get-go. Still do.

"Now I go out to the beach and see these little kids lined up on the shore like little soldiers, standing beside their boards while some kook *supposedly* teaches them how to surf. 'Get on your stomach. Jump to your feet. Crouch. Weight on your back foot. Swivel your hips.'"

"That's bullshit. If you've got to have a teacher to teach you how to surf, you shouldn't be in the water. When I was coming up, if we'd seen some kid taking surfing lessons, we'd have laughed his ass off the beach. If he came back, we'd have kicked his ass. Now all the soccer moms are driving their little darlings out to the beach in their minivans and dropping them off. They drink their double lattes in the parking lots while a generation of surfer wannabes clog up the beaches."

I shook my head, amazed. "That's the first time I've ever heard you string more than three sentences together."

"Well, I'm pissed, dude."

"I know what you're saying. I think that's why I liked surfing so much. Surfing was my escape from all that LAPD regimentation—and from everything I saw on the streets."

He extended a hand, a languid gesture. "That's it."

"Okay. No surfing schools. I'll take him out with me and show him a few things."

"Showing the kid a few things is fine. Nothin' wrong with that. But then let him make some mistakes, figure out where he went wrong, and develop his own personal style. Like I did. Like you did."

"Good advice," I said. "Now pick me out a board."

I followed Razor along the aisles as he slid a palm over the rails of various boards. Near the back of his shop, he lifted a board that looked to be about seven feet.

"This might be just the thing. The board's basic enough so he can ease into it, but I gave it enough oomph, so he'll be able to shred when he learns what he's doing." He ran his fingers around the tail. "It's a fun-shaped round pin." He pinched the nose. "It's got a slight rocker, about three inches." He patted the rails. "Fairly thick. Stable with some paddling punch." He lifted the board above his head so I could see the bottom. "As you can see, it's a thruster with glassed-ons." He set the board on the ground, crouched, and ran a palm along the sleek surface. "It's got a sweet look, yeah? I gave it a nice aqua air brush, fading to clear on the nose, and a Western Red Cedar stringer."

"You're an artist, Razor. I'll take it."

"I'll give you what I give all my partners in crime—or surf—twenty percent off."

"Excellent. When I was a kid, my mother always gave me three pieces of advice: 'Look both ways before crossing the street. Don't talk to strangers. And never buy retail.'"

"Right on. When your nephew sees this, he'll be stoked."

"Definitely. Now here's the work-related thing I need from you—your metal detector." On a few occasions when we went surfing and the waves were blown out or flat, or we were waiting for the tide to change, he'd pulled the metal detector out of the back of his van and scanned the sand. He always came up with something—usually a handful of coins and, on a few occasions, watches and jewelry.

He ambled to the back of his shop, and I could hear him rummaging through boxes. A moment later, I saw him cradling the detector, a black metal device, about four-and-a-half-feet long, with a metal rod, a screen at the top with a digital readout, and a round coil at the bottom. "Here it is," Reed said. "You've seen me on the beach with it. It's easy to use. Just slide the coil along the surface, and when it senses coins or jewelry or bullets or buckles or any kind of metal, you'll hear that long beep."

"How deep will it scan, like if someone buried something?"

"About two to three feet. Typically, a guy with a shovel won't bury anything much deeper."

"Why not?"

"Because he's usually in a hurry. It's usually at night, and he doesn't want anyone to hear him or see what he's doing." He flicked his finger on the side of the screen. "See this toggle switch. There're three settings: Relic, Coin/Jewelry, and Prospecting. Set it on Prospecting. That's the deepest read."

"You ever work on anything besides sand?"

"I haven't, but when I was surfing in Mexico, I saw people scan adobe walls and dirt floors and things like that and come up with stuff. Every village has a story of buried treasure. During the Mexican Revolution people hid a lot of their valuables to keep them safe from the Americans and from Pancho Villa. I saw a guy once find a sack of gold coins stuffed in the rafters of a hacienda."

"Any advice?"

"Keep it simple. Crisscross, so you don't miss any spots."

He handed me the metal detector and said with a sly smile, "Do I get ten percent of what you find?"

"If I gave you ten percent of what I'm looking for, you'd be able to buy half of Malibu."

I parked down the street from Revenco's West Hollywood apartment. The days were short this time of year and the streets were already in shadow, the Hollywood Hills purple silhouettes in the dying light. I retrieved the metal detector from the trunk, hauled it to the front door of the manager's ground-floor apartment, and rang the bell. The manager, a skinny woman in her seventies with brittle orange hair and a face covered with angry red blotches, opened the door and said, "No vacancies."

I badged her and told her I needed to examine Revenco's apartment.

She stared at the metal detector and said, "What the hell is that?"

"Just an investigative tool."

She looked at me skeptically and said, "I've never seen one of these on CSI. They use cutting-edge technology, and none of the trace technicians on the show has ever brought one of those to a crime scene."

"Can you let me in the apartment? I'm a little short of time."

"I knew it would come to this," she whined, as I trailed her up the stairs.

"Come to what?" I asked.

"Cops rousting the place." She halted at Revenco's door and pivoted on her heels, facing me. "I've rented to Russian girls before. I know their game. But I promise you, detective, I didn't know—I still don't know—exactly what kind of business she was running. If I did, I can assure you, I'd have called Hollywood Vice pronto."

"Sure." I was eager to get rid of the woman. I plucked the key from her hand, opened the door, and handed it back. "Thanks again," I said, gently closing the door.

I carried the metal detector to the kitchen, flicked it on, and slid the coil over the linoleum floor in a crisscross pattern. No hits. I'd seen Razor do it dozens of times when he'd surveyed the sand at the beach. In the living room, I ran the coil over a large throw rug. A loud beep. I shut off the detector, wrestled back the rug, crouched, and discovered a metal hair pin. After I finished in the living room, I moved through every other room, scanning the floors and walls. I then ran the detector through every cabinet and drawer in the apartment. Again, no hits.

I hustled back to my car, feeling foolish. Why was I letting Maksimov jerk my chain?

CHAPTER 30

Back at PAB, I flipped open the murder book. I'd been hurtling along for the past week, pursuing a concatenation of leads that seemed to converge at a logical destination, with a logical conclusion: the arrest of Kolya and Ziven. I certainly had enough to arrest them. I had enough to convince a D.A. to file murder charges. But did I have enough to convict them? Kolya had the money to afford a dream team of defense attorneys and an army of PIs calling into question every aspect of my investigation. It was my job to continue solidifying the case against my best suspects, the suspects who I believed had killed Ambrose—and Winfield and Pinkney. So I planned to do what I've always done since my days as a detective trainee at South Bureau Homicide: keep working the case until the prelim, and try to find out if there was any truth to Kolya's story.

I wove through the downtown streets in the light morning traffic, parked, rode the elevator to my loft, shut off my cell, climbed into bed, and slept all day. When I awoke, I crawled from beneath the sheets and stumbled to the kitchen where I made myself a sandwich and opened a bottle of Sierra Nevada ale. Afterward, I decided to update my chrono. I booted up my computer and gazed out the window. A helicopter lifted off from the roof of the PAB, loudly reverberating above me, almost drowning out the sound of the ringing phone.

"Levine here."

"*That's* how you answer the phone now?"

"Hello, Mom. I thought it was Duffy."

"Where are you?"

"I'm working."

"That's not what I mean. Everyone's here but you. It's the first night of Hanukkah."

"I thought it was tomorrow night."

"What's wrong with you, Asher?"

"I've been really busy on a case."

"So what else is new? How was your weekend?"

"It was cut short."

"Cut short?" she said. "I thought you and Robin had a romantic weekend in Santa Barbara?"

"Who told you that?"

"Your brother."

"That loudmouth. He wasn't supposed to say anything."

"Well? How was your romantic weekend with Robin before it got cut short?"

"That's not something I want to discuss right now."

"When can you get here?"

"About twenty minutes."

"Hurry, or we'll light the candles without you."

It was almost dark when I peeled off the freeway at Fairfax, cut east on Pico, drove about a mile, and then swung a few blocks south and parked in front of the duplex where I'd grown up and where my mother still lived. I paused on the sidewalk and looked around. The street was lined with run-down apartment buildings with oil-stained driveways and dusty patches of dirt instead of lawns. I could see the spray-painted tags of the Mansfield Family Crips on a few of the garage doors.

When I was a kid, the neighborhood was mostly Jewish. Now most of the apartments were hung with Christmas lights, and I could see trees, festooned with ornaments, in many of the windows. Rap and loud Mexican ranchera music blared from the apartment building next door to my mother's Spanish-style duplex. I passed beneath the Moorish archway, large chips of paint peeling from the stucco, walked over the cracked tiles in the courtyard, touched two fingers to the mezuzah on the door frame, gave them an distracted kiss, and rang the bell.

The door cracked open. "Nice of you to grace us with your presence, Asher," my mother said sarcastically. Short, fair, and freckled, with lacquered red hair, she generated such an aura of intensity that when she spoke, people instinctively stepped back. "I wanted to light the candles five minutes ago, but Ariel wouldn't let me." I followed her into the living room. After my older brother Marty and I had moved out, my mother had decorated the living room entirely in shades of pale green:

the carpeting, the sofa, the lamps, and the walls. I felt slightly claustrophobic, as if I was trapped underwater.

Ariel, my eight-year-old nephew, dashed across the room and jumped into my arms. "I made them wait for you, Uncle Ash."

"Thanks, buddy."

"Did you bring me a present?"

"Of course."

Marty—a smaller, older, pudgier version of me—said, "Hey, bro, Happy Hanukkah."

I could never understand how a highly paid corporate lawyer could pick up a heroin-smoking habit. Marty had recently spent six weeks at a rehab center when his wife, Muriel, gave him the ultimatum: get clean or get divorced.

Muriel, tall and skinny with short red hair and nervous eyes, hugged me and whispered, "Ariel was so worried you wouldn't make it. Thanks for coming."

My eighty-four-year-old great-uncle Benny, who was bald, wizened, and hunched over, stood beside the sofa and waved to me. "Hey, boychik. Glad you decided that we were more important than one of your stiffs."

"Okay, okay," my mother said. "We've wasted enough time waiting for the big shot detective. It's time to—" She narrowed her eyes, her nose twitching like a rabbit. Looking up at me, she snapped, "Do I smell alcohol on your breath?"

"I just had a beer at home."

"That woman has a nose like a bloodhound," Benny said, chuckling.

"Drinking alone?" she said in an accusatory tone. "Do you have a drinking problem?"

"Big deal," I said. "A single beer."

"Coming *shiker* to the first night of Hanukkah *is* a big deal."

"That's ridiculous," I said. "I am not *shiker.*"

Benny shouted, "Just light the candles! Who wants to do the honors?"

"Since you used to live in Israel, your Hebrew's the best," Marty said. "You do it."

"It's been a long weekend. I'm fried. Why don't you?"

"Sure," Marty said. He lit a candle and used it to light another candle on the end of the big brass menorah.

"Do you know why we call the candle we use to light the others the *shamash*?" my mother asked Ariel.

"You ask me that every year," he said, trying to sound bored. "It means servant in Hebrew. Everybody knows that."

Marty stuck the *shamash* back in the candleholder and recited two Hanukkah prayers.

"Ariel," my mother said, "are we done with the prayers?"

"Yes," Ariel said. "Two prayers and then the presents."

"Wrong, Little Mr. Know-It-All. On the first night of Hanukkah we say a *third* prayer."

"I knew that," Ariel said sullenly.

She turned to Marty and said, "You spend more than twenty thousand dollars a year to send him to a Jewish day school, you'd think he'd learn how many prayers we say on the first night."

Marty hugged her with one arm and said, "Mom, will you do me a favor?"

"Of course."

"Shut up."

Marty recited the third prayer before she could respond.

"Can we open the presents now?" Ariel asked.

"After dinner," my mother said.

Ariel trudged off to the dining room table and slumped into a chair. As Marty, Benny, and I joined him at the table, my mother and Muriel served plates layered with braised brisket, latkes, and sautéed green beans. Uncle Benny uncorked a bottle of red wine and filled all the glasses—except Marty's. I reached across the table for the dish of applesauce and smeared a dollop on each latke.

"That's Muriel's homemade applesauce," my mother said with pride. "Works all week as a psychologist and she still has time to make her Hanukkah applesauce."

The applesauce was so sour I felt like spitting it out.

"What's wrong?" my mother asked.

"Tart—just how I like it."

"Muriel's like Robin," my mother said. "A professional woman who still knows her way around a kitchen." I nibbled the latke, staring at my plate, hoping someone would change the subject.

"A little while ago, on the phone, you were telling me about your romantic weekend to Santa Barbara with Robin."

"I was *not* telling you about the weekend," I said.

"Well, why don't you tell us now. How *was* the weekend?"

"Like I said on the phone, it got cut short. I caught a case."

"Well, at least you got to spend *some* time, just the two of you. When are you and Robin coming to your senses and getting back together?"

"That's not a subject I wish to discuss right now."

"You're not getting any younger. You're going to end up an *alter kocker* living by yourself. And why? Because the murder of a stranger is more important to you than your own wife."

Muriel covered Ariel's ears. "Estelle. I don't want him hearing about M-U-R-D-E-R," she said, whispering the letters.

Marty winced. "Does every family gathering have to end up like this?"

Benny pinched my cheek. "We're all worried about you. Don't be a schmuck."

I lifted a fork and dinged it against my wineglass. "Everybody listen up. Because after this announcement, the subject is closed." I glared at my mother and said, "And I mean closed. I will not discuss it further." I drained my glass and said, "We separated two years ago. All of you know that. It wasn't my choice. But that's just the way it is. This weekend didn't work out. I don't know what's going to happen in the future with Robin and me. But I do know that I don't want to discuss it. So that's it. End of discussion."

My mother smiled broadly. "So there's hope?"

"Like I said, 'End of discussion.'"

For the next few minutes the dining room was filled with the sounds of forks and knives clattering against plates, the slurping of wine, small talk about all the changes in the neighborhood. "When are we opening the presents?" Ariel asked.

"After we clear the table," my mother said as she stood.

Muriel clasped her shoulder and pushed her back down. "Estelle, sit. We'll take care of it." She and Marty cleared the dishes, and I rinsed them—twice—because I knew how particular my mother was, and put them in the dishwasher. When we finished, Ariel began playing dreidel with Uncle Benny and Muriel. Marty stood by the picture window, staring out at a group of young Hispanic men, their forearms scrolled with tattoos, wearing baggy black pants and oversized white T-shirts, sitting on the curb, smoking and drinking beer.

"We gotta get Mom out of this neighborhood," Marty said.

"I've tried. But she refuses."

I crooked my arm around Marty's shoulder. "How're you doing?"

"I've got seventy-nine days clean and sober. I'm still doing it one day at a time," he said with a wry smile. "What's up with you and Robin? I can ask you this, because, after all, I fixed you up with her. Any chance it's going to work out?"

I smiled and crossed my fingers.

"My money's on you, bro. Lay some of that patented Levine charm on her."

My mother returned to the living room with a tray of coffee and jelly donuts while the family gathered on the sofa or the celery-green up-holstered chairs.

"When I lived in Israel, all the bakeries made jelly donuts for Hanukkah," I said.

"Why?" Ariel asked.

"Because of the oil. Just like the latkes. The oil represents the mir-acle—"

"*Now* can I open my presents?" Ariel interrupted.

"Yes," Marty said. "Whose present do you want to open first?"

"I don't care. I just want to open Uncle Ash's present last. He al-ways gives me the best one."

Marty disappeared into a back bedroom and a moment later rolled out a new Trek bicycle, black with bright yellow trim. Ariel scrambled onto the seat, gripped the handlebars, and said, "Thanks, Dad. Thanks, Mom."

"Not in the house!" My mother shouted. She crouched beside the bike and inspected the carpeting. "If you've stained this, Marty, I'll kill you."

"What's next?" Ariel said, looking frenzied.

Benny presented him with a slender, rectangular gift-wrapped box. Ariel tore off the ribbon, ripped the paper, and wrestled out a skate-board. "I can't wait to ride it," Ariel said. "It'll get me ready to go surfing with Uncle Ash, when he thinks I'm old enough."

Benny whispered to me, "I got it for half price, downtown, in the toy district."

My mother handed Ariel an envelope. "This is a check. For your college education."

"Thank you, Nana," he said in a monotone, kissing her on the cheek.

"Now you, Uncle Ash," Ariel said, eyes shining.

"One second," I said, hustling out the door. I eased the surfboard out of the back of my Saturn and deposited it at the front door. I whistled and Ariel bolted out, spotted the board, and shrieked, "Yes!" He grinned and hugged me.

A moment later, while Ariel admired the board, Muriel motioned me inside the house. "Do you know how dangerous surfing is?" she asked.

"Are you meshuga?" my mom chimed in. "He's only eight years old."

"My friend Zoe Liebenthal's son broke his nose surfing," Muriel said. "My son's not getting anywhere near that board."

Ariel stomped inside the house and shouted to his mother, "Yes, I am! You're ruining Hanukkah for me! I hate you!" He burst into tears.

Muriel looked stricken. She tried to hug Ariel, but he pulled away. "Well, maybe when you're a little older," she said. "But you have to take lessons, first. I insist on that because—"

"Listen up, everyone," I shouted. "We'll continue this conversation for another time. But I've gotta get to work. I'm on a big case and I have an interview tonight." Before anyone could respond, I hustled out the door and into my car, burned rubber, screeched around the corner, and roared toward the freeway.

Back home I collapsed onto the sofa and shut my eyes, savoring the quietude of the empty loft. When was the next major Jewish holiday? In the spring. I felt a wave of relief. I needed a four-month break before the next big family gathering.

I could hear the Santa Anas blasting through the urban canyons, whistling between the tall buildings, sending cans and boxes and other downtown detritus skittering down the sidewalks. I raked my hand through my hair, which crackled with electricity, and licked my lips, cracked from the parched desert air. I wished I had some ChapStick and a bottle of hand lotion. My fingers were as dry and scaly as a snake's.

I called Robin and said, "I was thinking of stopping by."

"I know what that means," she said, laughing. "In court today, I was a wreck. I've got to get some sleep tonight. I have a big cross tomorrow. But this weekend, I'm all yours."

PART V

A RIGHTEOUS SHOOTING

CHAPTER 31

The streets were quiet the next morning as I ambled up Main to PAB. Only two days until Christmas, and many of the downtown workers had the week off. The cavernous fifth-floor squad room, which housed all the RHD units, was only about a quarter full, and many of the detectives who remained were chatting at their cubicles, getting an early start on the holiday.

As I dropped my briefcase on my desk, Duffy stuck his head out of his office and called out, "Ash, I need to see you."

I entered his office. He looked as if he'd had a rough night. His face was puffy, his eyes red-rimmed and watery, and he seemed uncharacteristically somber.

"The case," I said, "has taken an interesting—"

"Grazzo wants to see you."

"Now?"

"Right now."

"What's it about?"

"I don't know what it's about," he said, raising both palms. "That's the truth." I knew he was lying.

I rode the elevator to the tenth floor, wandered down the hall until I found Assistant Chief Vincent Grazzo's office, and rapped on the door. Without greeting me, he jabbed a finger at the chair opposite his desk. The last time I'd seen Grazzo he was at least fifty pounds overweight and could barely squeeze into his midnight-blue LAPD uniform. I'd heard that he'd had lap-band surgery, but I was surprised at how thin he was. Now he was as skinny and wrinkled as some prospector who had just wandered down the side of a mountain on a burro.

Grazzo sipped from his *Semper Fidelis* coffee cup and said, "You've got a big problem. Which means this department's got a big problem."

"Yeah?" I said warily.

"The shooting's squirrelly."

"What shooting?"

"*Your* shooting."

"That was a righteous shooting. Self-defense from the gate."

Grazzo massaged his Adam's apple with his thumb and forefinger. "It's out of policy. You said the shooter fired at you multiple times, but the Force Investigation detectives couldn't find any points of impact or projectile perforations on the building behind you."

"That can happen."

"It can, but you've got a bigger problem. No gun."

"What do you mean, no gun?"

"Nobody could find a gun at the scene. The uniforms couldn't find it. The Force Investigation detectives couldn't find it."

"I saw the fucking gun. It was a chrome revolver. I saw him aim at me. I heard the shots. The G.S.R. on the vic has got to back me up." I knew the coroner tested the hands of all victims of controversial shootings—when self-defense is an issue—for gunshot residue.

Grazzo cut the air with a palm. "Negative."

"What do you mean negative?"

"The test was negative."

"That doesn't make sense. I saw the muzzle flash."

"You've always done things your own way," Grazzo said smugly. "The Israeli Army cowboy way. You've never much respected the LAPD way. If you had, if you'd followed LAPD guidelines when confronted with a threat, you might have saved this department a lot of embarrassment and a lot of problems. I don't care if you were in Special Forces over there."

"I wasn't. I was in a paratrooper unit."

"Doesn't matter what you did in Israel. Over here, once again, you've shown poor judgment. You might have shot an unarmed man without provocation. Now we've got to clean up your mess. Because—"

I leapt to my feet and bolted from his office, slammed the door, hurried down seven flights of stairs, and burst into Duffy's office. "This is fucked up."

"It gets worse," Duffy said. "A shyster, Wally Petrinos, dug up an aunt of the shooter and is filing a civil suit against you and the department. Says you racially profiled the guy. Claims you panicked because he was a Mexican, mistakenly assumed he was going to jack you, and shot him in cold blood."

"That's insane. What the fuck is going on? That guy didn't look Mexican."

Duffy shrugged. "Patrinos is a total sleaze. The shooter's name was Alex Mullin, but his middle name is Sanchez, so Patrinos is running with that."

"I can't believe this shit."

"That's not the worst part, Ash," Duffy said softly. "The DA's looking into filing charges against you. Grazzo says I've got to suspend you. But here's a bit of good news. You're being suspended *with* pay."

"I'm overjoyed."

"So you're off duty until the investigation is finished and the DA makes the call on whether to prosecute."

"Prosecute for what?"

Duffy sucked in a deep breath and slowly let it out, the air whistling through clenched teeth. "If you're lucky, manslaughter."

My chest constricted, and I couldn't breathe. Sweat dripped down my rib cage. My throat was so dry I could barely speak. "What's going on here?" I croaked.

"It's the gun that no one can find. They're basing their whole case on that."

"And the upcoming election?"

"That dickhead of a DA needs the Latino vote to get elected. He thinks that by going after you he's going to win over the East Side and Pico Union."

"Jesus," I muttered. "I can't believe this."

Duffy gazed at me with a compassionate expression, and said earnestly, "Is it possible that you just *thought* the guy had a gun, that you made an honest mistake?"

My forehead was hot, feverish. I was truly frightened now. I've asked countless suspects the same kind of question, with the same tone of mock sympathy. Now I was on the other side, and I felt my stomach clench.

"Let me make this as clear as I can," I said. "Asshole had a gun and he was firing it at me."

When Duffy saw I wasn't going to deviate from my story, his expression hardened. "One more thing working against you," he said flatly. "There's a wit. He claims he saw the whole thing. He says there wasn't any gun. He says the guy was just asking for directions and you whirled around and started blasting him."

"That's total bullshit! The guy's a fucking liar. This is some kind of setup. Who is the wit?"

"You know I can't tell you that."

"Have they polyed him?"

"Not yet. The investigation is in its early stages."

My heart hammered in my chest. I couldn't breathe for a moment. All the colors in Duffy's office faded to gray. I dropped my chin to my chest and dug my fingernails into my throbbing temples. Duffy was saying something, but his words were garbled. I glanced up at him. "I don't understand."

"You better hand them over."

"This is a bogus beef and you know it."

"I hate to do this, Ash, I really do."

I unclipped my badge from my belt, slipped my gun from my holster, my ID card from my wallet, and dumped them on the desk. "I want an honest answer from you. Do you believe me?"

"Sure I believe you, Ash." His tone wasn't convincing.

"So now what?"

"Lay low. Wait it out. Hope for the best. Another piece of good news, as you know, the Police Protective League will provide you with a lawyer. You don't pay a thing. And they hire some of the heaviest hitters in the city. I'm talking big names. So call the League ASAP and set up an appointment."

He scrawled something on a notebook, tore out the page, and handed it to me. "I'm the product of a good Jesuit education with three years of high school Latin. Here's something that might give you some guidance during this difficult time."

I stuffed the note in my pocket, pushed myself out of the chair, and stumbled through the squad room. As I wandered, dazed, out the building, I considered what would happen if the DA filed manslaughter charges against me; if I was tried; if I was convicted; if I was sent to prison. I thought of the worst moments of my life: When my best friend in the IDF, Ilan, was atomized by a Hezbollah RPG. When the wit I'd had promised to protect and moved into a safe house, was gunned down. When her family filed a lawsuit against me and I was suspended. When

Robin told me it was over. When my father died. But I couldn't remember feeling as fucking low as I felt right now.

Oscar Ortiz caught up with me in the PAB lobby. "Anything I can do?"

I shook my head. "I'm drowning here, but I don't want to take anyone down with me."

"Don't worry about that, homes. You just let me know how I can help."

"Thanks."

He clapped me on the shoulder. "Don't let the bastards get you down."

As I wandered out the front door of PAB, my eyes misted and my throat tightened. I wondered if I would ever again work as a police officer. What the hell would I do? I didn't know how to do anything else. How would I ever get a job with a felony conviction on my jacket? Now I couldn't even investigate the most important case of my life. Where would I start? Duffy had shut me down and shut me out. I had no access to the victim's body, to the LAPD computer files, to the victim's records, to the ballistics report, to *anything* connected to the investigation. I couldn't call in any chits, either. Since I was the subject of the investigation, no cop would risk his pension by feeding me sub rosa data or documents.

I lingered at the corner of Second and Spring and sucked in a few deep breaths, hoping to quell my panic. My headache was so bad I could barely see across the street. I couldn't think. I was never much of a drinker, but maybe a few pops would calm me down enough so I could figure out what to do. I walked down to Eighth Street, cut over to Grand, passed the run-down Hotel Stillwell and, next door, lingered outside Hank's Bar, staring at the sign outside, DELIGHTFUL DINING AND DRINKING. I didn't want a trendy place where they served cocktails in jam jars or featured thirty-dollar shots of single malt Scotch. I needed a dive bar. I staggered into the dim tavern, paneled in dark wood, climbed up on a stool at the bar next to a rheumy-eyed pensioiner staring into his beer, and ordered a draft and a shot of Jim Beam. While waiting for the drinks, I stared at the turtle flapping around in the aquarium behind the bar and spotted a sign: WELCOME TO HANK'S. WHERE EVERYBODY KNOWS YOUR NAME. EVERYBODY IS GLAD YOU CAME. I flinched when the bartender dropped my drinks on the wooden counter. I downed the whiskey in a gulp. It tasted like hell, but I was intent on getting drunk. How could Duffy drink these boilermakers and enjoy them? I guess the cliché was true: Jews can't drink. I ordered another round.

I thought back to the meeting with Duffy, and squinted at the piece of paper that he had scrawled on, but I couldn't read a single word; it was all in Latin. After I downed another round, my cell phone rang and, without thinking, I answered it. It was the Asian detective from the Force Investigation Division.

"We'd like to talk to you, Ash."

I didn't respond.

"We have a wit. We got his side of the story. We'd like you to come in so we can talk to you and get your side."

Hundreds of times I'd wondered why suspects, after being Mirandized, still blabbed their way to the joint when they could have simply kept silent until their attorneys arrived. I've always told friends and family if they got arrested they should keep their mouths shut until they talked to their lawyers, even if they were innocent. I decided to heed my own advice. I clicked off the phone and ordered a third round. After I drained my bourbon and beer, I was still too anxious to think clearly. I tossed two twenties on the bar, walked out, and called Robin's cell.

"Hello, Ash," she answered.

"Where are you?"

"I'm in my office. I'm supposed to be in court, but the judge had emergency root canal surgery this morning so we're dark today."

"Can I stop by your office? I have to talk to you."

"Meet me at the Starbucks on the ground floor."

"I'll be there in fifteen minutes."

Robin was waiting at a corner table dressed in a navy pinstripe suit, white silk blouse, a string of pearls from Tiffany's and matching earrings. I'd bought the jewelry for her on our fifth wedding anniversary. She was sipping a latte.

I stumbled into a chair across from her, and she said, "I heard."

"Heard what?"

"I've got a friend from law school who works in the DA's office. She filled me in."

"When do you get off? I really need to be with you right now."

She fiddled with a pearl earring and stared into her latte. "Listen, Ash, I know this is a tough time for you. I feel for you. I really do. But I'm coming up for partner this spring. You know my firm evaluates the spouses and significant others of all the potential partners. My firm is very, very image conscious. I'm a lock for partner now, but this kind of controversial incident could very well derail me."

"So that's why you didn't want me coming to your office, why you wanted to meet at Starbucks. You don't even want to be seen with me."

"If this was a freak thing, I might have some hope we could get through it. But you know how you are, Ash. You can't just get along, like other detectives. You're always pushing it. The department tells you to stand up and you sit down. They tell you to do X, but not Y; so you do Y and not X. You think you know more about police work than anyone else, and you won't listen to a damn thing anybody says. I've changed. And I thought you had, too."

"I have changed. And this *was* a freak thing."

"I don't know, Ash. Right now, it feels just like the old days. Being with you is like subscribing to the crisis-of-the-month club. I know that even if you squirm out of this one, there'll be another crisis next month. There always is with you. You do crazy things without thinking of the consequences. You always have. And I'm tired of having to deal with the consequences, afraid I'm going to see you on the front page of the *Times*, for the wrong reasons. So, no, I'm not going to risk everything for you."

"Tell me what I did that was so crazy."

"My DA source told me you didn't follow LAPD policy. She told me you shot an unarmed man."

"And you believe that?"

She flashed me a look that was as cold and devoid of emotion as any killer I'd ever hooked and booked for murder. "It's over," she said.

I stood and teetered toward the door.

"Ash," she called out in a loud whisper.

I pivoted toward her, my stomach lurching.

"Get a good lawyer."

I jolted awake, my throat so dry I couldn't swallow. Where the hell was I? What happened last night? I flipped on my side. I was in a bed I didn't recognize. The sheets were pale blue and felt like satin. Next to me, a woman with a small diamond stud in her nose slept on her back. I had no idea who she was. I inched forward. She appeared to be in her early thirties with smeared red lipstick and blonde hair with dark roots. I pushed myself out of bed and onto my feet, but my headache was so intense I almost toppled over. After negotiating my way in the dark and finding the bathroom, I stuck my head in the toilet and, in a hot, blistering cascade, vomited, followed by several minutes of dry retching and coughing. I fell to the floor, and when I felt the cold tiles on my stomach, I realized I was naked.

I tiptoed back into the room and spent several minutes tracking down my clothing. A sock was beneath the bed. The other sock was flung onto a chair. My Jockeys were on the bedpost, my pants were crumpled in the doorway, and my shirt was draped over a lamp. Her panties, jeans, and bra were piled across my shoes. I've reconstructed hundreds of cryptic crime scenes, so this scenario was pretty easy to figure out. But my memory was still hazy. I remember talking to Robin, making my way back to Hank's, ordering another beer. I closed my eyes, nauseous and dizzy, as I tried to recall the previous evening. At Hank's, I drank more beer and, eventually, bought a round of drinks for three loud, raucous, women at the other end of the bar who worked as secretaries for the city planning department, one of whom had blonde hair and a tiny diamond nose stud.

I dressed and as I crept out of the room, the woman murmured sleepily in a smoker's raspy voice, "Call me."

"Sure," I said, trying to escape as quickly as I could.

Outside her ground-floor apartment, I circled around a small swimming pool, through the front gate, and onto the street. It was dark out, and I had no idea where I was. The street was flanked by blocky three- and four-story apartment buildings, ringed by ficus trees and giant bird-of-paradise plants. I clicked on my cell and checked the time. It was 4:15 in the morning. I called Yellow Cab, glanced at the street signs on the corner, and gave them the intersection.

I stamped my feet to keep warm, recalling fragments of my conversation with Duffy, and wished that I was still asleep, or vomiting, or drinking myself insensate, anything to mask the memory of what had happened and the fear of what I faced. The cab finally arrived. Twenty minutes later it skidded to a stop in front of my loft. I rode the elevator up to the top floor, opened my front door, and when I spotted someone sprawled on my couch, asleep, I reached for my gun—which wasn't there. Quietly unplugging the table lamp, I wrapped the cord around the base, and approached the couch.

My brother opened his eyes and abruptly sat up. "Don't you have enough problems without adding fratricide to the list?" he shouted.

"How'd you get in?"

"You gave me a key last year, remember? Where have you been? You don't answer your cell. You stay out all night. I've been worried about you, bro. I want to help you."

I slumped on the couch. "Nobody can help me," I said, embarrassed by the tinge of pity in my voice.

"You hung over?"

"Very."

"Sit," he commanded.

A few minutes later he brought me a tall glass of water, three Tylenol, and two slices of buttered toast. I gulped the water, ate a piece of toast, and swallowed the Tylenol. After dropping my head in my palms, I muttered, "My life is over."

"You just gotta get through the next week or two. You can figure out what really happened and—"

"How can I? I'm not a detective any more."

"The detectives who are investigating the shooting will figure it out."

"How do you know so much about the case?"

"I've got a friend in the DA's office."

"You, too? Robin knew all about it."

"It's the Yiddish lawyer grapevine, bro."

"I'm fucked, Marty."

"You need to calm down. And fortunately I have something that will help you." He yanked a vial out of his right front pocket, shook out two large white pills, and dropped them in my palm. "Take these. You'll wake up in about four to six hours and you'll feel better, calmer. I prom- ise." He retrieved another vial from his left front pocket and set it on the coffee table. "For the next few weeks, when you're starting to get real anxious, take one of these. They'll cool you out."

"What are they?"

"You don't want to know."

"Tell me."

"It's something I used to take in the old days, when I was in prehab. I'm clean and sober now. I stay away from that shit. But you need some industrial-strength chill pills. And these make Valiums feel like M&Ms."

I swallowed the two pills he'd handed me and finished the water. By the time he brought me another glass of water, I was already feeling drowsy. I took a few sips.

"Time to hit the sack," he said.

After I undressed, I sat on the edge of the bed for a minute, massaging my temples, then crawled under the covers and fell asleep.

CHAPTER 32

"What time is it?" I asked groggily, looking up at Marty as he shook me awake.

"It's two."

"A.m. or p.m.?"

"P.m. You slept a good seven or eight hours."

"What're you doing here?"

"I called the Protective League and set up the appointment with your attorney. We've got a three o'clock appointment."

He gripped my shoulders and led me toward the shower. I turned on a blast of cold water, trying to clear my head. After I'd dried off and dressed, Marty called me over to the sofa. He'd made me a cup of coffee, two scrambled eggs, and two pieces of rye toast.

I sipped the coffee and said, "I'm not hungry."

"Force yourself. You need something in your stomach to counteract that Mickey Finn I gave you last night."

"What the hell was that?"

"Like I told you, you don't want to know. I gotta give you plausible deniability. You're a cop."

"Not any more." I pushed aside the plate of eggs. "I've lost my job, my pension, my reputation. I've lost everything, and I can't do a thing about it."

"We'll talk to the lawyer and—"

"You know the worst place in the world for an ex-cop? Prison. And that's where I'm headed."

Marty crossed the room, filled a glass of water from the sink, and shook out a large white pill from a vial. I swallowed the pill and drained the glass. Within a few minutes my pulse slowed and my panic subsided.

"Why do we have to see the lawyer?" I asked, my voice sounding strange to me because I was slurring my words.

"Gotta take care of business. Make sure you don't do anything stupid."

I followed Marty out of the loft, down the elevator, to his new midnight-blue Mercedes CLS. We cruised west on the Santa Monica Freeway. "I still can't believe you'd buy a German car after what happened to Dad and his family."

"Are you going to hold a grudge for a hundred years? It's a different world today."

"In some ways, yes; in some ways, no."

"I read an article in the paper a few weeks ago that helped me figure you out, bro. Some Austrian psychiatrist said there's something called the torchbearer syndrome. It's supposed to be common in Holocaust families. There's always one person in the next generation, or the generation after that, who's fixated by the family stories, the history, all the stuff in the past. This is a person who just can't let it go. Guess who's the torchbearer in our family?"

I shrugged off his question, and we rode in silence the rest of the way. He turned off the freeway at Robertson, drove up to Beverly Hills, and parked beneath a gleaming new four-story office building, inlaid with strips of pale-pink marble, a half block north of Wilshire. As we rode the elevator up to the eleventh floor, Marty said, "I leaned on the rep at the League, made a few calls, pulled a few strings, and got you the best defense lawyer in the city: Marv Romanoff. You know what they call him, don't you?"

"Yeah. Get-'em-off Romanoff."

"He's busy as hell and isn't taking new cases right now, but my firm has sent him a few big clients, so he owes me one. This is how I'm collecting."

Marty gave the receptionist our names, and she directed us to the end of a long hall flanked by the cluttered offices of the associates, which were almost all empty because it was Christmas Eve. Romanoff's door was ajar. With a phone cradled beneath his chin, he motioned us to wait on the black leather sofa opposite his desk. His office was almost the size of my loft, a vast, walnut-paneled expanse, one wall lined with framed newspaper stories about his biggest cases and magazine profiles, and on the other wall framed pictures of him with athletes and politicians and Israeli ambassadors.

Romanoff held the phone out, muffled the receiver with his palm, and whispered to us, "This will only take a sec. I'm helping out a friend of my mother's. You won't believe this conversation." He clicked on the speakerphone and winked at us.

"Why don't you call the Anti-Defamation League, Mr. Cohen," Romanoff said.

"They won't do anything. And this is a clear case of anti-Semitism."

"I'm sorry your grandson didn't get into the camp for his winter break, but I hardly think it's anti-Semitism that kept him out, Mr. Cohen."

"I know anti-Semitism when I see it. I've been dealing with it my whole life."

"Then you should know that this is something entirely different."

"And you call yourself a lawyer. You wouldn't know a case if it bit you in the *tuchas*," Mr. Romanoff. "I'm telling you this is a very big lawsuit I'm dropping in your lap. But it's not about the money."

"Of course not."

"It's the principle of the thing. I want those anti-Semites to get what's coming to them."

"And to get your grandson in the camp."

"That's right."

"Did you talk to your son about helping you? He's a lawyer."

He snorted. "A tax lawyer. My son's a pencil pusher, a complete *luft-mentsh*. He doesn't know how to rattle cages and get things done."

"Maybe you shouldn't have sent in your application at the last minute."

"What's that got to do with it?"

"For God's sake, Mr. Cohen, listen to me!" Romanoff bellowed, no longer amused. "How could it be anti-Semitism? It's a Jewish camp, for God's sake. It's affiliated with the temple!"

He hung up and twirled his chair toward us. "That man's a nudnik. It's the third time he's called this week. That's the last time I offer any pro bono services to friends of the family." He stood and said, "Good to see you, Marty. Nice to meet you, Ash." He shook our hands and eased back into his chair. Romanoff looked like he was in his early seventies, but a nervous energy, a vitality, made him seem younger. Bald, with a fringe of reddish-silver hair, he was dressed as if he was about to leave for the golf course: tan slacks, a pink polo shirt, and a pale green sweater.

"Thanks for seeing us on Christmas Eve," Marty said.

"What's that?" Romanoff asked, in mock confusion. "All I know from is Hanukkah."

"Well, thanks for seeing us during Hanukkah."

"Anything for you, Marty. I know the league pays legal bills for cops, but they might squawk at my rates. I usually charge an arm and a leg, but for your brother I'm only going to charge an arm."

"I appreciate that," Marty said. "So, how does it look now?"

"Doesn't matter how it looks now. What matters is how it will look in front of a jury."

"A jury, Jesus Christ," I muttered. My face felt hot and sweat pebbled my forehead.

"Don't worry, Ash. It probably won't even get that far."

"What angle you going to take?" Marty asked.

"As you know, Ash will never be on trial."

I felt a tinge of relief. Romanoff glanced at me and said, "I mean that metaphorically. The first person who'll be on trial will be the victim. I've got some of the best investigators in the business. A few ex-RHD guys you might know. If this guy ever got a ticket for jaywalking, if he ever spit on the sidewalk, if he ever cheated on his wife, if he ever farted in church, I'll know about it. By the time I get through dirtying him up, the jurors will think he was the shooter and you were the victim. Then we'll put the witness on trial. I'll make him look like a cross between Osama bin Laden and Jack the Ripper. The jury will think every word he said was a lie, including 'and' and 'the.'"

Marty was beaming. "You're the best, Marv. When Ash got into this trouble, I told my wife we gotta call Get-'em-off. I feel a lot better already."

"Ash," Romanoff said, "you look like you've got *shpilkes*, like you're going to jump out of your skin. Don't worry so much. I had a case last year, a cop from Inglewood P.D. who shot some *shvartze* in an alley who was just taking out his trash. Why? Who the hell knows. And this victim had a job and a family, not like the putz who had the unfortunate encounter with you. By the way, during the trial we'll never refer to this as a shooting, just an unfortunate encounter. So, by the time I finished with this *shvartze*, the jury was practically thanking the cop for getting rid of a cancer on society and making the world a better place. So my strategy—"

"I didn't do it," I interrupted.

"What?" Romanoff asked, distracted.

"I didn't shoot an unarmed man. I saw him aiming the revolver. I saw the muzzle flash. It was a righteous shooting. It was self-defense all the way."

"Fine, fine," Romanoff said impatiently. "All that will come out in good time."

"I was framed." I said, immediately feeling embarrassed because the words were such a hollow cliché. How many times had I heard the same protestations of innocence from suspects? How many clients had uttered the same exact words to Romanoff? The first thing you learn as a cop is that you never arrest anyone who is guilty. And the second thing you learn is the prisons are filled with innocent men.

"Yes, yes, that's good, of course," he said, sounding uninterested.

"So what's next?" I asked. "At what point would the DA decide to charge me?"

Romanoff held up a palm. "Whoa! Let's not get ahead of ourselves. At this point, all you have to remember is six simple words: Do. Not. Say. A. Fucking. Thing. *Fershteyn?*"

I felt like a child, being told what to do, what to say and not to say. How the hell did I get into this bind?

"Did you hear me, Ash? This is critical."

"I understand," I said.

"That means no talking to anyone. Not the detectives investigating the case. Not to the reporters. Not to any of your friends in the department."

"The detectives in the Force Investigation Division called me yesterday, but I hung up on them."

"Good boy."

"In a few days I'll have a better idea of what's happening," Romanoff said. "Why don't you call early next week, and we'll set up another appointment. Now let me have a little private time with your brother."

I waited in the lobby, and a few minutes later my brother ambled in, looking particularly downcast, but he flashed a forced smile. "You're in great hands, Ash. Nothing to worry about. You heard Romanoff."

"Yeah, I heard him."

"Well, cheer up. You got the best in the business representing you. If anyone can get you off, he can."

"But in the meantime, I've been suspended, I'll be ripped in the press, I'll be subjected to a humiliating trial and—"

"You're too negative, bro. I think you need to eat."

"You sound like Mom."

Marty laughed. "There's no problem too big that can't be solved with some decent deli. You up for Canter's?"

"Why not?"

Marty drove east on Wilshire, cut over to Sixth Street, and hung a left at Fairfax. Inside Canter's we lingered at the glass display case—packed with whipped cream cheese, knishes, whitefish, lox, chopped liver, and kosher salamis. I thought of my father.

"Remember what Dad would say?" I asked Marty.

He smiled wistfully. "In that thick German accent he'd say, 'Look at all this food. Achh! You American kids are so spoiled. You don't know what it is to be hungry.'" We slipped into a corner table, and Marty said, "We're upholding one half of the Levine family holiday tradition." My dad used to take Marty and me to Canter's for lunch every Christmas Eve, and on Christmas night our family, like many Jewish families in my neighborhood, would always dine at a Chinese restaurant. I scanned Canter's and felt my stomach tighten. When we were dating, Robin and I used to stop here after we'd check out a jazz set at the Catalina Bar & Grill. We'd talk for hours, one time until just before dawn. We drove out to Malibu and watched the sunrise. I had my board in my station wagon, so I caught some waves. We spent the rest of the morning at her place, in bed—A heavyset woman wandered over, breaking my reverie. "What'll it be, hon?" she asked.

"Coffee and *matzo brei*. With cinnamon and sugar on the side."

"Make it two," I said. This is what we always ordered when we were kids. Maybe because of the stress of the past few days we both craved familiar surroundings and Jewish comfort food. The waitress brought the coffee, and I stared into my cup. "This whole thing is fucked up. Every shooting I had in the IDF was by the book. Every shooting I had in the LAPD—including this one—was by the book. But Grazzo doesn't believe me. I don't even think Romanoff believes me."

"Shh," Marty said, raising an index finger to his lips. "You're shouting."

I glanced around. A few of the customers glared at me. "Somebody decided to lay me out, to fucking frame me," I said in a loud whisper. "And I've had it with everyone calling me a liar."

"You've got to stop feeling sorry for yourself."

"Right," I said without much enthusiasm.

"Let's see how well you know your Israeli history," Marty said. "During the early days of the Yom Kippur War when Israel was caught with its pants down and all those Egyptians crossed the Suez; when the Syrians knocked us off the Golan; when Moshe Dayan was freaking out and moaning how the country was doomed; when Golda Meir was crying and talking about suicide—"

"I know all about that," I said. "In Israel they call it 'The Black Day.' In the pit, where the IDF brass and Meir gathered, the mood was so low they called it 'the Holocaust basement.'"

"They were Jewish neurotics, which might be a redundancy," Marty said. "They were psycho-Semitic, just like you. But they were warriors." Meir went into the hall, smoked a cigarette, came back into the pit and said, 'Let's go back to work.' Dayan pulled himself together and assessed the battlefield. Then they launched one of the greatest counteroffensives in military history, kicked the asses of the Egyptians and the Syrians, and saved the country."

"What's your point?"

"Go in the hallway, smoke your cigarette, pull yourself together, and figure out how you're going to save your ass. Because nobody else is going to do it for you."

The waitress slid our dishes across the table. I stirred the dish of cinnamon with some sugar, sprinkled it over the *matzo brei*, and ate for the first time in more than twenty-four hours. When we finished, Marty dropped me off in front of my building.

I stood beside the car for a moment, feeling numb.

"Hang in there, Ash. It'll work out."

"Thanks for lining up Romanoff and coming with me today."

Before he drove off, he stuck his head out the window and said, "I know you, Ash. You always work better when you're pissed off. Leave the martyr routine to Mom. She's the pro."

CHAPTER 33

I staggered into my loft and kicked a chair across the room. Someone was trying to destroy my life and railroad me. But why? I was angry about the frame-up, I was angry at Grazzo, and I was angry at the DA. Grazzo had sold me out before the detectives had conducted much of an investigation. The DA's office was leaking the story and torpedoing my reputation. I wasn't angry at Duffy—he was just the conduit. While I was disappointed that he didn't extend himself to help me out, I wasn't surprised. Duffy always followed the route that served his own interests. I stood and rifled through my pockets for the note he'd handed me yesterday, but I couldn't find it. I searched for the pants I'd worn yesterday, found them balled up beside my bed, grabbed the note out of the pocket, and read it: *Cui licitus est finis, etiam licent media.*

After switching on my computer and Googling the words, I discovered that the phrase was a Jesuit motto: For whom the end is lawful, the means are also lawful. When Duffy was in high school, his Jesuit Latin teacher must have written it on the blackboard. This was also a typical Duffy move. He was telling me, in an oblique way, that if I could get information that would exonerate me, he would back me up. But if I tried, and failed, he'd help the DA prosecute my ass and push for my firing because I'd worked a case while on suspension.

Did Duffy want me to clear myself because he cared about me and believed that I was innocent? Or because it would make him look bad if one of his detectives was prosecuted and convicted?

Yes.

I didn't have much confidence in the Force Investigation detectives; they might just take the path of least resistance if the brass wanted me nailed to the wall. I had a lot more faith in my own investigative abilities.

Pacing my loft now, I realized that Duffy and Marty had told me the same thing. I couldn't sit on my ass and hope the investigation went my way. I had to hit the street and start knocking and talking. I needed to brace some of these assholes who had tried to bury me. If I had to violate a few dozen LAPD rules and regulations in order to clear this case, well—*Cui licitus est finis, etiam licent media.* It was worth the risk because the alternative was doing a dime at Tehachapi State Prison.

I picked up my phone and punched in the number for the LAPD's Records and Identifications Division. I said to the clerk, with as much bonhomie as I could muster, "You must have pissed someone off to be working on Christmas Eve."

"You got that right."

"This is Detective Ricky Brown over at Long Beach PD."

"So who'd you piss off to be working today?"

"It would be easier if I told you who I *didn't* piss off."

She laughed. "My kind of detective."

"I wonder if you could help me out, darlin'."

"What do you need?"

"A crime report. A RHD detective by the name of Asher Levine shot and killed a vic by the name of Alex Sanchez Mullin." I told her the time, date, and address of the shooting. "I heard through the ghetto grapevine that a witness to the shooting might be involved in a case I'm working in North Long Beach. You know what they say: Today's wit might be tomorrow's vic."

"You got that right."

"I need the name of that wit."

As I waited for her response, I felt a spasm of panic. What if she asked for a call-back number, for verification? Fortunately, I'd found a lazy clerk. "Lemme check," she said.

About two minutes later she said, "Aaron Ellison."

"You got an address for him?"

She yawned and gave me an Echo Park address.

"I really appreciate you helpin' me out."

"Merry Christmas."

"And a Merry Christmas to you."

I knew that Ricky Brown, whom I met on a case last year, had retired a few months ago to Belize, where he was born. It was unlikely anyone would ever follow up with him. I tried to plan out my next move, but I was still so jittery I couldn't concentrate, so I gulped down one of Marty's magic pills, drank a beer, and passed out on the sofa.

When I awoke I glanced at the west window and was surprised to see that it was dark. I checked my watch: 7:02. I stuffed my cuffs into my jacket pocket, jogged to the corner lot, started up the Saturn, and parked down the street from the PAB parking garage. I had turned in my badge, gun, and ID card, but not my car keys. Fortunately, the lot was deserted, so I walked to my Impala, flipped open my trunk, and snatched my flashlight and stun gun.

As I navigated through the deserted city streets, I could see Christmas trees in the windows of some loft buildings, and in the distance tiers of red-and-green lights on the tops of the Bunker Hill office towers. I never was too fond of traditional Christmas music, since it evoked a holiday my family never celebrated, but I've always liked Christmas jazz. I punched in KKJZ on my FM radio and listened to Kenny Burrell playing "Little Drummer Boy" as I hooked left on Sunset and right on Lemoyne, and climbed the hills of Echo Park, winding around streets until I parked down the street from Aaron Ellison's place. He lived in a peeling pink clapboard house that had been split into two apartments. Someone had wedged an old, stained mattress between two spiky yucca plants on the side of the house. The overgrown lawn was striated with weeds, and a pair of mottled Mexican fan palms, dense with dead, desiccated fronds, bordered the broken concrete pathway to the front door.

Before turning off my cell, I checked the time: 9:58, about two hours until Christmas. The duplex was dark, so I assumed he wasn't home, but I decided to reconnoiter to make sure. As I loped down the sidewalk, I realized the Santa Anas had died and the temperature had risen. A faint breeze from the west carried the scent of roses. It might be a sunny Christmas morning in the mid-seventies. Christmas lights, a few of them spelling out FELIZ NAVIDAD, adorned most of the houses, and a cottage on the corner displayed a crèche on the front lawn.

I soft-stepped around the side of Ellison's duplex, peered through a window, and inspected the living room and the kitchen, which were empty. Through a window in the back, I could see the bedroom. The bed was made and the lights were off. I returned to my car, hoping Ellison was at a Christmas party and would arrive within the next few hours, drunk enough so he'd be easy to handle.

Slumped behind the wheel, listening to the Christmas jazz, I kept my eyes on Ellison's front door. Marty's pills had calmed me down, but I was still so pissed off that I wasn't drowsy. I felt sharp enough to deal with Ellison, however he played it. A few minutes after midnight, an old Toyota weaved into the side of Ellison's duplex and a slight man, dressed in jeans and a bulky fishermen's sweater, climbed out and approached his front door. I jumped out of my car, hustled down the street, and called out in a cheery tone, like I was a long-lost friend, "Hey, isn't that Aaron Ellison?" It was a tactic I'd picked up from a process server who, years ago when I was a young detective, had tricked me into identifying myself before he slapped me with my first subpoena.

"Yeah." Ellison said warily.

I glanced around. I could see a few cars zipping by in the distance, but Ellison's street was quiet.

"Don't you remember me?"

A twitch of alarm passed across his face. "Take whatever—"

I gave him a Krav Maga hammer punch to the side of the neck. I cuffed him as he writhed on the sidewalk, hauled him to his feet, and led him to my station wagon, where I tossed him in the back. After I'd tied his ankles together with twine, blindfolded him with an old silk tie, and gagged him with a rag, I sped back downtown.

At my loft, I tore off the blindfold, kept him cuffed, and tied him to a chair. He was as small and wiry as a jockey, his feet barely touching the ground. I studied him for a moment. He was about thirty, but he had the features of someone much older: a bulbous nose flushed red, incipient jowls, and crow's-feet around his bloodshot eyes. He looked like a drunk who slept under an overpass. He reeked of alcohol and sweat, and I noticed that his hands shook.

"What's this all about?" he asked in a high squeaky voice, summoning up outrage that didn't sound genuine.

"I think you know."

"I don't know what the fuck is going on."

"Let's try the easy way first. How would you like a drink?"

"I won't say no."

"How about a cold beer? I can pour it in a frosty mug. You can chase it with a shot of Knob Creek. Very smooth. Aged nine years in a charred oak barrel."

"Please," he said.

"I'll serve them up if you answer one very simple question. Why'd you lie to the detectives about my shooting?"

"I don't know what you're talking about."

I recalled what Gideon Landau, my Sergeant Major in the IDF, used to say: "When force doesn't work, try more force." I had abducted Ellison, tied him up, and threatened him. And he still wouldn't talk. Now was the time to put Landau's adage into practice.

"Okay, Aaron. I guess we'll have to do it the hard way."

I taped his eyes and mouth shut with black duct tape, gripped his neck, and guided him to the roof of the building. In the corner was a heating unit, encased in heavy metal sheeting, about six feet off the ground. I slid a bench next to the unit, led Ellison on to the bench, and hoisted him to the top.

"Okay, Aaron. We're on the roof. On a ledge looking straight down. It's a twelve-story building, so you're about a hundred twenty feet from the concrete. One little push and you'll go splat on the sidewalk. Let me give you a preview of what you can expect."

Fortunately, Ellison was a lightweight. I crouched, clutched his knees, lifted him over my shoulder, and while he was squirming, gripped his ankles, swiveled around, and dangled him over the edge of the heating unit. The drop was only a few feet, but he didn't know that.

"Do you know how many bones there are in the human body, Aaron? Two hundred six. There's a good chance you could break all of them. Think of that moment of excruciating pain you'll have, right before you die."

I dropped him back onto the heating unit and listened to his muffled screams for a moment. "You ready to talk now?"

He jerked his head up and down. I ripped the tape off his mouth. "Talk."

He was hyperventilating, and between breaths said, "Somebody gave me some cash to say what I did, but I didn't know the guy, so I just did what he said, and told the detectives what I was told to say, but the guy was someone I'd never seen before and—"

I taped his mouth back up and dangled him again, this time for about a minute, until my shoulders burned and my neck throbbed from the strain. I pulled him up and said, "In this game, like baseball, it's three strikes and you're out. So if you bullshit me again, you're going overboard. So I'll ask you for the final time, you ready to level with me?"

Again, he nodded violently. I tore the tape off his mouth.

"The guy's name is Delfour."

"That's better. Let's get off this ledge and discuss the situation in a civilized manner."

Back in my loft, I tied him up again to the chair and set my briefcase—with the voice-activated digital recorder—next to him. "You mentioned the name Delfour."

"Can I get that drink?"

"First I want a little more information."

"Just a beer would be—"

"Let me guess. It all started in Iraq."

"That's right."

"Take it from the top."

He licked his lips and said, "I served with Sergeant Delfour. He was a Jew-maican."

"What's that?"

"He was from Jamaica, but grew up in New York. I'm from the East Coast myself. We call them Jew-maican, 'cause they ain't like regular niggers. They're pretty, smart, do good in school, save their money like, you know, Jews."

"I don't like that expression."

"Why not?"

"What's Delfour's first name?"

"Carlton."

"Third battalion?" I asked.

"Yes."

"Eighty-second Field Artillery?"

"Yes."

"First Cavalry Division?"

"That's right."

"You served with Teshay Winfield?"

"Yeah."

"And Mullin?"

He stuck out the tip of his tongue and pretended to spit. "That guy's a total scumbag. You did the world a favor by waxing that psycho."

"He was in your unit?"

"For a while. Until he got a bobtail."

"What's that?"

"Dishonorable discharge. Raped some Iraqi chick, but they couldn't prove it. So they got him on something else. You know he was a worthless piece of shit if they shipped his ass out of Iraq. That was a time they were desperate for bodies. Recruiters would take anyone with a pulse. And the guys who were in, well, they were stop-lossing everybody."

"When did he get discharged?"

"That was years ago, during my first tour."

"But Delfour kept in touch with him?"

"Apparently."

"When did you leave the service?"

"About a year ago."

"Delfour?"

"A few months earlier."

"So you and Delfour shot Winfield and Pinkney?"

"Whoa, whoa, whoa," he said, lifting his hands and shaking them, like a Bible-thumper in the grip of divine inspiration. "I'm just an errand boy. I didn't shoot anyone. Delfour contacted me a few days ago. Said he'd give me twenty thousand in cash to grab a gun off a dead guy. That's it. And that's all I did. And the only reason I did it was because the dead guy was going to be Mullin. Anyone else, I would have told Delfour to pound sand. But I was glad that someone was going to take Mullin out."

"Don't feed me a load of shit or—" I paused and jerked my thumb toward the roof.

"Listen to me. I've got a substance abuse problem."

"What substance?"

"I'm a fucking drunk. Delfour knows it. Everyone knows it. He doesn't trust me enough to kill anyone. My job was simple. When Mullin went down, grab the gun." He chewed the inside of his cheek. "How about that bourbon?"

"Run down the night you set me up."

"Delfour's a very uptight dude. He set this thing up military-like. Drew the whole thing out on a big piece of butcher paper. Even stayed at my place the previous twenty-four hours to make sure I was sober when the deal went down."

"So how'd it go down?"

"Mullin had the revolver. But there weren't any bullets. Just blanks. But Mullin didn't know that. The blanks were weighted down, so they felt right. You live on a pretty deserted street. Mullin was told to wait until night and make sure no one was around when he fired at you."

"Why was I set up?"

"That's intel way above my pay grade. My job was just to get the gun."

"Take a guess?"

"No idea. Delfour's a closed-mouthed SOB."

"So what happened to the gun?"

"Where's my boilermaker."

I retrieved a bottle of Sierra Nevada from the refrigerator, opened it, slipped it in his palm, and said, "Here's a cup of coffee."

Looking confused, he took a long pull. I didn't want anything on my digital recorder indicating that I'd given him alcohol because it could compromise the confession.

"What happened to the gun?"

He drained most of the Sierra Nevada. "After you blasted Mullin, you started taking fire from a different direction than where Mullin was, right?"

"Yeah."

"What did you do?"

"You tell me."

"First, you dove for cover. Then you moved toward the shots. You forgot all about Mullin. So while you were moving away from the body, I was moving toward it. I grabbed the gun. And I had plenty of time because you were so distracted trying to save your own ass."

"In fact," I said, "you had so much time, you wiped down Mullin's hands, and that's why they couldn't find any gunshot residue. What did you use?"

He guzzled the dregs of his ale. "One little Handi Wipe," he said.

"What did you do with the gun?"

"Dropped it in the trash right before the garbage man came by with the big truck."

"Shit," I muttered. The gun was probably at the bottom of some landfill now, rusting beneath a few tons of garbage. "What do you know about a valuable mask, covered in jewels, from Iraq?"

"Don't know nothin' 'bout that."

While he tipped the bottle, lapping the last drops of ale, I decided to ask him the money question. "You ever hear Delfour talk about a guy named Maksimov?"

"Never heard of the guy."

"Ziven?"

"Negative."

I figured Delfour was working for Maksimov, just like Ellison was working for Delfour.

I questioned him for a few more minutes, gave him another beer, questioned him some more, but couldn't get much more out of him. I tended to believe his explanation that he was a flunky hired to do one job and that he wasn't privy to Delfour's other plans. The only additional piece of information I gleaned was that Delfour had become friendly with Winfield's mother and had visited her several times. Ellison guessed they had a natural connection because they were both black. I had another take.

I untied Ellison from the chair and cuffed him. He stood and I said, "Sit down, shut up, and don't move."

I called Duffy's cell. "I want you to send someone to come by my place and cuff and stuff the lying sack of shit who was the wit on my shooting."

"What the . . . where are . . . who is going to . . .?" Duffy stammered, confused. He sounded like he was half in the bag, on one of his legendary benders. "Are you out of your fucking mind? You're only suspended, but Grazzo will fire your ass if he finds out you're working that case."

"I wasn't working the case. This wit comes by my house tonight, pays me a surprise visit, and tries to extort me. Says he'll change his testimony if I give him ten thousand dollars in cash. I got it all recorded, except for the money part, because I didn't have my recorder set up. But I got the part about why he set me up and how he and his partner tried to lay me out."

"I don't want any part of this."

"Okay, I'll make a citizen's arrest and walk him to Central Division myself."

"You're a pain in the ass, Ash, laying all this on me on Christmas Eve. Listen, Ortiz and Collins caught a case this morning. They're at the station writing reports. I'll send them by."

A few minutes later, the two detectives arrived. Collins, a dour, laconic newcomer I barely knew, said, "Let's all go to PAB and sort this out."

"I'm not leaving my loft. You can talk to me here."

Collins glanced at Ortiz, who said, "Let's do it his way."

My loft was one vast room, so Ortiz ushered Ellison into the hall, while Collins interviewed me. I told him a more elaborate version of the story I'd given Duffy. When I was done, Collins nudged open the door, and Ortiz led Ellison back into my loft.

"Hey!" Ellison shouted to Collins. "Like I told your partner, this guy abducted me from my home, took me to the roof, hung me over the side, and threatened to drop me if I didn't tell him what he wanted."

I jabbed a finger at Ellison. "This man is an acute alcoholic, subject to hallucinations and fantasies. After he tried to extort me, he blacked out for a while. I think you'll discover he's a pathological liar, suffering from sporadic memory loss, and an advanced case of the DTs."

Ortiz gripped Ellison's shoulders and shoved him out the door.

"I'll talk to Duffy and fill him in," Collins said as he followed Ortiz.

A few minutes later, I heard a knock on the door. I squinted through the peephole and saw Ortiz. When I swung open the door, he handed me a paper shopping bag.

"What's this?"

"After dragging me out on Christmas Eve, you deserve a punch in the jaw," he said with a crooked smile. "But in honor of our years of service together, I brought you some leftovers that my wife packed for me this morning: menudo and tamales. I was going to nuke it at the station's microwave. But after the night you've had, you need it more than me."

"Thanks," I said, choking up. "That means a lot to me."

"Happy Hanukkah, homes."

CHAPTER 34

Delfour figured the deal should be done in a few days and he could fly to Jamaica, buy a small Blue Mountain coffee plantation, and live the life of a gentleman farmer. He just had to take care of a few things—and the Aaron Ellison deal was at the top of the list. He did his job, and he did it pretty damn well. Unfortunately—for Ellison—instead of the twenty thousand dollar payoff he was expecting, he'd be receiving a B.O.D. payment—bullet on delivery. A .22 slug in the temple.

Delfour could never get used to Southern California and all its freeway numbers. When he mustered out of the army at Fort Hood and first arrived in L.A., and people discussed the various routes they commuted to work, it sounded like a foreign language to him. He must have acclimated and learned the language, he decided, as he mapped out his route to Echo Park: the 1 to the 22 to the 605 to the 210 to the 134 to the 2.

When he exited the 2, rolled south on Glendale Boulevard and hung a right, climbing a steep street into Echo Park, he felt a twinge of remorse. He'd been through a lot with Ellison. There were even times when he liked the weasely little wino. But now he was a liability, and the stakes were too high.

Delfour checked his watch, the numerals glowing in the shadows. Zero one hundred, Christmas morning. Right on time. Ellison was expecting him. He coasted in front of Ellison's duplex and—*What the hell?* Ellison's Toyota was there, but the lights were all off in the house. Maybe he'd passed out. Delfour reached into the glove box for a flashlight and opened the duplex door with the backup key Ellison had given him, but the place was quiet, the sofa empty, and the bed neatly made. *Where the hell was he?* That wasn't like Aaron. For a drunk, he was pretty damn punctual. And even a drunk will keep an appointment if he's expecting a sack of cash.

Delfour decided to examine Ellison's car again. He shined the flash-light ahead of him, peering inside the Toyota, and then lingered by the overgrown lawn. Crouching, he illuminated the area. A large patch of grass had been compressed, with small divots at the edges. It looked like an area where a man had fallen and, perhaps, struggled.

"Gordie won't like this," Delfour muttered. "Gordie won't like this one bit."

CHAPTER 35

It was dawn, Christmas morning, when I cut the engine in front of Mrs. Winfield's Oakwood bungalow. For the past decade, I'd surfed every Christmas morning, the best day of the year to catch some waves in Southern California without the crowds. Now, instead of paddling out to a break, I was trying to rescue my career, my reputation, and maybe my life. I didn't care if I woke Mrs. Winfield. She might be able to tell me how I could find Delfour, and he was the key to the case.

Since the Santa Anas had died, the prevailing winds from the ocean had picked up, blowing a damp breeze. The withered bougainvillea on the side of the house rattled fitfully against a window. I teetered up the creaky wooden stairs, stopping in the middle of the sagging wooden porch when I heard the faint sound of footsteps—or was it a radio or television—inside the house. I rang the bell. When no one answered, I rang again. Finally, I banged on the door and jiggled the knob, but it was locked.

I circled the house, past a listing fence draped with orange bugle vines, and inspected the back door, which was locked. But it rattled when I shook the knob, so there was plenty of give. With a swift knee to the rim of the door, it sprang open. I eased into the immaculate kitchen, its overhead light shining, the porcelain sink a lustrous white. The chrome faucet gleamed, and the floor emanated the faint scent of Pine-Sol. I recalled Winfield's tidy cottage and figured he'd learned his housekeeping skills from his mother, with the army providing the finishing school.

"Mrs. Winfield?" I called out. Leaning against the refrigerator, I held my breath for a moment, but still couldn't hear anything. The living room was dim, just the sunrise flushing the walls with a glimmer of light.

"Mrs. Winfield?" I shouted.

I edged my way across the living room and into the bedroom. A shape emerged from the closet. I reached for my gun, but there was nothing but air—no pistol, no holster. I glanced up: a tall slender black

man in his late-twenties loomed over me, aiming a blue steel Heckler &
Koch at my chest. I figured he was Delfour.

Why does the last thing I see before I die have to be a German gun?

"Stay down and put your hands to your side!" With precise diction,
he slowly enunciated each word. He was neatly dressed in blue slacks,
brown loafers, and a green cardigan sweater with a diamond pattern.
Delfour looked like a high school math teacher.

He waved the gun at a chair in the corner of the room. "Take a seat
nice and easy. No sudden moves."

I slowly backed into the chair, while he eased onto the edge of the
bed.

"I must be the stupidest cop in L.A.," I said with disgust. "Maksimov sets the trap for me and like a fucking sucker, I fall right in it."

"That's ex-cop," he said with a half smile.

"Where's Mrs. Winfield?"

"Do not talk until you are spoken to. Do you understand?"

I nodded faintly.

"I am going to ask you a few very basic questions about something
that I know you are very familiar with."

"Maksimov's got all the answers about the mask, not me."

"Do not say a word."

"Okay. But let me tell you one thing about Maksimov before you
get in any deeper. He's currently—"

The man jabbed the barrel of the HK at me. "If you answer my
questions, I may let you walk out of here. And if you don't—"

"I'll end up like Ambrose."

"I want that mask and I think you know where it is."

"I have no idea where it is."

"I have information that—" He broke off in mid-sentence and
cocked his head. I heard the back door swing open and rap against a
cabinet. Footsteps echoed in the kitchen.

"Levine, you there?" a voice called out.

Delfour inched toward me and said, "Shh," the sound a soft tremolo
as he pressed his index fingers to his lips.

"Careful!" I shouted, as I glimpsed out of the corner of my eye the
HK sweeping toward me. "He's got a—"

Then my head detonated and I saw, against a black background, a
corona of brilliant white flashes.

CHAPTER 36

"You been out all this time?"

I opened one eye. Duffy's big moon-shaped face and long narrow nose, striated by broken blood vessels, hovered over me. I fiddled with the controls and raised the hospital bed to a sitting position. "Naw. I came to in the ambulance. But I got tired out after the doctor here kept shining that light in my eyes and making me do stupid drills like naming the past five presidents, in reverse chronological order."

"How you feeling?"

I touched the thick bandage a few inches above my temple, a searing pain shooting from the side of my head to the base of my neck. "Terrible. How long you been here?"

"For a while. I was just talking to the doctor. He says you have a concussion. But your CT scan was clear. So it could have been much worse."

"When can I get out of here?"

"He wants you here at least one night. Maybe two."

I heard a shuffling in the corner of the room, craned my head, wincing, and saw FBI Agent Emery Peck studying me. "What's he doing here?" I asked Duffy.

"That's a fine thank you," Duffy said. "He'd be opening Christmas presents right now, but he saved your ass, so now he's here with you instead of with his family."

"How'd he save my ass?"

"He capped that shithead who banged you in the dome."

"Ah," I said. "It was *you* at the back door. What the hell were you doing there?"

"Staking out the house."

"Why?"

"We'd picked up on the wire Maksimov expressing a lot of interest in Mrs. Winfield's house."

"He's locked up."

"Apparently, he had an associate working for him. Unfortunately, the associate got there before me. But at least you got there a little after me."

"You're goddamn lucky he did," Duffy said.

"Is Mrs. Winfield okay? I didn't see her inside the house."

"Fortunately, she was at some prayer meeting when Maksimov's associate showed up."

"So you saw me go in," I said to Peck, raising the bed a few inches. "Why didn't you wave me down or back me up?"

Peck nervously glanced back and forth between Duffy and me. "I didn't know what to think. I knew you'd been suspended. I read the article in the paper. I knew you weren't supposed to be there. I wasn't sure what to do."

"So you sat around with your thumb up your ass," Duffy said.

"After a few minutes," Peck said, "I decided to find out what you were doing there and what you were looking for."

Duffy stepped toward Peck, hitching up his pants over his gut. "Normally, I'd be very pissed off and I'd be raising hell with your agent in charge for poaching on our case. But under the circumstances, it worked out pretty damn well. You agree, Ash?"

"I do. If we'd gone in the house together, the shooter could have dropped both of us." I kicked off the sheet and sat up. "Did you take him out?"

"He was in the ambulance right behind you," Peck said. "But he didn't make it."

Duffy pretended to wipe a tear from his eye. "I'm really broken up by that. The loss of any of God's children is a tragedy for us all."

"Who was he?" Peck asked me.

"His name is Delfour, but my head hurts too much to explain it all right now. Listen to the tape I gave Ortiz. The guy who tried to extort me laid it all out for you."

"I'm ready to add another few charges to Maksimov's list of offenses," Duffy said. "Powers and Guzman, those Wilshire dicks who worked with you on the Ambrose hit, are chasing that down right now. I briefed the Wilshire D-3 and asked if I could have those two on loan since they're familiar with this case and you're on suspension."

Duffy flashed me a look of strained forbearance and said, "The question of the day is: What the fuck were you doing at Mrs. Winfield's house? You're not supposed to be anywhere near this case." He slammed his palm on the table next to my bed and shouted, "I should fire your ass right now." I got the feeling he was trying to impress Peck, rather than admonish me.

"I thought I'd left my sweater on her sofa the last time I was there. I wanted to stop by and pick it up. With those winter Santa Anas, I've been freezing my ass off."

Duffy flipped me the finger.

"After the confession I got from that so-called witness, am I still suspended?" I asked. "Will the DA still look into charging me?"

"Yes to the first question; I don't know to the second. We all have to listen to that tape and make the call."

I turned to Peck. "You said you heard on the wire Maksimov chattering about Mrs. Winfield's house. What, exactly, was he interested in?"

"You know I can't discuss anything we obtain on a tap. There's a confidentiality that would violate—"

"Typical FBI bullshit," I muttered.

"Don't think," Duffy said, "that you're going to worm your way back into this case while you're on suspension."

Ignoring him, I said to Peck, "How long have you had Mrs. Winfield's place staked out?"

"Ash," Duffy said, "your conversation with Agent Peck is now over."

Duffy turned to Peck and said, "Sorry to make you work on Christmas."

"I'm stuck working this week, anyway. So it's not a problem."

After Peck left the room, Duffy dragged a chair across the linoleum and sat beside me. "Thanks for ruining my Christmas, you dickhead," he said with a half smile. "But what do you care about Christmas. You're a fucking infidel. You should—"

"Where do I stand with the department?"

"Too early to say. We haven't even had a chance to question that wit who you *claimed*," he said, emphasizing the word, "tried to bribe you. But let me repeat: stay away from this case. I don't want you ending up on dream street again. You're on suspension. Wait it out."

"But if I wait it out, I might get fucked over. I don't trust Grazzo. Frankly, I don't trust you. And I don't trust those Force Investigation detectives. They haven't done shit. I'm the only one who's come up with anything."

"Back off, Ash. Let the detectives do their job. Just relax and spend the next few days trying to look up your nurse's skirt."

"But how about that note for me that you scribbled. Weren't you telling me just the opposite?"

Duffy sauntered out the door and said over his shoulder, "What note?"

The clicks of metal on metal roused me from a deep sleep. I frantically searched the end table. Where the hell was my gun? Where was I? Who was coming after me?

"What do you need?" asked my mother, who was slumped in a corner chair, knitting, clicking her needles. I rubbed my eyes and asked, "What time is it?"

"Ten."

"Morning or night?"

"Night," she said, a look of worry creasing her face. "Do you know who I am?"

"Of course," I said. "Joan Rivers."

"Knock it off. With head injuries, you never know how a person will be affected."

"You don't have to worry about me. It's just a concussion. No fracture to the skull."

"A concussion is serious. I know because I just talked to Dr. Schneiderman. Anyway, I'm glad you're here—in a Catholic hospital."

"You are?" I said, surprised.

"Nuns as nurses and Jewish doctors—what could be better?"

She lifted a blue insulated food pack onto the bed, zipped it open, and smacked a Tupperware container. "I brought you some matzo ball soup. No noodles. Just how you like it. I've already talked to the nursing supervisor. She agreed to take it into the employees' lunchroom—where there's a microwave—heat it up for you and—"

"I'm not hungry."

"Maybe not now. But maybe later."

"I don't think so. But thanks, anyway."

"I know how you like the corn rye at Factor's. So I brought you a few slices, along with some rugelach," she said, holding up two plastic bags. "And for tomorrow morning, I've also packed you a little something." She pursed her lips, an expression of distaste, and said, "Hospital food is dreck!"

I faked a yawn and slit my eyes. She leaned over, kissed me on the cheek, and said, "Don't worry. I've talked to the night nurse and written down all the food preparation instructions on a piece of paper."

She crossed the room, flung open the closet, and said cheerily, "See, I got all your clothes from the ER and hung them up. I noticed that your shirt was stained. You should take more of an interest in your personal appearance. You shouldn't be going out like that."

I decided not to tell her the stains were blood. "Thank you."

"When I picked up the *Times*, I had a *shrek*. I saw that article about you, how you supposedly shot a man in cold blood. I never—"

"It's all a lie."

"I know that. Marty filled me in. Told me he got you Marv Romanoff, who I hear is the best in town. Marty said Marv will get you off. But I still worry because—"

"I don't want to deal with all that right now. I'd like to get the hell out of here."

"Have you lost your mind? You need to—"

"Thanks for stopping by, Mom. I appreciate your concern. But I'm tired."

"Of course, of course. I'm going to let you get some sleep now. We'll talk later. But before you doze off, there's someone here you might want to say hello to."

I saw my mother motion in the doorway. A moment later, Robin ambled into the room as my mother scampered out with a hurried wave. Robin was looking good in her tight jeans, clingy, pale-blue cashmere sweater, and high-heel brown leather boots. I was about to reach for her hand, when I remembered how she'd dumped me.

"How you feeling?"

"I'm okay."

"You need anything?"

"I won't be here long." I inched up in bed, smoothing the sheet over my lap. "You reconsidering?"

She squinted, hand over her mouth. I knew that expression well. She was trying not to cry. "This isn't a good time to discuss all that."

"Then why'd you come?"

She dabbed at her eyes with a thumb.

"Did my mom arrange this?" I asked.

Robin gripped the bed's railing. "Well, she did let me know you were hurt."

"You could have told her no."

"You ever try to talk your mom out of something?"

I stared out the window at an overcast sky. "Any chance for us?"

"I just wanted to stop by and see how you're feeling. We can talk about the other stuff some other time."

"You're here. So let's talk."

"Ash, now is not—"

"Stop playing games."

She snatched a Kleenex from the end table and wiped her eyes. "I'm seeing someone."

"Why didn't you tell me before we headed up the coast, before all those long phone conversations we had?"

"Christopher and I had been going out," she said, smoothing a cuticle, avoiding my gaze. "Things were going well. Then they weren't. So we kind of split up. That's when you and I started talking again."

"You mean that's when you called me, when we drove up the coast. And now you're seeing Christopher again? Boy, you don't waste any time."

"It's more complicated than that—" she said, her voice trailing off.

"And he's a lawyer," I said.

"He is."

"And I'm sure he makes a lot of money."

"That's not it."

"Is he a partner at your firm?"

"What if he is?"

"Right after we got married, and you took me to your firm's Christmas party, you told people I was in law enforcement, instead of just saying I was a cop, I should have known then."

"Known what?" she asked angrily.

"Known that you'd never be happy. Duffy said he knew it from the get-go. I wish I'd have figured it out then."

"Let's not start all this again," she said softly. "What's the point?"

I patted my bandage and winced. "No point. No point at all."

"You in pain?"

"It's been a long day."

"Ash, I'm sorry."

"Okay, you've said what you wanted to say. Now you can leave." I settled my head back onto the pillow.

"Don't be like that, Ash."

"Goodbye," I said, closing my eyes. A moment later, I heard her heels clicking on linoleum, echoing down the hallway.

PART VI

FUBAR

CHAPTER 37

Delfour was a dumb son of a bitch. Now a dumb, dead son of a bitch. He always showed too much fucking initiative. That was his problem in the service. That was his problem on the street. And now he was taking a dirt nap because of his initiative.

Gordie lit an unfiltered Camel, picked a piece of tobacco out of his teeth, and sucked down a drag. This whole deal had spun out of control. Totally FUBAR. Delfour dead. The rummy, Aaron Ellison, in custody. The only guy who did his job right was Mullin. He followed the script to perfection. He got himself killed, and he got Levine suspended. Who'd have thought that psycho Mullin was the only competent one.

Good thing, Gordie thought, he paid attention when his dad taught him how to reload his own ammo back in the garage all those years ago. After dabbing the inside of some empty casings with melted lead, and then loading them up, they had the heft of a real round—not a blank. Mullin never suspected a thing.

Taking a deep, angry drag, he decided he'd never delegate in the future. He'd do the fucking job himself now. But he hardly had the time. He'd been working full time while trying to oversee a platoon of idiots searching for the fucking mask.

He had to admit he was a bit overzealous when he put the soldering iron and the spiked knuckle dusters to Winfield and Pinkney. He learned those techniques from the police commandos at Iraq's Interior Ministry. Unfortunately, those tricks weren't useful enough. Winfield wouldn't talk. So he had to go. And if he had to go, Pinkney, who was with Winfield when Delfour made the grab, had to go, too. Unlucky bastard.

It was Delfour's idea to dump them in Oakwood. Gordie knew he had to stay away on that job because it would be hard for a white boy to slip in and out of the alley unnoticed. That, at least, was a smooth operation. No wits. Delfour blasted the shotgun to keep looky-loos away.

Fortunately, Delfour had scrounged a Special Forces scanner—which could tune into any frequency—and he picked up that Pacific Division was calling in Felony Special, and a Detective Asher Levine would be taking over the investigation and working solo. A .22 slug rattling around in his skull wouldn't be smart because it would bring down too much heat.

He was pretty proud of himself for figuring out how to push Levine out of the way and muddy up and stall the investigation. He told Delfour to find a shooter and a phony witness. The shooter did fine. Unfortunately, Levine tracked down and squeezed the phony wit.

Now was the time to punch Levine's ticket. That was Delfour's job. But he decided to search Winfield's mom's place and look for the mask before eliminating Levine. Gordie would have searched the place himself, weeks ago, but he knew the FBI was watching the house. He just hadn't told Delfour. He only disseminated information on a need-to-know basis.

Because Delfour didn't punch Levine's ticket, Gordie knew he would have to do the job himself. Levine was getting a little too close the ten ring.

Levine was smart, but not smart enough. He'd connected the dots from Mullin to Aaron Ellison to Delfour, but he probably thought the dots led eventually to Maksimov, a false trail Gordie had laid out. Levine assumed that Maksimov was calling the shots. In fact, Gordie knew, it was the other way around. He was damn proud of himself for leading everyone astray.

Anyone who'd think that he would work for a sleazy Russian like Maksimov had to be out of their fucking minds. Maksimov was working for him. He just didn't know it.

He shared only one thing in common with Maksimov: the mask. Gordie had found out years ago, back in Iraq, that Maksimov was batshit crazy over that mask. And Gordie had concluded that Maksimov was more likely to find it. After the fiasco with Winfield and Pinkney, he'd decided to track Maksimov. He figured the Russian, with more money and more muscle at his disposal, would lead him to the holy grail. So Gordie had dispatched Delfour to tail him.

Gordie smiled. A few times when Maksimov was tailing Levine, he was tailing Maksimov. That's how Maksimov and Ziven found Jerry Ambrose. Because the Russians were interested in Ambrose, he was interested in Ambrose. After the Russians left, he'd paid the grunt a visit. And that was the last interview Ambrose ever gave. Unfortunately, Ambrose didn't know shit. Gordie hated to waste a bullet on him.

Still, that worked out pretty damn well. Levine had arrested the wrong guys, and nobody had followed the trail to Gordie.

Now Delfour was gone. Gordie was surprised he didn't even feel a pang of sadness. They'd known each other for almost ten years. When he was at Centcom, Delfour served with the First Cav. Word got around about Sergeant Delfour. He'd boosted a cache of loot from some camel jockey who'd ransacked the museum. Delfour strong-armed the guy and was selling this ancient shit off—vases, little statues, jewelry, coins—one by one, in the back-alley bazaars. Getting pennies on the dollar. Gordie shook his head with disgust. When he heard about this, he'd figured they could help each other out. So he got in touch and had a confidential little confab with Delfour. A beautiful partnership, with Gordie's contacts and Delfour's goods.

No one ever suspected Delfour. He came off like such a straight fucking arrow. Must be that Jamaican accent.

They were making pretty good money, but they had to close up shop after the looting of that big national museum hit the news. After all the bad press, internationally, Washington mobilized. The Pentagon rustled up a task force with officials from about a dozen agencies, including all the service branches, FBI, CIA, and Customs. Their mission was to track down the most valuable and ancient Iraqi treasures that had been ripped off from the museum. Gordie remembered trolling for intel from the task force.

He fired up another cigarette. Yes, that day changed his life. That's when he heard about the mask. Gordie and his team had grilled some towel heads they'd just busted and discovered that this Russian Mafia from Southern California had ponied up a hefty cash bounty on the mask. This Russian, Gordie heard, was also running other looted items out of Iraq and over to Japan, some European countries, and the U.S.

Gordie knew if he could secure this mask, he wouldn't have to wait for his twenty and out and then, after he retired, work some chicken-shit job to supplement his pathetic pension. That's when Delfour heard that a guy in his unit had stumbled onto the mask. But before he and Delfour could move on him, Winfield had shipped back to the States, and then on to Afghanistan, where Gordie couldn't get to him. It was years before Winfield was back in L.A. and Gordie could arrange to work in the city. Winfield was living in that crappy little rental, so Gordie suspected he hadn't sold the mask.

Gordie took a long, slow drag. It wasn't a bad plan. Let Maksimov bird dog the mask and he'd bird dog Maksimov. He figured Maksimov would lead him right to it.

Maksimov thought Levine would do the same for him. That's why he and Ziven tailed Levine, why they questioned Ambrose, and why they ended up in the brig for a murder they didn't commit.

CHAPTER 38

The soothing peal of what sounded like wind chimes woke me. When I looked out into the hallway, however, I realized that it was an orderly pushing a trolley, rattling bedpans. I sat up and coughed. My mouth felt like sandpaper, my tongue was swollen, and a piercing pain radiated from the side of my head.

A few minutes later an orderly rolled my lunch in. My mother was right: the food *was* dreck. Stale bread and pressed turkey, pea soup, and macaroni salad glazed with mayonnaise. I slurped down the watery apple juice and pushed aside the plate.

"Hello there," a cheery Filipino nurse said, moving my tray to the end table and setting a raspberry rugelach in front of me. "Your mother brought this for you last night. How are you feeling?"

"Not too bad."

"The doctor will be by to see you during his afternoon rounds. And if you don't care for our lunch, I have the soup that your mother left for you." The nurse smiled sweetly. "She gave me detailed instructions on how long to heat it in the microwave."

"I bet she did," I said. "Maybe I'll have the soup later."

I sipped the weak coffee and chewed a bite of the rugelach. Delicious. Now I was glad to have an alternative to the hospital slop.

"Here's a Vicodin," she said, handing me a small plastic cup with the pill inside. "If the pain becomes a problem, take it."

As I curled up on the edge of the bed, my head throbbed, so I popped the Vike, lay back down, switched on the television, and dozed off.

When I woke, I glanced at the unappetizing lunch on my end table and called for an orderly to take it away. I climbed out of bed, gulped a glass of water, and slowly rotated my head. The ache was tolerable enough for me to stand and get dressed. I strode down the hallway to the elevator, slipping past my nurse. I didn't want her telling me to stick around another night or to wait all afternoon until the doctor finished his rounds.

My brief conversation with Peck was illuminating, a new path to follow. I knew I had to return to Mrs. Winfield's house, but it had to be when Peck was on surveillance. Since he saw me at dawn, I knew he was working the FBI's morning watch: midnight to 8 a.m. I hurried out of the hospital and called a cab. As I slumped in the backseat, I checked my watch and realized I had almost twelve hours to kill before Peck was back on duty. I was ravenous—during the past twenty-four hours, all I'd eaten was a single rugelach—and I craved a cheeseburger and fries. I told the driver to swing east on the Santa Monica Freeway, turn off at Overland, and drive north. I called Richie Powers's cell, reaching him at home.

"You've had a hell of a few days," he said.

"Glad to hear you're on the case."

"You should be, too, if this department wasn't so—"

"I knew the job was dangerous when I took it."

Powers laughed. "I think I saw that spy movie, too."

"Look, feel free to say no. I know this is the day after Christmas and you want to be with your family, but I wanted to talk to you briefly. Away from the station. Off the books."

"When and where?"

"You hungry?"

"I can always eat another meal."

I heard the shouts of children in the background. "Can I drag you away from your family for an hour?"

"Absolutely. It's almost three now. My kids are driving me crazy with all the video games they got for Christmas. I've been looking for an excuse to get out of the house. And you know more about this case than anyone. I want to hear what you have to say."

"You know the Apple Pan in West L.A.?"

"I've never eaten there."

"Let's meet out front, at Overland and Pico."

A few minutes later, the driver dropped me off, and I waited for Powers. In a city that had contempt for the past, where neighborhoods seemed to change overnight, I found it reassuring to visit the Apple Pan, a spot that had remained unchanged since I was a boy.

When Powers arrived, wearing jeans and a hooded sweatshirt, I said, "Let's talk for a few minutes outside. The place is pretty crowded, I don't want anyone overhearing us. We can gab, then we can eat."

"You look like hell," he yelled over the drone of traffic. I pivoted and studied my reflection in the restaurant's plate-glass window. A jagged purple bruise flared from the corner of my eye to my ear.

"I look worse than I feel."

I scrawled a number on the back of my card and said, "This is my cell number. You might be working this case for a while. I don't know when I'll be back. If you have any questions, call me any time."

"So where do we go from here?" Powers asked.

"Where do *you* go from here. Remember I'm off the job."

"You'll be back soon."

"I'm not so sure. And while I'm waiting this out, I'm not supposed to be working this case, so keep it on the down low. It's probably best you don't even tell your partner about this meeting."

"What meeting?"

I briefed him on my talk with Aaron Ellison, how Ellison had set me up and the way Delfour had ambushed me.

"Was Delfour working for Maksimov?"

"Probably."

"Should I try to talk to Maksimov?"

"No point—yet," I said. "He thinks he's pretty fucking smart, jamming me up like that. When he finds out it turned to shit, he's going to be bent out of shape. Let's let him stew for a while. After you can definitively link him to Delfour, head over to the jail and see what he has to say. I doubt he'll tell you anything, but it's worth a try. You have to find that link between Delfour and Maksimov."

"That's the key. If you can find that link, you can clear the Winfield and Pinkney homicides. You'll be the hero of the department because Councilman Pinkney will be so grateful he won't slice and dice our budget. Hell, he may even push for an increase."

"Where do you suggest I start?"

"Contact the place where they keep all the military records. It's in St. Louis and the official name is the National Personnel Records Center." I checked my watch. "It's way past five, central time. So you're not going to be able to get anyone on the phone right now. When are you back at work?"

"Both my partner and me will be back at work tomorrow."

"Work the phones tomorrow morning. Get a list of all the soldiers who were in the First Cav's Third Battalion, Eighty-Second Field Artillery at the same time as Ellison, Delfour, and Mullin—that guy I shot. Start interviewing the discharged soldiers, one by one. Interview the soldiers in the unit who are now stateside. Then talk to the injured ones at the army hospitals—from the local VAs to the big facilities back East. Maybe one of these guys will help you find the link between Maksimov and Delfour."

"I know you're on suspension but that, obviously, didn't stop you. You got any more tricks up your sleeve?"

"One. I've got something I'm going to chase down tonight. See where it takes me." I clapped him on the shoulder and said, "Let's eat."

I was angry that I had to run the investigation from the sidelines, but when we pushed through the swinging doors, my mood lifted, soothed by the familiar surroundings: the weathered wooden walls, the cozy plaid wallpaper, the worn terra-cotta floors, the aromatic scent of hickory burgers, the pies in the window, the ancient brick grill. With its U-shaped counter, the Apple Pan could pass for a 1940s-era roadside diner, if patrons ignored the Westside Pavilion and the other massive projects that loomed over the tiny restaurant. I recalled midnight meals here when I worked the p.m. shift with one of my first partners, a dyspeptic old cop who patronized the restaurant since it had opened a few years after World War II.

The waiter brought us a paper cone of water encased in an old-fashioned metal holder and took our orders. A few minutes later he brought our fries and burgers, which were laced with a hickory smoke flavoring and layered with Tillamook cheddar. Later, we ordered coffee, served with a small glass beaker of heavy cream, and wedges of hot apple pie dripping with cinnamon sauce. Powers wiped his mouth with a napkin and said, "That was a hell of a meal. Beats my wife's rubbery Christmas ham leftovers any day."

"Can I ask you another favor?" I said. "I need a ride to my car. It's in Venice, across from Mrs. Winfield's house."

"Sure."

When we climbed out of the booth, I slipped on my jacket and perfunctorily patted my chest, but the absence of my shoulder holster and gun made me feel vulnerable and exposed. When I was a street cop, I always carried a back-up gun: a hammerless .38-caliber two-inch Smith & Wesson Airweight. After my promotion to detective, I didn't want the Smith jutting from my ankle holster and scaring witnesses when I interviewed them. Next time I went out, I decided, I was going to retrieve the Smith from my dresser and pack it so I could protect myself from assholes like Delfour.

CHAPTER 39

I swung open the door to my loft, kicked off my shoes, and stretched out on the sofa. My temple was pounding where Delfour had whacked me. I winced when I touched the stitches. I switched on the jazz station and was glad they were still playing Christmas music. Listening to McCoy Tyner's version of "I'll Be Home for Christmas," I felt a vague sense of longing, just like when I was a kid. I didn't dislike the holiday; I just felt left out. The entire world, it seemed, was enjoying Christmas, while my family spent the day arguing over which Chinese restaurant had the best almond chicken and what time to make the reservation.

Hanukkah was traditionally a minor holiday, but Jewish leaders in America inflated its importance to give Jewish kids a Christmas substitute. Because it's spread over eight days, the impact is diluted, and as a kid, I always felt shortchanged. When I was about ten, I asked my father if we could have a tree. He slapped my face and said, "I didn't survive Treblinka for that."

When "Snowfall" by the Ahmad Jamal Trio came on the radio, I closed my eyes and focused on the music, not the memory. As the piece faded out, I tried to sleep. I knew Peck was working morning watch, so midnight would be the best time to make my play. When I heard an LAPD chopper hovering overhead, I bolted up. It felt like I'd dozed off for a few minutes, but when I checked my watch I realized I'd been asleep for hours. It was almost eleven.

I changed into black pants, black sneakers, and a black long-sleeved T-shirt. After grabbing my little zippered case with the lock picks and tension wrench, I reached into the back of a dresser drawer for my Smith Airweight, which was wrapped in an oiled rag. I spun the cylinder to make sure it was loaded, then jammed it into my leather shoulder holster, which also held my handcuffs. I draped a dark brown trench coat over my shoulders, locked my door, and rode the elevator to the ground floor. I drove back to Oakwood and parked on a desolate side street. I tucked my Maglite into a back pocket, slipped the metal detector beneath my trench coat, negotiated a desolate alley, and spied Peck in a dark-blue Buick LaCrosse parked a half a block from Mrs. Winfield's house. The FBI must be suffering budget problems like the LAPD because, fortunately, he was on stakeout alone.

I rapped on the passenger-side window. Peck whirled around, eyes wide, both hands gripping his Glock. When he recognized me, he mouthed, "What hell are you doing here?"

I motioned for him to roll down the window. "I need thirty minutes inside the house."

"Are you crazy? You're not supposed to be anywhere near this investigation."

"Just give me thirty minutes, and no one will ever know."

Peck reached under the dash for his radio and said, "I'm calling the FBI duty officer right now and telling him to get Pacific patrol over so they can haul your ass away."

I held up a palm. "Hold on. Last week, you entered Teshay Winfield's house without a warrant. In fact, you broke in. When you were spotted, you assaulted an LAPD officer. Me. And I'll testify to that. You lowered your shoulder and knocked me to the ground, like you were running for the goal line. The second time I spotted you at Winfield's house, I called Pacific patrol and they apprehended you. The only reason you weren't booked is because I stepped in and called them off. Now if you don't give me my thirty minutes, I'll report all this to your supervisor. I've got you on several felonies. If I follow through with this, you'll wish you were in Pierre, South Dakota. Because, instead, you'll be spending the next few years inside a six-by-eight foot cell at Terminal Island Federal Prison."

Peck glared at me. "You're one shady street cop."

I checked my watch. "It's five minutes after midnight. I'll be back at twelve thirty-five."

"If you're not back by then, I'm calling Pacific."

I hurried down the sidewalk, crossed the street, and made my way to the back door. Flipping on the Maglite and balancing it under my arm, I picked the lock and stepped inside the kitchen. I retrieved the metal detector from inside my trench coat, switched it on, and scanned the floor. When I traced the coil over a rug by the kitchen sink, I flinched when I heard a loud beep. I knelt and lifted the rug. A quarter.

Although the house was cold and dank, my forehead was beaded with sweat. I skimmed the floors and walls in the living room and the bathrooms, but registered no hits. As I entered the small bedroom, I heard a rattle in the kitchen. Quietly, I removed the Smith from my shoulder holster and inched toward the kitchen. Again, I heard the sound. I held my breath. A moment later, I exhaled loudly when I realized that it was just the freezer's icemaker plunking cubes into the collection pan.

After I'd moved through every room, I rushed to the backyard. I recalled how Maksimov had predicted that I'd get, as he put it, *infected with the virus of obsession.* Maybe he was right. Maybe it was an obsession. Or maybe it was simply persistent police work. I knew that I had to follow each lead to see if it linked to another lead, and another, until, ultimately, I could solve the case and resolve the investigative uncertainties.

I checked my watch: only fourteen minutes left. My heart hammered in my chest. I hurtled out the back door. Fortunately, it was almost a full moon and I could negotiate the space without the flashlight. I frantically swept the front of the yard, scurrying from one end to the other, praying for a beep. I then raced to the back half of the yard. When I reached the west corner, beside the naked branches of a plumeria, the detector sounded like the blast of a foghorn. I shut it off, fell to my knees, and traced my hand over a ragged patch of grass. Scanning the yard, I spotted a trowel on the wooden deck beside a planter brimming with geraniums. I ran across the yard, snatched the trowel, and furiously ripped up the grass in the west corner, sweat trickling down my forehead. A few inches beneath the grass, the scooping was easier, the dirt soft with a few pebbles. I dug down about a foot deep. Then another foot. Then another.

Shit. Razor said the metal detector had a three-foot range, and I hadn't found anything. Maybe because of the iron content in the soil, the detector had registered a false read. I wiped my forehead with my palm.

I scooped out another layer of dirt. Still nothing. And only four minutes to go. I angrily stabbed the trowel in the dirt and heard something: a faint metallic ping. Digging frantically, I unearthed the edges of a metal box. Jamming both hands into the hole, I hauled out a box and flipped it open. In the center was a cloth bag. I jiggled loose a thin, oval-shaped object. Flicking on my Maglite, I illuminated the surface. The hair on the back of my neck stood up. I murmured, "My God. That's it."

The face was so life-like, the expression so animated, the gaze so intent, I was startled and almost dropped the mask.

The seconds ticked by, I couldn't stop staring at the face. And that's exactly what it appeared to be: not a mask, but a human face, staring back. Aware. Cognizant. Alive.

In that moment I understood why Maksimov had spent decades searching for the mask, why Delfour had killed for it, why its value was inestimable.

It was the most beautiful thing I'd ever seen.

The ivory glowed a fluorescent white in the moonlight, with streaks of silver and gold radiating like neon. Framing the edge of the mask were silky pearls, lapis sparkling with specks of yellow, and other jewels that I couldn't identify. But I could clearly see that the eyes were rubies. Glowing like coals, they were magnificent, the most intense, vivid, and purest red that I had ever seen. My flashlight caught the facets, brilliant, shifting spangles of light. A razor-sharp, incandescent, six-rayed star shone from the very center of each ruby, like fiery pupils.

I knew I was running out of time, but I was mesmerized. Finally, I glanced at my watch. Damn. I was five minutes over. On my hands and knees, I shoveled the dirt back in the hole and tamped clumps of grass over the spot. I found a hose in the other corner of the yard, turned it on and quickly watered the area. The yard was raggedy and veined with weeds, so unless someone carefully examined the grass, my excavation would probably go unnoticed.

Jumping to my feet, I stuffed the mask inside my Jockeys, adjusted it like the cup I wore in Pony League when I played third base, slipped the metal detector under my coat, and dashed back to Peck.

When he saw me, he rolled down his window and said, "I was just about to blow the whistle on you. What were you looking for?"

"Nothing in particular. I just wanted to get a better feel for my vic."

"I don't believe you."

I opened my fingers. "See. I entered empty handed, and I'm leaving empty handed."

"Now we're even," Peck said.

"Definitely."

I stepped back into the alley and tugged a handkerchief from my back pocket. I wiped the detector for prints, snapped it over my knee, and dumped it into a trash can. It would be safer to buy Razor a new one, than risk someone discovering it in my car or my loft.

When I returned to my car, I fished out my keys. I was just about to crack open the door when I collapsed, racked by an intense pain. I tried to scream, but only moaned, a low, guttural gurgle. I attempted to rise, but all I could do was writhe on the ground, my legs, shoulders, and arms twitching and burning.

I caught a glimpse of a man, face blurred with green camouflage paint. He rolled me over on my stomach and ripped off my shoulder holster. He must have found my handcuffs because I could feel him cuffing my wrists behind my back. He bound my ankles with twine, wrapped a blindfold around my head, hoisted me up, and tossed me in the back of a van. Fortunately, he did not discover the mask. Just as a tingle of feeling seeped into my legs, I realized what had happened.

I'd been Tasered.

CHAPTER 40

As the blast from the stun gun wore off, I struggled against the cuffs. The van rumbled through a rutted alley and sped down the side streets. Rolling over on my stomach, I scraped the blindfold on the van's floor, but the binding was too secure to tear off.

My chest tightened. The sound of crashing surf echoed in my head. I tried to quell the panic and concentrate on my next move.

If I couldn't see, what defenses did I have left? Although my wrists were cuffed, my hands could still feel. Fortunately, there were a few inches of give in the cuffs. Maybe I could feel my way to an escape. But first I needed to familiarize myself with my surroundings. I squirmed onto my back, stretched out my legs and swiveled around to gauge the width of the van. It was big, more like a FedEx vehicle than a minivan. The driver, I figured, would have a hard time monitoring me. I touched the floor of the van with my hands. It was covered with a thin rubber mat. I inched forward, stretched out my legs again, my feet banging against two boxes. I pivoted around, hands cuffed behind my back, and shook the boxes slightly. Something was inside, but I couldn't tell what.

The van smelled like gasoline and dirty oil. I wriggled to the back and fingered some greasy rags. If I could scramble to my feet, maybe I could grip a handle and wrench open the door. The van suddenly swerved. I lost my balance and pitched forward with a thud, pain radiating from my stitches.

"Shut the fuck up back there!" the driver shouted. His voice sounded vaguely familiar, but I couldn't identify it.

I curled on my side and concentrated on the van's route. We'd been traversing the side streets of Oakwood, I guessed, but now it felt like we were speeding down a major thoroughfare. Traffic was light but, occasionally, I could hear the rumble of idling cars, the hydraulic hiss of bus brakes, the thrum of salsa and rap from passing cars. A moment later, I felt the van descend steeply, level out, and gather speed. The brackish scent of fog and saltwater drifted through the window. I was certain we were near the beach, probably cruising north on Pacific Coast Highway. When I'd enlisted in the IDF, I suspected that a letter to my parents—"We regret to inform you that your son has made the ultimate sacrifice for the nation of Israel"—would signal the end of my life. When I joined the LAPD, I accepted the possibility I could die after a routine traffic stop. I never thought it would end this way, alone, in the back of a van, surrounded by rags that stank of oil and gasoline, a cop's worst nightmare. Ambushed and shackled with his own handcuffs. Groaning, I tried to free my hands.

"If you don't calm down," the driver snarled, "I'm going to Taser you again. You think the last time was bad? You don't know what agony is until you've been drilled in the nuts."

I rolled over on my back. I sucked down a few deep breaths, exhaling slowly. Now is not the time to panic, I told myself. Conserve your energy. Wait for an opening. Then exploit it.

I could feel the van picking up speed and negotiating turns. We were rolling towards Malibu, I figured. A few minutes later, the van skidded to a stop. The driver stepped out, and I could hear a house door creak open and slam shut. I immediately struggled to my feet. This might be my only chance to escape. My feet were bound so I could only take tiny steps. I felt with my hands along the side of the van until I found a metal handle and jiggled it up and down. I wasn't surprised to discover the van had been locked from the outside.

Slowly, I inched my way to the front of the van, searching for something sharp that I could use to spring the handcuffs. Sweat dribbled from my forehead into the blindfold. I blinked hard. When my heel caught a rent in the rubber mat, I lost my balance and tumbled to the floor. Holding my breath, I waited for the van's rear door to fly open and braced myself for the excruciating electric shock.

But thirty seconds later it was still quiet, so I struggled to my feet. I groped between the two front seats, but the only thing I could find was what felt like a metal coffee cup. Crouching, I patted the empty driver's seat. In the corner of the passenger's seat I felt a soft fabric—maybe a sweater—and beneath it a metal box. I tried to open it, but it was locked. It felt like the metal gun box I kept at home to store my Beretta when Ariel visited. I shook the box. It sounded like there was a revolver inside. If I could just get that box open—

I heard footsteps. Scrambling to the back of the van, I collapsed on the rubber mat. I heard the driver talking to a man.

"Not much of a swell this week, Gordie," the man said.

"That's okay," said the driver, whom I assumed was Gordie. "I'm not the thrill-seeker I used to be."

The man laughed and then emitted a phlegmy cough. He sounded like a smoker.

"Thanks for the board. I owe you one," Gordie said.

"No problem, Gordie. It's a log. I'm glad to get rid of it."

The back of the van opened. Someone tossed something heavy onto the mat, a loud clunk. As the van sped off, I rolled to my side and reached out. I felt an enormous canvas sack with a hefty object inside, emanating a faintly tropical smell, the scent of surfboard wax.

While we rumbled up the coast, I decided to divide the back of the van into four sections and carefully search for something to spring the cuffs. Although my hands were behind me, I could still, while on my back or side, pat down each quadrant. I kicked off my shoes. Dabbing with my toes and running my fingers along the rubber mat, I discovered the front half of the van was empty. I wriggled around, examining the bottom left section, and only came upon the oily rags. The remaining section contained the two cardboard boxes, one large and one small.

The driver was talking on the phone, so I hoped he was distracted. I did a half sit-up, stomach muscles quivering, hands behind my back, and tried to quietly lift the top. Pain radiated down my arms. I discovered what felt like manila folders filled with loose pages, then searched inside the smaller box. I found a cache of paper. Snatching a paper clip from some pages, I slid it into my back pocket, maneuvered the top back on, and crumpled to the ground.

I quietly gasped for breath, and my shoulders burned. When I caught my breath, I bent open the paper clip and scraped it on the side of my palm. My old mentor, Bud Carducci, had taught me to break into houses, lock boxes, and desk drawers with a set of picks and tension wrenches. He had taught me to pick handcuffs—so I'd know what to expect after I hooked up sneaky suspects—using paper clips, bobby pins, needles, and wire. I had never sprung a lock with my hands behind my back but I didn't need to see the lock. I just needed to feel it.

A strip of metal bordered the mat. I bent the paperclip into a straight line and softly honed the tip to a needle point. After squirming around in the back of the van, I felt the mask slide down my Jockeys to my thigh. This was a major problem. As long as I had the mask, and my abductor didn't know its location, I might have some leverage. I had to spring those cuffs and settle the mask back into my underwear so he wouldn't discover it when he reached his destination and forced me out of the van.

I sat up and stuck the tip of the paperclip into the keyhole and tweaked the tip into a forty-five-degree angle. I removed it, stuck the tip in again and twisted the top of the clip into the other direction. Now it looked like a mini-hand crank.

The van screeched to an abrupt stop. I dropped the clip, and toppled onto my side with a thud.

"If I hear any more noise coming from the back, I'm coming back there," the driver shouted. "And this time, instead of the Taser, you'll get a lead slug between the eyes."

The van didn't move for several minutes. I was afraid if I searched for the clip, the driver would hear me. We'd probably hit a stoplight at Malibu. The van climbed—probably near Pepperdine University, I guessed—then barreled down a steep hill. When it leveled out, I started searching for the paper clip. After we teetered on a curve, I found it.

I inserted the tip of the clip into the keyhole and applied steady pressure. I hoped this would release the latches that would open the jaws of the cuffs. Straining, my wrists biting into the cuffs, I felt as if I was almost there, when the van hit a pothole. I lost my grip, and the paper clip clattered out of the lock and onto the mat. My stomach churned.

Squirming on my side, I traced my hand along the surface of the mat. I could hear the pounding of the surf in the distance, and I figured we were speeding by Point Dume. I inched down the mat and my fingernail brushed against metal. It was the clip. I inserted it back into the keyhole, pressed and jiggled, but couldn't release the lock latches. *Damn! I can't get these handcuffs off.*

Taking a deep breath, I slowly exhaled and focused on maneuvering the paper clip.

The van made a U-turn, a sharp right turn, rumbled over a dirt road for a few minutes, and skidded to a stop, pebbles banging against the undercarriage. I knew we were perched at the edge of the ocean because I could hear the hiss of the surf and smell the beached seaweed.

I have to get these cuffs off right now. Before the driver walks around to the back of the van and pulls me out. What do I have, twenty seconds? Maybe thirty?

I began to hyperventilate.

This is my last chance. My only hope for survival is getting these cuffs off.

I continued to jostle and wiggle and twist and press the tip of the paper clip.

I can't panic. I have to concentrate. Or I'll drop the clip. Or I'll lose the feel of the mechanism.

I heard the driver's door slam and footsteps crunching on gravel.

Finally. A beautiful sound. A faint click.

I collapsed and rolled onto my back, panting, wrists sore, fingers cut and bloody, forearms cramped with pain.

The cuffs were open.

CHAPTER 41

As I heard the man swing open the van's door, I freed my left hand, eased the mask back into the center of my Jockeys, and jammed my hand behind my back and into the open cuff. The element of surprise was my only advantage.

"Out," the man shouted, leaning forward to cut my ankle bindings with a KA-BAR army knife.

I teetered out of the van, facing him, so he wouldn't see that the cuffs were open.

He stripped off my blindfold.

When I saw who was pointing a pistol at my chest, I was stunned. It was Captain Rex Rilonas, the Army P.R. guy who had stopped by Felony Special with that female major.

"I see that you're being all that you can be, Captain Rilonas. Or is it Gordie?"

"I'm a Nascar fan."

"And Jeff Gordon's your main man. So your men call you Gordie."

He was wearing my shoulder holster and aiming my Smith. "Take a step back."

"I've got to say, I'm surprised that you're working for a sleazy Russian mobster like Maksimov."

"You don't know what the fuck's going on, do you?"

I glanced around, tried to familiarize myself with my surroundings, and search for an escape route. The desolate beach was set in a small scenic bay. A serpentine mound of cliffs dotted with ice plant and yucca cut us off from the highway. I guessed the beach was somewhere between Paradise Cove and the Ventura County line. I couldn't see any cars, campers, or night fishermen. The waves lapped against the shore and the moon cast ribbons of silver on the shimmering water.

"Don't even think of trying to bull rush me."

I felt like an idiot. Carducci had told me once when I was a young detective trainee that my single-mindedness was what made me—potentially—a great investigator. But single-mindedness, Carducci had advised me, was also my Achilles' heel. If a detective is focused only on the task at hand, Carducci warned, and is oblivious to his surroundings, he is vulnerable to predators. Like Rilonas, I thought.

Rilonas zipped open a large blue canvas duffel bag and tossed a pair of swim trunks and a wetsuit top at my feet. "I'm going to uncuff you. Then you're going to strip and put these on."

"After you get me into this wetsuit, you're going to pull a sap out of that duffel bag, bang me on the head, dump me and the board in the water, and try to make it look like an accident. Right?"

He plucked the handcuff key from the shoulder holster. "Turn around."

When he saw my cuffs were loose, he smiled, lifting just his top lip, revealing an even row of small yellow teeth. "Very enterprising. But not enterprising enough. Strip and put 'em on."

"So when your tour in Iraq was over, you got yourself assigned to Southern California because you knew that's where Winfield was."

"If you know so much how come *I'm* holding the gun on *you*?"

"And your visit to our office was simply reconnoitering?"

He threw the trunks and wetsuit at me and said sharply, "Now."

"I'm figuring the major didn't know shit and was just along for the ride. Am I right?"

"Start stripping or I'll start shooting." He jabbed the gun at me. I slowly peeled off my jacket and shirt and shoes and socks. I stood on the bluff, shivering in my pants, which I was reluctant to take off. I wanted to spring the mask at just the right time.

Rilonas kicked the trunks and wetsuit with the toe of his cowboy boot. "Get out of those pants."

"How'd you know I was a surfer?"

"Strip! Now!"

"You know you're not going to be able to pull this off."

"You're in no position to tell me what will and what won't work."

"Believe it or not, I've got all the leverage here," I said, appraising him coolly.

"And why's that?"

"Because I've got the mask."

He stepped toward me and said, "I don't believe you."

I reached into my pants and whipped out the mask, cocked it behind my ear, and hurled it into surf. I glanced out at the water and caught a glimpse of the mask—floating face-up, lifted by a swell—the ivory glowing vividly against the slick dark water, ruby eyes glittering in the moonlight.

Rilonas turned toward the water and froze for a split second, wide-eyed, and screamed, "Nooo!" As his eyes darted from the mask to me, I tackled him. We wrestled on the sand, Rilonas straining to point the gun at me. I clutched his wrist and tried to shake it loose. With his other hand, Rilonas squeezed my throat. I struggled to yank free, but he shoved me onto my back, straddling me. He slowly lowered the gun. With both hands, I tried to grab the barrel, but Rilonas was too strong. As I watched him lower the front sight toward my chest, I summoned all my strength and thrust my knee into Rilonas's crotch, just as I heard a deafening blast. A pool of warm, sticky blood dripped down my stomach to my legs.

No. Not this. A gut shot. How much time did I have? One minute? Five?

I was about to close my eyes, when I saw Rilonas tumble onto the sand. As I rolled over, I was surprised I had the strength to push myself to my feet.

After tracing my fingers over my stomach and examining Rilonas, I realized what had happened. My knee to the crotch had altered the trajectory, and Rilonas had shot himself in the thigh. As he lay bleeding and moaning on the sand, I turned toward the surf. Strong rip currents, kicking up sand and rippling the water with brown streaks, ran parallel to shore for a few dozen feet before angling out to sea.

The mask was gone.

CHAPTER 42

It was mid-morning by the time I'd finished talking to Duffy, Councilman Pinkney, and the lieutenant in press relations. I then typed up a detailed memo to the DA, explaining how Rilonas—not Maksimov—had committed the double murder in Oakwood and had killed Jerry Ambrose.

While I was printing out the memo, Duffy stuck his head out of his office, called out, "Ash!" and motioned me into a chair.

"Sometimes I wish I was back at South Bureau Homicide," I said. "I could use a simple ghetto drive-by every once in a while."

"What a convoluted mess this case was."

"Well, I know one guy who's going to be happy this morning—Maksimov."

"But not for long," Duffy said. "I just talked to Peck. Before the DA springs Maksimov, Peck will transfer him to a federal joint. He's just about ready to book him on conspiracy to smuggle, transport and harbor illegal aliens, white slavery, and a bunch of other shit. But not murder. So in this case," Duffy said, crossing his hands over his belly, "even the innocent are guilty. The final insult for him will be when he finds out that mask is gone."

"Forever?"

"Probably not," Duffy said. "They've got every lifeguard from Santa Monica to Zuma doing a grid search of the ocean bottom right now. The Coast Guard's there, too, searching with sonar. Someone will end up snagging it."

"I hope to hell they find it."

Duffy reached into his pocket and handed me a key. "Here's your car key back. A uniform dropped your beater back at your place."

"Thanks."

He smoothed his thinning hair and let his hand linger. "Well, Ash, this is a hell of a way to end the year. You took some foolish fucking risks tonight."

"This wasn't just another case. Everything was on the line for me. Don't forget, the department suspended me."

"Well, obviously, that's over."

"So now do you believe me about the way my shooting went down?"

"I have to. Ortiz and Collins just finished interviewing Rilonas. He's in the jail ward at county hospital. He copped to it all. Told them how he set you up. They can't shut him up. Maybe it's that military thing. You ask a career solider a question and it's, "Yes, sir. Here's the answer, sir. Let me elaborate, sir."

"How'd he come up with that surfing accident scheme for me?"

"He Googled you and read that write-up the *Times* did on you after you caught the Spring Street Slasher. When he found out you were a surfer he figured a surfing accident was the best way to get rid of you. A straight assassination of a cop, he knew, would bring too much heat. An accident was the way to go."

"How'd he get on the trail of the mask?"

"He was with U.S. Central Command in Baghdad, a captain in the public affairs unit. He dealt with everyone, all different shades of shady: military contractors, civilian employees, Iraqi merchants, arms dealers, smugglers. Delfour, who had the loot, and Gordie, who had the connections, decided to team up."

"They were making pretty good money. But then Rilonas hears about this task force put together by the Pentagon to track down the most valuable and ancient Iraqi treasures that were ripped off from that big national museum. That was an enormous PR nightmare. Well, Rilonas was picking up any intel he could from the task force. That's when he heard about the mask. The task force interrogated some Iraqi thieves they'd just busted and discovered that this Russian mobster from L.A.—who is running other looted items out of Iraq and over to Japan and some European countries, and the U.S.—had put a bounty on the mask. So Rilonas got very interested. When he found out the value, he had to have it. He wanted it. I mean bad. That's when Delfour got word that a guy in his unit stumbled onto the mask.

"But before they could move on him, Winfield got shipped out of Iraq and, eventually, to Afghanistan. It was years before he was finally discharged. He ended up back in L.A. and, surprise, surprise, that's where Rilonas got stationed. Rilonas figured he'd let Maksimov—find the mask for him. He figured he'd lead him right to it."

"How'd he know I was at Mrs. Winfield's place last night?"

"He'd put a transponder under your hood." Duffy tapped a pencil on his palm. "We got to step up security on that LAPD lot on Main."

"I sweep my engine periodically for devices like that."

"They make them so small these days it's hard to see them."

I traced a palm over my stitches.

"How's the head?" Duffy asked.

"I'm used to headaches."

"It's pretty obvious that you're a Jewish cop."

"Why's that?"

"You keep getting hit in the temple."

I groaned.

"After that concussion, you should be taking it easy. Get away from the squad room. Let's blow. I'll take you to breakfast."

"I do need something to eat, but I want something light. I think I'll walk over and get some *mochi*."

"What the hell is that?"

"Kind of like a sticky rice cake. An old guy in Little Tokyo, just a few blocks from here, makes them the traditional way—washes the rice, soaks it overnight, steams it in a kettle, beats it in a granite bowl—same way they've been doing it for thousands of years. He sweetens them with bean paste. You should try one."

"Bean paste," Duffy said, shaking his head with distaste. "I'll pass. I'm more in the mood this morning for bacon, eggs, and hash browns."

"Suit yourself. But he only makes them this time of year. It's part of the traditional Japanese New Year's celebration. Japanese families drive down from all over Southern California to Little Tokyo for this guy's *mochi*."

Duffy nodded at a window, where we could see the *Los Angeles Times* building. "I'll eat in the Kremlin cafeteria over there before I eat bean paste."

I returned to my desk, called the City Council rep who handles rewards, and told her about Ambrose, Winfield's old army buddy, how he gave me my first lead and how he was killed, probably because he talked to me.

"Looks like he won't be needing that fifty-thousand-dollar reward," she said.

I told the rep about Ambrose's daughter he'd never seen, how he wanted her to have the reward.

"You find her, I'll make sure she gets the reward."

"I'll find her."

I exited PAB and wandered to First Street. I walked a few blocks, cut down a narrow side street and into a steamy, storefront bakery. At the counter I ordered green tea and picked out three small *mochi*, all different colors, from the display case: white with a snowflake imprinted on the top; pale pink to represent a chrysanthemum; and orange, the color of a persimmon, a popular winter fruit in Japan.

I nibbled the snowflake *mochi*, savoring the chewy, delicate taste, then I ate half of the orange and pink ones. As I slurped my tea, my cell phone rang.

"I saw the story online in the *Times*."

"Hello, Robin."

"You're a hero."

"I don't know about that."

"You're the Jewish Rambo. If they make a movie of your exploits they can call it Rambowitz."

"That's the second bad Jewish joke I've heard in the last thirty minutes."

"You okay?"

"Yeah."

"Well, listen, I feel bad about how we left things. How *I* left things. When we were married we both made a lot of mistakes. I think that when I saw you a few days ago, I made another one. I don't want things to end like that. I think if we could have had that weekend in Santa Barbara—well, I had high hopes for that weekend. For us. Then this thing happened to you and—" I could hear her sniffling. "I'm sorry, Asher."

"So am I."

"We were married five years. I'm not willing to throw all that away."

I didn't respond.

"Let me make you dinner tonight."

"How about that partner at your firm that you're seeing?"

"I'm not married to him. I'm married to you."

I lifted my cup, swirled it around, and watched the tea leaves drift toward the bottom.

"Aren't you going to say anything, Ash?"

"Yeah. Happy Hanukkah." I clicked off the phone. Ten seconds later it rang again.

"Where you been, boychik?" Benny said. "Your mom and I have been calling you all last night and this morning. Don't you check the messages on your phone?"

"Didn't you read that story online?"

"What story?"

"Don't you have a computer?"

"Of course not. I'm afraid of all that online betting they've got. Remember, I used to be a bookie. If I had a computer, I'd be broke in two days."

"I thought you were in the business of taking bets, not making them."

"You know me. I'll follow the action wherever I can get it."

"When you get your paper tomorrow morning you can read about my case."

"What case? What happened?"

"I'll fill you in later."

"So I can tell your mother that you're coming for Shabbos dinner?"

"Why doesn't she invite me herself?"

"She's mad at you."

"Why?"

"Because you haven't called her in a few days."

"I've been a little busy."

"Make it for dinner and maybe she'll forgive you," he said, chuckling.

"I'll try to be there."

"I should hope so, after that *farkakte* surfboard you gave Ariel. Your mother and sister-in-law are still mad at you. You're going to have to make nice with them."

"I can't wait." I hung up and strolled back to my loft. After stuffing my wetsuit, booties, two towels, and a large bottle of water into a canvas bag. I stepped out the door. I dumped the bag into the backseat of my car, started the engine, sped onto the Harbor Freeway, and then veered over to the Santa Monica, toward the ocean. I cruised onto the Pacific Coast Highway from the Santa Monica tunnel, squinting when I emerged into a wash of bright blue sky ahead of me, the glittering cobalt ocean to my left.

My cell phone rang. I checked the screen, and saw that it was Oscar Ortiz.

"Duffy filled me in on what happened last night," he said. "That was a close motherfucking call."

"That's not the way I want to go out."

"Listen, homes, we're having some people over tonight. Kind of a pre-New Year's Eve party. Can you make it?"

"Wish I could."

"You don't want to miss this one. My wife's got a friend from work she wants you to meet. She's beautiful. Twenty-seven-years-old, long black hair. *Muy caliente.* You'll be glad you showed up. She's not like the lady lawyer you married. That bitch dumped your ass, not once, but twice. Forget Jewish women. We've got a nice Mexican girl for you. Mexican women know how to treat their men."

"I'll meet her, just not tonight. I'm heading somewhere right now, and I don't know when I'll be back."

"Where you going that's so important?"

"I'm heading up the coast. I've got my wetsuit. I'm going to stop at a dive shop in Malibu and get a snorkel, mask, and fins. I want to hit the water and join the lifeguards on the grid search. I can't stop thinking about that damn mask."

Acknowledgments

I would like to thank LAPD Detective Rick Jackson for his assistance and good company over the years. LAPD Detective Marcella Winn's insight was very helpful. I enjoyed the many meals I shared with LAPD Detectives Dan Jenks and Debra Winter, and I learned a lot from them. I would also like to thank Jason Davis for his military expertise. Hamilton Cain's editing suggestions were excellent. I am grateful to retired LAPD Detective Pete Razanskas for sharing his knowledge about crime and homicide investigation.